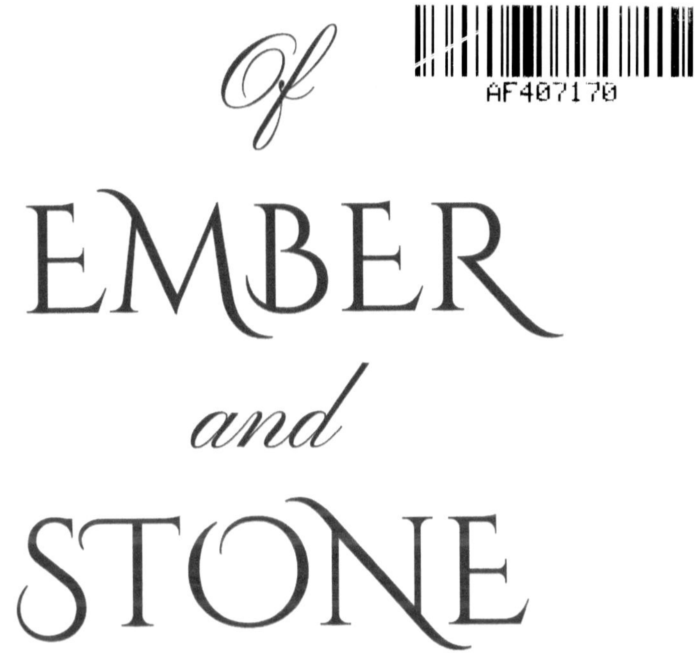

Of EMBER *and* STONE

BY L. J. NICOLSON

CORVUS & QUILL
PUBLISHING
YORK, PENNSYLVANIA

This book is a work of fiction.

Names, characters, places, and incidents are the product of the author's imagination and are used in this book fictitiously. Any resemblance to actual persons, living or dead, events, or locales is entirely coincidental and not intended by the author.

Trigger Warning: This book contains content that may be difficult for some readers, such as: explicit sexual content, attempted sexual assault/restraint with intent, violence/death/combat scenes and death of an animal. Please take care of yourself.

Library of Congress Registration Number: TX 3-531-820

First Edition: 2026

Edited by: Ashleigh Worley (www.ashleighworley.com)

Cover Design by: L. J. Nicolson via Adobe Photoshop and Canva

Interior Map(s) by: L. J. Nicolson via Inkarnate

Author Photography by: Darcey Walthes

ISBNs: 979-8-9941439-0-2 (Paperback), 979-8-9941439-1-9 (EPUB)

Corvus & Quill Publishing
www.corvusandquill.com
Printed in the United States of America.

For J —
Thank you for loving me in every form and through every flame.

RITHMOR
THE VEIL
TEMPLE RUINS
DRAYVIEN CASTLE
RITHMOR ROYAL CITY
THE AETHERIUM
NORTH GATE
THE BLACK DRAGON INN
CLIFFBORN SANCTUARY
RUINS OF SNOW CREEK
THE OLD WOOD
OLD WOOD OUTPOST
ENDARIA
ENDARIAN ROYAL CITY
HOLLOWBEND
BELLMERE
OAKLANDS
RIVER'S EDGE
BLACK PINE BAY

HISTORIES OF THE DIVINE

As written by Romanth Dawnmere, Aetherium Master Origin Scribe Translated A.D. 205 from Sacred Scroll Fragment I

In the beginning—before breath, before thought—there was only the Seam. A vast silence neither full nor empty, where time and void lay bound, humming with the promise of all things yet to come. From this sacred aether rose the Four Pillars—the origin gods, firstborn of the Seam and weavers of all that would be.

Aurelia, the Dawn-Bearer and All Mother. Flame of Becoming, light of life and judgment, and the first to emerge from the Seam. The one who tore through the void and held the threshold open so that others might follow. Where her fire touched, darkness retreated. From her radiance came the spark of life itself, and with it, the first realm dwellers. The Aetherian fae—luminous, long-lived, made in her image. Firstborn children of the realms, charged with protecting all that would follow them. Their magic was not fixed but infinite in potential—power that could be forged by those who carried it. And though the most powerful magic burned with Aurelia's flame, Aetherian gifts answered most truly to what the All Mother loved: the mountains, the rivers, the great wild world that Kaelor raised at her feet.

Malorith, God of Death, the Depth of Undoing. Shadow Sovereign, lord of the void, keeper of endings. He did not create. He waited. Where Aurelia guided the living, Malorith kept vigil over the dead. He ruled the halls of the fallen, tending the silence between what was and what would never be again. He was Aurelia's mirror opposite—light and shadow, becoming and undoing—and so he waited for what he believed must come: a summons to join Aurelia's side, to rule over every divine plane.

Kaelor, the Wild Lord of Air and Stone. Malorith's brother and steward of form. From his hands came the peaks, the valleys, the tides. He summoned the winds, seeded the forests, breathed life into every beast, bird, and branch. From this great shaping came the first humans, whose brief lives beat in time with the earth he raised, whose mortal souls found eternal rest in his brother's care. But where his power ran deepest—in the bones of cliffs, the breath of storms—he forged others. Shifters who could don the forms of beast and bird. Elementals who bent wind and tide to their will. These were near-immortal children of his wild world, their magic rooted not in divine fire, but in the land and sky their maker had wrought.

Nytheris, Queen of Dream and Memory. Sister to Aurelia and keeper of what lingers. Where Aurelia gave life and Kaelor gave form, Nytheris bestowed gifts of mind and soul. She alone could walk through the veil of life and death, bearing messages between her sister's realm of light and Malorith's dark, silent halls. In her keeping lay the Eye—a sacred scrying mirror through which all futures trembled into view. But she did not only gift souls and sight. She also made. From her came the rarest children of the world. The Whisperfolk, whose blood and bone carried secrets and dreams. The Witches, who moved between what was and what would be—seers, weavers of the liminal, their gift of sight a pale reflection of the Eye their maker held.

For a time, the Pillars moved in harmony. Each sovereign within their own domain, each thread woven true. But divine does not mean incorruptible.

Malorith gazed toward Aurelia, toward her fire and light, and longed. Not only for love, but for conquest. In the order of things, he believed his place was by Aurelia's side. Light and shadow. Beginning and end. Two halves of an eternal whole in divine rule. But Aurelia did not look toward his darkness, toward the keeper of endings. She looked toward the beauty of the mountains, the rivers, the forests that Kaelor—Malorith's brother—had raised for her from nothing. She chose him. Not for the sake of power, but for joy, for life, for love.

And Malorith, who had waited so long in his halls of nothing, found his patience curdling into madness. Desire rotted to venomous wrath, and since he had not been chosen, he instead plotted to steal the Flame of Becoming and unmake the balance. To fold her fire into his darkness, to become the One Eternal: keeper of all cycles, every beginning and every end.

Nytheris saw his plan in the Eye. Every thread of ruin, every fracture yet to come. She went to Aurelia with the truth, begging her sister to act before his shadow could devour her flame. But Malorith learned of her betrayal, and for it, he killed her. In his great cruelty, he bound her soul within the very mirror she had used to see, trapping the Queen of Dreams in an eternity of watching what she could never again prevent.

So began the Gods' War.

Malorith breached the Seam between the living and the dead, dragging darkness and torment in his wake. He corrupted Kaelor's wild beings, poisoned the tides, and turned Aetherian against human. What he could not create, he claimed—twisting the children of the other gods into monstrous reflections of what they once were. Shifters became feral, losing themselves to the beast within. Elementals turned violent, throwing the seasons into chaos. Even the Whisperfolk were not spared—their gift of secrets and dreams curdled into cruel memories that could be weaponized. These were Malorith's children now—not born, but broken. Not made, but unmade and reforged for destruction.

The Seam frayed. And the world bled from the battle he brought with him.

To stop Malorith, Aurelia and Kaelor forged a tomb of voidstone, intending to mute his corruption forever. But at the final moment, when their blades were meant to strike as one, Kaelor faltered. Even now—brother to brother—mercy stayed his hand. Aurelia was forced to act alone. She gave her full flame, her very essence, to seal Malorith beneath the world.

When the smoke cleared, only one ember of Aurelia's power remained. One ember, blown away on the great winds, tucked away somewhere in the world—waiting for the breath that would stoke it back to life.

For Malorith had not been destroyed. Only imprisoned, his corruption still pulsed beneath the voidstone, patient and seething. Waiting to seep into a new world and hunt what remained of Aurelia's light.

And so, in his grief and shame, Kaelor raised the Veil—a primordial barrier between the fractured realms where the Seam tore. It held his brother's shadow at bay, divided Aetherian from human, and scattered what remained of Kaelor's children and Nytheris' children to the far corners of the world.

When the inferno of war receded, when the mountains stopped crumbling, when the dust at last settled, Kaelor swore eternal vigil over the ember and vanished into the wild wood that she had loved. When the great silver pines welcomed their grieving lord, the Four Pillars fell silent.

And thus began the Age of Division. (0 A.D.)

I have studied every surviving scrap and scorched scroll. Every whispered tale still bearing the names of the Four. And yet, I cannot say with certainty where Kaelor keeps his vigil. Some believe he wanders the wild wood still, cloaked in grief. Others say he became the wood itself—that the great silver pines are his bones, and the wind through their branches is his breath. The war reshaped everything. All fixed points are lost.

The Aetherians remained North of the Veil, forgetting their All-Mother. In their delusion, they believe Malorith is the One Eternal, wrongfully imprisoned, and have dedicated themselves to freeing him through rituals I will never speak of. The humans settled in the South. Kaelor's children and Nytheris' children scattered to the edges of the world—the shifters to the cliffs, the witches to the wilds, the Whisperfolk to shadow and silence. Few remain. Fewer still remember what greatness they once were.

Of Nytheris, I dare not write much. Her Eye still exists—shattered, some say, its pieces scattered like her children. If her soul remains bound within, she sees still. She watches.

I believe Aurelia's last spark drifted southward to what we now call Endaria. Hidden, perhaps soon forgotten, but not extinguished. And so we must pray the Flame returns when we need the light.

For it is my greatest fear that Malorith's prison was never truly sealed. Without Kaelor's full commitment, the voidstone lacks its final binding. The rot festers—slow, insidious, creeping. If her light does not rise again, all shall be lost.

Of Sacred Quill,
Romanth Dawnmere, Origin Scribe Aetherium Records, Hall III, Shelf II

PROLOGUE

Spring, Northern Endaria

H e'd been chasing the Flame for a long time.

Vaelric Drayvien crossed the threshold of the Black Dragon Inn as if the night had been waiting for him. Rain clung to every line of his frame, dripping from the hem of his cloak to darken the inn's already warped planks. The few patrons scattered along the bar kept their eyes fixed on their tankards. None dared to look up. Woodsmoke and sour ale hung thick in the air. Shadows pooled in every corner—thick, watchful things—heaviest near the back table where the mercenary waited for him. Scarred, filthy, dressed in soaked leathers worn for weeks on the road.

And face first in a tankard of ale. He didn't notice the Aetherian until Vaelric had already slid into the chair across from him. The man startled with a barked laugh.

"Godsdamn, is that really you?" He wiped his nose across his sleeve as he lowered his head, trying to peer through the shadow cast by Vaelric's hood. "Couldn't find a royal courier with the balls to meet me here?"

Vaelric said nothing, fingers drumming a slow and steady rhythm on the scarred wood.

Mistaking his quiet for weakness, the mercenary's confidence swelled. "No use hiding under that hood, Aetherian. No one here cares what you are. You're just a pawn like the rest of us."

Slow and fluid, Vaelric lifted his head. Hearth-glow sliced beneath the hood, catching the carved planes of his face and the storm-dark gleam of his eyes. A dagger ghosted from the bracer at his wrist. He turned it easily over his gloved fingers, the blade reflecting the fire's amber light.

"I am the last piece moved when the game is nearly lost." He let the steel catch the light and flash again. "Remember that."

The mercenary's hand twitched toward his own belt but went still as he thought better of it. "Right," he muttered, mouth suddenly too dry. "I'm Kreg, by the way."

Vaelric didn't give a damn about what his name was. He'd come for the information he claimed to have. If this were all a bluff, if the trip through the North Gate had been a waste of his power and time, he'd hand this man his own guts before leaving him to bleed out behind the stable.

Kreg visibly gulped, shifting in his seat. "There's this girl. Farther south, in a fishing village called River's Edge. Off the Oakwood, near Hollowbend. Barely a smudge on the map."

"Get to the point. Description, location, what you've heard." Vaelric was carved stone, utterly still on the opposite side of the table.

"Early to mid-twenties, unmarried. Works the tavern there. Beautiful, but real standoffish. Downright vicious from time to time. But I've now heard the same stories in different towns from different mouths." Kreg risked a lean in, voice dropping. "Claims the river never floods there. Crops grow stronger, the winters lighter. And the fire—"

"What about fire?" Too calm to be casual.

"They say she can light it with her bare hands. Even soaked wood. One man hid behind the barn and swore she summoned it. Flames moved like they knew her," Kreg whispered. "And didn't burn her, neither."

"When did you last hear such claims?" Vaelric asked, spine straightening.

"Week or two ago. If she's still there, you'll find her. Think they call her Ren. Or Reny."

Vaelric rose, every movement unhurried and absolute. "If you follow me, or speak of this to another soul," he said, "I'll hang you by your ankles, gut you like a silver boar, and leave you for the things that hunt along the Veil."

"Wait—you're going? Just like that? What about—" Kreg's earlier bravado collapsed like rotten timber, all color draining from his face.

A black coin pouch landed in the center of the table with dull finality. When Kreg looked up, the looming shadow had receded as if it had never been there. The inn door was already whispering shut. The glamour spell took hold as Vaelric stepped into the rain, his true features folding beneath a shroud of human flesh.

Deceptively mortal.

Through the settling fog, the road stretched south, rain-slick and waiting. Vaelric had spent the last year tracking rumored flame-bearers across Endaria, coming up empty-handed at the bitter end of every clue and crossroad. Witches draped in borrowed lore. Half-breeds who'd wandered too far from the sea cliffs. All of them dead ends, while Rithmor continued to wither from its blight. He could feel it even here, in this godsforsaken human realm. The slow drain of his own magic, thinning with each season and every crossing through the North Gate.

His homeland was dying. Orchards bore no fruit, rivers ran dry, and the once-lush hillsides had turned gray, buried by ash. His people were dying, too. Not with the grace of centuries, as their kind once had, but in misery and pain. Mortal years claimed by mortal ailments. Their bodies had forgotten how to heal, how to keep their once-divine given power.

Even King Maelor Drayvien, the original architect of their decay, and, more unfortunately, his father, was rotting too. Age, merciless and cold, coming to collect on a debt long overdue. But the king's growing frailty wasn't what kept Vaelric hunting. Not when the innocent suffered beside him. Not when helpless, Aetherian children wandered the streets empty-eyed and starving because of one mad king's desperate, ignorant choice.

He'd already failed so many times before, forced to walk through Rithmor's streets without answers.

Nothing he had ever hunted before had been called unburned.

Vaelric knew one thing. If the whispers were true, if the Flame was in River's Edge, he would find it this time. It would be his.

One way or another.

Otherwise, everything he'd sworn to protect would crumble to dust, and the blood he'd spilled in oath for a man he hated would all be for nothing.

CHAPTER 1

A raven cut the sky above her, its cry a raw war call.

The sky was red. Not the warm blush of a summer sunset, but blood-red like a wound. It was all she could see until black billows gathered at the bottom of her vision. When she looked down, the entire village was burning. Flames engulfed cottages up to the rooftops, their support beams splintering in violent pops. Stone walls groaned as they collapsed from the heat. Screams rose in unison—human and animal—creating a chorus of terror.

She started running.

But the village only fell farther away, dropping back into the warped haze of heat with every step she took. Her legs grew heavy, dragging her down like chains. She looked down to find small, pudgy hands balled into fists.

Her own hands. She was a helpless child again.

A woman stumbled into view from a cloud of smoke, eyes wide and blind with terror, face blistered beyond recognition. But Reny knew who it was. Knew this place, knew this very moment her nightmares forced her to relive.

It was her mother.

"Help us, Aurenya," she rasped, grasping at her throat.

Reny reached toward her, but her arms passed only through air, her little hands clutching nothing. Helping no one. One by one, more figures bled from the fire to surround her, pleading for either a miracle or death. She heard her father screaming off in the distance. Saw her cousins trapped beneath a table. But she couldn't help them, couldn't save them. They turned to ash before she could touch them. Reny tried to scream, but only silent agony tore from her throat.

As they faded from view, the wall of flames before her split apart like a curtain. A towering darkness loomed in the space beyond, a form of distortion and torment. Elongated, human-like, with grotesquely long limbs that angled into unnatural points. Contorted antlers gnarled upward like dead branches, crowning an angular, tilted skull. In the void of its eyes, the firelight didn't reflect. Only vanished, devoured by pure nothingness.

"The flame does not belong to you." The hissing voice slid through her bones as the creature's jagged mouth parted, fangs dripping black tar. The world folded inward, the smoke forming claws that grabbed her throat. Her skin unraveled down to the bone, her soul already stripped bare by a darkness so suffocating—

Reny jolted upright with a strangled gasp, hands clutching her neck. For a minute, she could only sit still, heart thrumming in her ears like a drum. Her hands—adult, now—trembled as if they still belonged to the child she had just been. She dragged clammy palms down her face, trying to wipe away the image of her mother burning and the agony in her eyes in those final moments. It refused to fade, haunting her like it always did.

Get up, Reny. Don't think about it. Just get up and get to work.

Her legs swung to the floor as she cast aside the bed into one twisted heap. She dressed swiftly and without ceremony. A light tunic, snug brown pants, well-worn boots. Her fingers moved with practiced grace, weaving her long auburn hair into a loose braid. At last, she drew the narrow door shut, leaving the rumpled battlefield of her bed in shadow behind her.

Downstairs, warm air carried the scent of cedar and spiced chicory. Garron was already at the stove, a solid bulk with shoulders bent against the morning, feeding kindling into the fire like he had something to prove.

"You're up early," Reny noted, slipping into a chair.

He grunted without looking up. "Aye, no. You're up late."

His beard was thicker this year, more white streaks cutting defiantly through the peppered gray. His arms, roped with the strength of his soldier's past, moved with precision born of decades. Shoveling, chopping, carrying. Even now, he wore his battered leather apron, scorched and patched in a dozen places, like tavern-keeping required a uniform.

"You look like death warmed over," he added teasingly over his shoulder. When his gaze finally caught hers, the roughness eased just enough to betray the worry beneath. "Nightmares again?"

She didn't answer. *Didn't need to.*

He nodded, pressing a steaming mug into her hands instead. Garron's dark chicory brew, bitter and perfect. Silence settled easily between them, broken only by the stove's crackle and the soft scrape of his movements.

But Reny's eyes never rested. She watched him closely over the rim of her mug. The way his jaw tightened when he bent over too far, how his hand splayed across his lower back when he thought she wasn't looking. The slight hitch in his breath as he straightened again.

She set the mug down and rose without a word.

Garron turned at the scrape of the chair. "What are you—"

But Reny was already beside him, lifting the heavy iron pot from his grip before he could protest. She moved it to the hook above the fire before reaching for the sack of oats he'd been about to haul from the corner.

"Reny." Her name alone carried the warning of a man who hated being coddled.

"Sit down, old man." She didn't look at him. Kept to the work with efficient movements and focused eyes. Measuring oats, adding water, stirring.

"I don't need—"

"Your back is seizing. I could see it from over there." When her eyes finally met his, her expression left no room for even his resistance. "Sit. Drink your chicory. Let me do this."

For a moment, the air between them held taut. Garron had never been a man who accepted help easily. Decades of soldiering had taught him to push through pain, to never show weakness. But nearly twenty years of raising Reny had taught him something else.

She was as stubborn as he was. More, maybe.

"Bull-headed girl." He exhaled, a sound caught between frustration and something softer, and lowered himself into the chair she'd vacated.

"Learned from the best." She moved through the kitchen with ease, finishing what he'd started. The porridge was stirred. Bread was sliced. Firewood was well stacked for the afternoon fire. Her hands never stopped, her focus a wall between her and everything else.

Because if she kept moving, she didn't have to think about the nightmare that plagued her so frequently. About the flames. About the voice that still echoed in the hollow of her chest.

"The flame does not belong to you."

She pushed it down deep. Buried it where she buried everything else.

Garron watched her from the table, the steaming mug cradled in his scarred grip. She wasn't his by blood, but she was his all the same. Made of the same downright belligerent iron will. Shaped by the same sorrow that refused to break them.

Work is the kinder companion, girl, he told her years ago. *Asks nothing of the heart.*

But he knew she understood the truth beneath those words, even if she never said it aloud.

The work keeps the ghosts quiet throughout the day. Until night falls, and the memories find their way back in.

With the tavern rooms prepped for a new round of guests, Reny stepped out into River's Edge, bucket handles biting into her fingers. The scent of damp earth and wood smoke enveloped her.

Thick. Grounding. Home.

The village lived up to its name, curled along both banks of the river, cottages scattered with the uneven charm of a place shaped by hand rather than plan. Smoke drifted from crooked chimneys in lazy ribbons, carrying the savory promise of breakfast through the morning air.

Deep in the Oakwoods of southern Endaria, River's Edge had become a haven for the war-weary. Widows. Former soldiers. Families who'd traded steel for distance and the kind of quiet only the trees could offer. Garron had brought her here almost two decades ago when she was still small enough to carry.

When both their memories were too raw and their hearts too broken. They never spoke of where they'd come from.

Reny rarely thought of the far north. Endaria's Old Wood, where even shadows moved wrong, and travelers' stories were kinder than the truth. Rithmor loomed beyond that—the dying realm of the Aetherians, where the once-great fae grew more desperate with each passing season. Travelers whispered that the Aetherians had lost most of their magic and their immortality. That the raids which reduced border villages to smoke and bone had stopped only because crossing through the Veil's North Gate cost them too dearly.

Her village had been among the last, in the year of the Northern Slaughter. Just before the Veil crossings forced the fae to pay with their lives. The Veil was still fraying at its enchanted edges, bleeding Rithmor's corruption into the Old Wood. But it still held the line between Endaria's people and that slow decay.

For now.

Politics and history between the realms were complicated. So were the rules of magic. But in the Oakwoods, in River's Edge, life was slow. Simple.

And Reny intended to keep it that way.

The bridge—one of two arches connecting the village's banks, carved of thick pine and lashed with the sturdiest rope—groaned its familiar song beneath her boots as she crossed, buckets swinging against her thighs. On the far bank, Old Harl had already set out his line. A crooked feather stuck in his cap, a long pipe clenched between what teeth remained. He was the first to the water every morning, reliable as the dawn itself.

"Mornin', girl," he called out without looking, smoke curling lazily from the bowl. "River's generous today."

"She likes you," Reny called back, smiling despite herself.

"Aye. Most do, you know." His grin peeked out behind the pipe.

She smirked and moved on, the waking village swelling around her. Children darted between cottages, shrieking with delight as a fat white goose gave chase. The blacksmith's hammer rang steadily farther up the hill. Steel on steel, a heartbeat of its own. Maren, the smith's daughter and Reny's closest friend, would make her way down to the tavern kitchen soon enough.

The river ran clear and fast, fed by the very last of the late-summer snowmelt still spilling from the highest ridges. Reny crouched at the bank and slipped her hands into the shallows. The water bit cold enough to steal her breath, but it roused her in a way sleep never could. She dipped the first bucket.

And paused.

A bright glow shimmered along the surface of the water, centered in the reflection looking back at her. Strange, golden light bled from her mirrored image, threading outward from her chest. Moving like a living flame, it rippled beneath the surface as if fire burned in the water itself. It didn't follow the current or match the angle of the rising sun, instead pulsing to its own rhythm. Breathing, reaching toward her even as she pulled back. Heat bloomed deep in the center of her palms despite the water's cold. That unwanted thing always beneath her skin, pressing outward, seeking release.

No.

Reny clenched her fists, forcing the warmth away. Smothering it the way she'd taught herself years ago. She didn't want it. Didn't trust it. Whatever it was—whatever it meant—was too painfully similar to what had once stolen everything from her.

The light flickered and died. The reflection became only her reflection again. A woman with guarded green eyes, jaw too tight, knuckles white around the bucket handle. The river rushed on, indifferent and clean, but the warmth in her hands refused to fade. A reminder that no matter how deep she buried it, the fire always remembered her.

Even when she refused to remember it.

Reny filled the second bucket with sharp, deliberate movements, willing her hands to stop trembling. A sound from the branches above stopped her short. A raven's croak, loud and sudden and too close to the one from her nightmare.

She looked up, heart tumbling. The bird sat hunched on a low branch, black eyes fixed on her, its stare too knowing. She willed herself to hold its gaze, water dripping from her fingers as the morning's peace crumbled around her.

Just a bird, she told herself. *A coincidence.*

But her palms were still too warm. And the raven was still watching.

Chapter 2

Sunset draped River's Edge in crimson and amber, but the tree line had stolen the tavern's share. Inside, hearth and candlelight held the room in soft, easy warmth. Venison stew and roasted root vegetables made the air rich and heavy—a hearty anchor beneath the clatter of tankards and half-drunken laughter. Men crowded the tavern, eager to trade hunting tales and bad jokes over talk of darker things. The thinning Veil to the north, birthing monsters and madness through its cracks. Endaria's slow march toward another Rithmor war. Mercenaries playing both sides for coin.

No one mentioned the Aetherians—once divine-marked, now losing their magic and their minds. Their growing desperation had sent Endarian recruiters flooding the southern roads, peddling glory to a new generation of naïve soldiers still too young to have any business leaving home.

Late summer bowed toward autumn, bringing the first big round of huntsmen with mud-caked boots and coins to spend. In the coming weeks, they'd pass through in droves, stockpiling meat and stories before another Endarian winter. The tavern would make the most of it with fires burning bright and men needing distraction before the long, dark cold.

Garron manned the bar like a captain in a storm. Gruff and fast-handed, his voice rose above conversation and clatter with effortless command. "Don't hold my cutting board like that, boy, unless you plan on buying me a new one!"

The boy in his crosshairs—Flinn—yelped as he clutched a half-chopped carrot in one hand and Garron's cutting board like a shield in the other. "Tell her to quit throwin' things at me, then!"

Reny ducked just in time to avoid a flying cleaning rag. Maren grinned from where she stood, already reaching for another.

"Stop throwing things and get those tankards to table three," Reny scolded without looking up. Her hands were full, balancing a tray of steaming stew bowls and a half-pint of blackberry cordial. Her braid hung long over her shoulder, dark auburn catching the firelight when she moved.

"They're staring at you again." Maren slid up beside her with a fresh pitcher of ale, voice bright with amusement.

"Lonely men always stare." Reny shifted bowls to balance the tray, her tone flat. "Doesn't mean I have to look back."

It had always been this way. Men's eyes leered when ale loosened their restraint. Reny had long since perfected the art of dismissal, flirtation sliding off her like rain on oiled leather.

Maren sighed, predictable as the sunrise. "You could at least try. That one by the bar has been watching you all night. He's not bad looking."

"Then you go talk to him."

"I'm not the one he's watching."

Maren was always dreaming of knights and grand romance, sighing over any man with a good jaw and a decent horse. Reny tried—for a time. Kisses beneath stars, whispered promises in the dark. But all of them had been sparks too brief to ignite anything real inside her. All of it was too fleeting to make her forget everything that fire could take away.

Reny had chosen a smaller, steadier life. She'd accepted it.

And if ale or arrogance gave a man more confidence than sense, there was her training to contend with. Garron had seen to that since she was five. Punches thrown in the back yard, arrows loosed at straw targets, blades swung until her arms burned. He'd insisted on raising a daughter who could protect herself.

She rolled her eyes and crossed to a hearthside table, where a trio of hunters argued loudly over the best way to gut a silver-boar. As she bent to set down the bowls, one leaned in too close. Drunken confidence sent his hand creeping toward her backside.

Reny didn't flinch. She drove the final spoon down onto the table dangerously close to his wandering fingers. The sharp crack of metal on wood made him jerk back hard enough to nearly topple his chair. The rest of the table erupted in laughter.

"Told you," one bellowed, slapping his startled friend's shoulder, "The godsdamned woman's got teeth!"

By the time the moon crested over the forest's edge, the tavern's crowd had dwindled. Reny leaned against the kitchen doorframe to catch her breath, an empty tray hooked at her hip. She was more than ready for the long, tedious work of closing.

But then the door opened.

The shift was instant. A string pulled taut from her core. The air grew dense and hard to draw, muffling the tavern clamor until every sound became distant, like her head had been shoved underwater. Whatever entered with him settled into the marrow of the room.

Into her own.

The man framed in the tavern's threshold was no hunter. Of that much, she was certain. He stood over six feet, draped in a long, road-dusted cloak, black and weather-worn across broad shoulders. His hood was up, pulled low enough to hide his face. Darkness clung to him as if it had sworn an oath—summoned by dusk and now unwilling to let go. He moved with controlled grace, every step forward slow but deliberate. He paused to ensure the door latched behind him, then swept the room from wall to wall like he was cataloging exits.

Or threats.

He drifted to a small table in the far back corner, angling his chair so he could face the entire room with only the wall at his back.

Reny tracked every movement, a chill rolling down her spine. The way his hand slid and repositioned the chair with quiet precision. The single nod of greeting from beneath the hood when Maren gingerly approached. The brief flash of gold that passed from two black-gloved fingers to her open palm without fumble or hesitation. Like a man who'd done this a thousand times before in a thousand different taverns.

But never this one. Reny would have remembered him if he had.

When Maren finally turned toward her, ocean-blue eyes wide as saucers, she lifted a single finger.

Their silent signal for one tankard of ale.

Reny wasn't even aware she had been staring half-open-mouthed until Garron barked her name, snapping her back to herself. Like a violent tide, every sound rushed back into her ears at once. The tray in her hands suddenly felt weightless, her thoughts too scattered to gather.

What the hells was that?

Across the room, the man's hood fell back and pooled on his shoulders. She wasn't ready for the sight. Handsome in a terrifying way. Granite jaw dusted with dark stubble. His mouth curved with a half smile, subtle but assured, like he carried secrets the rest of the world had yet to learn. Storm-gray eyes caught the firelight, sweeping the tavern in another slow pass.

Reny's chest tightened. She needed to be anywhere else.

Now.

She darted into the kitchen, seizing the nearest tasks. Tying herb bundles she had already tied. Wiping down a counter already clean. Anything to justify her retreat, even if it was to herself.

Because she wasn't hiding. Just... regrouping. The lie tasted sour even in her own mind. Her pulse betrayed her, hammering fast, and she cursed herself for it. Maren's foolishness must be rubbing off.

It was just a man. Just another traveler passing through.

When Reny finally re-emerged from the kitchen, reluctant but duty-bound, she found Garron had poured the stranger's ale. The lone tankard still sat waiting on the bar, untouched and expectant, catching the low amber glow of the distant hearth.

Her stomach sank.

"Take that over," she hissed at Maren, who'd appeared at her elbow with an empty tray and flushed cheeks.

Maren allowed a turning glance to follow Reny's quick nod toward the far table and immediately shook her head, blonde curls swinging. "Absolutely not. That one's too broody. Too many secrets."

"I thought you loved men with secrets," Reny said, forcing her tone light. Failing.

"Not when they look like that." Maren leaned closer, quiet words tucked close to the curve of Reny's shoulder. "Besides, he hasn't taken his eyes off *you* since he sat down."

Because of course he hadn't.

Reny's breath caught. Before she could stop herself, her gaze drifted to the corner. Their eyes met instantly, vivid emerald crashing into unforgiving slate. Not leering, like most men. He studied, as if he had been patiently waiting for her to acknowledge his arrival, and now that she had, he wouldn't let her forget it. She couldn't place the tug in her chest toward his table. Unsettlingly foreign, but undeniable. *And she hated it.*

Reny tore her attention away, heat claiming the back of her neck.

"See?" Maren was grinning. Like an idiot. "He's watching you like you're his prey."

"You're foolish," Reny muttered, but her hands moved, grabbing the tankard with more force than necessary to place it on the waiting tray.

"And you're so brave, Reny Stonehelm," Maren teased. "Make sure you smile."

Reny huffed a curse before walking away. Shoulders squared, chin high, her face already set into her most unapproachable and unfriendly mask.

She'd never forgive her for this. Perhaps tomorrow, it would be Maren's chore to pick out all the rotten potatoes from the bottom of every barrel in the kitchen.

Floorboards creaked under her boots as she closed the distance between them. Sound fell away once more, muffled by the pounding of her own heart. His gaze devoured her approach, but he never moved. A statue, save for the steady drum of his fingers on the tabletop, even as she set the tankard in front of him.

She tucked the empty tray against her side. "Your drink."

He gave it a brief glance before meeting her gaze again. The slow drag of his returning focus sparked heat low in her center. This close, every detail of him was alarmingly amplified. Shadow and firelight carved sharp cheekbones, fair skin bronzed by summer sun. Dark stubble roughened his jaw, thick enough to suggest he wasn't bothered with daily conveniences. His hair gleamed deep chestnut, swept back with minimal effort. As though he'd stopped caring how he looked a long time ago and, infuriatingly, looked better for it.

By her guess, a skill gained over years of serving men from every corner of Endaria, he was only a handful of years older than she was. But rough, untamable energy clung to him—not from age, but from a life lived hard and unforgiving under open sky.

And his eyes. They churned with a deeper restlessness, as if a storm had gathered at the table, and its lightning had learned to stare her down.

"I was beginning to think I'd been forgotten." His voice curled low, coaxing, like a current in deep water.

Her teeth clenched at the comment, forcing out something civil. "Maren would forget her own head if it weren't attached. It's been a busy night. The next round's on the house, for the trouble." She turned, eager to leave, when his voice caught her mid-step.

"I was hoping it'd be you."

Spine now rigid, Reny looked back. "What?"

"To bring me my drink." The corner of his mouth lifted into a private, fleeting smirk. "Looked like you and your friend over there couldn't decide who would brave the journey to my table. I didn't realize I required such deliberation."

He'd picked up on that? Watched her from across the room with such unnerving, invasive precision, despite her years of building a fortress around herself?

She'd worked too hard to become a wall of unreadable iron for him to sit here like she was made of mere glass. The observation was just unacceptable. Even worse, it stirred what Reny fought to contain. Warmth bloomed in both hands, enough that she had to adjust her hold on the tray. She gestured toward the tankard as if the motion alone could dampen his effect. *Or whatever the hells was wrong with her tonight.*

"Drink it or don't. There it is."

He raised the tankard and took a lengthy sip, his eyes locking her in place. One brow arched higher, the briefest clue that he was savoring more than the ale.

"I'd like something else, too," he finally said as he lowered it.

"Stew?" The word simmered with impatience. "We might have some left."

He nodded. "And a name."

"Your parents didn't give you one?" Reny's own brow arched now, mirroring his. Her tone turned sweet enough to rot teeth. "That's sad."

His storm-laden stare darkened, dangerous and magnetic. And instead of getting offended by her rudeness, he smiled with newfound amusement. "I'm just curious who I'm speaking to." Focus never wavering, he sat up straighter, like he was daring her temper to turn on him.

Reny wouldn't disappoint.

His fingers continued their slow drum on the table. Small as the motion was, she glanced at his hand, and the glint in his eyes told her he'd noticed. She cursed herself, the silence stretching between them like a dare.

"Alright. Annoyed and Tired. That's who you're speaking to," she snapped, hating the way his voice curled like velvet through her insides and stayed there.

"Nice to meet you, Annoyed and Tired. I'm Rook Blackvale." Pride glinted in his expression as he leaned back, too content in the aftermath of his own joke.

"Is that what you want to eat or not?" It was a war for her not to snarl every word.

"If you'd be so kind," he answered, studying her intently.

She turned again, even more eager to leave than before.

"Is the service here always so... welcoming?" he asked, overly pleasant. Taunting her.

Reny froze mid-stride, pivoting. "Only for our most distinguished guests." Her words dripped honey. She bowed, deep and slow in exaggerated courtesy, mocking every polite gesture she'd ever been taught.

Both of his brows rose in a slow arc. Reny didn't give him the chance to retort, barreling full force back across the tavern floor. Whatever game he was trying to start, she had no intention of playing. Shoving through the swinging kitchen door with her whole body, she thrust the serving tray at Flinn, nearly toppling the poor boy backward.

"Easy, Ren!" he yelped, scrambling to steady it with wet hands. "What the hells is your problem?"

Maren was already waiting by the potato bins, grinning like a fox in a henhouse. She had no business knowing what had just happened at that table, but she was stealthier than Reny gave her credit for. The gleam in her expression betrayed her.

"So?" she purred. "When's the wedding?"

Flinn dramatically faked a gag over the tray he was scrubbing. Maren shot him a scolding glare, but Reny already had one waiting for them both.

"He's *exactly* what you'd expect."

"Tall, dark, handsome?" Maren's gaze lit up. She twirled a blonde curl around her finger, lips curling with mischief. "He looks like he'd ruin your life, and you'd thank him for it."

Yes. Maren would absolutely be spending her morning searching for rotten potatoes.

"Insufferable is what I meant." Reny yanked a dish towel off the hook. "Smug. Arrogant."

"And gorgeous! Who cares for one night if he's an ass? Gods, Reny..." Maren rolled her eyes, but her playfulness remained. She leaned closer. "Aren't you... bored? Aren't you, *you know*... lonely?"

Her question hung heavily in the air. Flinn stopped scrubbing mid-plate, furiously blushing, but unwilling to miss a word.

Reny went rigid, refusing to look up, attacking the dinner plate with a wet rag like she could scrub Maren's words away. "I'd rather be *lonely* than fawn over some pompous ass with a tragic jawline and a superiority complex. I'm not desperate."

Maren burst out in throaty laughter. "I suppose not. Not with Brannic passing through soon for his yearly roll behind the h—"

"Shut up!" Reny hissed, her eyes wide.

Flinn coughed out a laugh, ears burning bright pink. Maren, still grinning, glanced to the far side of the room before snatching Flinn's elbow, jerking him away from the sink. Reny's cheeks were still hot as the pair darted out of sight through the kitchen door.

As if on cue, Garron lumbered in from his small office like a bear roused too soon from hibernation. The unmistakable clatter of Reny taking her temper out on the dishes had drawn him out. He'd stepped into the kitchen just in time to watch his staff scatter.

"Did that newcomer insult you?" Dry as old leather. "Or just have the audacity to breathe too loudly in your presence?"

He never missed a thing.

Reny scowled, wiping her hands on her apron to busy them. Her gaze stayed fixed on the floor. "Neither. He's just... odd."

"You mean handsome!" Maren's voice chimed, bright and too loud, from somewhere beyond the door.

"I mean odd," Reny insisted, ignoring her. "He doesn't sit right with me."

Flinn reappeared through the kitchen door, flour dusting his gangly forearms. He was back to prepare dough for the morning bread, though Reny suspected Maren had sent him to listen.

"The tall one in the back?" Big brown eyes sparkled. "With the broody stare? Aye. He looks like he bites."

"That's what dogs do," Reny muttered.

Garron folded his arms, eyeing Reny with the kind of look that somehow always found its way through her armor. "You look ready to take on a beast from the Old Wood. Now tell me. Did he do something you aren't telling me?"

Reny mirrored him, crossing her arms, and met his stare head-on. "No. He did nothing. I just... feel it. In my bones. He asked for my name too quickly. Watched me for too long. Talks too much."

"Maren and Flinn talk too damned much," Garron grunted, hands finding his hips. "Men get stupid around beauty. Doesn't always mean danger."

He cast a pointed look at Flinn, who was now elbows deep in dough. *Oblivious.*

"Sometimes it does." Reny's eyes stayed on the floor.

Garron's face softened, amused suspicion fading. He stepped closer, cast one pointed look at Flinn, and then at the doorway. Taking the hint, the boy sighed and shrugged, slipping out of sight.

The old man placed thick hands on Reny's shoulders and gave her a gentle shake. "I taught you to watch, aye. Taught you to fight." His voice became calm and quiet. "But girl... You can't spend your whole life scanning for threats. At some point, you've got to let yourself live in the room instead of always guarding the door."

Reny continued looking toward her feet. "This is my life."

"I know it is, child." He lifted her chin with a calloused thumb, forcing her to meet his gaze. "But it doesn't have to stay so damned small. So lonely, made up of sharp edges and empty spaces. Just... make sure you're not mistaking survival for living."

Beyond the kitchen door, she could make out muffled whispers and stifled laughter. Maren and Flinn. Predictably together. Predictably not minding their own business.

Reny groaned. "Can we not do this right now?"

Garron chuckled, clapping her on the shoulder. "Some walls protect. Others cage. Make sure you're not building the wrong kind, Ren."

She didn't answer but took up the tray instead, slipping back through the kitchen door as Maren and Flinn held it wide open for her. Across the tavern, Rook Blackvale hadn't moved from his seat, still watching with that maddening, unshaken calm.

And godsdamnit. When their eyes met across the room—

He smiled.

CHAPTER 3

Reny set the tray down on Rook's table harder than intended, wood striking wood with a crack that drew a few glances. She ignored them, folding her arms across her chest.

A shield and a challenge.

He didn't flinch, gray eyes sweeping the tray's arrangement before climbing to meet hers. "Let me guess," he murmured, devilry in every word. "No one else wanted the honor of bringing this out either?"

She arched an eyebrow. "You think you know a lot, don't you?"

"Hardly." He offered her a half shrug. "Only enough to be right."

Oh gods, he was maddening. And he knew it. She could see it in the way he watched her, tracking every crack in her composure. She opened her mouth to fire back, but lost every word when his attention dropped to her lips.

It was brief. But obvious enough. Red bloomed on her cheeks.

His head tilted curiously, eyes keeping her pinned. "You still haven't given me your name."

"And you still haven't said why it matters," she countered with bite. "What do you care?"

"I'm just making conversation."

"We aren't having a conversation."

"Strange. Could've sworn that's what two people talking back and forth is called." Lips quirked in a half smile as he leaned back, propping one arm on the back of the chair. "Do you have some reason not to give it to me, or are you just being difficult?"

There was no reason. None besides her own urgency to escape that suffocating focus that made her legs feel like water.

No damned way she would let him know that, though. She opened her mouth but quickly shut it again, caught at the end of her own deflection.

"That's what I thought." The faintest hint of impatience bled into his tone, and the soft, distracting drum of his fingers on the table stopped. "Perhaps I simply like to know who I'm speaking to, especially when they bring me dinner with such... *spirited enthusiasm.*"

Reny huffed, resisting the urge to laugh. Or throw his ale in his face. "So, you want stew and pleasant small talk? That's going to cost you extra."

"Will it now?" That infuriating smirk returned, intent and provoking. "Because I'll gladly pay it."

"You can't afford it." Reny's lips formed a thin line of false disinterest.

"A bold assumption," Rook said, eyeing her from face to feet and back again. "I was actually hoping for... more." He let the pause stretch until he'd fully seized her attention, absently pulling a coin purse from his pocket and setting it on the corner of the tray. His voice dropped, intimate and quiet. "Not food."

The words yanked the floor out from under her. Hot, mortified crimson flooded her face. "Excuse me?"

"A room," he clarified with just enough speed to catch her in full embarrassment over where her mind had gone first.

And by the look on his face, he'd enjoyed every second of it. Far too much.

Her jaw tightened, molars grinding. "You're really enjoying yourself, aren't you?"

Rook lifted the spoon from the tray but didn't eat, deftly rolling the utensil between his fingers before he pointed it at her. He couldn't help but break as he held her stare. Not with a smirk this time, but a full wolf's grin, predatory and triumphant. "More than I have in days."

The unguarded flash of teeth ignited a traitorous flame in her chest. She should turn and leave.

But didn't.

Don't leave. Stay and throw the tray at his insufferable head.

But her body refused every command, her posture locked like she'd been nailed to the floorboards. She should *say* something, at least. A cutting remark. A rejection loud enough for the whole room to hear.

Anything. But nothing came.

"I'm passing through," he began. "But not too quickly, if I can help it." He glanced over the warped floor and smoke-darkened rafters above his head, one hand lazily sweeping over the room. "I must say, this place has a certain... humble charm."

"Interesting way to describe falling apart," Reny observed flatly, unimpressed with the hollow compliment. "What are you getting at? What do you want?"

He tracked the shift of her weight from one leg to the other, and she felt the attention like a hand pressed to her skin. "I meant no insult. It's only an offer." Rook braced his forearms against the table, leaning forward. He was still rolling that damn spoon between long fingers, too comfortable in the tension she stubbornly refused to fill.

"I'm a carpenter by trade, among other things," he said casually. "Couldn't help noticing a shutter upstairs hanging off its hinges, a few porch posts are bowing, and the gate outside could wake the dead with the way it drags. Thought maybe a set of strong hands around the place might be useful."

Reny's head tilted in sharp assessment. "And what, exactly, gave you the impression there aren't already strong hands here to handle it?"

If the viper poised to strike surprised him, he didn't show it. He smiled anyway, right in the face of her fangs and venom. All feral charm. "I think you misunderstand me. Perhaps I could—"

"No," she snapped like a blade drawn. "I don't think I do. I'll be right back." Her braid whipped over her shoulder as she turned and marched toward the kitchen. The tray sat forgotten on the table. If he said anything behind her, she didn't hear it over the furious thunder of her pulse.

She hated that smile. *Hated infinitely more what it did to her.*

Reny blew through the swinging kitchen door like a summer storm to find Maren and Flinn already hovering by the frame's edges, faces full of unsuppressed glee.

"He's complaining about you, isn't he?" Flinn's eyes went wide with mock horror, his whole face alight with mischief. "Does he want to report you to the owner? Excessive sass? *Surly stew service?*"

Reny shot him a look sharp enough to gut a fish. "I'm going to break your nose, Flinn Remming, if you don't shut your mouth." She jabbed a finger over her shoulder. "He wants to speak to Garron. Says he's looking for a place to stay and wants to barter repairs in exchange."

Flinn, all lanky elbows and knobby knees despite turning twenty the previous fall, threw his head back in a full laugh, sandy hair flopping into his eyes.

Maren perked up, blue eyes sparkling like cut glass. "He wants to stay? Oh, Reny. You're doomed. This is wonderful!"

"I am *not* doomed." Reny chewed on the words as she slammed a bowl into the sink. The clatter made her wince, forcing her to check for cracks before subjecting it to another furious rinse. "Go find my dad, would you? Stop standing there like idiots."

"Surly indeed!" Flinn chuckled, darting off in search of Garron.

Reny snatched a towel and dried her hands. Maren sauntered closer, propping her chin in her hands against the counter. She looked smug, her eyelashes batting against her rosy cheeks. "You're taking this very well."

Only receiving a glare in return, the laughter in Maren's eyes burned brighter. Before Reny could open her mouth, Garron stepped in from the small storeroom, wiping his hands on his apron.

"The customer in the corner wants a word with the owner." Reny's voice was tight and cold. "He'd like to inquire about room and board. Says he's a tradesman. Offered to make repairs in exchange."

Garron's bushy brows lifted. He cast a quick devil's glance at Flinn, who was struggling and failing to stifle a giggle. "You mean he doesn't want to compliment your *glowing* hospitality?"

They'd told him already.

Reny didn't answer. Her deadpan stare said more than enough. Now well out of her reach, Flinn and Maren erupted with laughter.

Garron snorted, jerking his chin toward the common room. "Come on, then. Let's go see what's got you all riled up tonight."

The old man strode across the tavern, head high and shoulders back. Reny followed reluctantly, two paces behind, wishing the floorboards would open and swallow her whole.

He stopped next to Rook's table, his broad chest squared, while she hung back in his shadow. "You wanted to speak with the owner?"

Rook rose in one fluid motion, his chair barely whispering back against the wood. He dipped his head in a respectful nod. Reny tracked his movement as he straightened to full height. Taller than Garron, broader through the shoulders. From where she stood, she'd been reduced to little more than a forehead and a pair of furious green eyes peering over Garron's shoulder.

Something flickered across Rook's face, and he smiled widely.

She did not return it.

"Yes, sir. Rook Blackvale. I'm a traveling tradesman, among other things." His face, every word, carried effortless confidence. "I've been on the road for some time and hoped to settle for a few days. Longer, if it suits. I noticed this place could use a hand. If you're short on help, I'd be glad to barter repairs for room and board."

There it was. Reny nearly grinned. Any second, Garron would thank him for the offer and then refuse. Politely, because her father was nothing if not civil. But he'd be firm in his decline, the way he always was with drifters who thought charm or chore could buy them a bed.

Garron cast a glance over his shoulder at Reny before turning back. "We manage. But extra hands never hurt. What kind of work are we talking?"

Reny blinked, throat going dry. *Wait a minute.*

"Carpentry. Masonry. General upkeep." Rook ticked them off on his fingers. "I know my way around a forge, though I won't claim to be a smith."

"Well, now." Garron scratched his beard, rolling the thought over with visible deliberation as the woman behind him went rigid. "Can't say I love strangers moving in uninvited. But—"

He stepped back and shifted to Reny's side, revealing her. Weathered brown eyes glinted with pure mischief as he flung a muscled arm around her shoulders and gave her an affectionate squeeze. "My darling daughter here just told me this morning I ought to ask for more help."

No, no, no. What the hells—

Reny's mouth fell open, eyes wide. "I didn't mean—!"

Garron cut her off with a sly grin and a shake of his head. "You said what you said, dear."

Rook watched the exchange, amusement breaking through before he could catch it. "So, it's just you and your daughter, then?"

"Garron Stonehelm." The old man offered a massive hand as his arm dropped from Reny's shoulders. Approval flickered in his bearded smile at the strength in Rook's grip as they shook. "Owner of this fine and, apparently, crumbling establishment. Got my help, Maren and Flinn, lurking around somewhere." He gestured toward Reny with evident, fatherly pride. "And this is Aurenya, though we call her Reny. Truth be told, she runs the place. Keeps the rest of us from running it right into the ground."

Reny met Rook with a narrow glare. He accepted it warmly, dipping his head in the same polite tilt he had given Garron. His gaze lingered on her lifted chin, and something in his expression sharpened.

"Aurenya," he drawled slowly, tasting each syllable like a fine wine.

"Reny." She corrected him with clipped precision, already deciding she never wanted to hear her full name from his mouth again.

Garron, either oblivious or intentionally ignoring her discomfort, kindly continued. "There are no open rooms tonight with all the huntsmen passing through. But tomorrow, check the ledger hanging near my office door. Take any unclaimed room." He shrugged. "For now, all we've got is the cot in the barn. It's dry, at least."

"That'll do. Thank you, sir." Rook dipped his chin to Garron as he reached back toward the table, plucking the coin purse from the corner of the tray where it still sat. He pressed it into Garron's palm. "For dinner. And the incredibly wonderful service."

Garron accepted it without suppressing his amusement, his weathered face brightened with a toothy smile as he pocketed the pouch. "Much obliged."

A muscle twitched in Reny's jaw. His immaculate manners with Garron, the ease with which he navigated the entire exchange, the smug jab about service. All of it grated against her very bones.

Rook's eyes dragged from Garron to Reny, but she was turning away. "I'll do my best not to be a burden."

"Oh, I'm sure you will be." With that thrown over her shoulder, she was gone, vanishing into the kitchen like a fuse lit from both ends.

CHAPTER 4

R ook stayed.

Long after the last of the hunters stumbled out in slurred farewells and the final mugs were stacked behind the bar, he remained, settling in with easy belonging.

And much to Reny's growing irritation, he didn't merely linger. *He was helpful.*

Moving between the tables, lifting chairs one by one so Maren could sweep without obstacles.

"Oh, you don't need to do that," she chirped, eyelashes fluttering.

Rook offered her a lopsided smile in return. "My hands were empty. Your chore list wasn't. Seems a fair trade."

Flinn emerged from the kitchen, arms loaded with clean tankards. He stopped short when he spotted Rook lifting chairs for Maren.

"I can get those," Flinn said, stiff.

Rook glanced up, took in Flinn's rigid stance, the defensive set of his shoulders, and his mouth twitched. "I'm sure you can." He gestured to the teetering stack of tankards in Flinn's slender arms. "But you've got your hands quite full already. I, however, do not."

Flinn gave a grudging nod, shoulders loosening. "Fair enough." He headed for the bar but paused beside Rook, leaning closer. "Just... don't let Reny catch you reorganizing anything. She likes things kept her way."

"I bet she does." Rook's mouth quirked. "Wouldn't dream of disrupting the order of things." The knowing glint in his eye said otherwise.

Flinn chuckled and shook his head before moving to put the tankards away.

"Unbelievable," Reny muttered under her breath, scowling at the exchange from her place at the farthest end of the bar.

Garron, tired and heavy-eyed, didn't look up from tallying the night's earnings. "What is?"

She jabbed a thumb in Rook's direction, voice dropping for Garron alone. "That. *Him.* Acting like he belongs here. Helping like he's part of the family."

"By the fallen Four Pillars, child," Garron grumbled, head shaking over the ledger. "He's making himself useful. Put your hackles down and your claws away."

"He's getting on my last nerve," she hissed.

Garron's quill stopped mid-stroke. He looked up, removing his reading glasses with deliberate slowness. Eyes that once commanded soldiers, that had stared down her temper more than once, fixed on her.

"Reny." Just her name. Quiet and final.

She folded her arms in defiant reply.

"Show him to the barn." He set his glasses down with pointed care. "And mind your manners while you're at it. I raised you better than this."

Reny's mouth opened for the argument already brewing on the tip of her tongue. Garron's stare was unforgiving. The kind of look that had ended many battles before they began—especially with her.

"Now, girl."

Muttering a curse that Garron chose to ignore, Reny flung the rag onto the counter before marching back to the kitchen's narrow storage closet, lined with shelves of folded linens and supplies.

She'd come for one of the guest blankets. The simple, brown, scratchy wool ones. But her hands didn't move. Instead, she refolded a stack of towels that didn't need refolding. Straightened jars of preserves that were straight.

Finally, her hand reached for a guest blanket. But then she faltered, her fingers drifting one shelf lower. To her own blanket. The soft blue one she always curled up with to watch the sunrise on cool autumn mornings. She glared at it, angry at her own impulse for mercy. For kindness. She huffed in disgust and snatched it up.

Out front, Rook lounged against the bar, one boot crossed over the other. His head inclined toward Garron as the old man recounted a story with animated hands. Their laughter rose, easy and genuine. Garron's deep rumble met Rook's low chuckle like they'd shared a hundred conversations before this one.

"—and so I told him, 'You want to fight a man twice your size, you better fight twice as dirty,'" Garron finished, slapping the bar.

Rook grinned. "Wish someone had told me that before I fought three brothers in Hollowbend."

"Three?" Garron's brows rose. "At once?"

"Wasn't my finest moment. Or my most sober."

Garron laughed again, so full and rich it made Reny's chest twist.

When was the last time she'd heard him laugh like that?

Rook had carved out space for himself in their lives without permission, like he and Garron had known each other for years instead of hours. Reny blew by on her way to the front door, the blue blanket clutched tight against her chest. She braced herself against the frame and waited, arms crossed and jaw firmly set.

Rook's gaze cut toward her mid-sentence. "I believe that's my cue," he said, pushing off the bar with easy grace. His mouth curved slowly, knowing and insufferable.

Garron clapped him on the shoulder. The motion was warm, almost paternal. "Just ignore her, boy. She's got more fire than a dragon on a good day." He shot Reny a pointed look. "Best to let her blaze and keep your hide clear 'til she burns herself out."

That look lingered on Rook's face, but Garron's words sank deeper. "I've weathered harsher greetings."

"Aye, I bet you have," Garron said, his words dropping to the safety of a whisper. "But few are quite as stubborn as that one."

Rook gave him one last nod before drifting forward, hands in his pockets. Each stride closed the distance until he stood near enough that she could feel the warmth radiating off him. For the span of a few agonizing seconds, neither moved. Reny's fingers tightened on the blanket, restlessly shifting from one leg to the other. Rook watched her with that shadowed, unreadable stare.

"Well?" She snapped the question impatiently.

"After you, Reny." He swept the door open wide with an exaggerated flourish. She brushed past him without a glance, but she felt his gaze track every step.

The village lay quiet aside from the river's murmur and branches stirring in the breeze. Above, a waxing moon hung silver and watchful. Silence stretched between them, thick as the fog rolling in from over the ridge line.

"So," Rook said at last, tone all play, "are you always this friendly?"

"Only when I really like someone," Reny muttered.

"Lucky me." The words were low and resonant. She blamed her immediate shiver on the night air.

The barn sat crouched beneath the trailing arms of an old willow. Reny heaved the groaning door aside, wood rasping along its worn iron track. The space exhaled as it opened, the air heavy with hay, aged timber, and the faint ghost of tobacco long surrendered to time.

"Hooks on the back wall, cot in the corner. Fresh straw to keep out the damp. The cat handles the mice." She waved a hand toward the darkness, not stepping any closer. "Don't track mud everywhere. And don't scare my chickens."

Distaste flickered across his face. "...You keep the chickens in here?"

She didn't bother hiding the roll of her eyes. "No, but their coop's outside. They hear everything, and if you spook them, they won't lay. Just keep it down."

Rook scoffed, brushing past her close enough that the air changed in his wake.

The scent of him hit her. *Summer rain on the mountain. Well-worn leather. The faintest curl of woodsmoke.* And beneath it all, an older note that wove through her like a half-remembered song. Earthy and achingly familiar. She stiffened, but not because it repelled her.

Gods, it wasn't repelling at all. It made her want to lean in, to breathe him deeper and close the distance she'd intentionally carved between them.

Which was completely unacceptable.

He crossed to the narrow cot and set his bag down, forcing its contents to shift. The hilt of a longsword poked free from the leather, briefly catching the dim light.

"Most carpenters I know don't carry swords," Reny said, her voice even cooler than before.

"Do you know many carpenters who travel across Endaria alone?" He straightened, that maddening half-smile tugging at his mouth. "Even a craftsman should carry the means to protect himself. Wouldn't you agree?"

She didn't answer, making no effort to hide her stiff posture and the way she stood poised to bolt right back out the door.

His eyes swept over her. "You don't trust people easily."

"Sharp as a tack, aren't you?" she asked, deceivingly sweet.

She let her gaze sweep over him this time. He straightened under the weight of it.

"I have absolutely no reason to trust you." She shrugged, her shoulders loose and careless. "I know nothing about you." The moonlight briefly caught in her eyes like sparks as she turned away.

"A clever girl." The words rolled out smooth and warm, chasing another shiver down her spine.

His expression lit up, some flicker she couldn't name. His lips parted—

And she slid the barn door shut in his face.

It took everything Reny had not to sprint back to the tavern. She'd only made it halfway across the yard when she stuttered to a halt.

The damn blanket. Still clutched tight against her chest. Her scowl deepened as she stared down at the pale-blue fabric, as though it had conspired its way into her arms. She was hugging it like some moon-struck fool. *Like Maren sighing over village boys with soft eyes and softer promises.*

She had been so focused on acting like his voice hadn't unraveled her that she'd forgotten to leave it behind. And he hadn't said a word about it, either. For all the times his eyes had raked over her, he'd let her walk away with it, knowing she'd be forced to return. Her cheeks flushed, fury braiding with embarrassment. She spun on her heel and marched back toward the barn, each stride heavier than the last.

Get it together, Reny. He's just a man.

She knocked three times, hard enough to rattle the wood on the iron track. The door slid open instantly.

Rook filled the threshold, his cloak discarded. A plain tan tunic softened him, his hair mussed in a way that made him look, infuriatingly, more approachable.

"Miss me already?" He braced one arm against the frame, his smile wicked and satisfied.

"Don't flatter yourself." She shoved the folded blanket hard into his chest with enough force to make him rock back a step. "I forgot to leave this."

"Maybe the service here isn't so terrible after all." He caught it easily, steady even as her shove rocked him, fingers grazing against hers a beat too long.

"But I thought you said the service was wonderful." Reny was walking away when the words escaped. "It's mine. Don't ruin it."

Rook stayed in the threshold, watching the sway of her messy braid, every defiant step carrying her deeper into the dark. Anyone else might have stripped his patience raw by now, but he found himself fighting the urge to follow her. The blanket hung absently in one hand. Almost against his will, he lifted it to his face and inhaled.

Her scent struck like a fist to the jaw. Smoke and warmth cut straight through his composure, flooding his lungs. For one reckless heartbeat, he let himself drown in it.

Notes of toasted vanilla and the char of banked embers. Earthen and unsettling in every right and wrong way. Like the echo of a life he'd never lived, yet one his body remembered anyway. It yanked on a ravenous, hungry need he'd learned to keep chained in this realm.

He'd crossed paths with countless Endarian barmaids, all of them excruciatingly dull. Meek, merry, mindless. Reny Stonehelm was none of those things. She was a wildfire burning fierce in a small, boring place that should have smothered her spark long ago, meeting the world with her teeth bared. That alone made her a rare, exquisite challenge.

Rook drew the blanket over himself as he stretched out on the cot, willing sleep to drag him under. But her scent clung stubbornly to the fabric, to his senses, tightening its hold with every breath he took. He stared at the rafters, the weight of it pulling down like the cruel pull of a riptide.

Learn what you need to and get what you came for.
Do not deviate. There's no other way.

At the tavern's back door, Garron lounged against the frame, thick arms folded across his chest. Amusement tugged at his beard as he watched her stalking back from the barn with thunder in her stride.

The porch blanket had vanished from its familiar shelf. She hadn't grabbed one of the rough guest throws reserved for travelers and strangers.

No, she'd chosen hers. The soft pale-blue one.

Pure fire and vinegar, his girl. Yet beneath all that bristle and fang beat a heart too tender, too naturally generous, to abandon anyone to a drafty barn with nothing but coarse wool for comfort.

Perhaps she wouldn't become the solitary spinster she seemed so determined to be.

Reny halted mid-step into the kitchen, catching him there. Watching her. One look at his face and her eyes narrowed. "Don't you dare," she cautioned, palm raised like a ward against whatever hovered unspoken between them.

He raised both hands in mock defense, laughter rolling deep in his chest. "Not a word from me, you miserable brute."

She expelled a sharp breath and swept past to tackle the soup kettle. The silence that followed held no residual anger. Only the quiet of everything she always left unsaid. Garron let the moment stretch before his voice softened into the cadence he saved for her alone.

For his daughter.

"Maybe just... see where it goes, Reny. Might do us some good. Might do you some good."

"I seriously doubt that." She kept her back to him, but her shoulders dropped. Slightly, but enough for him to notice.

Garron's tone went dry as old oak. "Though you'd best bolt your door tonight, aye? Wouldn't want our barn guest getting ideas about how hospitable we really are."

Reny groaned and caught his backside with the dish towel as he retreated.

His laughter echoed all the way to his worn chair beside the fire.

CHAPTER 5

The Eastern Cliffs towered white and jagged above the sea, their faces scarred from the ceaseless gnaw of waves. Salt spray and wind scoured stone in endless thunder.

A roar in the world that never ceased.

Where Endaria ended in storm and rock, the forsaken had created a sanctuary. Ghostly curls of smoke drifted from cave mouths veiled by moss. Rope ladders swayed against the cliff face, tethering paths that clung to its harrowing edges. One faltering step meant a plunge into the abyss below.

This was the refuge of the Cliffborn.

Those cast out by Endaria and Rithmor alike for their untamable magic. Etched with the traits of man, beast, and earth, they were branded half-breeds. Abominations born of the fractured realms.

Scorned, hunted, unwanted.

But here they endured, following scripture older than memory, keeping alive the legacy of gods both men and Aetherians had long forsaken. With calloused hands and unbroken hearts, they carved their lives into the stone.

Rhedda moved with quiet grace through halls worn familiar by decades of passage. To her people, she was the Cliff Mother, steady-handed and soft-eyed, the one who gathered the forsaken and opened her arms to those the world beyond had thrown away.

She'd come to them two decades ago, during the Hunting Age, when Endaria's witch hunts raged alongside Rithmor's Northern Slaughter. They had branded her a witch and cast her out.

To the Cliffborn, she'd become a prophet.

Her face mapped sea air and hard years, deep lines carved around pale eyes that had long stopped flinching at what they saw. Gray hair hung to her waist, unbound with sparse braids threaded with charms and shells that chimed when she moved. Her wisdom and the power of a seer's visions had become a compass to her people.

At her insistence, every child of the cliffs learned the Four Pillars by name, their stories of the old gods kept alive when the rest of the world beyond the rocks would rather forget.

Her shawl whispered against damp walls, her torch hissing where seawater leaked through in restless trickles from the tide. She did not hurry, though the man following her bristled with urgency.

"You'll drain yourself again," Brenn rumbled, his voice a rough echo in the passage. Broad-shouldered even in human form, the bear-shifter filled the corridor, his heavy stride a drumbeat of boot and protest. "Last time you looked into the Eye, you couldn't rise from bed for three days."

The charms in Rhedda's graying hair chimed as she glanced back, pale eyes calm and unyielding. "It was made to be seen through," she murmured. "We must be able to observe the realms."

"Then allow me to send scouts," Brenn pressed, wedging his bulk through a tight turn. "Or send me alone. But don't go near that cursed thing. It's warded and hidden for a reason."

"So that we may protect the relic," Rhedda reminded him. "That is our sacred duty as leaders of the Cliffborn."

The corridor tightened once more before releasing them into a cavern that breathed with the sea. Salt wind threaded through a crack above, moonlight slanting in a single, silver shaft.

At the cave's center rose the Eye. An ancient scrying mirror nearly Brenn's height, arched and wide as a doorway. Its black glass shimmered faintly as if lit from deep within. Water dripped in a steady rhythm at its base, ripples stretching its shadow across the floor. It didn't look placed so much as born—as if the cliffs had risen to cradle it.

Brenn went rigid, back hunching as if to shield against its pull. Even a man built like a wall, with the strength of the bear, seemed diminished before it. He kept his eyes averted, too wary of the glass that throbbed with its quiet lure.

Rhedda had never known him to find comfort in its presence. She doubted he ever would.

"It feels wrong," he growled, words falling heavy in the silence. He rolled his shoulders as if to shake free of some unseen weight.

"Nytheris, forgive him." Rhedda eyed him with a smirk, though her fingers tightened on the torch. A silent struggle against the instant draw of the black glass.

Her feet held fast, a chill racing up her spine. It was all the warning she needed.

"It carries answers of fate," Rhedda whispered. "But not the ones we seek tonight." For a long moment, she only listened. To the water dripping, to the mirror's hum, to the waves below battering against the rock. She drew her shawl close, finally turning away. "You are right, Brenn. Not tonight."

Relief left him in one long exhale that was more growl than breath.

"Send the scouts," Rhedda continued as they reentered the narrow passage. "Have Orwyn take Aric, the hawk girl, and the old wolf. To Rithmor's borders, then Endaria's capital. Quietly. Only to watch, to see what they are planning. They are not to engage."

"Not to engage," Brenn echoed firmly.

"Never," Rhedda agreed. "Endaria's king is too eager for another excuse, and the Drayviens are desperate."

"Korva will want to know," Brenn muttered, unease carved into his defined brow. "She'll want to follow her brother."

"Korva has her own task," Rhedda replied, her tone sharpening. "It is time she learns obedience for her people's sake. When she returns, and she should soon enough, we will tell her. He might even be back by then." Brenn followed her, as the bear had always done, his tread heavy in the corridors.

Behind them, the cavern sank into silence, filled only with the drip of water and the sea's hollow churn through the rock. The Eye answered with a shimmering pulse, looming beneath the single shard of moonlight. Its shadow stretched across the floor, patient and thin.

Waiting.

When Brenn eventually parted ways with Rhedda, leaving her to her chambers, he carried a sense of dread he couldn't shake. Torchlight blurred to streaks as he walked the long hall, his thoughts a tangle of questions that refused to quiet. For all her certainty, the Cliff Mother's words had lately left him feeling hollow. Life had grown into too many unknowns, and faith in the answers had worn thin.

He crossed the inner causeway where the cliffs opened to wind and sky. The night pressed in, the sea below battering the stone as if it sought to tear the entire refuge down. Smoke drifted from the lower caves in ghost-pale ribbons against the dark, and from above came the distant cry of gulls unsettled from their roosts.

Orwyn waited near the outer rock ledge. Even at a distance, Brenn could pick him out by the ease of his stance, the long-limbed calm that never left him. The owl-shifter's cloak hung dark against the pale stone, his black hair caught by the wind like threads of night itself. He turned as Brenn approached, immediate warmth in his expression.

"You've got that look again," Orwyn said, his voice carrying the dry affection of a man who had seen that look a thousand times before. "The one that says Rhedda's been weaving riddles with no answers."

Brenn huffed a sound too tired to form a laugh. "Half-answers. And none I feel good about."

Orwyn tilted his head, the gesture so naturally owl-like it drew a flicker of amusement even through Brenn's unease. "Then I take it you're sending me to find some."

"Rhedda wants eyes in the realms," Brenn sighed. "Take the hawk, the wolf, and the fox. Survey the border with Rithmor, then keep an eye on Endaria's roads to and from the capital. Quietly. You're not to engage."

"Never do," Orwyn replied, his stance loosening. His reply earned a skeptical huff from Brenn.

They'd walked through this ritual before. Orders given, assurances offered, faith exchanged without need for ceremony. It was the language they'd built over years of survival, of choosing each other when the rest of the world had failed them both.

Orwyn stepped closer, clapping a hand to Brenn's shoulder. His grip was firm, grounding, steady as the salt-beaten rock beneath them. "You worry too much, brother bear. The world's been ending since before we were born. We're just here to make sure it doesn't do it without fair warning."

The tension in Brenn's jaw eased, but the weight in his chest remained. He covered Orwyn's hand with his own, holding it there a moment longer than necessary. "Korva's still gone," he said. "On orders of her own. When she returns, and she should soon enough, I'll keep watch over her. You have my word."

Orwyn's expression softened, his easy humor giving way to deep affection. His sister. The only blood he had left. "Good," he said quietly. "She won't thank you for it, but she'll need it all the same. Don't let her come looking for me."

"I'd never allow it."

"I know." Orwyn squeezed his shoulder once more before releasing him. "That's why I can leave without looking back."

For a moment, they simply stood together. Two men who had found brotherhood in the margins of a world that wanted neither of them. The wind howled through the causeway, cold and relentless, but between them existed an easy quiet that had weathered far worse storms.

Brenn studied his friend's face. He wanted to say something. Some warning his instincts couldn't name. But he kept his lips clamped, afraid of sounding foolish.

"One of these days, you'll have to stop playing scout and help me run this place."

Orwyn's grin flashed, quick and genuine. "One of these days, you'll be the one to make such an order. You realize that, don't you?"

Brenn shook his head, half-amused, half-weary. "You've been saying that for years."

"And I'll keep saying it until you believe it." Orwyn adjusted the strap of his bow, his fingers brushing over the feathers woven into the elaborate trim of his collar. A gift from Korva, years ago, when she'd still been small enough to climb his back.

"The cliffs need a bear at the helm, Brenn. Not a fretting mother who sees too much, not an owl who flies too far. Someone who stands firm when the wind tries to tear us all away."

"The cliffs have Rhedda."

"Rhedda has unpredictable vision. But you have certainty." Orwyn met his gaze, unflinching. "There's a difference, and you know it."

Brenn said nothing, but the words settled into him, heavy and uncomfortable in the way truth often was.

They clasped wrists in the firm and sacred Cliffborn warrior's farewell. Orwyn pulled him forward with surprising strength, drawing the mass of him into a back-slapping embrace that forced a grunt out of Brenn.

"Keep the cliffs safe, bear," Orwyn said as he pulled back. He dipped his head in respect, not as subordinate to commander, but as brother to brother.

"Keep yourself safe, owl," Brenn answered, his throat tight. "That's an order."

Orwyn's bright smile returned, reckless as ever. "Yes, sir."

He turned toward the ledge, and the change took him mid-stride. Feathers rippled where flesh had been, his body collapsing inward and unfurling outward all at once. Wings stretched wide to catch the ocean wind, pale silver against the dark sky. He rose swiftly, powerfully, the sea spray scattering cold against Brenn's face as the owl climbed higher, a ghost against the clouds.

Brenn watched until he could no longer distinguish feathers from shadow, until the shape of his brother disappeared entirely into the teeth of the storm. Even then, he remained, the echo of wings fading into the endless rhythm of surf and wind.

He lifted his gaze toward the horizon, where storm and sky bled together into indistinguishable gray. He murmured a prayer. Softly, and only to the gods who might still listen. Who might still care for men the world had abandoned.

Safe travels. Swift returns. And if the worst should come, let it find him ready.

The wind carried his words away, swallowed them whole, and gave nothing back.

Brenn turned from the ledge and walked back into the stone halls, carrying the weight of farewells and the unshakable sense that something, somewhere, had already begun to shift.

CHAPTER 6

The dream shattered at her feet, leaving only shards of visions and broken memories.

Jagged mountains rose beneath a bruised sky. Black fog crawled across open fields like a waking beast. At the heart of the chaos loomed a tall looking glass, warped and vast, its surface splintering outward into a thousand broken truths. Each piece gleamed impossibly bright, razor-sharp edges hurtling toward her chest. In another heartbeat, they would pierce straight through—

Reny jerked awake. Pale morning light pooled around her, but dread sat heavy on her chest. Her sheets tangled around her legs, damp with sweat. Fog blurred the tavern windows, softening River's Edge into an unfamiliar haze. She pressed her palms against her eyes, willing the images away.

She chose simple, unadorned things and dressed quickly. Snug black pants, worn boots, and a white linen shirt with the sleeves rolled to her forearms. Her auburn hair tumbled wild from sleep, and for once, she left it unbound. Her own small defiance against the nightmare still coiled in her mind.

Outside, the fog thinned, unveiling the first golden rays of a late-summer sunrise through the tired trees. She walked barefoot to the water's edge, crouched, and splashed her face. The river ran cool over dark stones, the hushed babble pleasantly woven with the morning's birdsong.

A rabbit nosed through the clover nearby, unbothered by her presence. Two mourning doves pecked at the ground by her feet, indifferent to her movements. Reny drew her fingers through her hair with a measured exhale, teasing out the worst tangles before gathering it into a loose braid.

The air shifted, unsettling the morning's peace.

Birdsong faltered. The doves burst skyward. The rabbit darted into the brush, its white tail flashing. Reny froze mid-braid, spine straightening, every line of her body taut.

From the last row of trees, a shadow emerged.

A warden of the wild stepped free from the wood line. His antlers spiraled high, vast arcs of moss-draped bone crowned in silver from the remaining fog. His coat ran deep earthen brown, darker along the spine as though he bore the night on his back. His eyes carried the weight of ages, old as root and river.

The stag drifted through the clearing, each stride too certain, too measured, for any common beast. Each hoof-fall struck with authority until he reached the river and lowered his head to drink.

Reny drew a shallow breath and held it.

Endarian priests still wandered from village to village, preaching prophecy and a promised return, but their words never stirred her into faith. The gods had been absent for generations, their names and stories ground to ash. But watching the stag glide through the mist, drinking right beside her, she understood why others felt called to believe. Not because she did, but because the world still held things that defied explanation. When autumn neared, just before the hunts began, he appeared.

And every year, it astonished her.

She turned slowly, angling her profile toward him, and kept her voice soft as a welcoming prayer. "Good morning, your highness."

The stag lifted its head, droplets falling from its chin like dew shaken from a branch. Its ancient gaze fixed on her as it drew another step forward. Closer than it had ever dared in the seasons before. She held still, but not out of fear. Only respect, and a strange kind of recognition. The stag's great head dipped, nostrils flaring.

And then it eased even closer. When it stopped, its warmth reached her skin, nose lowering and stretching with inquisitive eyes. Reny lifted her hand. Velvet found her palm and nestled there.

"Thank you." A soft, knowing smile curved her lips. "You'd best move on now, before they all wake. Be smarter than the ones who hunt you."

The stag snorted in response, one deep note that resonated through the hush. It turned, antlers catching the morning light, and slipped back into the deep green of the forest, dissolving into fog and leaf until only silence remained.

Reny let out a long breath. She felt a prickle at the back of her neck, the unmistakable sensation of being watched. Her head snapped toward the barn. The doors stood slightly ajar, shadow pooling in the gap.

For a heartbeat, her face stayed soft with wonder, but it quickly hardened into stone. Her eyes narrowed, posture snapping back into familiar, guarded lines. The tenderness of the moment vanished behind her chill reserve.

Without a word, she rose, dusted her palms against her pants, and headed toward the tavern.

Rook had risen at first light, a habit too deeply ingrained to break.

He stood in the shadowed gap between the barn doors, watching the fog thin over the river. Then she appeared. Barefoot, hair unbound, moving through the morning like she belonged to it.

Her auburn hair caught the sun—caught *him*—ember-red threads flaring where the light touched. But it was the way she moved that held him there, as though the land itself had shaped her with its pulse. The rabbit at the clover remained at ease. The doves near her feet were unbothered. She carried none of the careless noise most people made, only a natural grace most would never possess.

He respected that.

Rook leaned against the doorframe, eyes narrowing. Every village had its secrets, and she was likely just another. An anomaly in a world fractured by tainted magic. Or the descendant of a lucky family missed in Endaria's past witch hunts.

That was what he told himself. And yet, a distant, primal recognition stirred in his chest at the sight of her, so he stayed in the barn's darkness. Watching. Waiting.

The air shifted, birdsong faltering. The doves exploded skyward; the rabbit bolted. Reny froze mid-braid, every line of her body pulled taut. From the threshold, Rook stared at her stillness. A mirror to his own—so precise that he caught himself leaning forward.

The fog curled as a shadow emerged from the trees.

A massive stag. Antlers spiraling high, covered in moss and mist. Coat dark as old earth. Eyes holding the weight of ages. Rook went rigid, every instinct pulled tight to the point of pain.

Creatures like this belonged to the far north, in the Old Wood along the Veil, where magic bled through root and stone, distorting the natural order. They weren't meant to exist this far south except in bard-songs and legends—stories traded between men that spoke of a world lost to time.

He'd seen a stag like this only once. As a small boy in Rithmor, just before the land turned bitter. Before everything did. It had watched him from the tree line with eyes that saw too much, and he'd been too awed to move. No one believed him when he recounted the tale at the royal table. A lying tongue, the king declared, and an imagination too wild for his father's court.

So it was whipped out of him.

And yet here one stood. Undeniable. Alive.

The stag drifted through the clearing, each stride too certain for any common beast. It reached the river, lowered its head, and drank. Right beside her.

Rook's hand found the hilt at his side. Stags could be dangerous this time of year. And here she was, facing one as though the wild world might yield to her.

Reckless twit.

But the animal did not charge. Didn't stamp a hoof or lower its antlers in warning. Its ears stayed loose, its massive frame radiating a calm so unnatural it made his skin crawl. The stag eased forward, and his nose lowered. Reny lifted her hand.

Rook's grip tightened—

But when the stag's velvet nose found her palm, it simply rested there. Her lips were moving, but he could only catch the shape of her words, not the sound.

It had to be nothing more than an Endarian stag. One foolishly used to humans.

The stag snorted in response to whatever she'd said before it turned, antlers bright in the morning light. It disappeared back into the treeline as easily as it appeared.

Rook's pulse hammered against his ribs. *What in the hells had he just seen?*

Approached by such a creature, yet she hadn't flinched. No startled gasp, no trace of fear, no call for help. Only unshaken calm, like such an encounter was ordinary. He let out a controlled breath.

As if the sound betrayed him, her head snapped toward the barn. Rook stilled, cloaked by the lingering dark. *She couldn't see him. Impossible.*

For a heartbeat, her face remained soft. And then it hardened again. Her eyes narrowed, posture snapping back to its usual defensiveness. He watched her rise and walk back to the tavern.

Rook forced his pulse to settle. He'd seen enough to pay close attention to this woman. This flame-haired creature who snarled at flirtation and moved like a gathering storm.

She was an errant thread tugging at the fabric of his understanding.

And he would not let go until he unraveled her.

CHAPTER 7

By midafternoon, from Reny's efforts alone, the day's tavern chores were finished. Tables wiped, hearth swept, linen folded tight across clean mattresses. The hunting party had long since gone, their boots and hounds and noise leaving nothing but the faint scent of leather and bow resin.

Outside, the hammering continued, underscored by the low thrum of men's conversation.

From her seat at a table, folding dish rags, Reny caught a glimpse through the window of Rook atop the porch rail, one leg braced as he leaned in to drive a nail into a fresh board. Garron passed something up to him. An iron square, maybe, or another sarcastic remark, and Rook smiled.

Reny didn't like how easily he wore it. That smile.

Or how soon into the day she found herself looking for it.

The kitchen door banged open from the bar area behind her as Maren swept in like a gust of wind. Before her usual shift.

Too early to be a coincidence. Kohl at her lashes, a smudge of soft red at her mouth, and a faint perfume behind her ears that smelled like sweet summer fruit. Her apron was flour-dusted, though Reny suspected it was more for dramatic effect than honest effort.

"You're here early," Reny remarked with an arched brow, not looking up from the rag she held mid-fold.

Maren whisked by her, adjusting chairs that didn't need adjusting, her gaze making an unsubtle sweep of the front windows. "Figured I'd be helpful."

Reny tilted her head, the corner of her mouth curving into a smirk. "A rare and potentially realm-altering impulse."

Maren only sighed and drifted to a table near the window, her posture shifting. Shoulders lifting, chin angling, expression softening into that practiced, dreamy glaze. Reny recognized the performance instantly and rolled her eyes.

"Thought maybe our new help needed another set of hands," she added breezily, scanning the width of the porch before throwing a sidelong glance over her shoulder. "From someone not covered in cobwebs."

Reny snorted, tossing another folded towel onto the stack. "You're a menace."

"He's the menace, actually," Maren countered, nodding to where Rook stood with his back turned. "The tall one. With the arms. And legs. And that back..."

"He also has a face," Reny said dryly.

"Believe me," Maren murmured, still staring, lips curving, "I noticed."

Reny didn't bother to reply. She had no interest in indulging Maren's fluttering lashes another second. Rising and untying her apron, she crossed the room to lift the egg basket from its nail by the door.

"I'm checking the coop."

"Don't hurry," Maren called after her, already moving back to the window. "I've got the floor. And the view."

The yard stretched beneath the sweeping afternoon light, gold and dappled where it filtered through the waving oak branches overhead. Reny moved briskly behind the barn, avoiding the more direct path by the tavern porch. Her boots crunched over straw and dry earth, the air thick with the scent of sun-warmed hay. The chickens stirred as she approached, ruffling their feathers and issuing their usual round of clucks in half-hearted protest.

She opened the gate and stepped into the coop. Dust swirled lazily in the sunlight, catching the breeze. A few hens continued to fuss at her presence before finally settling with sleepy indignation. A rhythm she welcomed. *Predictable and uncomplicated.*

Halfway through collecting the eggs, the air behind her changed. Not with movement or sound, but with a presence that swept over her like a winter chill. She didn't need to turn to know who it was. Instinct called her to look back anyway.

Rook leaned against the barn's edge just beyond the open gate, arms folded, one boot crossed over the other. His posture was loose, but his stare was not. A strip of shadow from an overhead branch divided his face in half. One eye swallowed by darkness, the other locked on her, expression intent but unreadable.

Her fingers tightened on the edge of the nest box. She crouched again, forcing her attention back to the hens, but her breathing had grown shallow. The familiar task she'd settled into moments ago felt strange and brittle.

Still, he didn't speak. He watched, letting the silence hum between them. She lasted another minute before rising, the basket steady in the crook of her arm as she turned to face him at last.

No cloak today. Only a pale gray shirt with sleeves rolled to the elbows and black trousers that fit close to his frame. Freed from hood and shadow, his face struck harder than her memory from the night before had allowed. High cheekbones, an uncompromising jaw, dark irises that absorbed the daylight and her along with it, offering nothing back in return.

Her gaze flicked to the corded muscle braced on the gate, to the flex of his arm as he shifted his weight.

A glance. A half breath. Enough to betray her before she dragged her focus back to his face.

"Is there something you need?" Her voice stayed cool and even. *Damnit.*

He tilted his head, one corner of his mouth lifting. His fingers drummed once on the rail, idle yet purposeful. She refused to follow the movement this time, and something in his eyes changed. Awareness, or perhaps recognition.

"Just thought I'd bid you good morning. Afternoon now, I suppose." His lopsided smile landed like a peace offering.

She answered only with silence, eyes sliding away in dismissal.

His smile faded, chin angling toward the trees. "That stag this morning. Big one, wasn't he? Caught sight of him just before the mist burned off. Thought maybe I was dreaming, or that I'd cracked my head on a barn post."

The joke didn't land. She adjusted the basket higher on her hip, body weight sliding to the other leg.

His gaze tracked the shift in her stance. She hated that he noticed. *Hated more that she couldn't seem to hold still under his attention.*

"He came so close to you," Rook continued, words overly light and careless. "Didn't bolt, snort, or pin his ears. Never seen anything quite like that. Bard songs tell of witches and Whisperfolk greeting beasts that way, you know."

Reny turned her head, feigning indifference. Her feet betrayed her with a small shuffle backward, instinctive as a heartbeat. She looked up, catching a smirk and what appeared to be satisfaction on his face. It made her teeth clench.

"Looked like two old friends catching up, if you ask me," he went on, shoulders rolling in a careless shrug.

"I don't remember anyone asking you," Reny said just as lightly, her chin lifting a fraction.

His mouth curled, almost predatory, his focus locked on her. She refused to flinch.

"So, what are you, then? A forest-bound nymph descended from the Cliffborn? Or a witch with an antlered familiar?"

Reny let out a short, humorless breath. "Not even close. Besides, magic hasn't been in this part of Endaria for a long time."

"Shame." His gaze tracked the stiff set of her shoulders, the tension pulling at her jaw. "You've got the look for it, though. Hair like spun embers, catching the sun the way it does? You might even fool someone into thinking that you're magical. If you ever smiled."

"I'm not in the habit of fooling people," Reny bit out, her voice becoming a serpent's strike against the flirtation. She took a wide, confident step toward the coop gate. Toward him. "Or pretending to be something I'm not. Especially when it comes to nonsense and hearthside fables that got Endarians *killed* in the Hunting Age."

A muscle twitched in Rook's jaw as she approached. Her expression was uncompromising, leaving no room for doubt. She expected him to move.

His gaze swept her face in slow assessment. "Ah, okay," he murmured at last, stepping aside. He held the gate open with his body, leaving just enough space for her to walk through.

Reny slipped past him, the narrow gap forcing her too close. Close enough that her shoulder brushed his chest as she passed. She widened her next stride, deliberately putting distance between them, the egg basket tucked on one hip. Keeping her back to him, her chin angled so her words could carry, clear and defiant, over her shoulder.

"That stag's lived in these woods longer than anyone. He's wiser than every man who's marched through with a bow or blade, convinced of his own importance."

"Or maybe," Rook replied, obvious amusement coloring his tone as he shut the coop gate, "he just keeps the right company."

Reny didn't answer. She kept walking, braid swaying with each measured step until she disappeared around the corner of the barn.

Rook stayed where he was, fingers still resting on the gate's latch. The chickens had settled back into their idle clucking, indifferent to the tension still coiled in the air. He let out a slow breath, replaying the exchange.

She'd given him nothing. Every question meticulously deflected, every probe parried with that sharp tongue of hers. But her body betrayed what her words refused to give him. The shuffle backward when he'd pressed too close to the truth. The way she couldn't hold still under his attention.

A doe with her ears pricked, ready to bolt at the first wrong move.

He'd almost had her. Almost cracked that iron composure wide open. *And then she'd surprised him.*

Instead of bolting, she'd walked straight toward him. Lifted her chin and met his stare with those blazing green eyes, daring him to hold his ground. When she'd slipped through the gate, her shoulder had brushed his chest. Deliberate or not, he couldn't be sure. And the smell of her, of whatever oils she wore or soap she used, hit him like a fist to the sternum.

Sweet and smoky and somehow, unmistakably her. Like incense curling through a forgotten hall. Like dessert and witchcraft.

He hadn't meant to breathe her in as she passed, but instinct outran discipline. Luckily, she'd been so focused on getting away from him that she didn't notice.

Poor little doe.

She had no idea what she was provoking.

He stared at the corner where she'd vanished, recalling the proud lift of her shoulders. The sway of her braid. The measured rhythm of her retreat. Unhurried, unbroken, refusing to give him the satisfaction of looking back.

Savage little tart. Against all better sense, heat sparked low in his chest. The kind he knew better than to trust. The kind that had no place in the task his king had set before him.

But he let it burn anyway.

CHAPTER 8

The few days since Rook's arrival had blurred into a pattern Reny couldn't quite escape.

Warm afternoons and cloudless skies. Shadows stretching long across River's Edge, painting the village in hues of gold and rust as the sun slipped behind the treetops. And always, without meaning to, she'd watch from the corner of the tavern yard, mindfully tucked out of their sightline as the two men worked side by side like they'd known each other for years.

Garron clapped Rook on the back with a laugh that seemed borrowed from some younger version of himself. She couldn't hear what he said, but she saw the way Rook's mouth curved. Something almost surprised in it, almost soft. He dipped his head in response, setting the last of the tools in the wooden box at the back corner of the barn.

Garron moved with a spring in his step across the cart path, shoulders loose, jaw unknotted in a way she hadn't seen in years. A former soldier's ease, softened by shared labor and the kind of male camaraderie she knew he missed. What Flinn's youth and inexperience weren't quite ready to provide. The sight of him so at ease with Rook twisted in her chest with a familiar ache. One that whispered the same, haunting warning.

If it feels this easy, this good, it will not last. If it can be taken from you, best never to let it in at all.

Chewing on the thought, Reny looked up as Old Harl crossed the yard, a string of trout swinging from his weathered hands. He gave her a gap-toothed grin, pride lighting his pale eyes.

"Nearly jumped into the basket, they did." He chuckled. "Figure the river's feelin' generous today."

Reny huffed a soft laugh, stepping forward into the amber wash of dusk. "I told you. The river just likes you better."

He pocketed the coins she placed into his palm, shaking his head with a kind, worn smile that could rival any grandfather's. "Ah, doubt that, deary. We all know you're the good-luck charm 'round here. More magic in that little finger than I've seen in my whole life. Don't go spillin' it, now."

"That's our secret, Harl." She rolled her eyes, but the smile curving her lips was real. "You'll get me in trouble."

The cheerful glint in his expression dimmed. "Mind yourself after sundown," he said, voice dropping though it was only them in the yard. "Word is, the Cliffborn half-breeds are runnin' the Oakwoods again. Veil's thinner up north, and when it weakens, things don't always keep to their paths." He jerked his chin toward the tree line. "Light the bridge lanterns early. Sing the river-rhyme if you're caught past dark. Can't hurt."

"They keep to their cliffs, Harl," Reny said gently. "I'll be fine."

"Aye." His mouth twisted, skeptical. "And rivers keep to their banks 'til they don't." He managed a smile, but the worry held firm in his furrowed brow. "You mind what I said, girl. I'm too old to go fishing you out of trouble."

She nodded, watching affectionately as he shuffled off toward the river bridge, humming now, the setting sun catching on the edges of his white hair.

By the time the firepit was ready, dusk had deepened toward true dark. Reny crouched beside the pile of split logs, threading the cleaned fish onto a fresh roasting line with deft hands.

She looked around the tavern yard and struck the flint. The fire caught far too quickly. The wood, still damp from the previous night's rain, should have resisted. Instead, it flared with impossible eagerness. The whisper of her breath, the slight tilt of her hands, and flame answered. A hungry bloom of orange and gold engulfed the logs.

Reny didn't flinch away from the sudden burst. If anything, she leaned forward, breath caught on a fine line between awe and recklessness.

Fire had taken everything from her once. The ghost forever with her—smoke and ruin threading through her dreams like a scar that wouldn't fade. She should have recoiled from it. Avoid it at all costs. But it remained the only seduction she'd ever truly surrendered to, warming her blood even as it scorched her memories.

It spared her. Let her survive when no one else did.

The flames danced higher, moving not by wind but by the unseen tether between them. A connection, ancient and eager. For a heartbeat, she heard the river rhyme Harl mentioned, unbidden on her tongue.

Root and river, bone, and rain. What was blessed, now bless again.

The one mothers sang at the flood line or on the hillside when the fields desperately needed rain. Her mouth didn't shape the words, but the memory of them thrummed through her bones as heat gathered, obedient and bright.

Of the ember, of the stone, protect my soul and see me home.

The fire was her curse and her blessing. A tangled ruin of both. She let her hand slip closer to the twisting flames, knowing she should bury it like she always did.

But tonight, she let it rise.

The bathing room's heat clung to Rook's skin, along with the faint scent of the pine and mint soap Garron had given him. After weeks on the road, the simple act of a hot, daily shower felt like royal luxury. Dressed in clean pants, he crossed barefoot and shirtless into his room across the hall. The floorboards groaned softly under his weight. He paused, rolling his shoulders as the quiet settled around him.

The last few days replayed in fragments. Garron's voice carrying easy instruction. The rhythm of hammer and nail. And at the end of every day, that clap on the back—firm, familiar, weighted with approval.

"That's a day's work well done, boy."

Boy. It should have grated down to the bone. From anyone else, it would have. But from Garron, it landed differently. More pride than slight.

Almost fatherly. The thought unsettled him more than he wanted to admit. He hadn't come here for belonging. Hadn't asked for the warmth that crept beneath his ribs when the old man looked at him with hope and pride and friendship.

It would make what came next harder.

Rook moved to the window, leaning one forearm against the frame. Through the cracked, foggy glass, the garden beds lay in shadow, the distant trees blurring with nightfall.

Movement caught his eye. Then light.

Fire.

Toward the back of the yard, Reny knelt beside the firepit. He'd seen her strike the flint, but what followed locked him in place. The fire didn't hesitate. It leapt, bursting upward, immediate and full. Her lack of surprise or recoil sent an icy ripple straight through him. Rook watched as her shoulders loosened, her lips parting slightly as the blaze leaned toward her.

He scanned the trees, searching for wind that wasn't there. When he looked back, he saw it plain. The fire moved wrong. It danced before her, bending closer with what looked disturbingly like awareness. The firelight caught her profile, illuminating the faint smile curving her mouth. Her fingers hovered closer to the heat. Closer than anyone else would dare.

Before he could tell if she was outright touching the flames, her head snapped up to the trees, eyes searching. Her body tensed as if sensing she was no longer alone.

Rook took a wide step back, letting the room's darkness swallow him before she could spot him, his expression blank. Beneath his feet, the tavern had come to life with the clatter of plates and Maren's laughter, but every sound was muffled, barely registering. His thoughts were far too loud.

She wasn't what she pretended to be. Either that, or she possessed something—some artifact, maybe a relic—that answered her. After years of chasing half-truths through Endaria's backwater towns and forgotten hills, perhaps one rumor finally led him in the right direction.

Fire clearly answered her. *But why? And from where?*

He wasn't going to leave until he understood what she was or where her power came from.

Because he couldn't afford to be wrong again.

High above the tavern yard, wings sliced through the last of the light. A raven drifted low on the cooling air, feathers black as deep water, drinking the last of the sun's gold. She circled once, twice, before settling onto a branch in the crooked oak at the garden's edge.

The world far below flickered in miniature. Woman and fire, darkness and flame. The blaze should not have sprung so fast, nor curved so close. The damp wood should have resisted. Instead, fire ignited with startling ease, bending toward the woman's hand like a spirit recognizing its master.

The raven caught what Rook's eyes had not. For a fraction of a second, Reny's fingers slipped directly into the fire, her hand, unharmed, wreathed in flame.

This was what Rhedda had sent her to find. She was the unburned.

Korva, cloaked in feather and hollow bone, had spent weeks watching nearby rivers and rooftops, soaring over the roads threading around River's Edge. Weeks in silence, waiting for the signs. Now prophecy blazed right below her, bright as noon despite the nightfall.

The Flame was rising.

Her focus shifted to the tavern's second-floor window, where her keen vision picked out the figure half-hidden in shadow, rigid and watchful. The man's intentions were obscured, his face unreadable. She sensed a deep concealment, beyond shadow or clothing. He carried an energy she couldn't place. And couldn't investigate further without risking discovery.

Her instructions were explicit. *Watch. Observe. Do not engage.*

The raven's feathers ruffled, whispering against the leaves. The branch trembled beneath her, springing free as she launched skyward, arrowing east. Behind her, the horizon surrendered its last small fraction of light.

It was time to tell Rhedda.

The sacred fire of a new dawn was nearly upon them, and she would be the one to tell her people that the first sparks were catching.

CHAPTER 9

I n the kitchen, Reny moved in a well-worn rhythm between the chopping board and clay oven. Her braid had unraveled hours ago, loose strands curling against her temples from the long day's work.

Beside her, Maren was laughing with Flinn, who stood at the counter, elbow-deep in dough. He kept giving crooked smiles as Maren giggled, looking one ill-timed joke away from upending the whole mixing bowl.

A broad hand settled on Reny's shoulder. Garron stood there, his expression caught between stern and amused. He tipped his chin toward the stairs. "Go wash up before the crowd rolls in."

"Why?" Reny blinked, genuinely confused.

"Look at you, girl. Soot on your face, sweat on your brow, and you smell like fire and fish."

"Better than armpits and ale," she shot back with a smirk.

His full, easy laugh rolled through the kitchen. "Maybe. But you look like you wrestled the fish first. Pretty faces make the men spend more. Don't argue."

"Calling me pretty, old man?"

"I'm calling you profitable. Now, git." He lumbered forward, shooing her like a stray cat.

Reny rolled her eyes, unfastened her apron, and tossed it to the hook by the door. "If the stew burns while I'm upstairs, you're to blame."

"Blame me all you want. Just don't come back in here smelling like pond water."

She was halfway up the stairs when she heard his voice boom from the kitchen.

"Lock the door when you shower, girl," Garron called after her. "Half the men coming in tonight already have more ale in 'em than sense."

Her laugh drifted down the stairwell, light as ash on the wind.

In the bathing room, Reny tested the water until it hissed and warmed, then stepped beneath the spray. Heat poured over her shoulders, sliding down her spine. She tipped her face back into it, eyes closing as water rushed over her.

Her thoughts drifted to him before she could stop them.

Rook.

The lean cut of him. The way he'd cornered her at the coop. That unsettling gaze, always trying to see through her defenses. Even when she dried off, heat clung to her like a secret.

She wiped the mirror clear with her wrist, revealing a softer version of herself. Fresh-faced, her hair free and falling in clean, loose waves. She gathered part of it, pinning it with two hairpins from the small drawer, leaving the rest to spill over her shoulders. A touch of color dabbed to her lips, faint as a whisper.

He'd consumed her thoughts, even as she dressed. Uninvited, insistent.

She chose her crimson dress. Form-fitted, daring in its neckline, with her shoulders and collarbones left bare. By no means her usual choice, but her hands found it anyway. Knotting the ties at her waist, she glanced once more at her reflection before stepping into the hall.

Nearly colliding with him.

Rook stood outside the room beside hers, a dark silhouette in the low light. Arms folded loosely over his chest, one boot braced against the doorframe. His navy shirt clung to his frame. His hair, still wet from bathing, was swept away from his face. He looked refined, every edge carrying quiet precision. Like a blade fresh from the forge, built for beauty as much as use.

Her pulse stumbled at the sight.

He let the silence hang between them, eyeing her. His study of her was deliberate, tracing a slow path from her feet upward. The look wasn't crude—only curious, full of questions. Which somehow felt even more disarming.

She froze, air catching in her lungs. Every part of her went rigid as she lifted her chin and jerked a thumb toward her door. "That's my room."

Panic set in. *How the hells did she not notice sooner? It had been days.*

Rook arched a brow, feigning surprise far too obvious to be sincere. "Is it now? Well, I suppose that makes us neighbors." With open palms and a dramatic sweep of his arms, he gestured to the door beside hers. "Because this is *my* room."

She didn't move. Her jaw locked tight, every insult she wanted to spit scorched to ash behind her teeth. He watched her with deepening interest, the corner of his mouth threatening a smile.

"Who's that for?" He noted her dress, letting the question fall easy as rain.

Her eyes narrowed. "Tonight's ledger. For patrons who tip better than you."

Hunger flashed in his eyes. There and gone, quickly replaced by something safe and neutral. "Is that so?"

"I know it is," she said. Angling past him in the cramped hall, she paused to throw one last cool jab over her shoulder. "If we're sharing a wall, you better not be noisy."

He leaned against the frame to let her pass, and she felt his gaze trail her as she went. "I can't make any promises about that." His words landed slick. A dare and an invitation all at once.

A vivid flush, unwanted and undeniable, crept into her cheeks despite herself.

Bristling like a feral cat, she refused to acknowledge the comment and hurried away, her steps clipped as she retreated down the stairs.

Rook's grin finally broke wide as he watched her go.

That dress. Gods, that dress.

Crimson fabric clinging to every curve, shoulders bare, collarbones catching the low hall light like an invitation. She'd lifted her chin like she was daring him to look, even as her cheeks flushed pink at his words.

She had no idea what she did to him. Or maybe she did, and that was worse.

His grin faded as the silence of the hall settled around him. He cast one glance at her door, his instincts beginning their familiar whispers.

Find the relics, the tomes, the siphon she keeps. Proof that her power came from anywhere but herself.

His hand twitched toward the handle.

It would be easy. A few minutes while she worked the floor below. Answers waiting right behind an unlocked door.

But Rook remained where he was, staring toward her room with his mind caught in a more dangerous war. The one between his mission and this woman, who was becoming an unbearable distraction.

He pushed away from the doorframe, hands sliding into his pockets as he strolled toward the tavern stairs to follow her. The search could wait.

Tonight, he wanted to watch her work.

The dinner rush was a flurry of shuffling boots, overlapping voices, and tankards hitting tabletops in quick succession. Hunters, merchants, and regulars had already filled the room. Two recruiters in Endarian cloaks took up a small table in the corner, satchels fat with golden bribery, their eyes in search of gullible candidates to join the ranks. Dice rattled over the strained tuning of an old lute.

Rook had stationed himself near the bar with his sleeves rolled up, helping Flinn wrestle kegs into place. He settled behind the mahogany counter like he'd been there for years.

Listening. Catching more than anyone suspected. He always did.

Let the eyes wander elsewhere. Let the voices forget that anyone could be listening.

"She's still here, huh? Not married off somewhere?"

"Too protective of her old man to leave," another answered. "And too mean."

The men chuckled.

"Same bow hanging on the wall, I'll wager. Bet she's still sharp. Remember when she beat all three of us at the target rings?"

"I still say that third arrow curved."

"Curved?" a third man laughed. "She enchanted it, that's why."

"Don't say that so damn loud," the second hissed, glancing around. "She's got fire in her hands. You've seen it."

"You're a gods-damned liar," another muttered into his ale, half-drunk and skeptical.

"Garron raised her smart. If she were mine and worked in a place like this, I'd keep her close and train her well. Wouldn't cross her, not even with a blade in my hand."

Rook wiped a smudge from a glass, filing every word away. He glanced toward the front of the room, finding her without meaning to.

Reny was standing by a large table, smiling. A genuine smile, given freely to a man with messy golden hair. The lopsided grin he kept flashing showed too many teeth. He leaned into her, whispering something that made her laugh. Not the polite or practiced kind for tips, but a bright, unrestrained laugh that cut clean through the room's noise.

Rook's fist tightened around the glass.

A wave of heat swept through him—irrational, unwelcome. He didn't like the way the man leaned into her. Or that Reny didn't stiffen or dismiss him the way she did everyone else.

You idiot. What's wrong with you?

He had no claim to her, no right to the tension coiling through every inch of him, and yet it twisted in him anyway. The woman moved like salvation and laughed like freedom—neither of which he had any business wanting.

Swallowing hard, Rook forced every thought and feeling back down. Reminded himself why he was here in this insignificant, backwater village in the first place. One thought burned steady, desperate to override the rest.

Fulfill your oath.

CHAPTER 10

The rush ebbed just enough for Reny to slip into the kitchen, her arms finally free. She leaned against the counter, the oven's warmth seeping into her spine, a few stray strands of hair sticking to her cheek. A familiar presence brushed beside her, an elbow nudging her ribs.

Maren.

"You know," Maren purred near her ear, tone too innocent, "if your goal was to rile up the tall, broody one, you could've told me. Would've helped make a real spectacle of it."

Reny blinked at her. "What?"

Maren's brows danced a sly waltz. "Please, Reny, don't play dumb. I'm starving for entertainment. I saw the way Rook looked when you smiled at Brannic after he came in with his cousins."

Reny groaned, rolling her eyes with the kind of despair only Maren could wring from her. "All hells, Mar, you're relentless—"

"No, no, no," Maren cut in with full theatrics, half-collapsing against the counter, the back of her hand pressed to her brow. Her eyes sparkled with mischief. "This is delicious. That man practically ground his molars to dust watching you laugh at Brannic's stupid jokes."

Turning back to the simmering pot, Reny stirred with more force than necessary, refusing to acknowledge the flush creeping up her neck.

Maren grinned, savoring every second of Reny's discomfort. "Dark and Dangerous out there hates the thought of someone else making you smile like that. Mark my words."

A huff escaped her, but Reny didn't bother hiding the amusement glinting in her eyes. "You're imagining things because you're bored."

"Mm-hmm. I am bored," Maren conceded, her voice a sultry song. "But I'm not imagining anything. And you know it."

Reny didn't answer but made no further effort to deny. A dangerous thought, small and nagging, sparked to life, taking root before she could talk herself out of it.

This might be a little fun after all.

Reny returned to the tavern floor with a new sway threading her steps. Subtle, but impossible to miss. She caught Maren's eye across the room and the silent applause glinting there. Rarely did Reny join in her schemes.

Tonight, she'd uncharacteristically accepted the challenge.

Her smile came quicker, her banter warmer as she drifted table to table. She topped off tankards with easy laughter and light in her eyes. Coins slipped from pockets more freely, conversations bent toward her, jokes landed easier. Even the hearth itself seemed to flare higher, coaxed to burn hotter as if it too had chosen to answer her.

She drew every eye in the room like moths to lanternlight.

And she felt it, that forbidden heat rising in her chest. The wild tether she usually kept buried. Tonight, she let it simmer closer to the surface, let it warm her skin and brighten her presence.

Her warmth swept over the tables, her voice clear as a bell above the layered clamor, until her focus caught near the bar. And found him.

Rook stood half-hidden in shadow, the distant firelight catching the hard angle of his jaw. His stare seized hers, gathering like a storm on the horizon. The weight of it cinched around her ribs until the air between them felt like a single, taut thread. She couldn't look away.

"Hey, Reny!" Brannic stepped into her line of sight, lamplight catching the gold in his curls and the blue of his eyes. His voice carried a hope he didn't have the sense to hide.

Over his shoulder, she caught the faintest shift in Rook's expression. Not a frown. Only ice-cold observation, and the entire room grew heavier for it.

"I gave the bard a coin to play something," Brannic said, sheepishly rubbing the back of his neck. "Thought maybe you'd dance with me?" His hand extended toward her, earnest and awkward.

Reny hesitated for a breath. With a soft huff—half exasperation, half affection—she let her hand slip into his. The bard's tune changed, turning slow and honeyed.

Brannic led her toward the open space between the tables. Their steps weren't graceful, but they carried familiarity and shared history. Something that had been, perhaps, almost love.

Her laugh broke loose when Brannic spun her, and for a moment, everything felt deceptively unburdened.

Her hair slipped over one shoulder, catching the glow of the hearth. From across the room, Maren raised her cup in a subtle salute, eyes gleaming with triumph. Reny didn't bother hiding her grin. But even as she laughed, her attention kept drifting toward the edges of the room.

She felt Rook's focus like a hand pressed to her back. Still rooted near the bar, tall and unyielding. She didn't need to look to know he hadn't moved. Hadn't sipped from his tankard. Hadn't looked away.

The bard's melody dipped, half-mournful notes curling through the tavern as his voice spun verses from stories the hills of Endaria had nearly forgotten.

"And flame called to stone, and the stone bowed down low, in echoes of names that they no longer know..."

As the song ended, Brannic dipped into an exaggerated bow. Reny curtsied in return. Not with mockery, but with grace and a warm smile. When she stood upright, she saw the question lingering in his eyes. The hope he'd carried since they were young.

She gave a playful punch to his arm and a platonic pat on his shoulder. His smile turned weak as he turned back toward his table, defeat softening his shoulders.

Reny passed the bar without a glance in Rook's direction, her skirts whispering around her legs as she breezed through the kitchen door. But she felt his attention chase after her, along with Maren, who was eager to pounce and share everything she'd seen.

Rook stood rooted where he'd been most of the night, one hand braced on a stool, the other curled around the tankard he still hadn't sipped from.

The kitchen door swung shut behind her, and the hearth fire—the whole room, really—seemed to dim in her absence.

He forced himself to exhale, his thoughts a torturous replay.

The way she'd emerged from the kitchen with that new sway in her step. The crimson dress catching the firelight. The easy laughter she'd given to everyone in the room.

Everyone except him.

And then the magic. He'd felt it the moment the shift took hold—a hum rippling through the air, prickling his skin, lifting the hairs at his nape. The hearth had flared higher without anyone touching it. The room had bent toward her like flowers turning to the sun.

She'd woven something over that tavern, whether she knew it or not.

But it was the dance that had nearly undone him.

Brannic's hand at the small of her back. The way the huntsman kept glancing at her curves. The easy way she'd let him hold her, spin her, make her laugh.

His grip on the tankard had tightened until his knuckles ached.

She can laugh with anyone. Dance with anyone. Smile at anyone.

He took a long swallow of ale, its bitterness doing nothing to douse the heat rolling in his center.

Just not with the likes of him, apparently.

Despite every logical reason to stay where he was, his mind had whispered wild commands. To step in. Cut between them. Take over.

No.

But then she'd turned Brannic down. Gently, but unmistakably. A punch to the arm. A most disappointing pat on the shoulder. The huntsman had walked away with slumped shoulders and a weak smile, and Rook had felt a small, private victory at the sight.

He hated himself for it.

"You'll break that thing to pieces if you squeeze it any tighter," Garron rumbled to his left.

Rook startled. A rarity. He hadn't heard the old man approach. White-knuckled on the tankard, he forced his hand to relax.

"It's just one dance," Garron said mildly, almost amused. "You're not about to start a war over it, are you?"

"Me? No, not at all. Just tired." The denial was too quick. Too flat.

"Mm." Garron didn't press, but the sidelong glance he cast said enough.

Silence stretched between them. Rook's focus held on the kitchen door a beat too long, willing her back through it.

Beside him, Garron leaned against the counter, hands clasped together. He let out a breath that seemed to come from the depths of his bones as he took in the main room, now quieter. Settled.

"She doesn't act like that often," Garron murmured, half to himself. "Usually carries herself like she's got more scars than skin. But Brannic always gets a dance when he passes through."

Rook said nothing, his jaw tight, his attention drifting back over the crowded room.

"They were close once," Garron continued without prompt, as if sensing Rook needed explanation to avoid combustion. "Childhood sweethearts, you might call them. Never believes anything good will last, so she never lets anything grow roots."

Rook's brow furrowed. "Yet she stays rooted here."

Garron's eyes slid toward him, laden with sad acknowledgment. "She could've left this little village a dozen times over. Had offers to marry.

Good ones, too. But she won't. Someone's got to look after us, she says. Me, Maren, Flinn."

Turning toward Garron, Rook met his eyes with assumed understanding. "A sense of duty makes her that stubborn."

"No, boy," Garron said, low, shaking his head. "It makes her lonely."

The words settled between them like a stone.

Rook looked away, staring into his drink, throat constricting.

"Women usually want to be taken care of," Garron added, lifting his tankard for a thoughtful sip. "But she insists on taking care of everyone else." A pause. "You ever know anybody like that?"

"Once or twice." Pressure built in Rook's chest, more suffocating than the entire evening's restraint. A feeling swelled, deeper than the jealousy he'd been battling.

Guilt. What a useless thing to feel.
Especially for someone like him.

Chapter 11

The air thickened as Korva sliced through it, salt stinging her lungs. Ahead, the Eastern Cliffs rose like a wall of silver, scarred white stone holding fast against the endless rage of the sea.

To others, they were jagged and treacherous. To Korva, they were salvation. Here, she was safe. And it was here she would soon be celebrated, because she'd found *her.*

The flame-bearer Rhedda had prophesied, the one who would usher in the new dawn. After weeks of watching and waiting, there she was. A woman with fire in her hands and ancient power threading through her veins like a song older than kingdoms.

No more isolation, no more hiding. No more losing their people to Aetherian butchers. No more children orphaned the way she and Orwyn had been.

Orwyn would be so proud of her.

Her talons scraped rock, feathers dissolving into flesh as her boots hit the path. Black hair whipped in the wind, her cloak snapping tight around her narrow frame.

Home.

Orwyn had carried her here when her world shattered, when their parents were slaughtered for having power Aetherians wanted to steal. He'd been six years her elder, but her mirror in every way that mattered. Her anchor in every storm. He'd trained her, encouraged her, coaxed strength out of her until she could fly without fear. It was for his sake as much as her own that the Cliff Mother had trusted her with this mission.

To watch the human lands for signs of the fire-bearer.

And she succeeded. Against all odds, against weeks of uncertainty, she had found her. The sacrifices and hiding and endless years of loss would all mean something now. The new dawn was coming, and Korva would be the one to tell them it was on the way.

She quickened her pace. Orwyn would be waiting like he always was, probably halfway down the path because he could never wait patiently. Brenn, too, with his stubborn steadiness and the crushing embrace of the bear he was. She could already imagine their faces when she told them. Orwyn's whoop of triumph and Brenn's rare, genuine smile.

I'm home! The thought warmed her, filled her ribs until they ached. For the first time in weeks, she breathed.

But when her eyes found Brenn on the path, torch in hand, the rising joy instantly faltered. He made no move to meet her. No grin split his face, no arm raised in welcome. He stood carved from the shadows, firelight carving hollows across his face, his jaw clenched tight.

And he was alone.

"Brenn!" she called, forcing brightness to her voice. "You won't believe it! I found the fire-bearer!" Her laughter came light, almost desperate. "Only you tonight? Where is my brother?"

He didn't answer. His shoulders sagged, and his silence was heavier than the roar of the sea below.

Dread swept through her, cold and immediate.

Brenn had spotted her long before she touched down.

The raven came racing across the moonlit sky, wings beating against the salt air with reckless speed. She flew as if nothing could touch her, as if the world was still whole, waiting for her to fly home.

Home.

The word caught in his throat and turned to ash. The torch in his hand sputtered against the sea wind, no stronger than the grief crushing the air from his lungs. He watched her approach, all wild and urgent, and felt his chest fracture clean through.

She didn't know. *Gods help him, she didn't know.*

Only an hour before, Aric had staggered into the tunnels. The fox shifter collapsed in the Great Hall, caught between forms, breathing in broken, animal sobs. Blood streaked his fur, his human skin. The words tumbled out incomplete, but Brenn pulled sense from the ruin.

All of them were dead. The Hawk. The Wolf. And Orwyn.

His brother in all but blood. The man who'd laughed too loud and loved too fiercely, who'd sworn he'd outlive them all.

Gone.

And the others with him. Erysia the Hawk, barely twenty summers old, who'd earned her wings only last spring. Rennar the Wolf, grizzled and steady, who'd taught combat alongside Brenn to every young shifter learning their primal form.

Three of their strongest. Three of their best. Their power had been torn away through siphons. Their souls swallowed whole. And the Aetherians had taken the bodies, denying the Cliffs their most sacred ritual.

The Death Rites.

Without the rites, they couldn't return them to wind and wave and ancient rock, to the Lord of Air and Stone who'd forged them. Their souls would wander, lost between the worlds, beyond even the reach of Nytheris.

Brenn had sworn an oath when he'd become commander, his hand pressed to the heartstone in the main hall. That he would keep them safe and bring every soul home. Now three were gone by his command, and he stood here whole and living, waiting to shatter the youngest of them all.

Korva.

Orwyn's little sister. The girl they'd raised together since she was barely old enough to shift. Brenn had taught her combat, sat beside her through scripture lessons, helped fill her with hope for a brighter future for their people. But she'd looked up to Orwyn the way fledglings looked to the sky. With absolute faith that he would always be there, steady and un-touchable.

Now she was hurtling home to a truth Brenn could not soften.

He set his jaw, squared his shoulders, and tried to remember how to breathe. Somewhere in the rock below him, the Cliff Mother was sum-moning the others. Soon, there would be council meetings and strategies and the cold logistics of survival.

But first, there was this. First, he had to break the heart of a girl who still thought her brother was immortal.

Orwyn's face rose unbidden in his mind. That crooked grin he'd worn since they were boys, the one that always meant trouble was coming, and he'd gladly walk into it anyway. The way he'd pulled Brenn into that back-slapping embrace before he left, surprising him with its fierceness.

Their final goodbye, and neither of them had known.

Brenn's grip tightened on the torch until his knuckles went white. Korva's silhouette grew larger against the moon. She would land at any moment, shifting mid-flight the way she always did. Impatient, eager, too young to have learned the caution that came with loss.

Gods guide my words, Brenn prayed to deities he wasn't certain were listening anymore. Had ever listened to him at all. *Grant me the strength.*

The raven descended, wings cupping air, talons reaching for the cliff's edge. And Brenn, who had led men into battle without flinching, who had stared down death a hundred times and never blinked, felt his courage falter at the approach of shadow and feathers.

Her boots hit the path. Black hair whipped in the wind, and even from here, he could see the triumph blazing in her face. She quickened her pace, and every step she took toward him drove a nail deeper into his chest.

"Brenn!" Her voice carried bright across the wind. "You won't believe it! I found the fire-bearer!" Her laughter came light, almost desperate. "Only you tonight? Where is my brother?"

His throat closed. His shoulders sagged under the weight of everything he needed to say.

When words finally came, they ground out rough, crumbling in his throat. He'd chosen the coward's route and loathed himself for it. "The Cliff Mother will explain."

He watched the joy drain from her face. *Watched understanding begin its terrible work.*

"No." She closed the space between them in three strides, fingers digging into his arm through the leather of his bracer. "She might be a prophet, but you are my friend. My family." Her voice cracked on the word. "Tell me. Where is Orwyn?"

He turned to face her fully, letting the torchlight bare what his words could not. He owed her that much. The truth, written plain on his face before he could even speak it.

"They're gone, Korva." His voice broke. "Orwyn. Erysia. Rennar. Only Aric returned, and barely."

The words hung in the air between them. He watched them land, watched her face shift from confusion to denial to the first cracks of devastation.

"How?" The word scraped out of her, raw and desperate.

He didn't want to say it. Didn't want to make it more real than it already was. But she deserved to know.

"Tareth Drayvien." The name tasted like poison. "He ambushed them near Rithmor's border. Used siphons to drain their power before—" His throat closed. He forced himself to continue. "The Aetherians took the bodies. Aric barely escaped."

He watched her process it. Watched the horror deepen as she understood what no bodies meant.

No rites. No offerings to the sea. No chance to speak Orwyn's name one final time or honor the man he was. Her brother. Her compass, her north star, the one who had held her together.

"No." The word barely made a sound. "No, that's—Brenn, that's not—he promised. He promised he'd always come back. You don't understand, he always comes back, he—"

Her knees buckled. Brenn caught her before she hit the ground, but she was already shoving against him, fists pounding his chest. Wild, frantic blows wrenched from the grief, splitting her open.

"You were supposed to protect him!" The accusation tore out of her. "You're the commander!"

Brenn took every blow without flinching or defending himself. He'd been waiting for this. He deserved far worse than her anguish could deliver.

"I failed him," he whispered. "I failed you both."

The admission shattered her. Her strikes weakened until she was clinging to him, fingers twisted in his cloak. "He can't be. Brenn, please. Please tell me you're wrong."

But his arms closed around her with unbearable gentleness. He could feel her body realize its worst fear in the way she tensed and trembled.

Her scream rose vast and uncontained, so terrible it rattled the cliffs themselves. A sound of primal loss. The waves below carried it out into the endless night, and somewhere in the tunnels behind them, the Cliffborn would hear it and know.

She sagged against him, her breath coming in uneven gasps. His own tears soaked into her hair, his broad body shaking with an anguish that matched her own. They held each other in the ruins of what remained, two orphans who had just lost another piece of everything.

Then he felt her change. Felt rage rise through her grief, cold at first, then searing.

"Tareth Drayvien," she hissed into his cloak, the name a curse scorching her tongue. When her face lifted, her eyes had blackened to the raven's stare. "I'll kill him. I'll kill every last Drayvien bastard that draws breath."

"Korva." Brenn cupped her face, thumbs brushing her cheekbones. For a moment, he just held her there, trying to ground her. "You must go to the Cliff Mother. Tell her what you've seen. She needs to know about the fire-bearer, and where—"

But her breath caught, fury surging again. She shoved her palms to his sternum, pushing him away.

"Damn the Cliff Mother!" The words cracked against rock, echoing down into the tunnels. "This is her fault! Her visions, her missions. She sent them to die!"

"Korva, please—"

"No!" She stumbled back, away from his reach, away from comfort she couldn't accept. "She sees everything, doesn't she? That's what you all say. She sees the future; she sees the threads of fate. Why didn't she see this? And if she did, why didn't she stop it!?"

His face twisted. His throat worked, but no words came.

"You didn't know, did you?" Her voice dropped into a quiet, broken thing. "She didn't tell you. Didn't tell anyone."

The realization settled like poison. Brenn saw it take hold. The Cliff Mother had agreed so quickly to send the scouts. And he, loyal and dutiful, had obeyed without question.

"I thought they'd be safe," he whispered, the words barely audible. "I thought—"

"You thought wrong." Her words were ice. "My brother is dead because of it."

He watched the truth of it destroy something between them. Felt no path back to what they'd been.

"I loved him too," Brenn offered, his voice breaking. "He was my brother, Korva. My best friend. I would have died in his place if I—"

"But you didn't." The cruelty was intentional. "You're here. And he's not. Never will be again."

Brenn absorbed her words like he'd absorbed her fists. Like he deserved it, accepting whatever punishment she could deliver. And he saw it devastate her all over again, because hurting him changed nothing. It wouldn't bring Orwyn back.

Nothing could.

"I can't—" Her voice splintered. "I can't be here anymore. I can't breathe here."

Before he could respond, before he could try to hold her together one more time, feathers erupted where her body had been. A sudden rush of air struck his face, and then she was gone, wings black against the night, vanishing into the open sky above the cliffs.

Fleeing the truth. Fleeing the place that no longer felt like home without Orwyn in it.

Brenn stood rooted in the dark, the torch guttering low in his grip. His face was soaked with tears he didn't remember shedding, chest hollow where his heart should have been.

He'd lost his best friend. And instinct told him that now he'd lost Korva too.

At last, he turned deeper into the caves, each step heavy with the duty that remained. He would have to tell the Cliff Mother that Korva had fled.

That she'd found the flame, but the cost of that discovery might be more than any of them could bear.

CHAPTER 12

R iver's Edge had finally tucked itself away beneath the rising moon.

Customers had either retired to bed or gone home, leaving the tavern still and quiet. The hearth had burned down to embers but still provided steady heat into the main room, throwing low light and long shadows across the floor.

"See you tomorrow, Reny," Maren called. "You survived the evening's suitors."

Reny arched a brow, smirking. "Barely."

"I'm going to make you relive all of it tomorrow in excruciating detail, you know."

"Looking forward to it."

Maren paused at the doorway, eyes glinting with mischief as she hooked her arm on Flinn's. "Will you be taking a late-night *stroll* with Brannic?"

"No, Maren." Reny gave her a pointed look. "Too tired."

"Interesting." Maren dragged the word out, studying her with far too much interest. "Reny Stonehelm, turning down her yearly *stroll*. Very interesting."

"Goodnight, Maren."

Maren shot a wink and one last grin before tugging Flinn away, the two of them dissolving into the cool night.

Alone now, Reny hung by the back door, letting the late-night stillness seep in. Fatigue hummed in every inch of her, but restlessness stirred even deeper.

And disappointment. *And guilt.*

Brannic had looked at her with that familiar question in his eyes when she'd patted his shoulder and walked away. The same question he'd asked every autumn since they were seventeen. And for the first time, she hadn't even been tempted.

She'd crossed her own boundaries tonight. Laughed louder, moved freer, let some wildness slip through her careful guard. It had been irresponsible and dangerous. But it had also been intoxicating.

It couldn't happen again.

With a heavy sigh, she padded through the kitchen toward the small office where Garron sat bathed in candlelight. Spectacles perched low on his nose, he counted the evening's earnings without looking up.

"Well?" she asked, leaning on the doorframe, kicking off her shoes.

"Best night in over a month." He stacked coins with a practiced flick. "Might've been the music. Probably the food."

"Maybe the pretty and profitable help?"

He glanced over his glasses, mouth twitching. "Doubtful."

She scoffed and crossed the floor to plant a firm kiss on his forehead. "Goodnight, old man."

"Night, girl. You did good."

Smiling with a tender pull in her chest, Reny left him to his numbers.

Rook had been waiting in the hallway for over an hour.

He leaned against the wall directly across from her door, one boot braced behind him, arms folded across his chest. Moonlight spilled thin and silver through the high window at the hall's end, carving the space into blades of shadow and pale light. The hall's darkness hid him well.

He'd listened to the night winding down. Maren's giggling, fading once she stepped out the back door. Garron's low humming. The creak of a chair. The clang of the soup kettle. Her voice—Reny's—from the kitchen. Quiet, brief.

And still he waited. Told himself it was all strategy. That he needed answers about the magic she thought no one noticed. But standing here in the dark, the lie had worn thin. Strategy didn't make his blood run hot. Strategy didn't keep replaying the sound of her laugh or the easy way she'd let another man put his hands on her.

This was something else.

Footsteps on the stairs. Light. Barefoot.

Rook went still, every sense sharpening as she appeared at the top of the staircase. She moved quietly past the guest rooms, past the broom closet, her silhouette soft in the darkness.

She paused outside his door, still and silent. Alert.

What do you see, little doe? A dark satisfaction swept over him as he watched her shoulders loosen when she saw no light coming from his room. Watched the exhale of relief as she reached for her own handle.

Now.

"So."

She spun, and even in the dim light, he caught the way her body jolted, how her pulse instantly hammered at her throat. The sharp intake of her breath echoed inside his chest. When her eyes found him in the shadows, it was what simmered there that caught him off guard. Surprise, alarm, but something that almost looked like... *Anticipation.*

"Did you have fun tonight?" He kept his voice low, unhurried, as he studied her.

"How long have you been standing there?" She hissed the words, fighting to keep her voice from disturbing the sleeping hall.

He ignored the question, pushing off the wall with fluid ease. "You looked like you really enjoyed yourself this evening. Just thought I'd ask."

"Just thought you'd ask, at one in the morning?" Her eyes narrowed, but her breathing had quickened. He tracked the rise and fall of her chest, the flush creeping up her throat.

"Well, up until now, you've been very..." He let his gaze trace her face. "...preoccupied."

"You mean working."

"Dancing." He took an easy step forward, and she stepped back. He fought the urge to smile. "Laughing." Another step. Another retreat. "Drawing every man's eye in the room." His voice dropped to a deep, dark tease. "That doesn't sound much like work to me."

Color flooded her cheeks. Anger. At him, or herself for being caught, he wasn't sure. *Didn't care.*

"I'm a barmaid. That is the job."

He kept moving, slow and measured, until her back met the solid wood of her bedroom door. She lifted her chin, stubborn and defiant in his shadow. The sight of it drove his thoughts somewhere hungry and dark.

"Oh? See, I wasn't sure," he murmured, close enough now to catch the scent of her. Smoky and sweet, that same intoxicating blend that had been tormenting him for days. "That wasn't exactly the service I received when I arrived as a patron here."

"Oh, I'm *sorry.*" Every word was clipped and venomous, but her voice had gone breathy at the edges. Her body was betraying her. "My apologies for not catering to your arrogance. If your ego needs stroking that badly, try the mirror next time."

That's it.

Rook lunged, one hand shooting up to brace against the doorframe above her head, caging her between his body and her door. This close, he could see the rapid flutter of her pulse, could feel the heat radiating off her skin. His other hand hung at his side, fingers curling and uncurling against the urge to grip her face and silence that smart mouth with his own.

"Interesting," he said, barely above a whisper. "Because it seemed like you spent the entire night trying to bait me."

Her breath caught on the accusation. He saw the embarrassment flicker in her eyes, saw the way her lips parted and quickly closed again over what she couldn't deny. *Some reckless part of her had wanted this.* She'd pushed and provoked on purpose.

And gods help him, knowing that was driving him mad.

Even with him exposing her motives, even with him pinning her like this, her chin tipped up, stubborn and blazing. She'd willed a strength to her voice he hadn't prepared for. "If I wanted to make you jealous, you'd know it."

He saw red. The challenge hung between them, igniting every part of him. Rook clenched his hand harder and dipped his head, his mouth hovering beside her ear. So close he could feel the shiver that ran through her. So close that when he spoke, his bottom lip was a ghost against the shell of her ear.

"You'd better be careful, little flame." He felt her stiffen at the endearment. Felt another sharp intake of breath, the way her body unintentionally melted toward him before she caught herself.

"No," she breathed. "You'd better be careful."

For half a heartbeat, neither of them moved. The moment stretched taut as a bowstring, threatening to snap, to give way to the hunger he knew was clawing at them both.

But then she twisted the knob with the hand she'd tucked behind her back and slipped through the gap. The door slammed between them hard enough to rattle the frame.

Click. Click.

Both locks, fast and final.

Rook stood in the aftermath, one hand still braced on the doorframe, the other frozen mid-reach where she'd been. The sudden absence of her heat left him cold and ravenous, blood burning with pressure that had nowhere to go. Every instinct—the ones he'd kept buried so deep he could pretend they didn't exist—screamed to follow her. To tear through the damn door. To take what his blood was demanding.

He dragged a hand through his hair, forcing himself to breathe. To rein in the part of himself he'd kept contained for so long that it had become second nature.

Reckless. That was reckless and stupid, Rook.

Only then did he notice it. A small, blackened mark along the wood grain of her door. Right where her back and hands had been pressed.

He raised his hand slowly, pressing his fingertips to the mark.

Still hot.

Triumph and concern tangled together until he couldn't separate them, forming a near-painful knot in his chest. Whatever flared between them had set her on fire, too.

Literally.

The evidence was seared into the wood right in front of him. Proof that her control had slipped almost as much as his. Proof that she was dangerous in ways he was only beginning to understand.

And that only made him want her more.

Inside her room, Reny leaned against the door, palms flat against the wood as if she alone could keep him out. Her hands shook as she checked the locks again for good measure.

Her body hummed, heat licking through her veins, that rogue flame still uncoiling in her belly. Responding to him in ways it never had to anyone or anything else.

She'd lost it. For just a moment, pressed between him and the door with his voice in her ear and his breath on her neck, she'd lost control. Let the fire slip through and scorch the wood at her back.

What is he?

Because no normal man should make her—or her magic—react this way. Like he was fire and she was mere kindling, desperate to catch. She closed her eyes, willing it away. The heat. The hunger. The way he'd called her *little flame,* like he knew exactly what she was. The terrifying awareness that if he'd pushed just a little harder, if he'd crossed that final line, she didn't know if she would have stopped him.

When she lifted her hand from the door, power still tingled in her palm. Her fingertips glowed faintly in the darkness of her room before she clenched her fist and forced it down. Hidden away where it belonged.

"Damn you," she whispered into the quiet.

Whether to him or to herself, she didn't know. What she did know was that this could never happen again.

Would never happen again.

She'd make sure of it.

CHAPTER 13

I t had been two days since Rook cornered Reny in the hallway. Two days since he'd come dangerously close to losing all control.

And whatever had come over him that night hadn't let go. It prowled beneath his skin like an animal caged too long and starving for release.

He needed distance.

Space to think without her scent filling his lungs or the ghost of her defiance echoing in his ears. Without that scorch mark branding itself into his mind alongside every other bit of evidence he'd witnessed.

Evidence he should have reported already.

When dawn broke, he wasted no time. He'd talked to Maren the night before, and she, soft-hearted as ever and easily swayed by his smile, had persuaded her father to lend Rook their old gelding. By the time the sky blushed with the first morning light, he was already in the saddle.

"Hollowbend. Side job." With a quick nod to Garron at the woodpile, he was gone. The old man didn't bother asking for details. Not out of indifference, but in the way of men who knew when not to pry.

The wind grew sharper with every mile, pulling him farther from the warmth of the tavern. From everything tangled within.

From her.

By dusk, the forest swallowed the trail whole. Roots clawed across the path, and the canopy knotted tight overhead. The deeper he rode, the older the trees became. Ancient sentinels that had witnessed the rise and fall of realms.

As the last light bled from the sky in shades of purple and dying gold, he reached the highest ridge above Hollowbend. He slid from the saddle and tethered the gelding to a crooked birch leaning precariously toward the slope. Below, lanterns glimmered in scattered pinpricks across the village, their weak amber light struggling against the encroaching dark.

He stood there, one hand on the saddle, the other on the hilt at his hip, eyes lifted to the stars scattered through the canopy's gaps. For a moment, he let himself exist in the quiet as nothing more than a man beneath an indifferent sky. But then the air thickened, too distinct not to notice. The back of his neck prickled with the oppressive sense of being watched.

An owl descended and settled on a half-fallen pine ten paces away. Too large for the Oakwoods, too perfect in its stillness. Silver-ash feathers caught the moonlight, and its gaze fixed on him with intelligence no natural creature could possess. Eyes like polished coins blinked once. Twice.

Rook's jaw tightened. He glanced away for a single breath, long enough to steel himself and don the mask he'd perfected over years of walking on lethal edges.

When he looked back, the branch bore a man instead.

For a treacherous heartbeat, Rook didn't see the crown prince.

He saw a boy of ten, said to have their mother's eyes, reaching for his smaller hand in the cold corridors of Rithmor.

Come on, Ric. I'll show you where she used to sit.

Tareth had been the only one willing to speak of her back then. The only one who didn't look at Rook like he'd stolen something precious just by being born. He'd led him to her garden when their father wasn't watching, crouched beside Rook among the roses she'd planted, and told him stories of a woman Rook would never know.

She smelled like these, Tareth had said once, crushing a crimson petal between his fingers. *Like flowers on the summer solstice.*

A softening in his brother's face that Rook had never seen directed at anyone else.

She would have loved you, Ric. I know she would have.

Two boys with no mother and a father who looked at them like chess pieces waiting to be moved. For a brief, stolen window of time, they'd had each other.

But that was before the high priest and the king claimed Tareth. Before the rituals began. Before he changed.

The memory guttered and died, because the man perched above him bore no resemblance to that boy.

Tareth Drayvien lounged with effortless arrogance, gloved hands braced against the bark, one boot propped up with the other hanging loose. He studied Rook like a tool that had once shown promise but was beginning to dull.

Dark-haired and golden-eyed, he looked every inch the prince in his finely crafted, gold-trimmed black leathers. Moonlight carved the clean-shaven planes of his face, revealing beauty curdled by cruelty in every angle. Where Rook was rough-hewn stone, Tareth was a sharp blade of lethal perfection. Polished, precise, and deadly in ways that had nothing to do with swords.

He didn't smile. His presence alone chilled the air.

"Nice trick," Rook muttered, chin angling toward the branch.

"Siphoned from an avian shifter we caught near the border." Tareth's voice carried a light, conversational tone, as if he were discussing the weather. His hand brushed the white siphon brooch at his shoulder.

His mouth curved, but the smile held no warmth. "I'm partial to this one. Flight has a certain... freedom to it." He tilted his head, thoughtful. "I have a wolf form I could give you, if you'd like. Fresh. Quite potent. Might make your time here more interesting."

Rook's stomach turned, but he kept his face blank. "I'm fine, thanks."

Tareth's nose wrinkled with delicate distaste. "Suit yourself. But it would seem with all the recent activity that the half-breeds are trying to insert themselves into this war." He examined his nails with studied disinterest. "Foolish, but predictable."

Rook kept his voice carefully neutral. "They no longer have the numbers to mobilize into a significant threat. But their presence along the Veil and into Endaria has increased. The locals speak of sightings."

"Let them." Tareth shrugged. "They've always skulked in their caves, clinging to the scraps of what they once were. Their movement now is nothing more than desperation. And for us, an opportunity." His tone sharpened. "Every half-breed we siphon is only taking back what their mongrel breed stole from us. What is rightfully ours."

Rook had heard this same rambling speech before from Rithmor's high priest. From the king himself. The grand justification for the relentless push toward the south.

"If that were true, Tareth," Rook's voice went flat, "why does the magic never hold? Why do the vessels empty within a week or less?" He pointed at the brooch on Tareth's shoulder. "If it's our magic, why doesn't it last?"

For a single heartbeat, Tareth's composure threatened to break. Rage flared in his eyes, brief and vicious, before aristocratic disdain smothered it. He dismissed the question with a wave of his hand.

"A matter of refining the process. The high priest is working on it." He spoke with finality, leaving no room for argument. "Truth is what matters, Rook. They are diseases, and we are the cure. Soon, the Veil will fall, and Aetherians will be god-touched again." He spoke the words like gospel. "As we were always meant to be."

A bitter, metallic taste clung to the back of Rook's throat. He had watched too many draining deaths, too many siphons crack and empty after stolen power faded to nothing.

He'd carried that magic once. Felt it sing through his blood like borrowed divinity. And then felt it leave in one sudden rush, leaving him emptier than he'd felt before.

Never again.

Tareth dropped from the branch, landing with a grace that came as natural to him as breathing. He reached into his cloak and pulled out another siphon. Larger, fist-sized, its black surface drinking in the light instead of reflecting it. The runes etched into the sides of the stone pulsed with a faint, sickly glow.

Binding runes. Protection sigils carved by Rithmor's high priest to keep the stone from turning on Aetherian flesh the way raw voidstone would.

Because they were never meant to touch it.

Tareth turned it once in his hand, admiring it with a cutting smile.

"Make use of this," he said. "Hungry and waiting." He tossed it carelessly to Rook. "If this new lead is nothing but another abomination, some hedge witch with stolen elements, drain her and be done. Stop wasting my patience and time."

The siphon landed heavily in Rook's palm. It radiated a constant thrum of restrained appetite, like a living thing eager to feed.

For a moment, Rook let himself consider it.

Pressing the vessel to her chest. Watching her magic pour into the hollow stone until only her husk remained. If she were a witch, a half-breed, or some other stray thread in the wild weave of their distorted world, using this would prove it. Contain it.

End it.

But siphoned magic never lasted. It was never strong enough to heal their dying land. Never real enough to restore everything they'd lost.

Power without permanence. Theft without transformation.

Rook despised it in silence. Speaking out against it would be treason.

"She's not like the others," he said instead, forcing his tone flat. "She's different."

Tareth began to circle him in loose, prowling steps. "Different how?" The question was casual, but Rook knew better than to trust Tareth's tone. "Where did you even find her? River's Edge, like the mercenary said?"

Rook shook his head, the lie coming with practiced ease. "No. A different nameless hovel east of there. Blink, and you'd miss it. She was hiding."

If Tareth knew she was at the tavern in River's Edge, knew Rook had been living under the same roof, knew how close he'd gotten while keeping it to himself—

He wasn't willing to risk Tareth deciding to handle this of his own accord.

Suspicion gleamed in Tareth's eyes as he studied Rook's face. But after a moment, it smoothed into something close to amusement. "You've chased this trail for more than a year with nothing to show for it." He folded his arms, the gold trim of his leathers catching the moonlight. "While you drift on this side of the Veil in that human mask, playing peasant, Rithmor weakens. Our court decays." His voice dropped, each word becoming a carefully placed blade. "Our people starve."

Rook's hands curled into fists at his sides. "I know that, Tareth."

"Perhaps you need to hear it again."

Tareth closed the distance between them in two confident strides until they were nearly nose to nose.

"You're only here because of me," he reminded gently, almost whispering. "I convinced Father to give you this chance. To pursue your little theory based on a feeling. He thinks you are mad for believing our salvation lies in Endaria."

Rook said nothing, glaring into Tareth's eyes. Finding nothing there that he recognized.

"Don't give me cause to regret it, Rook. Don't make me look like a fool for defending you."

Tareth wouldn't just withdraw his support if he failed. He'd ensure Rook paid for making him look weak. Rook kept his face locked, neutral. Only a small tremor at his jaw betrayed the fury simmering beneath the surface.

"We're dying, brother." Tareth leaned in, chest puffed. Rook could smell the expensive oils he always insisted on wearing. "You feel it, don't you? Every time you cross back through the North Gate, every time you see what we've become."

Rook did feel it. The memories rose before he could stop them.

Rithmor's deserted streets the last time he'd walked them. Gray dust choking the air where magic once shimmered. A mother clutching an infant too still, too silent, while a priest marked the doorframe for collection.

"If we are to raise the One Eternal, drop the Veil, and seize Endaria, we need the flame. Without that power, our people starve. Our magic bleeds away. The Veil suffocates us, and we become nothing more than mortals." The last word dripped with disgust. "Is that what you want? To watch your people—your *family*—wither to human weakness?"

Family. The sharpest blade his brother wielded against him.

"I need more time," Rook said, winning the war to keep his voice even. "She's worth observing. Endarian recruiters loiter in the taverns. Military presence is increasing. If I'm not careful, I risk exposure." He met Tareth's stare without flinching. "When I am certain, when I know what she is and how to use her, I'll bring her to Rithmor. Alive."

Alive.

Tareth studied him for a long, suffocating moment.

Finally, he gave a reluctant nod and stepped back. "Fine. One month. You have one month to deliver, or I'm coming back to handle this myself."

His smile was all teeth. "And we both know I'm far less... *delicate* in my methods than you are."

Rook was far from delicate. Tareth was monstrous.

"Don't fail, Rook." His words were deceptively soft. "Father already believes you will. You don't want to prove him right again, do you?"

Tareth grinned at him as he turned away.

With a shimmer of cloak and shadow, feathers erupted where flesh had been. The faint rush of wings marked the owl's return to the skies. Tareth vanished into the canopy with the same eerie silence he'd arrived in.

Rook remained beneath the trees. Alone with the ghosts of Tareth's words and the cold weight of the siphon still in his hand. He stared at it, its awful hunger pulsing against his palm like a second heartbeat.

One month.

With a sharp flick and minimal thought, he flung the siphon toward the nearest birch, where it struck bark and tumbled down, lost in a bed of dead leaves and ferns at the tree's base.

He turned away and didn't look back.

As he swung into the saddle, the gelding shifting beneath him, the silence of the night pressed in from all sides. It felt nothing close to peace.

With a click of his tongue, Rook coaxed the horse forward, pulling the reins to the south. Back to River's Edge.

Back to her.

And Rook, who'd never questioned his service to Rithmor, felt something break loose in his chest he'd never been willing to acknowledge before tonight.

Doubt.

CHAPTER 14

R eny hadn't breathed a word about Rook in the hallway.

Not to anyone.

There were chances. In the mornings with Garron, when mugs of chicory brew steamed between them and his presence radiated warmth. The kind of moment when honesty was easy.

Simple.

But whenever she tried to shape the words to tell him what happened, her throat would close around them. Reny told herself it was shame and embarrassment that kept her quiet.

But nothing about it was simple.

It was all infuriatingly complicated.

She didn't let herself think about why. Tried not to replay the heat of him so close, the way her magic rose in his presence before her mind could catch up. Like he'd summoned it out of her somehow.

And while she knew it couldn't happen again, telling Garron meant Rook would be gone, cast out faster than he'd walked in. Garron would see to it with fists first, questions never.

And the thought of Rook leaving—really leaving—sat like a stone in her chest. So Reny kept her mouth shut.

Two days after the night in the hallway, Rook left before dawn. *Hollow-bend*, Maren had said.

Side work. A few days, maybe longer. A few days stretched into a week.

In that time, summer fell away in sudden surrender. Autumn bled into the countryside in vibrant shades of crimson and rust, smoke curling from chimneys while the fields lay bare. By week's end, rain had come. Cold, relentless, glazing the bridges until they gleamed black under the swaying lanterns.

And through it all, Rook was gone.

Maren cornered Reny in the storage closet when she'd had enough of her sour mood and silence.

"Alright, what's going on with you?" she hissed, eyes narrowed. "You've been miserable for days. Snapping at customers, burning bread, staring off into nothing. Spill it, Ren."

He cornered me. Almost kissed me. Made me want things I have no business wanting. And now he's gone.

Reny shoved it all down, swallowing it like broken glass. She blamed her moon time with enough bite that Maren backed off, murmuring sympathies and offerings of willow bark tea.

The lies came so easily. Every excuse, every dismissal. All of them intentional choices she made on his behalf, each one feeling more damning than the last.

Reny told herself it was a relief that he'd left. Convinced herself that perhaps she'd finally driven him off, made herself too cold, too unapproachable. Not worth the effort it would take to scale the walls she'd built.

Good, she thought fiercely each time the hollow ache settled in her chest. *Perfect. He's gone. Finally.*

But every time the front door opened, she had to look, her pulse leaping. Only to crash back down when it was just another patron shaking rain off their cloak. When it happened for the sixth time in one evening, Reny was forced to admit it to herself.

She cared. And that knowing sat in her gut like poison.

He was a drifter. A stranger. Someone who would eventually leave regardless.

And she told herself she'd be just fine when he did.

Maren breezed into the kitchen in her usual whirl of vibrant warmth, an empty breadbasket crooked over her arm. Her focus shot straight to the threshold of the back door where Reny stood, catching her there yet again.

"If you're looking for Dark and Broody," she drawled, a knowing grin tugging at her mouth, "he just came in through the front. Shaking the rain off his cloak right now."

Reny quickly straightened, feigning indifference. "I wasn't looking for anyone. I just needed fresh air."

Maren's brow arched high, but she gave her friend the gift of letting it go.

With a swing of the now-full basket and laughter already spilling from her lips, she swept back to the bar, her voice intentionally loud as the kitchen door swung shut on its hinges. "Good to see you, Rook!"

He was back.

Despite herself, despite every rational thought screaming at her, warmth bloomed behind her ribs.

She didn't let herself name it but knew what it was anyway. Relief.

Rook had chosen the forest for as long as he could bear it.

Days bled into nights beneath the changing trees, the meager warmth of a campfire his only companion. He'd told himself distance was what he needed. Space to remember his motive and to wrestle with the raw, shameful lack of discipline that had seized him that night in the hallway.

Each dawn found him no steadier than the last.

The season shifted in tandem with his restlessness. Every evening carried sharper winds. Every morning, the ground woke silver with frost. The bite of autumn was easier to endure than the constant knowledge pressing against his chest. Easier than the realization that he'd defied the crown when he'd hurled that siphon into the leaves outside Hollowbend.

What he ought to do. What Tareth demanded. What his realm required of him.

A mission so simple. And necessary.

And yet none of it felt simple at all.

From his camp high on the ridgeline, the tavern sat in the distance, just visible through the trees. His eyes found it every night as lantern-light appeared in the windows like runaway stars.

And there, framed in the back doorway, she would appear night after night. Light gilded her silhouette, catching the copper fire in her hair. She'd stand motionless, staring into the dark. Into the same woods where he was hiding.

When the rains came on the seventh day, heavy and unrelenting, they soaked through both his leather and resolve. The campfire sputtered and died, too soaked to relight.

Through the rain and mist, he could see the tavern's lights, and the pull grew unbearable.

By week's end, he gave in. Broke camp, saddled the gelding with hands trembling from more than cold.

And he went back.

As the tavern appeared through sheets of rain, Rook told himself it was for the mission. For his homeland. He would uphold his blood oath and do what he'd set out to do.

But as he pushed through the front door, water dripping from his cloak, nodding to Garron's surprised look, Flinn's easy grin, and Maren's bright welcome, the lie crumbled inside him.

He simply wanted to see her again. Needed to, with an intensity that bordered on madness.

And as his eyes found her across the tavern—caught mid-motion in the kitchen threshold, her focus pinning him with an expression he couldn't name—Rook knew he was lost.

The only question left was whether or not he'd be able to find his way back.

CHAPTER 15

The following morning broke crisp and cloudless, a pale blue sky stretching wide over River's Edge. The smell of woodsmoke and ripe apples drifted through the yard, mingling with the sharper tang of bowstring resin.

Behind the tavern, a gathering of huntsmen and townsfolk had set up a makeshift archery range, their current target a bruised apple balanced atop a weathered post. Garron sat nearby with a tin mug of steaming cider while Flinn strutted between shots like a peacock. Coins passed hands along the edges of the group as each man took his turn.

Two figures stood apart from the rest, their cloaks marked with Endarian military stitching. Recruiters were still prowling through the village. They didn't join the betting or the banter. Only quiet observation, cataloging every steady hand and clean release.

No one acknowledged them directly. If recruiters had come as far south as River's Edge, it meant the war effort was getting desperate.

Earlier that week, Flinn had taken a few eager steps their way, eyes bright with the idea of noble adventure. Garron latched onto his arm with a glare fierce enough to stop him cold. He hadn't tried again.

"Sooner or later, one of us'll bag the lord of the woods," a man called across the yard, nodding toward the distant tree line. Laughter rippled through the group, all of them men who'd been hunting a legendary stag for years without success.

Rook stood apart along the fence rail, half-cloaked in the shade of the old maple. He smirked at the bravado, knowing with certainty it would be none of them.

Reny appeared in the back doorway off the kitchen, arms folded, focus distant.

From his spot by the fence, he studied the furrow in her brow, the flat line of her mouth. Something held her back, keeping her rooted in the threshold rather than joining the easy noise beyond.

"You coming in for a round, or just judging from the sidelines today, sweetheart?" One of the older hunters called out to her, no mockery in his tone. Only the warm familiarity of someone who'd watched her grow up knew this tradition.

She didn't move, her eyes cutting briefly toward the fence where Rook stood before landing on the old man. She took a small step back into the safety of the doorframe, offering a smile that never reached her eyes. And shook her head.

A muscle in Rook's jaw twitched. The only disappointment he allowed himself to show, as another voice cut over the crowd, louder and harsher than the rest.

"Bet she can't shoot half as good as she looks. Women never can!"

Laughter and chatter faltered, a distinct quiet falling over the yard.

The speaker was a broad-shouldered man with a jagged scar carving a brutal line from his left temple to his jaw. The kind of mark left by a blade that nearly killed him. And probably should have.

He was not from River's Edge. Everything about him made that clear. His smirk stayed fixed on Reny, wide and expectant, as if he'd already won whatever game he thought he was playing.

"Hasn't learned yet, huh, Garron?" Old Harl called from the fence line. A few chuckles rippled through the crowd.

Rook straightened from his place on the rail, his casual ease giving way to sharp awareness. His focus landed on the man now staring at Reny.

The stranger doubled down, strutting forward with a stack of silver coins in hand. "Twenty says she can't even hit the post, let alone the apple." He kept eye contact with her. "Pretty little thing like that's probably never held a real weapon in her life."

Garron didn't look up from his mug. He waved a lazy hand toward Flinn, who was already hurrying over with Reny's bow and quiver.

Reny had been utterly still in the doorframe, but then her chin lifted, shoulders pulling back. That half-hearted smile vanished, replaced with something harder. Colder.

From the corner of the stoop, Maren held Flinn's bow for him in both hands. When her gaze caught Rook's, she winked, tipping her head as Reny passed. She leaned back against the tavern wall and let out a quick whoop of encouragement.

Rook couldn't hold back his own smirk as he watched Reny descend the stairs and cross the yard, the crowd parting for her instinctively. She took her bow from Flinn, fingers curling around the leather grip like greeting an old friend. Unhurried and expressionless, she tested the string's tension and grabbed one arrow, never once glancing at her target.

Drew back and fired in one smooth motion.

Thwip.

The arrow split the apple clean through. Both halves tumbled into the grass, the shaft left quivering in the fence post.

Cheers broke across the gathering.

Without pause, Reny turned, took another arrow from Flinn's ready hand, and let it fly toward the fence line. A faint smile curved her mouth as the arrow threaded through a narrow notch in the post and struck dead center in a crude bullseye painted on a hay bale far beyond. A gap no wider than two fingers.

An impossible shot. And she'd made it look effortless.

The crowd erupted. Hollering and applause mingled with pointed jeers aimed at the man who'd doubted her. He stood frozen, mouth wide, as his twenty silver vanished and the full weight of his humiliation landed.

Garron chuckled as men clapped him on the back, and Flinn beamed as if he'd made the shot himself.

Reny handed the bow back to Flinn without a word. She didn't gloat, didn't so much as glance at the man she'd just fully embarrassed. She walked back into the kitchen as though she'd done nothing more remarkable than fetch water from the river. As she passed, Maren swatted her playfully on her behind, grinning ear to ear with pride before hopping off the stoop to join Flinn.

From his place by the old maple, Rook couldn't look away. The easy set of her shoulders, the unhurried sway of her steps, the way she vanished into the kitchen without even looking back.

The crowd moved on, placing new bets, setting up another round.

But at the edge of the gathering, the scarred hunter hadn't moved. His oily smirk was long gone, jaw grinding over curses he kept to himself. His eyes stayed fixed on the doorway where Reny had disappeared.

His hands opened. Closed. Opened again.

Garron's laughter rang out as Flinn attempted to recreate Reny's shot, and Rook let himself smile for the first time in days.

When he glanced back over the yard, the scarred hunter was gone.

With everyone drawn to the yard, the tavern felt hollow.

The noise outside had dulled to a distant hum as Reny moved behind the bar, bending for a rag and pitcher. In the incessant tangle of thoughts over Rook, that ass who challenged her, and everything she still had to do, she never heard the front door open.

When she straightened and turned, he was already there.

Too sudden. Too close.

The hunter with the scar.

"Didn't mean to ruffle your feathers out there," the man said, tone slick with false apology. His eyes—brown, nearly black—dragged over her, from face to feet and back again with nothing good in them.

Reny's jaw tightened. She shifted sideways to move past him, angling toward the kitchen door, but he mirrored her movement step for step, blocking her path.

"Just friendly sport," he continued, creeping forward. The smile he flashed never reached his eyes. "Hell of a shot, though. Shame it's wasted on a woman carved out of stone."

"Move." The command was solid. Ice cold.

He didn't. Instead, he crowded in, cutting off her escape entirely. The stink of him hit her first—stale ale and old sweat—as he reached for her arm.

She was faster. And thanks to Garron, trained.

Reny pivoted, driving her elbow hard into his ribs, following with the heel of her palm aimed at his nose. The first strike landed solidly, forcing a grunt from him. But to her surprise, he caught the second, grabbing her wrist mid-thrust. His iron grip jerked her arm down, using her own momentum to slam her back against the bar.

"Feisty," he breathed, crowding her against the wood, using his bulk to pin her there. "I like that."

The pitcher was still within reach. She grabbed it with her free hand and swung hard, catching him on the shoulder with a crack. He flinched, briefly loosening his hold. For one desperate heartbeat, she thought she'd broken free, but he recovered. Meaty fingers dug into her forearm as he dragged her close, all pretense of charm gone. He slammed her against the wall hard enough to knock the air from her lungs, one hand pinning her shoulder in place.

"Shouldn't have done that," he spat, breath rank against her cheek. His mouth lowered to her neck, dry lips scraping her jaw as she turned her face away.

"You put on that ice-queen act out there, thinking you're better than everyone." His body crushed her against the wall, words slick and venomous against her ear. "But you strutted out for that bow, didn't you? All those men cheering, all those eyes on you, watching you move." His hands roamed where they had no right. "You wanted it. I could see it. And I bet you want it now."

She twisted hard, trying to force space between them, but he anticipated it and leaned in harder, pinning her. His hands grew frenzied.

"Don't bother fighting," he murmured against her neck. "Nobody can hear you out there. They're all too busy laughing and drinking in the yard." His voice dropped, intimate in the worst way. "You're mine now. And I'm going to get my coin's worth out of you."

Fury rose beneath her terror. And with it, fire.

Heat seared beneath her skin, answering a call she hadn't consciously made. The scent of scorched oak filled her nose, cutting through the stench of him. The taste of ash grew bitter on her tongue. Flames threatened to gather in her chest, in the depths of her bones, in her hands. A hairline crack split along the bar's edge where her hand gripped, a thin tendril of smoke curling upward from the splintered wood.

"No—" Her voice shook as she pushed against his chest, desperate, feeling her control slip. Feeling the magic straining against its leash. "Let me go."

One moment of lost restraint and the flames would escape her, wild and devastating. They'd consume him. Consume the tavern. Take away everything she'd spent years protecting.

But gods, she wanted to let them.

The pressure built like a scream trapped inside her. The air around them heated, the center of her palm beginning to glow—

The kitchen door slammed open, jerking her attention to the side.

Rook stood on the threshold.

Everything about him had gone terrifyingly still. No charm, no easy smirk, no careless lean. He filled the doorway like a blade drawn from its sheath.

"Get your fucking hands off her."

The hunter's shoulders went rigid, but he made no move to release her. Instead, he hauled Reny tighter against his front, using her as a shield. "The lady and I just wanted some time alone—at her request." He smirked over his shoulder. "Mind your godsdamned business. You can have a turn later."

He turned his face back to Reny with a look carrying a clear warning.

Say nothing. Send him away.

"He's lying." She met the hunter's stare with eyes of wrath, each word landing like a hammered nail. "I would *never* want this."

The hunter's smirk faltered.

And Rook moved.

One moment, he was in the doorway. The next, he had the man by the collar, wrenching him away from Reny with brutal force. The man barely had time to curse before Rook slammed him face-first into the bar, then dragged him back against his chest. A dagger appeared in Rook's hand—sleek, polished silver—pressing against the hunter's throat. The hunter tried to break free, but Rook's hold was iron.

The blade shifted, tilting. Not enough to cut, but enough to promise that it could.

The man went still.

Reny couldn't move. Couldn't breathe. She had known there was more to Rook—sensed it in the way he watched her, in the predatory stillness that she could feel living beneath his easy manner.

But this... this was a different creature entirely.

"You want to run your mouth? Fine. Try your hand at archery in this village? Sure." Rook twisted his fist in the collar, forcing the man onto his tiptoes. The dagger slid, its edge biting flesh, a single bead of blood welling dark against the steel. "But if you ever touch her again—if you so much as look at her wrong—I'll bleed you out so slowly they'll think it was the drink that did you in."

The hunter's lips parted, but Rook leaned closer, his hold on the shirt collar tightening. An eager noose.

"Go on," he murmured like silk over iron. The dagger pressed deeper, the trickle of blood becoming a slow descent along the blade. "Give me a reason to finish this quickly." His head tilted, a smile touching his mouth that held no warmth at all. "Or tell me which finger you can spare for touching what doesn't belong to you."

The man couldn't answer. Not with his own death staring at him.

Reny stared at him, transfixed. Terror and fascination relentlessly warred in her chest. She should be afraid of this—of him. And part of her was. The part that recognized a predator, eager to kill, when she saw one. She refused to acknowledge what other parts of her were thinking.

"Rook." Her voice came out too thin. She hated how weak it sounded.

He didn't hear her. The promise of violence had consumed him entirely. A desperate whimper escaped the hunter, but Rook remained frozen in lethal purpose, watching the man's artery flutter under the blade's edge.

"Rook!" Louder now. Cracking.

His focus snapped to her, but everything else in his stance remained carved from stone. The look in his eyes stripped the air from her lungs, dark and burning and utterly unguarded. For one suspended moment, she saw past every mask he'd ever worn.

Just say it.

This man's life or death. Justice or mercy. He said nothing, but it was clear that he was ready to give her either without a breath of hesitation.

The realization should have frightened her. Instead, it ignited a different kind of heat low in her belly. Dangerous, but undeniable.

She exhaled slowly, shakily. "Let him go."

Rook hesitated for a beat as if she might change her mind. When she stood firm, her look stern, he took one stiff step backward, chest rising as he pulled himself from whatever edge he'd been too eager to cross.

The dagger vanished into a sheath at his hip. With an effortless shove, the hunter fell onto the planks. With Rook's eyes on every move, he scrambled for the door, clutching his bleeding neck. The tavern door bounced off its hinges as he fled, leaving only silence and the faint copper scent of blood.

Reny took in every detail. The rigid lines of Rook's frame, taunt with undelivered violence and unspent rage. The sheer weight of his presence consumed every inch of air between them.

This was what had always been there. Not a wandering carpenter. Not a charming drifter with an easy smile. This—this lethal, barely leashed thing—was the truth of him.

And instead of running, she felt a call to step closer.

What is wrong with me?

When his gaze lifted back to her, what she saw there defied language. Possession. Concern. A hunger so raw it made her breath catch.

"Are you okay?" His rough growl thrummed inside her ribcage. He shifted, shoulders rolling, as if calling back whatever still strained at its leash.

"I'm fine." A tight shake of her head. One hand braced against the bar, she pulled composure around her like armor. The lie withered beneath his stare.

He moved closer in two measured strides.

"Really. I'm fine." She lifted her hand, the one still bearing the phantom marks of the hunter's grip.

But he didn't stop. He closed the last of the distance and stood directly before her, his attention drawn to her raised hand.

She began to lower it, chin tilting up. "So, what? You're the only one who gets to pin me against walls?"

Darkness flooded his expression. Her words struck hard, and she watched them land. Watched a tremor pass through him, threatening to shatter what remained of his control.

Even now, she couldn't stop herself. Sharp-edged and defiant, even when she should be soft. Grateful.

His jaw flexed. For a breath, she thought the confrontation would break over her next. But when he caught her raised arm, he wasn't rough. His fingers circled her wrist with startling care.

She didn't pull away.

He turned her arm gently, searching. His fingertips drifted along the sensitive underside of her forearm, stilling over the faint red marks in her skin where the hunter's grip had branded her. His thumb hovered above the marks without making contact, but heat collected there, bleeding out from her skin. Not from adrenaline.

A separate pulse entirely. Intentionally reaching for him.

Despite herself, Reny gasped.

The sound of her breath must have done something to him—she saw it in the way his chest seized, the slight falter in his own breathing. His fingers loosened with what looked like agonizing reluctance.

Voices drifted in from the kitchen.

"Flinn, I swear, if you knock over one more godsdamned—*oh*." Maren's exasperation cut off as she stepped into the bar. She froze mid-stride, Flinn colliding into her from behind.

Rook's hand had only just fallen from Reny's arm. She stood rigid, face half-turned toward the interruption. He was leaning far too close, and though his hands were empty now, the charge between them was unmistakable.

Maren's gaze darted between them, already lit with suspicion. Flinn's cheeks burned crimson.

Quickly and urgently, Maren slipped a hand around Flinn's elbow, tugging him back, lips curving. "If we were interrupting anything—and I mean *anything*—we'll just see ourselves out and you two can—"

"Nothing." Too fast. Too harsh. Reny's eyelashes fluttered on flushed cheeks. "You weren't interrupting anything."

She hadn't meant for the words to bite so hard, but the heat—*and him*—were scorching her blood. She slid out from behind the bar without meeting anyone's eyes, muttering about bed linens.

Their stares followed as she rushed across the room. But it was Rook she felt most—tracking her up the stairs, burning into her back. He said nothing as he stood behind the bar, shadows clinging to him like a second skin.

As Reny fled to the fragile solitude of her room, she hated the truth of it. This thing between them.

It wasn't nothing.

Not anymore.

CHAPTER 16

T he tavern had filled with the wrong kind of crowd.

Rook stood behind the bar alongside Garron, sleeves rolled, expression locked tight. Lanterns threw their familiar glow, and the hearth hissed over fresh logs Flinn tossed across the grate, but its warmth couldn't cut the harsh air that had settled in the room. Autumn's chill had drawn in a rougher breed. Men cloaked in road-dust and drink, jingling coin and careless hunger.

Their laughter was too loud, their jests too crude. Too many unfamiliar faces and eyes lingering where they shouldn't.

Rook watched the room, too aware. Aside from a handful of locals and the two Endarian recruiters who'd been prowling around for weeks, he didn't recognize most of the men packed into the tables tonight.

And then there was Reny.

She threaded through the crowd with her usual grace, but her presence had changed. Her grip on the tray was white-knuckled by default, her movements sharper than normal.

He'd been watching her all week, trying to find the right moment to get her alone and talk to her. Perhaps bridge the gap that had widened even further between them. But she was frustratingly good at slipping away, vanishing around corners.

And when their eyes did meet in passing, hers were hard. Glaring. Not with fear, but fierce recognition. Her silent acknowledgement of the strange pulse that had surged between them when he'd held her arm in his hands, her magic rising to meet him like it recognized some part of him not even he understood.

She was keeping her distance, not because she was afraid of him.

Because she was afraid of *that*.

Neither of them had spoken a word about what happened with the huntsman, despite separate, fevered interrogations from Maren.

A door had cracked open between them, never to be closed again. He'd glimpsed a truth in her he was never meant to see, and she'd seen the same in him. Now it lived in every silence, in every look held a beat too long.

Her body moved through the evening's routine with a volatile force. He could feel it brewing like thunder banked behind clouds, pressure building toward the inevitable break. What bothered him most was that he had no idea what that would look like.

Their eyes met across the room. She looked away first, but she'd been unwilling to hold any man's gaze too long for the past week. He didn't blame her.

Stepping in, saving her, had gone against every instinct Rook had been trained to obey.

Observe, don't interfere. Shadow, never hero.

But the sight of her pinned beneath that bastard's weight had ripped loose the most primal part of him that defied years of discipline.

He'd lost his chance. If there was true, raw power in her, that moment should have forced it free in undeniable, merciless flame. But it hadn't had the chance because he'd answered some visceral demand to protect her.

A chair scraped near the hearth, loud enough to slice through the tavern's usual hum. A man's shout followed.

Reny's head snapped toward the sound. Rook's attention had already found the source. Four men, red-faced with drink, swollen with arrogance, were laughing.

Directly beside them, Maren flinched away, an empty tray clutched tight against her chest like a shield. Her smile was too weak and forced, the tension around her eyes giving her away. One of the men shot his hand out, fingers snagging the strap of her dress.

The fabric gave way, falling from Maren's shoulder to expose the pale skin beneath.

A hush claimed the room as the tray slipped from Maren's grip and clattered to the floor. She scrambled to claw the torn fabric back in place before it could fall any further, cheeks blazing as she stumbled backward. The man lounging in his chair grinned widely, dangling the dress strap from his hand like a trophy.

Rook shifted his stance to intercept Maren, to involve himself, but Reny was already moving. She reached the girl in two long strides, threw a protective arm around her, and steered her toward the kitchen.

"Go to the back," Reny said calmly. "Now."

Maren obeyed without protest, head bowed in embarrassment as she vanished through the swinging door. Rook's eyes swept to Reny as she straightened on the tavern floor, pivoting.

Her chest rose with one steady breath, both hands clenching from the effort it took to keep them still. To keep the heat already gathering beneath her palms from igniting.

Rook recognized the rage in her and knew it was far older than the huntsman's assault. What he saw wasn't new. It was an ancient storm built from every wrong gone unanswered, every mercy shown when her blood howled for judgment. The attack she'd endured had only cracked the dam. All week, the pressure had been building, growing more volatile by the day.

Now the storm was breaking. As she made for the hearth, Rook took a few steps in her direction without thinking, but fury had already locked on its mark.

The table of men didn't notice her at first. The one who'd grabbed Maren finally looked up, still lounging smugly in his chair. His smirk was distorted by an old, dimpled scar at the corner of his mouth, unevenly spread beneath a greasy, patchy beard.

"Thought I liked blondes," he drawled as the others lifted their heads from their tankards. "Turns out I need a red."

Reny's face betrayed nothing. She stopped at their table, unnervingly still, one hand resting on her hip, the other braced on the empty tray tucked at her side.

"Let's make this simple." Her voice was soft, almost gentle. The tone sent a chill down Rook's back. "You put your hands on a server, so you need to leave."

The men erupted into bellows and howls, some snorting into their mugs. The scarred one leaned back and lazily scratched his stomach, giving her an amused but cold once-over.

"Or what, wench?" he slurred. "You'll tell your daddy? Waggle your pretty finger at us?"

"No." Reny tilted her head, slow and fluid, watching him the way a cat watches a bird with a broken wing. "But I'll bury my finger in your fucking eye."

Nearby conversations collapsed, forks stilling over plates. A second man barked out a chuckle. "She's got fire."

"Bet she writhes real pretty, too," the scarred one crooned, his grin splitting wider, revealing uneven, yellowing teeth.

That was all it took.

Reny kicked out, her boot catching the leg of his chair. The chair pitched and spilled him backward in a tangle of limbs, ale sloshing across the floor. His curses rang out the whole way down.

Rook lunged forward, only for Garron's arm to catch him across the chest like a gate slamming shut. "Best you not," the old man muttered, never taking his attention from the scene. "She'll be fine."

Behind the bar, Maren had re-emerged from the kitchen, her eyes red and puffy. Flinn took up the space beside her, a lanky but protective arm thrown over her shoulders.

The fallen man had just begun to push himself upright when Reny stepped forward, slamming the heel of her boot into his chest. He grunted in pain, the impact forcing him flat again.

Another man surged to his feet with a wild swing aimed directly for her. Reny's upper body pivoted, the empty tray she'd been holding swinging up in her hand. It cracked across the side of his face in a clean arc, sending him toppling back into his chair. He groaned, cradling his head, as Reny let the tray drop to the floor.

Rook tracked every movement until his focus was drawn to the hearth. The fire was no longer steady. Flames began curling outward, rising, stretching.

Reaching for her.

Reny had no idea. Her green stare, oddly vacant, held an ominous gleam that sent ice through Rook's veins. It wasn't a surrender to her magic. It was a siege, and she was losing without even realizing it.

Beside him, Garron stood rigid, his gaze also fixed on the hearth. Not with fear, but with watchful, careful patience.

He's seen this before.

Rook's gut tightened. From the nearest table, he heard the first whispers.

"Did you see that?"

"Like she just summoned—"

"You boys might want to rethink what kind of place this is," Garron shouted, silencing them all. Every head turned.

"This isn't some rat hole in Bellmere," the old man continued. "You disrespect one of mine, you don't come back. Lay a hand on them, and you'll leave with fewer fingers than you walked in with."

The man pinned under Reny's boot groaned again, desperate for a deep breath. Another shoved to his feet in flustered rage, snarling, pointing. "Are you threatening us, old man?"

Garron lumbered out from behind the bar, guiding Rook aside with a firm hand. "No." His voice was level as he tipped his chin toward Reny. "But she is."

She hadn't moved. Balanced over him, she forced more weight through her boot, heel sinking into his sternum until breath stuttered from the pressure. The firelight caught in her hair, kindling her into something out of a bard's song.

The man heaved to throw her off, one hand fumbling for the knife in his pocket. She bore down harder in one slow lean, her face expressionless.

Rook advanced from behind the bar as a slender tongue of flame slid free from the grate and shot toward her. It licked Reny's bare forearm before coiling once around her wrist. An intimate, claiming caress answering a call only the fire could hear.

She didn't flinch. But with gaping mouths and stunned silence, nearly everyone in the room saw it.

Rook's pulse pounded in his ears. Her magic wasn't just elemental. The fire itself recognized her, answered her, held her.

And left her unburned.

The pinned man wheezed, his ribs jolting with every frantic gasp for air, but Reny showed no mercy. Her awareness had been pulled away, becoming lost in the hearth and the blaze bending toward her.

He could sense her teetering at a dangerous edge—one she wouldn't come back from. The air became oppressive, charged with her unraveling power. Her breath turned shallow, fingers twitching, reaching toward the flames. The fire climbed higher, more tendrils escaping the hearth to snake up her arm.

Chairs began scraping backward, forks clattering against plates of half-eaten meals. Only the locals muttered quick apologies, dropping coins with distracted haste as they moved toward the door. Their glances flicked to Garron in passing, heavy with concern, but not over coin.

Over the danger swelling out of control.

Garron met each look with a nod, forcing himself steady as the tide. He no longer bothered with the scattered payment. Instead, he held the door wide, ushering everyone out. One by one, they slipped past him into the waiting night.

Two men from the corner were slower to exit, catching Rook's attention. The Endarian recruiters. For a breath, he thought they might draw weapons, but they didn't. They exchanged pointed glances before hurrying out into the darkness with the others.

They'd all seen enough. Enough to report back to the capital city.

Flinn had drawn Maren closer to his side behind the bar, soothing worries Rook couldn't hear. Neither of them moved. Neither looked as startled as he'd expected.

They knew about this. About her. The whole damn village had known.

Garron shut the door with a dull thud when the last guest left. He stood there for a moment, palm flat to the wood, his face drained several shades.

He turned toward the hearth, toward Reny, and took a few steps back into the room.

The blaze surged higher, lashing perilously close to the dry beam above the mantle. For the first time, Garron's expression fell. The calm was stripped away, leaving behind haunting fear.

"Ren..." he called out, but much softer now. A father's voice.

But the inferno did not retreat. Her head turned, eyes focusing again on the man trapped under her boot, now slick with sweat, writhing in the growing heat.

"So pretty when you're writhing." Her head cocked to one side as she threw his words back at him. Her voice had changed. An eerie, second tone hummed along with her words. Rook shivered.

She was going to turn that man to ash, and everything around her, if he didn't do something.

He couldn't think anymore. There was no time. He moved.

Long strides ate up the tavern floor, every step drumming against the planks. The three remaining men jolted upright in a panic, scrambling in a tangle of limbs and overturned chairs as they made for the exit.

Leaving their companion to beg or burn.

But Rook didn't care about them now. His focus was only on her.

And gods, she was blazing.

Not just with fire, but a power he couldn't place. It surged through her like a second soul, golden and searing through her veins. Even through the scorched air, he could feel it. An awful, impossible tether taut between them.

His chest seized. *No. That's not possible.*

He caught her by the waist, yanking her back against him. The moment her boot left the man's chest, he gasped and rolled. With a hoarse curse, he stumbled up and out through the tavern door.

Reny twisted in Rook's hold like a feral animal in a snare. Her nails tore at his forearms, and a boot slammed back into his shin, but he held fast, even as her whole body thrashed to break free. He spun her around to face him, holding her by the wrists.

"Reny, stop."

The flames around her rose higher, dancing off her skin. Fire wrapped around his forearms, rolled forward against his chest. A wild heat that should have scorched, blistered, destroyed. But there were no marks, no pain. The fire found no part of him to consume.

Her eyes, now lit white and vacant, widened as she pulled harder to break free.

Rook struggled to steady his breath, trying to grasp what radiated off her. Not only fire, but a deeper force strung painfully tight between them.

Even as her flames lashed out with desperation, they banked, softening or recoiling where they touched him.

"Reny!" His voice boomed over the flare. "Look at me!"

She fought harder, more frantic now. The flames climbed up to her shoulders, licking toward her throat. Garron stood still nearby, his weathered face frozen in shock. Tears rolled down Maren's cheeks as she buried her face in Flinn's chest, his own wide eyes consumed by the sight. Stunned.

"You're not turning me to ash." Rook hauled her tighter, closer, growling through bared teeth. "Not tonight."

Reny yanked and twisted, her body bucking violently. The flames hissed, desperate to break free, but his grip never faltered. He'd become an immovable mountain of shadow to her furious light, even when she spat mindless curses in his face.

Pressure surged until it had nowhere to go, and something in her gave way. A ragged gasp tore from her throat before her knees buckled. The fire recoiled and collapsed inward as the brilliance in her gaze blinked out. She dropped, limp and unconscious, but before she could hit the ground, Rook caught her, gathering her up in his arms.

The hearth collapsed back to embers, pulsing faintly beneath the charred logs. Rook's eyes lifted, meeting Garron's, who was a statue a few tables away, eyes wide and face pale like he'd seen a ghost.

Behind the bar, Maren and Flinn were motionless. Maren's mouth hung open, no words forming. Flinn's arm stayed firm around her shoulders, his own expression unreadable.

Unable to hold Garron's gaze a moment longer, Rook glanced down at his arms, at a loss. For words and understanding. Her fire, alive and consuming moments ago, had burned itself out everywhere that it met him. And in his arms, Reny was still, her breathing steady. Her head on his shoulder, her breath warm at his neck, forcing a chill across his skin despite the clinging heat.

Like this, she looked deceptively harmless. Serene.

And now he knew with utter certainty that she was neither.

Rook was quiet. There were no words, no speculation, no doubt left. He was holding the undeniable, living proof of the very thing he'd been hunting. Held it gently in his own two hands, after all this time.

The flame.

CHAPTER 17

T he hour was late.

Calm had finally descended on the tavern, but it was far from peaceful. Smoke from the hearth hung in the rafters, restless ribbons that still carried the bitter tang of scorched wood.

Flinn stayed in the kitchen, the muffled clatter of dishes barely disturbing the hush. Upstairs, Maren had opted to stay at Reny's bedside, her usual brighter chatter notably absent.

Garron moved through the room with purpose, setting chairs upright, sweeping crumbs from tabletops into his hand. Rook worked alongside him, gathering abandoned tankards. His attention kept drifting to the blackened scars near the hearth, where Reny's control had finally shattered, confirming his gravest suspicions. His thoughts circled back to the man she'd nearly killed. The other huntsmen with him.

More like mercenaries than huntsmen.

And that was a problem.

Bending to retrieve a fallen fork, Rook noticed a satchel tucked beneath the table where those men had been sitting. He might have left it had he not felt the familiar thrum pulsing from within.

He crouched and slid it closer, its weight too dense for coin. His fingers brushed the clasp, unbuckling it. One quick look inside confirmed what his instinct had already been screaming.

A voidstone siphon.

Crude in its construction, but no less dangerous for it. The runework was amateur, hastily carved, but functional. And it was empty and waiting.

His jaw clenched, a cold knot settling in his gut.

They were mercenaries. Ones who'd been hunting for power to steal.

He snatched up the satchel and carried it to Garron, opening it and tilting it toward the old man. Garron peered inside and stilled.

Neither one of them spoke at first. Firelight flickered across the deep lines of Garron's face as his gaze settled on the siphon's ravenous gleam.

He exhaled. The sound of a man who'd spent decades waiting for the other boot to drop.

"I was afraid of this," Garron murmured, more to himself than to Rook. His hand trembled as he reached out, but stopped short of touching it. He pinched the bridge of his nose instead.

"How long have you known of her magic?" Rook asked. He caught the furrow in Garron's brow, the way his shoulders tensed. Perhaps he'd underestimated Garron, what he knew of the world beyond this tiny village. What burdens he'd kept tucked away beneath their simple life.

Garron braced his knuckles on the table, staring at the siphon for a long moment before his focus drifted far away. "Since I met her. She was only five."

Rook's brows lifted despite himself, surprise flickering across his features before he could smooth it away. "Five? I thought you said she was your daughter."

The old man's face twisted, letting the question go unanswered.

"It was the year of the Northern Slaughter. When the Aetherians broke treaty and crossed the Veil at the North Gate and took out Snow Creek."

Rook went still, his breath catching in his throat before he forced it steady.

He hadn't been there. But he'd known of it.

His father had kept him stationed at Rithmor that year, but he'd taken the men that Rook helped assemble and train. Every outpost had whispered of the attack for months after. An Endarian village, erased in a single afternoon, supposedly crawling with spies and mercenaries threatening the Drayvien crown.

Apparently, that had been a lie, too.

His father had given the order, speaking of it afterward with grim satisfaction as if Snow Creek was just another piece removed from his own private game board.

Watching grief carve itself into Garron's weathered face, Rook felt a festering crack form in his center. Snow Creek hadn't been a strategic victory at all. Hadn't been Rithmor defeating threats or its enemies.

It had been a slaughter that destroyed innocent people living quiet lives.

All because the crown had commanded it.

"I wasn't home when it began," Garron went on, the words thick with long-buried grief. His fingers traced invisible patterns on the tabletop.

"I'd gone to the next village over for supplies. When I returned..." He paused, swallowing hard. "Smoke and silence. That's all that was left. Every cottage burning, our people slaughtered in the streets where they'd tried to flee."

Rook wanted to look away, but he couldn't. He felt he owed Garron this. To bear witness to his grief. He could at least give him that.

"Some blamed rogue mercenaries," Garron's voice hardened. "Endarian raiders looking for easy plunder. But I know the bite of Aetherian steel when I see it. The precision and cruelty of it." His fists curled on the table. "They didn't just kill. They erased. Made sure there'd be nothing left to rebuild. The fucking monsters."

Monsters.

The word hung between them.

Rook's teeth ground together, the only sign of what churned deep within.

"She came out of a cottage that was fully engulfed," Garron added after a long pause, his tone softer. Quieter, as if he were giving away a secret. "The roof had already caved in, flames everywhere, the heat so intense I couldn't get within twenty feet of it. No one could have survived that inferno, let alone a child."

He swallowed, frozen in the memory. "But she did. Walked straight through the flames where the front door had been, barefoot, in nothing but a nightdress. Not a single burn or mark of soot." His voice cracked. "She just... walked to me. Looked up at me with those green eyes and took my hand as if she'd chosen me. So calm, so certain."

Rook's breath had gone shallow. "And you kept her."

"I'd buried my family one week before the attack." Garron's throat was raw. "Wife went into labor too early. I lost her and the babe within hours of each other. I had nothing." He dragged a wide palm down his face.

Rook caught a lone tear sliding down Garron's cheek.

"And then this child walks through a wall of fire to me. She stood there holding my hand while everything around us burned, and I thought maybe the gods hadn't fallen. Had sent me someone to save, since I couldn't save my own."

Rook kept his expression neutral, giving Garron room to continue.

"She didn't speak for three days. Just sat by our campfire, staring without a lick of fear into the flames. She'd reach out sometimes and let her fingers drift through the fire as if it were water. It never hurt her. Like the flames belonged to her. Or she to them."

Garron's gaze finally lifted, meeting Rook's directly. Nearly two decades of love and fear pressed into a single look. "What was I supposed to do? She'd chosen me. So, I chose her back. She was mine before anyone could ask questions, before anyone could take her away to one of those terrible Endarian orphanages. And she's been my daughter every day since. Not by blood. By choice."

Rook couldn't hold his eyes a second longer. His attention drifted toward the stairwell, where he knew Reny rested above, still unconscious the last time he'd checked with Maren.

"She's not a child anymore, Garron."

"No," Garron sighed. "She's not."

Rook eyed the satchel on the table between them. "Too many saw what happened here. Those men will return, or new ones will take their place. This siphon wasn't carried for nothing. It was likely for her. They'll come and bleed her dry to sell whatever they can take."

"Sell it to who?" Garron demanded, jaw set in a way that reminded Rook very much of Reny.

"The kind who can pay enough to tilt the world in their favor," Rook answered. "Endarian recruiters were here. Word will reach the capital within a week, maybe less. If the mercenaries don't get to her first, King Braivier's royal guard will. And she won't be warmly invited to join their ranks, Garron. She'll be taken, collared, and used as a weapon until there's nothing left of who she is."

The ember-veined logs popped in the hearth, sending shadows jumping across the walls. Garron stared into the remaining flames, and when he spoke again, his voice was grave, heavy with reluctant realization.

"She can't stay here."

"No." Rook shook his head. "No, she can't."

The opportunity was unfolding before him, easier than anything he could have orchestrated himself. Garron was not just going to hand her over willingly, but insist on it. Insist she leave and head north. With him.

No elaborate scheme, no resistance to overcome.

Rook had always been good at seizing opportunity whenever it presented itself. But this one didn't hold the same level of satisfaction he was used to. This one tasted like ash. Bitter and shameful.

Garron reached forward and snuffed the nearest oil lantern, allowing more darkness to gather around them. Only the dying firelight remained, painting everything in shades of amber and ash. "Some part of me knew that when she nearly lit the rafters ablaze tonight. When I saw that look in her eyes, like she wasn't even in there anymore. But where in all the realms could she possibly go? Where would she be safe?"

"There's one place," Rook said after a pause, choosing each word carefully. "Far north, inside the Veil. Carved into the Silver Mountains, where the realms first split millennia ago. It's called the Aetherium."

Garron looked up sharply, suspicion narrowing his eyes. "You're a tradesman. How would you know of such a place?"

"I told you," Rook said evenly, unflinching. "I do trades. And other things."

"Smart ass," Garron huffed, folding his arms. "The Aetherium's a bard's tale." The words carried an edge of desperation as if he wanted to believe but couldn't quite let himself.

"I assure you, it isn't." Rook leaned forward. "It's a sanctuary older than any kingdom. Bannerless, neutral ground. The master scribes there could teach her to control what's inside her instead of being consumed by it. She'd be behind ancient wards. Safe."

"How do you know all this?" Garron pressed.

"I hold an open welcome with the Aetherium. I've walked its halls, spoken with the scribes. They know me."

The words were mostly true. He had been there. They did know him.

Being welcome was another matter entirely.

Still, it all came out smooth and easy, natural as breath.

Garron's jaw worked, his stare recalculating everything he thought he'd known. "I saw you tonight," he said finally. "Her fire should've stripped the flesh from your bones. Yet here you stand without a mark on you. Not even a blister." The old man leaned closer, a hint of threat in the movement. "What are you, boy? Really?"

"Lucky." Rook shrugged, the gesture too casual, the faintest smirk tugging at the corner of his mouth.

Garron grunted, utterly unconvinced and unamused. The intensity in his expression eventually gave way to exhausted acceptance. The kind that came from fighting a battle already lost, and he knew it.

So Rook leaned into it.

"If she stays here, she'll be in constant danger. The entire village will be at risk. Every week, there'll be more hunters with siphons who've heard whispers of a flame-bearing girl. If she goes north with me, she could learn enough to protect herself. To choose her own path. But if she stays..."

He let the sentence hang, leaving Garron's imagination to fill in the terrible blanks.

"She could die," Garron finished hoarsely, just as Rook expected him to. "Or burn down the village trying to stop them." His face had gone pale despite the stubborn set of his shoulders. He gripped the table as if he could somehow hold onto her, onto the life they'd had, by force of will alone.

Rook's stare held steady. "The Aetherium keeps what the world has forgotten how to hold. Things too precious, too powerful, too dangerous to be left in the hands of kings and generals."

A rare whole truth.

"They will protect her and teach her before the wrong people decide her fate for her." He paused, then added, "I can get her there safely. I swear it."

"You really mean that?" The question came as a gruff plea. Garron pressed the heels of his palms against his eyes, the gesture making him look devastatingly old.

He didn't let Rook answer. "I guess if her fire spared you, there must be a reason. The flames don't choose without purpose."

Rook said nothing, refusing to let the words sink too deep.

"I'll let you tell her." Garron pushed back from the table. "But don't expect her to thank you for it."

He turned toward the stairs, movements slowed by his grief. At the first step, he hesitated, glancing back at Rook over his shoulder. The firelight caught in the silver of his hair, in the lines of his face that looked much deeper now.

"She's worth protecting. Worth more than any of us, more than my comfort in keeping her close. And if her fire spared you..." He paused, considering his words. "I have to believe that maybe you're meant to protect her. Maybe that's why you wandered into my tavern in the first place. Believing that is what'll keep me going when my whole world rides off with you."

Rook remained silent. He stood in the tavern's growing gloom, watching as the stairs creaked beneath Garron's weary climb.

Long after the old man had disappeared, Rook stood alone in the empty common room. The dying fire painted its last shadows across the walls.

"She's worth protecting. Maybe you're the one..."

Protection was never what he'd planned to offer. He'd come to retrieve, then hand her over to his father and brother. To claim his place in the royal court, to prove himself worthy of the power and position he'd been denied his entire life.

He'd come to betray her. And now, feeling the ghost of her fire on his skin—fire that should have killed him but had somehow refused—Rook felt that betrayal like a blade pressed against his own throat.

And realized, with grim finality, that it would have been far easier if she'd just burned him to ash instead.

CHAPTER 18

R ook had been watching her for hours.

He sat in the corner near the window, one elbow braced on the armrest of the rocking chair. His cloak hung from the chair back, the sleeves of his shirt rolled up to bare his forearms. A night without sleep had left him hollowed and worn thin.

He'd taken the chair from Maren shortly after midnight, sending her home with a quiet word and a promise to stay until Reny woke. The girl had been reluctant to leave, but exhaustion won out. Rook kept vigil through the long hours, watching the firelight play across Reny's sleeping face. Listening to every breath she drew.

Thinking of what he would say when her eyes opened. And how.

A gentler path might win her over. She would be frightened and confused. His kindness could ease that. Could draw her trust toward him instead of away.

But her trust was a luxury he couldn't afford.

He had come here for Rithmor. For his dying people. For his father's approval and his brother's grudging respect. If he cared too much, if he softened for her, he would lose his nerve entirely.

Better to be hated and useful than gentle and weak.

If fear was the lever that would move her, then fear was what he'd use.

Pale morning light spilled across the floorboards when she finally stirred. She pushed herself upright, blankets pooling in her lap. A visible shiver ran through her as the chill hit her skin. Her eyes found him instantly.

"What are you doing in my room?"

Rook let his focus slide to her, his face unreadable. "Keeping watch."

Her brow knitted together. "Garron's downstairs. He doesn't need someone to patrol the tavern wh—"

"I'm not watching the tavern." He cut her off, all warmth stripped from his voice. "I'm watching you."

She stared at him, unsettled by the change. The lack of charm.

Good. Let her be unsettled.

"I don't need someone to watch over me."

"See," he said, leaning forward, his forearms braced on his knees. He let his attention drift to the window. "That's the problem. You think you don't."

"Because I don't," she insisted. Her confusion finally peeled back, revealing the anger beneath. He could see it in the hard set of her jaw.

He gave a short, humorless laugh and leaned back in the chair. Ice and arrogance made flesh. "Last night says otherwise."

Better her anger than what had been building between them up to this point. Rage was easy. Rage, he could handle.

He watched as color rose in her cheeks, memories stirring from the night before. Recognition. And then denial.

"Maybe I lost my temper a little, but that doesn't mean I—"

"You really don't remember, do you?" His eyes cut to hers. "You lit up half the tavern with no ability to call it back. Next time, it could be worse. A lot worse. You nearly killed a man."

Her mouth opened, but nothing came out. He watched her struggle for words and swallowed against the tightness in his throat.

"You want to sit here and pretend life can go back to what it was?" Rook made his tone merciless. "It can't. Not after that display. The minute the wrong person arrives because they heard of your power—and they will—it's over. They'll run through this whole village, killing everyone, if that's what it takes to siphon the magic out of you."

He knew exactly what to say. Exactly where to press.

Rook watched her chest hitch, watched fury clash with fear across her face. A scalding retort rose visibly on her tongue. "Just who the hells do you think you are? What gives you the right to—"

"You don't get to stay hidden, Reny. It's not your little secret anymore. It's your whole village's problem now." He cut her off without mercy.

She reared back, mouth opening to argue, but he spoke first. Again.

"You need proper training. Somewhere that you can't hurt the people you love or burn this whole place down when you have another temper tantrum."

The words hit exactly as he'd intended. He saw her flinch, saw the shine building in her eyes, saw her teeth catch the inside of her cheek as she fought to hold herself together.

There was a sharp twist in his chest at the sight. He ignored it.

"Let me guess," she bit out, the words laced with venom meant just for him. "You know exactly where I should go."

He could ease back now. Soften. Offer her something that felt like a choice.

But that door had closed the moment he'd chosen this path. He had to stay the course.

"I do, in fact, know exactly where you need to be. And I'm going to get you there before someone else decides where you belong."

"I decide where I belong," Reny snapped, her voice breaking over the words.

Her tone tore through him. He choked down the urge to explain, to apologize. Nearly choked on the bitterness he summoned next.

"Not anymore, you don't. I've already talked to Garron."

He watched her go still. Watched the betrayal land, the realization that they'd spoken and decided without her input. Her eyes glistened, the war inside her rising to the surface. But beneath that rage sat what he'd been working her toward, what he'd been counting on. He saw it the moment she realized it.

She would never put them in danger. Not Garron. Not Maren. Not Flinn. Not this village.

"And if we were to leave," she forced the words through clenched teeth, "when would that be?"

There it was.

"The wagon's already packed." Rook reached for his cloak, the motion unhurried. Victory tasted like ash in his mouth.

"Wretched bastard." The words flew out of her, deadly and unrestrained. Her face was set like stone, refusing to give him anything close to her agreement.

He let the blow land. Let it carve into him because he deserved it.

He rose from the chair and shrugged on his cloak, pausing beside her longer than he should have, caught in his own war. But he let the moment go, crossing the room without another word, his shadow falling over her as he passed.

The door shut behind him with a firm, final sound. He stood in the hallway, hand still on the latch, and let out a breath that shook more than he thought it would.

This was the path he'd chosen. He just hadn't expected it to feel so much like ruin.

Just as Rook had said, the wagon was already packed when Reny stepped onto the tavern porch, the boards creaking under her boots. The air bit cold and crisp against her skin. She was dressed, though anything but ready, the weight of the day sinking in before dawn had fully broken.

Sal was waiting in the yard, hitched to Garron's modest covered cart, her brown-and-white coat dappled gold by the waking sun.

The old mare stamped once, tail swishing, and nickered softly when Reny brushed a hand along her flank. "Morning, girl."

Her reply was a snort that forced a plume of steam from her nostrils, but her ears turned toward the quiet steps approaching from behind.

Rook.

The mare stretched her nose toward him in a warm huff of welcome. Reny blinked. Sal had never given men such grace, not even Garron, who'd bought her from a rough-handed trader in Hollowbend when Reny was just a girl.

But him?

She rolled her eyes. *Traitor.*

Refusing to meet his eyes, Reny busied herself with the harness straps, though she knew they had already been checked twice. The wagon brimmed with food, canteens of water, hunting tools, and blankets. Everything Garron must have spent the night cramming into it while the rest of the village slept.

She wanted to be upset. To lash out at him for making this decision with Rook, for not consulting her the way he always had. But standing there, looking over the meticulously packed supplies, all Reny felt was a deep, aching sadness.

Above all things, Garron always protected her. Made every decision as a father first. And if he had agreed to this, whatever this was, it could only be because he believed, down to his bones, that she would be safe.

That this was the right thing to do.

For that, she couldn't be mad at Garron. She'd save all that rage for Rook instead. For however long she'd be stuck with him.

Maren was the first to cross the yard from the bridge path, arms wrapped tight against the cold morning. Her apron was askew, her golden hair falling loose from the messy braid she must have slept in.

She halted a few paces from the wagon, glancing between everything nervously. "I feel terrible for all of this. I'm so sorry, Ren."

"You didn't do anything wrong, Maren." Reny studied her friend's face, committing each freckle to memory. "None of this is your fault."

"When that man grabbed me, I felt so helpless." Maren's words, in rare form, had become barely audible. "But you just lit up. You're always protecting us, never thinking about what it does to you."

Reny's throat tightened. She chose silence, her hands clasped in Maren's. The girl moved first, pulling Reny into a fierce, breathless hug.

"Please come back as soon as you can," she whispered, face buried into Reny's hair to hide the tears. "Soon as you can, okay?"

Reny didn't answer. Didn't know how to. She had no idea the amount of time it took to master a thing she could barely comprehend.

Flinn arrived a moment later, pacing along the yard's edge before trudging over, his hands shoved deep in his trouser pockets. He bore every bit of angst and reluctance that his narrow frame could hold.

"You don't have to go," he muttered, his eyes darting to Rook, then down to the dirt. "They'll all forget. Drunks always do."

"Come on, Flinn. You know better. It's bigger than that." She tried to smile for him, but it was too weak. A fragile thing that never reached her eyes.

Flinn kicked at the dirt, the gesture so painfully familiar that it made Reny's heart clench. She'd seen it hundreds of times in the seven years since he started working at the tavern. A scrawny little boy trying to help his widowed mother make ends meet. "Place won't be the same."

"I hope not. I want it to be better. Safer."

He frowned, sniffling, before pulling her into a rough, one-armed hug, holding her longer than he ever had. "Try not to burn down the world, Ren. You're the only sister I've got."

She squeezed her eyes shut against the tears that threatened. "Try not to drink the tavern dry while I'm gone."

They parted with a scowl of affection before he stalked off to the barn, already swiping at his face with his sleeve.

Rook remained by the wagon through their goodbyes, his posture overly rigid. Whatever their words might have stirred in him stayed buried, his jaw set and shoulders locked.

A carved sentinel among the crumbling all around him.

The tavern door creaked open, and Garron emerged into the dawn's growing light, his broad shoulders carrying a heaviness that went far beyond exhaustion. His gaze swept the cart as if tallying the life he'd crammed into it over the night's restless hours.

"Everything's in order then."

Reny watched as he lumbered slowly down the porch stairs. The man who'd been her father longer than she'd ever been anyone else's daughter. Who'd taken her in when she had nothing and no one, and was now letting her go into a vast unknown.

"I gave Rook the northern routes I've mapped over the years," he went on, his voice a low, carefully contained rumble. "Avoid Silver Oak, there's a mercenary camp east of there. He knows all the ways, though, can get you through the Veil, too."

She swallowed the questions that arose from hearing that, all of them too much she wasn't ready to voice.

Not yet.

"There's enough coin and dried meat to reach the Aetherium if the weather holds. If it doesn't—"

"I'll manage, Dad."

His eyes found hers, pride and sorrow tangled in them. He drew a deep breath and let it go carefully. "You always have. I love you, girl."

"I love you more."

He pulled her into his arms, brief but firm. The kind of embrace that said everything words couldn't.

From the corner of her eye, she caught Rook shift. A small thing, barely perceptible, but Garron noticed it too. His gaze moved past her, pinning Rook where he stood by the cart.

A dense pause stretched between the two men. Reny couldn't name what moved through it, but she felt its weight. Garron released her and extended his hand. Rook clasped it without hesitation, their grip holding long enough to seal something unspoken.

"Swear to me you'll keep her safe."

"I swear it."

Something flickered across Rook's face. There and gone before Reny could place it. His voice held steady, but his words landed strangely hollow in her ears.

Garron released him and drew back, pulling an already weeping Maren close to his side. Like he could steady them both. She pressed her face into his chest and let the tears fall.

Reny climbed onto the bench of the wagon, sliding to the far side of the narrow seat. Rook took his place beside her, gathering the reins in both hands. With a soft click of his tongue, Sal started forward. River's Edge began to fall away behind them, peaceful and beautiful in the soft hush of the morning.

To Reny, it felt like the disappointment of waking in the middle of a pleasant dream. She couldn't bring herself to look back at the tavern. At Garron and Maren arm in arm on the porch step. At Flinn tucked by the corner of the barn, trying to hide his tears.

The tree line loomed ahead, shadows pooling thick beneath the canopy where morning sun had yet to reach. She focused on the forest before her. Quiet and still and ready to receive her.

Until movement caught her eye.

The stag.

It stood between two ancient oaks just inside the tree line, half-veiled in darkness, its antlers crowned by the sun's faint golden light. Still as stone, watching.

Its presence settled over her like a gentle hand. Almost tender, as if it too had come to say goodbye and see her off. Beside her, Rook stilled. His grip tightened on the reins, knuckles paling, his body straightening. She glanced over, finding his jaw set, his haunted gaze fixed on the animal.

As if he'd seen a ghost.

She looked back to the stag, but it was already gone. The words she'd offered every autumn when it appeared echoed in her mind.

Be careful in the wilds of the wood. Be wiser than those who hunt you.

As the cart rolled forward into the forest's waiting darkness, she realized that perhaps those words had always been meant for her instead.

CHAPTER 19

Five days of tense travel stretched between them, threadbare and fraying.

They rode side by side on the narrow bench, barely speaking, but the space between them was never truly empty. The wagon creaked and rocked, and their legs, no matter how often they shifted, kept brushing.

A press of knees. A bump of hips as the trail pitched.

Neither acknowledged the constant friction, but both felt it. Had become too aware of it.

Reny kept her arms folded, gaze fixed ahead and cold as the air between them. As they moved deeper into the Oakwoods, the trees grew wider, taller. Gnarled, silver-barked giants whose roots curled from the earth like sleeping limbs, bramble choking the underbrush.

Overhead, the canopy wove tighter with each mile, ablaze with autumn's fire.

The quiet settled like a third presence in the wagon, an uninvited guest that made the miles a miserable drag.

By the fifth night, dusk bled orange and violet behind the trees. They were still a few days from the Old Wood border, but the Oakwoods had already shed their softer face. Reny no longer seemed to recognize the landscape.

She looked like a woman who barely recognized herself.

The clearing Rook chose to make camp was small, half-sheltered by a low rise and ringed with ancient ash, birch, and clusters of narrow evergreens. Sal had already claimed a dense patch of moss, tail twitching, eyes half-lidded, trusting the dark wood in a way Reny clearly didn't.

They worked in tandem, silent. Pitching the tent, stacking kindling, setting the perimeter with practiced, weary efficiency. When the fire took hold, they settled on opposite sides, flames throwing restless shadows across the forest floor.

Rook studied her through the wavering heat. The hard line of her mouth, how the firelight caught in her eyes but gave back no warmth. Her arms were locked around her knees, chin resting atop them. Her stillness reminded him of a serpent in tall grass.

Coiled and waiting.

Whatever had been building in her started the moment they left River's Edge. He could feel it billowing in his own chest like it belonged to him. Every day, every hour, only served to feed the embers inside her. She hadn't looked at him since breakfast, and even then, it had been only a passing, reluctant glance.

Despite himself, he spoke first. "I thought you'd have stabbed me with a fork by now."

"Then I wouldn't have my pass through the Veil, now, would I?" Her reply cracked through the air, faster than he'd expected.

His brows lifted, the corner of his mouth twitching toward a smirk. She didn't return it.

"How is it you have permission to cross the Veil, anyway?" The question held no curiosity. No pleasantry.

Rook let the words sink in, and for the first time, he wondered if he'd misplayed his hand by being so cold to her about leaving. He'd done it to create a safe and necessary distance, but it had only made the air between them unbearably volatile.

Now, he was caught in the grass beneath a serpent's stare.

"I've done work for the Aetherium scribes in my travels," he said, the lie sliding smoothly from his tongue. He met her eyes, easy and unbothered.

"Did you fix their broken shutters and porch posts, too?" She tilted her head slowly.

The predator measuring distance before the strike.

The fire between them surged, its flames rising and leaning toward her.

Rook set his mug down beside him. "Alright," he exhaled, the edge in his voice born of exhaustion and temper. He leaned back on his elbows, eyes fixed on hers. "Go ahead. Ask me whatever you're dying to know so we can move on."

"How is it I went all these years with no one showing up with a siphon until you came along?"

The words found their mark, quiet and piercing. His mouth opened, but she cut him off.

"A word during your mysterious side job, perhaps? A trail of bread-crumbs that led straight to me?" Her eyes narrowed. "Or maybe you were hired to do this. How much coin to hand-deliver someone like me? How convenient that you show up, trouble follows, and you've got the damsel-rescuing answer right in your pocket."

The fire swelled with her voice, heat pressing against his skin.

She was wrong. At least, in the way she thought.

But gods, she was close enough that his chest tightened. Close enough to trigger the part of him he purposely kept locked away. Rook straightened but held his tongue, unwilling to answer her outright.

Ignited by his stillness, Reny surged to her feet. She didn't wait for his explanation. The one she'd already built in her mind was enough.

"Do the Aetherium scribes even *want* to help me? Or is that just the story you tricked Garron with? When I get there, will I be free to leave whenever I want? Or will it be a cell?"

The campfire roared, flames nearly as tall as she was, casting wild gold through the trees. Shadows writhed at his back, clawing toward the forest's edge to escape her.

"Are we even going to the Aetherium?" As her anger climbed, so did the heat.

He kept his expression locked, sweat lining his brow and jaw. He needed to steer her away from the truth she was unintentionally zeroing in on.

Needed to be careful with this gods-forsaken wildfire of a woman.

"I'm trying to help, Reny. That's all." He kept his voice calm and low as flames jumped to life along the backs of her hands, curling upward in slow spirals.

"Is that really all, Rook?" she asked, all accusation.

The fire climbed her forearms, snaking over her collarbone and throat until it traced the lines of her jaw, her chin. From the pit between them, tendrils crawled past the ring of stones he'd made, stretching toward her like they knew her name.

Behind him, a sharp crack split the air. A wide, blackened branch crashed down a few feet away, hissing and scattering sparks as it landed.

Rook flinched but didn't turn to look. Instead, he held her stare, rising to his feet. He closed the distance between them in a few quick strides. Her hands rose as he drew near, but swift as a striking whip, Rook caught her by the wrists, plunging his hands into the fire enveloping her.

Her breath caught, eyes wide and aware. The fire should have hurt. Gods, it should have hurt—skin blistering, bone searing—but the heat only sank into him like water into dry earth.

Impossible, unnatural.

Her gaze fell to where he held her, rage and confusion twisting her face as if the fire itself was betraying her. She tried wrenching against him, but he only held her tighter. And then he leaned closer.

"You don't remember," he said, his words almost teasing in the charged air between them, "but when you did this at the tavern... it didn't burn me."

Rook kept his grip tight and stepped forward, forcing her back, away from the campfire. "You didn't burn me then, and you won't burn me now."

The difference was striking. Just days ago, the same power had left her detached and reeling, collapsing unconscious in his arms. But tonight, she was a monument of fire and wrath, fully aware, every muscle taut with strength.

Part of him wanted to release her to see if she would yield or keep burning. But he'd spent too many years either hiding in violent shadows or becoming one to believe in naïve mercy or kindness.

By the look in her eyes, she wouldn't back down until the magic collapsed and forced her to. He couldn't help the dark, reluctant admiration that stirred watching the inferno in her grow, but he held fast against her efforts to tear away. Too stubborn and unwilling to fold.

"Believe it or not, Reny," he said, bringing his mouth near her ear, "I'm just trying to do the right thing."

Her arms kept straining against him, sparks spitting from her skin in rolling bursts. His patience frayed, and with one fierce pull, he dragged her flush to his chest.

As her body crashed into his, flames curled greedily around them both, the heat licking along his jaw without burning him. Her fire started folding inward, flickering out against the dark lines of his body until her strength began to falter over itself. He felt the softest tremor in her limbs. The first hint of surrender through the blaze.

And damn him, part of him hated to see it go.

"Even if I *was* being paid," he growled, keeping her against him as the last sparks died, "there's not enough coin in the damn realm to put up with your insufferable ass these next few weeks."

All at once, the clearing collapsed into quiet. Her fire retreated, sinking back toward the earth as if scolded. The great column of heat in the firepit returned to a low, crackling flame. Her body shifted, shoulders sagging under the power's toll, and her breath came slower. Steadier.

Still, her eyes didn't soften. Didn't yield an inch, nor had he expected them to. Furious, unbent, daring.

He met her glare in equal measure, his whole body taut with the control he'd seized. "Now," he said, still refusing to release her, "are you done throwing your little fit?"

A pause stretched between them, balanced on a lethal edge. She let out one breath. One sharp exhale through her nose.

He felt it. The faintest loosening in her spine, the smallest drop in her guard. The instant he slackened his hold, she tore free and stalked into the dark without a word.

That night, she curled up beside Sal, who'd settled next to the wagon. She chose the steady warmth of a sleeping horse's flank over the fire.

Chose that over being anywhere near him.

Dawn broke through the canopy, a slash of silver in a bruised sky. Reny sat at the back of the wagon, perched on the narrow wooden ledge with her boots dangling just above the damp ground. Light began filtering through the trees, soft and slanted, but there was nothing gentle about the morning.

The fog clung thick in the forest, around their camp, dense as everything left unsaid since last night's confrontation by the fire. She'd chosen the farthest edge of the wagon's rear plank she could without falling off into the ferns, claiming every inch of distance the clearing allowed.

Rook was a storm today.

She felt it before she saw him. Heard it in the way his boots struck the earth, hard and deliberate, from the moment her eyes opened. His usual loose, quiet gait was gone, replaced by a rhythm too charged.

The detached calm he usually wore was gone. Shredded. Whatever rope he'd been holding onto the night before had snapped, leaving something dangerous at its frayed end.

Something she wanted nothing to do with.

Reny didn't look up when he stalked by the firepit, nor when he began dismantling the tent with more force than finesse. Still, her heart betrayed her, thudding faster with the cadence of his movements.

This is just adrenaline, she told herself. *A spillover from too much magic. Nerves, maybe. Nothing related to him.*

But when a shadow spilled dark across her, she stiffened, her fingers curling hard around the plank's edge as her heart leaped into her throat.

Too late.

He was already on her, bent down face to face, heat and irritation rolling off him in waves. Before she could rise and retreat or cut into him with a cold, cruel word, his arm lifted and braced above her head on the back of the wagon, caging her there with his whole body.

A mirror of that night in the hallway.

Only now, there was no door for her to vanish behind, no locks to bar him out.

"Let's get one thing straight." His voice was rough. Angry.

She looked up at him, into eyes gone dark with thunder, but said nothing. Her chin rose, slow and deliberate.

A dare.

Rook's whole expression changed. It still held fury and frustration, but suddenly became threaded with something far too raw, too hungry. She was caught between the need to run and the desire to stay right where she was, just like the night in the hallway.

His gaze swept over her face, unhurried and unforgiving. The weight of it nearly forced her to look away.

"All last night did," he said, too calm, "was prove my point. You're dangerous. Uncontrolled. And you are done lashing out at me when I'm only trying to keep you alive. Do I make myself clear?"

His arm stayed braced above her head, but his body angled closer. Close enough that her heart tripped, her breath half-formed. He wasn't just angry. There was a different heat beneath his anger. A kind she knew but would not name.

Not now, not ever.

She gave him nothing but her silence and the cold narrowing of her eyes.

"I'm doing what I've been sworn to do," he snarled then, every word forced through gritted teeth.

She tilted her head, offering him not a single shred of remorse or kindness. "Which is what, exactly?"

A muscle in his jaw twitched. She could tell he wanted to say something, the way his mouth opened and then closed. But whatever it was, he'd swallowed it. She told herself she didn't care what it was.

Her gaze slid away in the stubborn hope that if she didn't meet his eyes any longer, he might let it go. Might free her from having to face him.

He didn't.

"You know," he continued, barely above a murmur now, as if he were giving away a secret, "not everyone you let into your life is going to disappear. Not everything you're given ends in loss."

Her eyes cut to him, brutal and sudden. The flare of a strike landing where a wound had never closed. She didn't ask how he knew, but the question lived in the smoldering of her eyes.

"Garron told me about Snow Creek," Rook said quietly. A whisper softer than she'd ever expected from him.

"Don't." She forced every bit of warning she could into a single whisper.

To her surprise, he obeyed, standing down when she'd anticipated him to push back. She shoved the memories back where they belonged. Her chin lifted again, shrugging off the pain she refused to acknowledge. A weakness she would not allow him to exploit.

"I know you're hiding something." Her voice came out too certain, too eager to change the subject. "I just don't know what yet."

His face darkened in an instant, the shift fast and harsh as lightning. "That's fucking rich," he said with a smirk, "coming from someone who's spent her whole life hiding."

She bit the inside of her cheek, bit back what she didn't know how to say. Rook stayed where he was, looming like a storm just before it broke.

"You can hate me if you need to," he said finally, "if that's what it takes for you to accept this. But you will stop fighting me every damn step of the way. If not for yourself, then deal with it for Garron."

He drew closer, narrowing what little space remained between them. His breathing had gone shallow, his body tight with the effort of holding some invisible line that was pulling him toward her. Reny didn't lean back, didn't make it easier for him.

Rook was the one who broke, pushing himself away as if the air itself scorched him. The space he left behind rushed in, cold and empty. She cursed herself for leaning forward, chasing the heat he'd taken with him.

Her heart was pounding as she watched him go, the storm of him still crackling in the clearing long after he'd vanished from her sight.

CHAPTER 20

A tension much older than the day's grief filled the Great Hall of the Eastern Cliffs.

Cliffborn had gathered from every corridor, filling the cavern with bodies and torchlight. The shifters had assumed human shapes for the meeting, though a few remained in their animal forms—perched, prowling, or drawn into shadows along the walls.

They were the fewest in number now. Powers passed down through generations were dwindling. A slow whisper against the roaring of a world that no longer had a place for them.

Rhedda stood on the raised stone platform at the hall's center. Brenn took his place a step behind her, jaw tight, hands clasped at his back.

"I have brought you here," Rhedda began, loud and clear, "because the Eye has shown me a path to our salvation. But as I have warned, we cannot walk this path without great sacrifice."

A murmur rippled through the crowd. The familiar words did little to calm them, fear thick as the salt in the air. Shifters, elementals, witches, and the few Whisperfolk in attendance were all searching for faces they'd never see again.

Rhedda's expression remained unwavering. "The scouting party we sent forth has not returned. Orwyn, our wise owl. Erysia, the young hawk, and Rennar, the wolf. All have fallen. Aric, the fox, is the lone survivor."

A unified gasp swept through the hall, broken by the young ones crying out. The fox-shifter, Aric, stepped forward, fists clenched at his sides. He stood tall and lean, high, sharp features framed by hair the same shade as his red fox coat. Grief had hollowed the fox-shifter's usually bright amber eyes.

"How?" A young woman demanded from the back of the hall, her tone raw with disbelief. "They were among our most powerful."

Rhedda held up a hand. "Powers were not enough. Even our gifts can fail us."

Aric shook his head, his lean face twisted with rage.

"No." His voice cracked, cutting through Rhedda's measured tone. "Powers didn't fail them. Crown Prince Tareth Drayvien and his royal legion ambushed us. A waiting trap with voidstone chains and siphons. They were slaughtered so their power could be stolen."

The Great Hall erupted, shouts and curses crashing against stone. The Aetherian royal family's name was a brand against each of them, carrying generations' worth of oppression and loss.

"We knew they were hunting us," another voice shouted. "The Aetherian power is failing. They're stealing ours to survive. Who sent our people into that?"

The question hung, unanswered.

Brenn's jaw worked. Before Rhedda could speak, he took a large step forward. His sheer size moving across the stone platform hushed the group, drawing every eye.

"It was me."

Shocked silence fell, heavier than their grief. Brenn let his head drop, shoulders bowing under the burden of confession.

"It was my idea," he rumbled, each word a distant thunder. "I asked for scouts to observe the Drayviens' movements instead of allowing Rhedda to consult the Eye again. We all know how it weakens her. How each vision takes from her." He lifted his head to face the crowd, meeting their eyes one by one. "I am the one who sent them to their deaths. I should have gone myself."

For a heartbeat, no one spoke. Then Aric laughed, bitter and hollow.

"Don't you dare," he said, stepping closer to the platform. The words carried the weight of old friendship, of someone who knew Brenn too well for what he was hearing. "Don't do that, brother."

Brenn's brow furrowed. "I'm telling the truth—"

"You're taking the fall," Aric cut him off, pain flickering across his bruised face. "You're standing there trying to shield her from what we've all been thinking for months. For years." He turned to face the crowd, throwing his hands up. "How many visions has the Eye shown her? How many paths has Rhedda told us to follow? Or chose not to? Think about where that's led us."

Murmurs of agreement rippled through the gathered Cliffborn. Soft at first, but growing louder. Faces that had been tight with sorrow began shifting into validation and deeper thought.

"Aric—" Rhedda began in warning.

"Orwyn questioned the last vision three months ago," Aric continued. "He asked how we could know the Eye was showing truth and not simply what—"

"Enough." The single word cut through the noise like a blade. Rhedda stepped forward, the sheer force of her presence commanding everyone's attention.

"You will not speak of what you *think* Orwyn's thoughts were." She'd become cold and cutting. "He questioned, yes, and I answered him. I showed him patience when he challenged the very foundation that has kept us alive."

She turned her gaze on Aric, pointing, and he stepped back from the force of it.

"And now you stand here, fresh from watching our people die, and you dare to use their deaths as fuel for your own faithlessness?" Her words rose, filling every corner of the hall. "You think I don't grieve for them? You think I haven't wept for every vision the Eye has shown me, knowing the cost?"

The crowd shifted. Some who had been nodding along with Aric now looked uncertain.

"The Eye does not show me simple paths," Rhedda continued. "It shows me the only path. The one thread of possibility in a world that wants us erased. You call it blind faith. I call it survival."

"Rhedda—" Brenn began, but she hushed him with a look.

"No, Brenn. They need to hear this." She turned back to the crowd. "Every one of you came to the Cliffs broken. Hunted, stripped of home and hope. The prophecy gave you purpose. The Eye showed us how to stay hidden when the Drayviens' raids intensified. It warned us about Endaria joining the voidstone trade before it reached our borders. It has saved more lives than it has cost."

"And Korva?" An air sprite's small voice rang out like a bell. "Where is she?"

Careful control settled over Rhedda's face. "Korva walks the path the gods have laid for her. She found the flame, just as the Eye showed me she would. Aurelia's ember, reborn in flesh."

Brenn went still.

"She returned to us with this news," Rhedda continued, ringing with certainty. "Confirmation that the prophecy is unfolding exactly as foretold. And now she follows where the gods guide her. Protecting the flame-bearer, ensuring the path to our salvation remains clear."

Brenn's jaw tightened to the point of pain. *That wasn't why Korva left. Not at all.*

"Convenient," Aric muttered, just loud enough to be heard.

Rhedda's eyes snapped to him. "What did you say?"

Aric met her stare, and the hall held still. "I said, it's convenient. She came back just long enough to tell you what you wanted to hear, then disappeared again? And you're calling it divine guidance?"

"How dare you?" Rhedda's words were fire and ice. "Korva is my student. My responsibility. She has done exactly what the prophecy required of her. Found the flame, confirmed its existence, and now ensures its safe passage to us."

She descended from the platform, the crowd parting before her. When she reached Aric, she looked up at him with unforgiving eyes.

"I have given everything to keep you safe." Quiet now, but no less fierce. "My strength. My sight. My own peace. The Eye takes from me with every vision, and still, I return to it because it is the only light we have in this darkness."

Aric's mouth pressed thin, but he said nothing.

"Korva found the flame," Rhedda continued, voice carrying to every corner of the hall. "The girl who carries Aurelia's ember is real. She exists. And Korva is guiding her here, to us, so that the prophecy can be fulfilled and our people can finally stop hiding in the dark."

No one spoke or moved.

Rhedda turned to face the assembled Cliffborn. "I will not apologize for the harshness of the path. I will not soften what I've seen to make it easier to swallow. This is survival. This is war, whether or not you choose to see it."

She climbed back onto the platform, standing tall beside Brenn.

"The prophecy has been our guide for generations. It is the only thing that has kept us hidden, kept us whole. Korva's success proves the Eye shows true. I ask for your faith, not your blind obedience. Have faith that I have led you well thus far and will continue to do so."

Thorne, one of the oldest earth elementals, stepped forward. "And if the flame-bearer doesn't come, Cliff Mother? If Korva doesn't return?"

Rhedda met his eyes without flinching. "She will. The gods have shown me this path, and I have never steered you wrong."

The crowd stirred. Some were nodding, most remaining uncertain but unwilling to speak. The fracture was there, visible now, but Rhedda had held the line.

"You are dismissed," she said. "Return to your quarters. Mourn our fallen. And tomorrow, we continue preparing for the flame-bearer's arrival."

The Cliffborn dispersed slowly, breaking into murmuring groups. Some cast uncertain glances at Aric. Others looked to Rhedda with renewed faith, or at least renewed fear over openly doubting her. When the hall had emptied, Rhedda remained on the platform. Her shoulders, which had been squared with authority moments before, sagged slightly.

Brenn stood beside her, silent. The words she'd spoken still echoed in his mind, scraping against what he knew to be true.

Aric remained, staring up at them both. "I'm not your enemy, Rhedda."

She looked down at him, and sorrow flickered across her face. "I know. But you're no ally right now, either."

"Orwyn was my friend," Aric sighed. "He questioned because he cared. Because he wanted to understand."

"And I mourn him," Rhedda replied. "But I cannot mourn and lead at the same time. Not now. Not when everything hangs by a thread."

Aric held her stare a heartbeat longer before shifting into his fox form in a flash of white and rust. He paused at the cave entrance, glancing back only once before disappearing into the tunnels.

The quiet stretched between Brenn and Rhedda.

"She didn't leave because the gods told her to," Brenn finally said, the bear in him waiting behind the words.

Rhedda's back stiffened. "She left because her path continues. The Eye—"

"The Eye didn't tell her to fly into a storm the moment she learned Orwyn was dead." Brenn fought to keep his voice neutral. Calm. "I was there, Rhedda. I saw her face. That wasn't divine guidance. That was grief. And rage."

Rhedda turned to face him, and he caught rawness in her expression, some twist of fear and desperation he'd never seen before.

"What would you have me tell them, Brenn? That my most gifted student fled in anguish? That she's out there alone, driven by sorrow rather than purpose?" Her voice dropped to barely above a whisper. "They need to believe there's a plan. That everything we've lost means something."

"Even if it's not true?"

"It is true," she said, but there was a brittle edge to her certainty. "Korva found the flame. That part is undeniable. And whether she's following the gods' path or her own grief, she's still moving toward the same end. The prophecy will be fulfilled."

Brenn said nothing. She sighed.

"I need you to trust me. Even when you doubt. Especially when you doubt. Because if you waver, they all will."

Brenn had no words. He dipped his head and turned, leaving the great hall behind him. But as he walked the spiraling stone corridors back to his quarters, doubt gnawed at him with teeth.

Rhedda had intentionally reshaped Korva's departure to fit the prophecy. Had made grief look like divine purpose. And the Cliffborn had believed her—or at least, most had.

How many other visions had she interpreted to match what she needed them to mean? How many truths had been bent to fit the shape of hope?

For the first time in his great, long life, the steadfast and loyal bear was doubting everything the Eye had ever shown the Cliff Mother.

Beginning to doubt the prophecy altogether.

Beginning to wonder if Rhedda's strength was the only thing holding them together, or if her need to believe had become more important than reality itself.

CHAPTER 21

After two days, they broke free from the Oakwoods.

The wild tangle of trees thinned to reveal a clearing. Rough farming cottages, weathered trading posts, and uneven garden beds. A stubborn foothold of farmers and fields along the border where light gave way to the shadow of the Old Wood.

Reny and Rook didn't speak much. Not out of peace, but because neither wanted to risk tearing open the heat they'd left banked in the clearing two days before.

Rook tied Sal to a crooked fence post. The mare pawed the ground, restless, ears flicking back, nostrils flaring. Without a word or backward glance, he started toward a narrow trading post at the end of the lane, walking like a man who'd been here many times before.

Reny slid down from the bench and stood beside Sal, arms crossed, watching Rook walk away. The afternoon light caught on the broad line of his shoulders, but did nothing to soften that brooding weight he carried. His shadow stretched long and lean across the path.

Familiar. It had fallen over her more than once.

His presence looked wrong in this little village. A dark, jagged silhouette against light and scenery too soft, too gentle.

Other eyes watched him, too. Both of them. Villagers leaned in doorways and perched on low stoops, their faces carved deep by sun and suspicion.

Reny kept her expression neutral, but their scrutiny dug in deeper than she cared to admit. Fear and judgment—what she'd spent her whole life evading. A weight she was eager to leave behind, even if it meant descending into the Old Wood.

With him.

A brown mutt pup burst from between two weathered sheds, yipping as it barreled toward her. A small boy followed a few steps behind, laughing, a mop of black hair bouncing as he ran. The pup skidded to a stop at Reny's feet, tail wagging so furiously it nearly knocked itself over. She crouched with her hand outstretched, a soft smile breaking through. It licked her fingers before bolting away again, the boy shrieking with laughter as he chased after it.

At the lane's farthest end, Rook passed two men hunched close, voices pitched low. He heard them anyway.

"... saw it again, a flash of the Mire."

"Old Wood's waking. Same rot as before, mark me."

Their voices faded when they sensed his presence, their silence as telling as their words.

Beyond them, an old trader slouched against a timbered wall, pipe smoke curling about his head. The one he knew. Rook gave the briefest nod, and the man tipped his head in return.

From his pocket, Rook drew a narrow slip of parchment, already soaked in whisper ash ink. He uncapped his pen and scrawled in a coded hand:

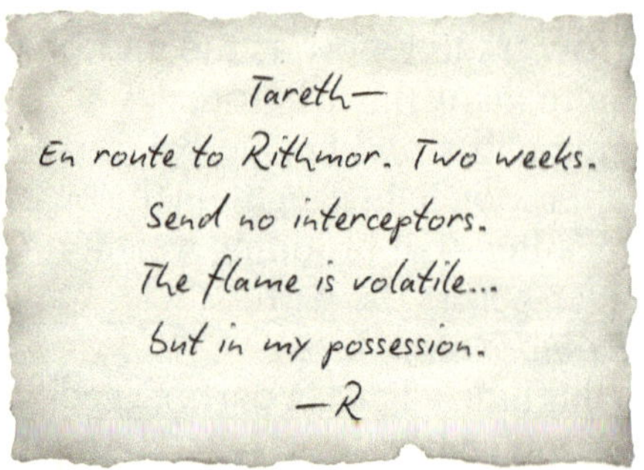

He folded the message twice over before pressing both parchment and gold coin into the trader's hand. Another dark transaction in a lifetime of them. Quickly executed, but far from clean.

Inside the post, he bought a loaf of bread, a wedge of hard cheese, and strips of dried venison for three more coins. Travel food, and the perfect cover for his true errand. When he stepped back into the afternoon sun, dust stirred around his boots. Halfway to the wagon, he stopped.

Reny crouched in the dust as the puppy circled her in chaotic, dizzy joy. The boy had looped a frayed rope around its neck, but the dog tugged free to leap at her again, tail thrashing.

And she was smiling. Laughing. Not the cold smirk she'd flash. No brittle glare born of defiance. Her face was soft. Real. It startled him with a jolt that went deeper than it should have.

Had he ever seen her without so much weight behind her eyes? And why did such a question cross his mind, anyway? Why did he care?

A tight knot formed in his chest, unwelcome and foolish. He was a blade, and she was a burden to be delivered. *Nothing more.*

Yet the sight of her genuine, open joy was a splinter he couldn't remove.

As if sensing his presence, Reny rose and brushed her hands on her pants. She waved after the boy and pup before turning toward him. Her smile dimmed, face shuttering back behind its usual guard as she returned to the cart bench.

Rook looked away as he crossed to her, the bundle of food in hand. He set it in her lap when he climbed up into the wagon beside her.

A small, simple gesture where an apology might have been, had he been anyone else.

He clicked his tongue, and Sal immediately surged forward, the wagon wheels groaning as the cottages fell away behind them.

Ahead, the Old Wood opened its wide mouth. The canopy—still thick and lush, and somehow still untouched by autumn—cut out nearly all light. Shafts of gold broke through in rare places, but the deeper they went, the darker the world became.

Like stepping into a place that had never once truly been touched by the light of day.

Tareth Drayvien counted the cracks in his father's throne.

Seven in the left armrest. Fifteen along the back. Lines that had not been there decades ago but were now splitting deeper with each passing season. As if even stone forgot how to hold itself together.

The throne was failing, riddled with the same rot gnawing on everything else in Rithmor.

Walls, wells, bones, minds.

He lounged in his chair beside the dais, one leg draped over the armrest, watching his father pace. King Maelor's boots scraped the same circuit they'd worn into the floor for months now.

Back and forth. Back and forth.

His lips moved around words meant for no one living, his nails raking raw lines down his forearms. The madness had worsened.

Good, a voice whispered somewhere in the back of Tareth's skull. *He weakens. You strengthen.*

Tareth no longer flinched from the voice. He'd stopped years ago, when the whispers first overlapped his thoughts after another trip to the voidstone chamber. They were as natural now as his own pulse. More natural, some days, than the thoughts he tried to claim as his.

Beyond the throne room's narrow windows, Rithmor sprawled gray and gasping beneath the mountain's shadow. Rivers that once glittered with starlight had become dry beds of dirt. Or gutters of thick, black muck. Trees twisted inward, trying to escape their own roots. And the people—

He tried to remember what their eyes had looked like before. When he was young, before his mother died, before his father first led him down those spiral stairs.

Had there been light in them? Color? The memory slipped away before he could grasp it. They always did, now.

It doesn't matter. They are yours to rule. To use. His fingers twitched against the armrest.

Behind him, the high priest lurked in the shadows, his breathing a wet rasp that set Tareth's teeth on edge. Holy men weren't supposed to sound like they were rotting from the inside. Then again, nothing in this castle was what it was supposed to be.

Black banners hung limp from the towers and from the massive double doors of the throne room, each marked with the serpent devouring its own tail. Tareth stared at them.

A fitting emblem for a house consuming itself from within.

But his focus broke as the doors burst open. A servant boy stumbled through, pale and trembling, clutching a folded parchment. He barely managed a bow before Tareth's hand lashed out and snatched the note away.

"Out."

The boy fled without ever looking at them.

"What message does the Rook send?" Maelor's pacing halted, his voice iron-tight, that spark of wildness flaring in his hollowed eyes.

The Rook. King Maelor never addressed him by the name the queen had chosen for her son with her dying breath. Referring to him as a game piece made it easier to treat him as such.

Tareth unfolded the parchment, sneering as he angled it away from the priest's craning neck and read it aloud. His brother's coded hand, sharp and efficient. No wasted strokes. No wasted anything. That had always been Vaelric's way.

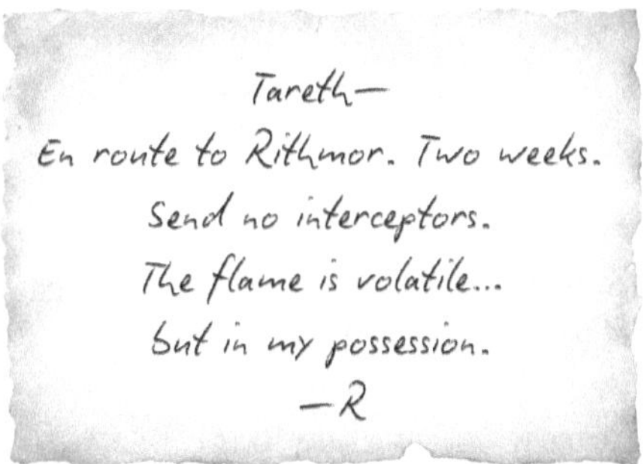

The flame. After all this time. After all the hunting, the failures, the whispered promises that salvation was just one relic away. Tareth read the words again, and he felt a twist in his core.

It wasn't joy or relief. Far from that. Something darker, with teeth and venom.

"In my possession."

His brother, in lush Endaria, with the prize they'd sought for decades. His brother, who still slept through the night without screaming. Who still owned every thought in his head. Who had looked their father in the eye and refused the voidstone's kiss, and somehow kept breathing afterward.

The memory surfaced before Tareth could stop it.

Vaelric, at twelve, dragged before the throne after yet another refusal. Yet another whipping. Again, when he turned fifteen. Their father's voice, thunder wrapped in silk. "You will place your hands upon the stone, or you will have no place in this house."

And Vaelric, bloody and defiant, offering his palm to the blade instead. "I'll give you my blood, my service. But never my soul."

Tareth scoffed aloud, drawing a sidelong glance from the high priest.

As if there was a difference. As if the blood oath hadn't chained him just as surely. It only provided a longer leash.

He'd watched his younger brother from this very chair, waiting for their father to strike him down. But back then, Maelor had understood what Tareth was only beginning to grasp.

A weapon was useful, but never beloved. A weapon that hesitated, that looked too long at the faces of those it was meant to cut down, that refused the very power offered to strengthen it, was dangerous.

But it could be conditioned. And so the second son lived, repeatedly banished back to the barracks where he'd been raised as a hound instead of a prince. Drilled and beaten and forged into something their father could point at enemies whenever he wanted.

All while Tareth sat, poised and perfect, at the right hand of the king, the voices in his head growing louder with every ritual completed in the hungry dark beneath their feet.

You chose power. He chose weakness. Do not envy the lamb for escaping the altar when you have the chance to become a god.

"Well, boy?" Maelor pressed. "What does he say?"

Boy. The word never landed with good intentions when it came from the king. Tareth's lip curled. "He claims to have found the Flame. A fortnight out, supposedly."

The king's face mottled, composure unraveling like loose thread. "Too long. What if she slips through his hands? We are not the only ones searching."

She. So he'd been right about that woman, then.

Tareth filed that away, wondering what poor creature his brother was dragging back to this rotting keep. Wondering if Vaelric still felt anything when he delivered innocents to slaughter, or if that part of him had finally calcified like the rest of him.

The priest's voice oozed through their silence. "Perhaps the One Eternal might bring her to us by other means. I shall summon his forces."

Tareth's spine stiffened. The voice in his skull purred in agreement, and he hated how his own anticipation wound tight with its hunger until he could no longer tell them apart.

For a long moment, father and son were quiet. Then, in unison—the same gesture, the same dismissal—their hands flicked toward the side door. The priest melted away, murmuring prayers neither of them cared to hear.

Tareth rose, and together they turned toward the stairwell hidden behind the throne.

A black stone staircase spiraled down into the belly of the mountain. The air grew damp, heavier with their descent. King Maelor's breath was labored, each step slower than the last. Centuries of borrowed time were finally demanding payment.

The Crown Prince didn't offer his king an arm. Didn't acknowledge the frailty.

Because he felt the same creeping weakness in his own veins. The same appetite that never faded, no matter how much he fed it. The same certainty, growing stronger with every step, that he was not walking toward power.

He was being digested by it.

The chamber opened before them. Vast, bare, each wall blacker than obsidian. Two torches guttered in their sconces, flames tinted green as swamp-light, casting shadows that pulsed in rhythm with whatever lay far below.

The pedestal claimed the room's center. Voidstone. Its surface swallowed what little light touched it. Runes sprawled across it in twisted loops, older than their race, older than kingdoms, older than the world. The script of the Seam itself.

Tareth's skin began to hum the moment he crossed the threshold. The pull was immediate, undeniable. A hook beneath his sternum, tugging him forward, feet moving without his full permission.

Yes. Come. It has been too long.

Had it? Days blurred together now. He couldn't remember the last time he'd been down here. Couldn't remember if it had been his choice or the voice's.

There is no difference. There never was.

Tareth tried to hold onto his focus, willing strength into any thought that was his alone. His mother's face. The sound of her laugh, before the blood moon took her. But the memory dissolved like sugar in water, gone before he could even taste it.

His palms met the cold stone. Beside him, his father did the same. Maelor had shown him this ritual when he was still a boy, young enough to believe his father's promises of salvation and infinite power.

Young enough not to understand what he was truly offering.

The runes woke, igniting not with light but infinite corruption. Their brightness guttered into decay, seeping up from the carved lines like infection in a wound. The stone exhaled, and Tareth inhaled it as his own.

His voice rose with his father's, chanting syllables of a dead tongue, words that scraped his throat raw and tasted rotten.

How many times had he said them? He'd lost count, each ritual binding him tighter to what waited for release. Each time giving a little more of himself until he wasn't sure how much was left.

You give until there is nothing left but me. Only then will you ascend.

The thought, the voices, came from everywhere and nowhere. Their whispers collapsed into a single, endless hiss that scraped until Tareth's mind was empty.

His father's eyes went first. Blackness poured in, erasing pupil and iris until only void stared back. Tareth watched it happen, knew his own would follow, tried one last time to hold onto something—

Vaelric. His brother's name. His brother's face. The one who got away.

But the thought scattered like ash as the darkness took him, and time meant nothing.

When Tareth surfaced, he had no idea how long they'd been in the chamber.

Hours? Days this time?

He was on his knees before the pedestal, palms still resting against the smooth stone. His father slumped beside him, breathing but absent, eyes still black and staring at nothing.

The stone floor had cracked beneath them, hairline fractures splintering away from the base of the stone. Tareth traced them with his fingertips.

The voices were whispering again, this time from the crack itself. In unison, they spewed living shadow, hungry and aware. Darkness slid deep under the mountain, threading outward into wells and roots and rivers.

Tareth stared at the fissure, at the narrow gap he knew was bleeding darkness out into the world. And felt nothing.

The lock is weakening, the voice whispered, satisfied. *The prison cracks. Soon, I will rise.*

Maelor had thought he was making a deal the first time he'd performed the ritual and touched this stone. Thought he was noble and still had a choice when he offered up his firstborn son.

But gods did not make bargains. They made vessels.

Tareth's mouth curved into something like a smile. It didn't feel like his. Nothing did.

Not anymore.

CHAPTER 22

The raven flew until her wings betrayed her, plunging at last through the ancient canopy of the Old Wood. She struck the earth in a scatter of feather and shadow, and from the ruin of that fall, Korva rose.

Human again, though she felt far from it.

She leaned against the gnarled trunk of an elder tree, its roots twisted and sprawling to hold her upright. Her eyes burned, swollen from days of grief and sleepless flight. The absence of Orwyn carved deeper than any wound. Pain hammered in her skull, echoing her faltering pulse.

"Why you, brother?" she whispered to the silence, her throat cracked from relentless flight. As if the trees themselves might know the answer. "I can't do any of this alone."

But you'd always been alone, hadn't you?

The thought came unbidden, bitter as bile. Even surrounded by the Cliffborn, Brenn's steady presence, and Rhedda's empty promises of purpose and prophecy, she'd always felt like an outsider.

The girl who'd arrived at the Cliffs half-starved and feral, with only her raven form and a brother who'd somehow survived the same hell she had.

Orwyn had been her tether. Her proof that surviving meant something.

And now he was gone.

She dragged herself toward the creek that threaded the wood, crawling over soil and moss until its babbling sound lured her to the water's edge. The current slipped over dark stones and gathered in shallow basins beneath the shelter of tangled roots. Every muscle in her body trembled, weary with sorrow, hollowed out by hunger and thirst.

Her hands shook as she cupped water to her lips. It burned going down, cold enough to ache. She drank greedily, gulping mouthfuls as if the stream might scour the grief from her bones.

The water tasted off. Strangely metallic. But she was too thirsty, too desperate, to care.

When had she last eaten? Days, perhaps.

Time had lost all meaning in the endless gray of her flight. She'd pushed herself past exhaustion, past reason, flying until her wings gave out because stopping meant thinking.

And thinking meant remembering.

Remembering Orwyn's easy laugh. The way he'd ruffle her hair when she got too serious, too intense. The way he'd always known when she needed space or anchoring. How he'd taught her to shift when they were children, both figuring it out together in the dark corners of places she wanted to forget.

"Never find yourself unarmed, no matter where you are," he'd told her once.

Just beneath the surface of the water, something stirred. Darkness seeped upward from cracks in the creek bed, bleeding like ink into the current. It moved with intention, drawn by her anguish.

She stopped drinking and pulled her knees close, setting her chin atop them. Silent sobs wracked her frame as she watched the ripples flow. The flame-painted canopy danced across the water's surface—until the reflection wavered. Fractured by unnatural stillness.

The air grew colder. Not the chill of autumn, but a bone-deep cold.

Wrong.

He did not have to die...

Korva's dark brows furrowed. The thought had her cadence, her grief, but it carried a fury that did not entirely feel like her own. She lifted her head, gaze sweeping across the small clearing. Every branch and leaf seemed to hold its breath.

She no longer felt alone.

But that made no sense. She'd flown deep into a part of the Old Wood far from any settlement or path. There was no one here. No one but—

The Cliff Mother sent him to his death willingly.

"No," she whispered, but even as she spoke, doubt crept in like frost.

Hadn't Rhedda sent them out? Hadn't she ordered the scouting mission that led Orwyn straight into Tareth Drayvien's trap?

Brenn asked for it, she reminded herself, trying to grasp the truth before it slipped away. *It was Brenn's idea. Not Rhedda's.*

And who let him? Who approved it? Who saw the future and sent them anyway?

The questions burrowed deeper, hooks sinking in. She pushed her palms flat to her temples, willing the relentless words away. Too long without sleep, too many scattered thoughts, too much grief. But the thoughts settled like stones in the depths of her.

The Seer is blind. Faith wasted on a prophecy she cannot read, on false gods she cannot raise. There is only one true Eternal.

"Stop," Korva breathed, but it came out weak and shattered.

She thought of the times Rhedda had consulted the Eye. The visions that led nowhere and the prophecies that shifted like smoke, never quite clear enough to act upon.

How many had died following those visions? How many would continue to die because the Cliff Mother saw pieces but never the whole?

Orwyn had trusted Rhedda, believing in her guidance, her wisdom, her connection to powers beyond their understanding.

And he'd died for it.

More whispers curled through her mind, layered and merciless. The words morphed into false, festering memories. Her head began to pound, the ground swaying beneath her as her eyes swept the trees again, seeing double of everything around her.

Korva's legs buckled. She folded into the grass, body surrendering even as her mind fought to hold on.

But sleep would not come. Could not come.

She lay there, staring up at the canopy, and let herself remember. All of it. Not just Orwyn's death, but everything that came before.

Her service to the Cliffs. The missions where she'd nearly died, where Orwyn had nearly died, all in service to prophecies that never quite came true. The way Rhedda looked at them sometimes—not as people, but as pieces on a board. Valuable, perhaps. Useful. But ultimately expendable if the Eye demanded it.

And Brenn. The bear who'd sworn to protect them both, who'd promised to watch over her when Orwyn left.

Where had he been when her brother fell? Where had any of them been?

The first stab came without warning. Blinding agony cracked through her skull from within. Her hands shot up, clutching both sides of her head.

A high-pitched ringing drowned her cries. The presence surged again—not a whisper this time, but guttural screaming that seemed to come from the earth itself.

THE CLIFF MOTHER IS UNWORTHY! UNWORTHY OF THE EYE! BRING THE EYE TO ME!

She rolled wildly through moss and leaves, body writhing as the pain spread like fire and fog, choking every breath she tried to take. Darkness laced through her ribs and down the length of her spine, spiraling around her bones, burrowing into marrow.

Through the haze of her agony, images flashed.

Orwyn, standing tall and proud before a mission. Orwyn, teaching her to navigate by the stars. Orwyn, laughing at one of Brenn's terrible jokes. Orwyn, promising he'd be back before she knew it.

And then—

The sinking of Aetherian blades into his back as he fell under the weight of chains. The voidstone siphon slammed into his chest, drawing out every ounce of his power and life until only the hollowed husk of his corpse remained.

"No—" The word tore from her throat, her face twisting.

Avenge your brother.

She curled up in a ball, seeking any angle of escape from the torment. "Why are you doing this to me? Who are you?"

The one who will help you avenge him.

The voice was almost gentle now, almost kind. A shadow wrapped around her broken heart like a balm, soothing even as it poisoned.

They failed him. They failed you. But I will not. I see your pain. I know your rage. I can give you the power to make them all pay. Every Drayvien, every false prophet, everyone who let your brother die.

"I don't... I can't..." Her words broke on a sob.

You can. You are stronger than she ever saw. But first, find the Flame for me. The girl who carries Aurelia's ember. She is the key to everything—to your vengeance, to your brother's justice, to remaking this shattered world.

Visions flooded her mind. Of a young woman with dark auburn hair threaded with red, caressing the flames behind the tavern in River's Edge.

Find her; tell me where she is. And when I ask it of you, you will take the Eye from the false prophet who let your brother die. You will be the one to claim it. You will be my eyes in this world, little raven, and together we will make them all pay.

"The... the Flame..." Korva's words were barely a rasp, her mind imploding under the onslaught of visions and voices.

Yes. She is with the one they call Rook.

The name dripped with venom.

He brings her north, thinking to deliver her to his king. Let him. She will never reach Rithmor's throne. She belongs to me.

Korva's body seized, breaking into wild convulsions. Her spine arched as though her very core had been wrenched skyward. A silent scream stretched her lips as her head fell back, jaw twisted to the side in a soundless, distorted shout.

In that moment of unbearable suffering, she saw him. Not with her eyes, but deeper. A presence vast and terrible, timeless, reaching up from depths that should never have been disturbed. It had been patient. Waiting for someone broken enough, angry enough, desperate enough to let it in.

And she was all three.

You will have your vengeance, Korva. I promise you that. But patience, child. Watch the Flame. Ensure her path north continues and await my command. The false prophet will pay for what she's done. They will all pay.

When her eyes snapped open, they were no longer blue as the sky but endless black. Darker even than her raven form, reflecting the venomous thoughts that had drowned out her senses. Whatever fragile breath of duty remained, vengeance smothered it. Until the thoughts she heard were no longer her own.

It was his.

I am the One Eternal, and now you belong to me.

Deep within the prison of her own mind, the real Korva screamed, the sound never reaching her lips.

The body that had been hers rose from the forest floor with unnatural grace. The sorrow was gone, replaced by a thrumming power that felt limitless. Intoxicating.

Grief remained, but it had been weaponized, sharpened into a blade that could cut through anything.

Good, the presence purred. *Now fly, little raven. Find the Flame. Stay close. Watch and wait. Your time will come.*

The shift came easier than it ever had before, the darkness smoothing away any lingering resistance. Feathers erupted from skin, bones hollowed and reformed, and within moments, a raven launched from the clearing.

But this raven's eyes did not reflect the sky. They held only void.

And they were hunting.

CHAPTER 23

The Old Wood closed around Rook and Reny with unsettling speed, its canopy knitting so tightly overhead that it choked out the remaining daylight. Reny had always found solace in wild places, the Oakwoods a sanctuary throughout her childhood.

But nothing here offered comfort.

The air was thick, as though the forest itself was holding its breath. Birdsong came rarely, and when it did, the cadence was strange, notes cutting short, swallowed by a silence that held no peace.

Even Sal sensed it. The paint mare kept tossing her head, muscles bunching, hooves stamping with restless irritation. Rook murmured something to the mare, his voice deep and sure, calming her with a patience Reny had not expected. Against her will, the sound of his voice calmed her, too. The same voice that enraged her could also steady her heartbeat as the world grew strange and foreign around them. She repeatedly cursed herself for it as they rolled along the trail.

Fog fell when the sun did, rolling in thick waves through the trees. Rook guided Sal off the trail into a narrow clearing shielded by fallen trunks and moss-draped boulders. Without speaking, they made camp. Reny secured Sal and offered her oats while Rook retrieved two canteens from the back of the wagon.

He looked up at her, and she heard it. The soft babble of running water beyond the first dense rows of pines and silver birch. Their eyes held a beat longer than they should have.

"I'll fill these," he said eventually, looking away. His tone hardened, leaving no room for argument. "The Old Wood isn't safe. Stay here."

Reny bristled even as she nodded, her spine stiffening at the authority in his voice. He hesitated, standing behind the cart for an extra moment before disappearing into the fog.

With nightfall, the air grew bitter and damp. A tremor ran through her, the forest's chill sinking deep. She moved for the cart to grab a blanket when, mid-step, a sound caught her off guard.

A whisper.

Faint and feminine. Too far away to catch the words, yet too clear to be dismissed as wind or the rustling of an animal. Reny stilled, glancing at Sal. The mare never lifted her head from her oats. She kept eating, content and blissfully unaware.

Another whisper, this one closer, like breath brushing past her ear. A shiver of warning traced down her spine, but she still felt a strange, primal pull toward the sound.

"Rook?" she called, her voice coming out small. The fog swallowed his name whole.

There was no answer. No rustle of footsteps or even the distant trickle of the creek's current. Only silence.

The voice again, even clearer this time. Not words, but a melody, woven with tenderness that made her chest tighten. It wasn't a stranger's tone, but a warm, familiar hum in her bones.

She wanted to hear it again.

It wrapped around her, beckoning gently at first, then with more insistence, reeling her forward with invisible hands. Each note promised understanding. Reunion.

Come. Come, I've been waiting.

Sal grunted when Reny stepped away, but dropped her head back to her oats, tail swishing with lazy indifference.

Reny's boots pressed soundlessly into the damp earth as she walked forward. The wagon, the clearing, the tether to the waking world all dissolved behind her as she moved through the trees.

She should stop. Some buried part of her was insisting on it. But the voice she followed was stronger. It promised things she hadn't known she was starving for.

Comfort. Belonging. Love.

The melody shifted, taking on the cadence of a heartbeat.

Her heartbeat. As though whatever called her knew the rhythm of her pulse, the pattern of her breath, the secret ache she'd carried since she was five years old.

I never left you. I've been here waiting. Always waiting for you to find your way back to me.

Silver trunks and black boughs arched overhead in a cathedral vault, fog unfurling between them like slow-moving smoke. The whispers beckoned, slipping past her ears and into her bones, commanding her steps.

Her strides softened until she no longer felt she walked at all but drifted, gliding weightless over the forest floor. The ache in her chest, the one she'd learned to ignore, bloomed into desperate need.

The trees opened suddenly, revealing a bend in the brook where the current slowed to a dark, glassy basin. Stones slick with moss and half-drowned logs stitched a crude path across the water.

And there, on the bank just beyond the water—

A figure.

Aurenya. There you are.

The woman stood at the water's edge, her back turned. The fall of dark, reddish hair—that shade of auburn that caught fire in sunlight—was achingly familiar. The narrow shoulders, the subtle tilt of her head at the sound of footsteps—etched into Reny's earliest memories.

Her heart stuttered. Heat and longing surged, choking out her voice, preventing her from calling out. When the woman shifted just enough to reveal her profile, the curve of her cheek, the softness of her mouth, recognition struck like a blade.

"...Mother?" The word barely escaped her lips, small and broken and desperately hopeful.

I've been waiting for you.

The voice trembled with such feeling that it hollowed Reny out completely. Every lonely night, every time she'd watched other children run to their mothers' arms. All rose up in a wave that threatened to drown her.

I've waited for you so long, my dear girl.

The world around her stilled at the promise that the nightmare might end. Reny stepped forward into the water, all logic falling away. The cold shocked through her boots, but she barely felt it. She tested each slippery stone with tentative steps, as though one wrong move might wake her from the impossible.

The figure waited, so close now that a single stride would bridge the distance between them.

This was her mother. The woman who'd sung her to sleep, who'd promised to always protect her. The woman whose absence had carved out a part of Reny's soul that nothing ever filled.

I'm sorry I left. I never wanted to leave you, Aurenya. But I'm here now. I'm here, and I'll never leave again.

She lifted a shaking hand and reached out. Desperate to anchor herself to the miracle before her. Her fingertips brushed the fabric of her mother's sleeve.

The figure turned.

And the world caved in.

It was her mother's face, but it was ruined.

Flesh pale and bloodless, shrunken and drawn tight over bones that jutted at wrong angles. The bottom jaw hung loose and distended, glistening with black tar that dripped down the front of her dress. Only gaping voids where her eyes should have been, charred and smoking at the rims as if fire had burned them out from the inside.

Reny's breath tore from her lungs. She staggered back, but the thing moved first. Faster than her thoughts, faster than her fear.

Its hand snapped to her throat. Fingers impossibly long and thin, joints bending half backward, dug into her flesh. Nails like splintered glass bit deep, drawing blood. The cold of its grip sank, flooding her body, icing her from the inside out. Air rushed from her lungs, black flecks blooming across her vision as she clawed at the hand, her own nails catching on slick, glassy skin that felt frozen and fluid at once.

The voice came again, but it was no longer her mother's. Male now, deep and guttural and ancient, dragging up from the darkest of depths.

I've been waiting for you.

The grip released, and a shove followed, violent enough to knock the rest of the world away. Reny reeled, arms flailing helplessly for balance. The brook surged up and swallowed her, the freezing water closing over her head in one merciless gulp. The current was impossibly strong for such a shallow stream, pulling her down, down into darkness that had no bottom.

The forest. The light. The air in her lungs and the warmth in her body. All devoured, until only cold darkness remained.

Chapter 24

Reny was lost in the black.

Her breath, her thoughts, the trembling thread of who she was. There was no up, no down, no sense of time. Only the crush of water and the suffocating weight of silence pressing in from all sides.

Then the visions came, breaking over her the instant she tried to breathe. Water rushed in, searing her lungs with cold, and with it came memory, merciless and bright behind her eyes.

Her parents burning. Her cousins screaming. The village drowning in blood and ash as black banners split the smoke. Steel rending flesh. Pounding hooves striking the ground in rhythm with shrill, maniacal laughter. Fire devouring everything.

Everything except her.

The nightmare that had haunted her steps was no longer a dull shadow at the edges. It had become a raging flood, drowning her from the inside out.

She tried to scream, but the water filled her mouth instead. Cold hands closed around her wrists, yanking her deeper. Black tendrils writhed up her arms, slick as oil, curling over her throat before forcing their way past her lips. She gagged, choking, clawing at them as they burrowed deeper, trying desperately to latch onto her magic, her fire, her very soul.

Another vision seized her, but this one felt wrong—another's memory forced upon her.

A battlefield shrouded in fog materialized before her, shapes lunging through the storm with eyes burning and mouths shouting in a tongue she'd never heard. Walls of stone erupted from the ground, trapping her while her body grew impossibly heavy, the cold rooting deep in her core.

And then pain. Searing and unimaginable as claws raked across her ribs. Inhuman hands reached up, grabbing hold of her ankle. They started dragging her down toward a vast and hungry presence waiting within the void with its mouth wide open.

You are mine. Reny heard every word as a shrill hiss.

No. The word formed deep inside her, where not even the darkness could reach.

A spark caught, a lone ember refusing to drown. Light ignited in her chest, white-hot and wild, bursting outward and tearing through the dark claws that held her. The water itself trembled, recoiling as if burned.

Another grip seized her, but this one was different. Real. An arm banded firm around her middle, anchoring her to everything real and alive.

Rook.

The instant he pulled her against him, the darkness's hold shattered. It wailed, fury at being denied, as he ripped her free and kicked hard toward the surface.

The world exploded around them in spray and air. Reny gasped, choking, foul, black water spilling from her lungs. Her body convulsed as Rook pulled her onto the bank, hauling her higher, farther from the water's reach. She rolled onto her side, coughing violently. Each breath was agony, her throat raw, her ribs burning. She retched until at last only air, raw and cold and clean, filled her lungs.

The forest came back into focus. In the newfound quiet, only the soft rasp of crickets and the wild hammering of her own heartbeat remained.

Rook gathered her into his arms, one beneath her knees, the other tight around her shoulders. His breath was ragged against her temple, his own body trembling. She didn't fight him. Her head fell against his chest, fingers clutching his soaked shirt as though she might slip back into the black if she let go. The drum of his heartbeat pounded beneath her palm.

"I've got you," he murmured, barely audible.

Beneath the stench of decay and malevolent magic from the water's depths, he smelled like silver pine and woodsmoke. Grounding. She shamelessly hid her face in his chest and let herself believe him.

Rook moved through the fog in silence. Halfway back, his breathing changed, shifting from urgency to something quieter. More guarded. She didn't have the strength to wonder why.

The clearing was dark when they returned, trees leaning in with branches heavy with fog. Rook drew a blanket around her shoulders before turning to the kindling. Flint sparked in his hands until a frail ember caught, the flame wavering before it finally grew steady. Reny sat upright, too pale against the glow, her gaze fixed on the fire as though it might burn away what had happened. Her hands stayed buried in the blanket, fists clenched against her own memories.

She was here, awake and breathing. But some part of her still felt lost in the void, lost in her mother's comforting words.

How naïve and foolish she had been to believe them.

Rook watched her. She could feel him looking but couldn't meet his eyes. When the cold finally drove him to move, he turned away. His soaked tunic clung stubbornly to him, water sliding in icy lines down his back. He pulled the shirt over his head and draped it near the fire to dry.

Reny told herself not to watch, but her eyes followed in immediate betrayal. The firelight sketched his form in alternating strokes of shadow and amber. He moved with the careful awareness of a man long accustomed to threat, every motion controlled, nothing wasted.

And the scars. So many scars.

Some were pale and fine with age, while others were carved deeper, rawer, brutal marks across his ribs and belly that couldn't be justified with the tools of a simple tradesman.

From the moment she saw him, she'd known there was more to him than the picture he'd painted. Seeing it right in front of her now left her transfixed, staring too long until his quiet motion broke the spell, forcing her eyes away.

Rook hung the tunic near the fire to dry before briefly disappearing behind the wagon. When he returned, barefoot and dressed in fresh linen, he carried a bundle.

Her clothes.

"You need to change." His words were quiet, but absolute.

Reny began to rise, the blanket sliding from her shoulders. The moment she straightened, pain lanced through her side, and her breath caught, body folding inward as she clutched her ribs.

Rook was already kneeling before her, hands hovering near the wet hem of her shirt, close enough that she felt the heat of him. His eyes held hers, wordless, waiting to see if she would lash out and drive him back.

She didn't. Her jaw tightened as she allowed his hands to lift the edge of her shirt, fingers brushing the soaked fabric and raising it with careful precision.

When the bruise came into view, he stilled. It sprawled across her ribs in an ugly, livid sigil that pulsed with stinging heat. It looked nothing close to a simple bruise, but a mark with intent, as though whatever had reached for her in the water wanted to stake its claim.

"Hold still," he murmured, pitched so low she felt the words more than heard them.

She obeyed, her breath catching and not wholly from pain. His gaze swept her with painstaking care, searching for other injuries, but kept returning to the mark on her ribs.

He grimaced. A hand reached for the bundle and placed the clothes in her hands. Fingers brushed hers, the contact sparking through her she refused to acknowledge. She shifted to rise again, pain twisting her face.

"Let me help you."

Reny hesitated instinctively, shaking her head.

She didn't want to need him, didn't want to show weakness.

Another attempt to straighten on her own again failed. The adrenaline from earlier had abandoned her, leaving her to her wounds. Pain slashed through her middle again, sharp enough this time to draw a startled breath and curse she couldn't contain.

Rook rolled his eyes. "You're impossible, you know that?" When he lifted his gaze to hers, there wasn't harshness. Only deep resignation. "If you'd listened to me, if you'd stayed where I asked, you wouldn't be in this situation. Now, please, Reny. Just let me help."

"You didn't ask me anything," Reny hissed through clenched teeth. "You ordered me."

Rook only narrowed his eyes, gesturing vaguely to her clothes with one hand.

She looked away, reluctantly nodding. He moved closer, one arm slipping around her back while the other braced her side, easing her upright with a gentleness too far at odds with his strength. The blanket slipped free, pooling at her feet.

Cold air bit her skin, but it wasn't the chill alone that stole her breath. It was him and the slow draw of his breathing through slightly parted lips, so close she could feel the warmth of it against her temple.

He stripped the soaked fabric from her with cautious motions, mindful to keep his eyes averted as much as he could. When his fingers grazed the edge of her bruise, he froze, waiting for the fang-filled recoil that never came. She swallowed the sound threatening to escape, refusing to show more vulnerability than she already was.

"I'm sorry. I know it hurts." The softness in his voice, combined with her shirt falling to the ground, forced a burning flush into Reny's face. He reached for the pants next, his eyes lifting to hers. The storm of them locked on her, cinched tight around her throat. She gave another small nod, careful not to meet his stare too long.

Rook worked quickly, undoing her pants and guiding her legs free, more careful with every flinch she made. When her bare feet touched the ground, he was already easing her into clean, dry pants. When it was done, he helped her back down by the fire and draped his own blanket around her shoulders.

Heat stirred in her chest at his kindness, curling into a place she intentionally kept hollow.

Rook sat down beside her, angling himself out toward the trees to keep a watchful eye on the forest around them.

"What was that?" she asked at last. "It sounded like my—"

"Don't." His head snapped toward her, the sharpness in his tone stilling her tongue.

Rook exhaled, some of the edge draining from his voice. "Don't give name to the form it wore. If you do, it can find its way back."

His eyes caught the fire's restless light. "It was a mimic. Supposedly, they were Whisperfolk at one time. Twisted spirits normally summoned by mages who know the old rites, but..." He paused, his own words tasting bitter. "Magic's been bleeding across the Veil for generations now. Hard to say what's been made that was never meant to exist."

Reny had gone rigid beside him. He hesitated before adding, quieter, "That one knew you. Knew exactly what would draw you in."

The admission unsettled him more than he would let her see. As did the lie that had slipped out so easily to explain it to her.

Mimics didn't simply appear. Someone with knowledge of the old rites and the earliest scriptures had to have summoned it. Sent it specifically for her. Memories rose in his mind of what his father and brother practiced in the private chamber beneath Rithmor, where he refused to go. His loyalty had been to the crown, to his people.

Not to long-lost gods or rites whispered in smoke and blood.

But he'd seen enough. Enough to want no part of what his father and brother had become obsessed with. The hours Tareth and King Maelor would vanish below the throne room, descending spiral stairs. Rook had been forbidden to follow after he'd refused to place his hands on the strange stone kept there. After their secret rituals, they'd return hollow-eyed, carrying shadow with them that never left.

His father's devotion to Malorith—*the One Eternal, they called him*—had grown from faith to fervor more closely resembling possession with each passing year.

Could the high priest have summoned it? His father? Tareth?

He had already sent word that he was coming, that she was with him.

Shouldn't that have been enough? Unless the message never made it. Or worse, the mimic had been meant to take her from him, leaving him to drown or arrive in Rithmor empty-handed and expendable.

Tareth always found humor in the cruelest ways.

For the first time, his loyalty felt less like duty and more like a noose tightening around his own neck.

And then there was the horrific pull in his chest when he'd returned to camp to find her gone. No overturned wagon, no sign of struggle. Only absence and one lazy, indifferent horse. An ache had gripped him, too sharp to be instinct alone, winding tighter with every step until it pulled him straight down into the creek's black maw.

Straight to her, the same way it had when the hunter attacked her at the tavern. He hadn't questioned it then. He wouldn't question it now.

What it meant. That was something he refused to consider.

"Like I told you, it isn't safe for you out here," Rook said at last, shaking free of his thoughts. "When we reach the Aetherium, you'll be behind wards. Protected."

Her brow furrowed, but her words were soft. "How do you know about all this?"

"A lot of travel." His jaw flexed, eager to redirect her. "Look, I know you're not happy about this. It isn't something you asked for." He sighed. "But I'll protect you, like I told Garron I would."

Her lips parted, words right on the edge of her tongue. "Rook, I'm s—"

"Don't." His voice cut her off. Short, but gentler now. "Don't apologize. Just listen. Trust me a little bit."

The fire crackled between them, throwing restless light across her face. She held his stare, and he watched something shift in her expression. Some small loosening of the walls she kept so carefully fortified.

"I'm trying."

CHAPTER 25

Four days had passed since the mimic, and the bruises along Reny's side had begun to fade. The breath-stealing ache in her ribs had dulled to a stubborn throb. The distance they'd traveled did nothing to quiet the memory of that night, even if they didn't speak of it.

Rook had little to offer by way of conversation. He simply kept them moving, driving the wagon forward as if speed alone could outpace the shadows behind them. Pauses came only when Sal refused to be coaxed forward, her ears pinned and hooves stamping with indignation.

Reny couldn't blame her.

In the late afternoon on the fourth day, the path began to climb. The trees thinned the higher they went, allowing the canopy to break open to the sky. As the wagon crested the ridge, sunlight struck Reny full in the face. She squinted against the brightness, drawing a sudden gasp of awe.

The Old Wood stretched away beneath them over sweeping hills, massive stone outcrops crowned with fire-bright leaves. Crimson and amber bled together beneath a sky gathering storm. On the distant horizon, heavy clouds began to knit into dark walls, sweeping toward them in ominous sheets. The air had turned cool and expectant. Reny pulled her blanket tighter around her shoulders as Rook slowed the wagon, scanning the skies.

"We'll need cover," he muttered, more to himself than to her.

Sal tossed her head and snorted as Rook veered off the trail, making their way down a narrow track choked by underbrush and saplings. They found a small clearing hemmed in by ancient boulders and the splintered wreckage of fallen oaks. Soft earth gave beneath their boots, the air growing heavy with the threat of rain.

Rook climbed down first, tying Sal beneath an overhanging branch where she'd have room to lie down if she wanted. Reny followed gingerly, ribs protesting the movement, though her face betrayed nothing. She stretched her legs as Rook began to unload rope and a tarp from the back of the wagon.

The forest's hush fell in around them. *Until it wasn't.*

Sound rolled through the trees. Voices. Men, careless and cruel. *And too close.*

Rook went still, rope and tarp falling soundlessly from his hands, gaze cutting through the darkening wood. The spot they'd chosen offered some natural cover—boulders and brush to break sightlines—but it was far from perfect. Without a fire, there was no smoke, no warm glow to betray them, but if someone looked from the right angle or strayed too far off the path to make camp of their own, they'd be spotted.

Sal's ears flicked, head tossing once. Rook was already at her side, leading her behind the largest moss-crowned mass of rock. Reny moved without thinking, falling into step to drop a small scatter of oats in front of the mare to keep her occupied.

Her hand brushed Sal's neck as she murmured a quick plea to stay put.

With a quick flick of Rook's fingers, Reny followed. They slipped deeper into the trees together, ducking beneath low branches and weaving between ferns. His pace was swift and silent, every nerve in her body tuned to the urgency in his stride.

Just off a narrow game trail, he stopped, pulling her toward the hollowed heart of a long-fallen oak, its split trunk veiled in a heavy drape of ivy. He swept the greenery aside with one arm and drew her through with the other. The dark, damp opening swallowed them at once. Bark slick with age pressed flush to their backs. The ivy fell back into place, sealing them behind a curtain of leaf and shadow.

There was no space for distance. No room for breath.

Her body fit against his out of necessity. Front to front, their hips aligned, every line of him burned into her through the barely lit space. His breath mingled with hers as he pressed his hands against the tree hollow above her, warm against her temple. Audibly uneven, as though he couldn't quite steady it. Her pulse thundered, racing harder still when a branch splintered nearby. Boots followed, heavy and careless, trampling down on sticks and leaves.

The voices drifted closer, loud and hateful.

"...the last one didn't even scream. Not worth the siphon."

"They won't react the same. The closer you draw to the Veil, the richer the pull. Fetches double if you sell to Rithmor's priests. Triple if you smuggle it south."

A third voice, thick with drink, broke into a wet laugh. "Endaria's king will throw half his treasury for a flame-bearer, after those recruits saw one out in River's Edge. His bounty's higher than the Drayviens' now. Gold up front, no questions asked."

The first man spat. "Let the kings choke each other with their coin. Makes no difference to me who bleeds for the siphon, so long as the price keeps climbing."

Another chuckled darkly. "Aye, let us get rich while they fight for the favor of dead gods."

A bounty in Endaria for a flame-bearer? A bounty for... her?

Reny's stomach twisted, bile threatening to rise in her throat. She looked up at Rook, her mouth set in a firm line. His eyes were already on her. There was no mockery in them. Only the truth he'd been waiting for her to see.

I told you they'd be coming. I told you it wasn't safe.

He was the first to look away, gaze finding the slit of forest visible just beyond the ivy curtain, every line of him coiled tight.

The hollow was too damn small.

Reny's back pressed hard into the rough curves of the trunk, every raised knot biting into her. Pain flared along her wounded side, lancing through her ribs. She shifted restlessly, the movement driving her harder against him. Their bodies aligned in an unyielding, unforgiving press.

Friction stole their breath in tandem, quick and ragged. The change in him was immediate. A sound—half growl, half warning—vibrated his chest, leaving the air quivering around them.

Her eyes snapped up. Rook was already looking down at her, his brow furrowed, expression carved rough with restraint. For a heartbeat, his eyes slipped unguarded—dark and edged, threatening to cut right through her.

It wasn't only the danger outside that had him like this.

It was this. Her. Here.

Heat rushed to her cheeks. She said nothing, the silence itself turning perilous. The moment stretched wide until the forest just beyond the ivy stirred with the mercenaries' passing.

Outside, laughter broke in sharp, ugly bursts. Boots crunched closer, snapping the slender branches littering the forest floor. Reny's pulse hammered. She could feel Rook's too, thrumming against her chest, charged with the same wild energy that radiated from the men outside.

Two dangers closed in at once. One of steel and cruelty, prowling through the trees. One of heat and hunger, caged in the hollow with her.

The voices echoed in the Old Wood around them, scraping against the hush as they stopped. The mercenaries weren't just passing through. They were settling in for the night, far too near the place where Sal and the cart were hidden behind rock and underbrush.

Their proximity tightened around Reny like a fist. One curious glance, one careless step, and it would all be over. She begged silently for the mare to stay quiet for a while longer.

Her side burned again, pain licking hot beneath her skin. She tried to hold herself rigid, a statue in the cage of his arms, to avoid what had happened before.

But as the pain grew, her body betrayed her, indifferent to how close they were. She shifted, only enough to ease the unbearable fire searing through muscle and bone. With nowhere else to go, she sank harder into him.

Rook's breath fractured against her temple, a hiss dragged through clenched teeth. His body shuddered as if holding himself still demanded more strength than he possessed.

She tilted her head up, apology caught in her throat. His eyes found hers in the low light, the mask he'd kept up for her falling away completely.

No smirk. No condemning glance. *Just want.* Undisguised and unforgiven.

His hands moved, tracing along the line of her waist before curving to her hips. His grip closed on her as he shifted her position, angling her body to ease the pull on her wound. But the way his palms stayed told a different truth. The flush meeting of their hips. The way his fingertips dug into her, memorizing the feel of her beneath them.

She could feel the truth in his hands. And other places. He needed to feel her. To hold her against him, to take whatever the darkness and danger would allow. Her pulse raced, heat curling through her belly as the hardness of him pressed unmistakably against her. The hollow around them shrank to nothing, air thick with their mingled breath, charged with everything they couldn't say.

She could feel him holding back, straining violently against his self-imposed leash. And against all better judgment, she moved again. Not by accident, not to ease the pain. She rolled her hips against his with deliberate intention, testing the boundaries of what he could endure.

This is insane, Reny. Why?

The reaction was immediate. Devastating and sinfully satisfying. His head dipped, breath hot against her temple. Her name tore from him, quiet and broken, barely more than a rasp.

"Reny." Not loud enough for the men outside, meant only for her. A confession of hunger he couldn't contain.

Her breath caught in a quiet gasp, trembling in the fragile space between them. Her hands, previously trapped stiff at her sides, lifted before thought. Her fingertips found him in the shadows, following the corded muscle of his arms, the hard planes of his chest, trying to anchor the storm building between them through her touch alone.

Only making it worse.

A sound escaped him, primitive and raw. Strong hands roamed her body in the dim, moving from her hips to her waist, over the curve of her ribs and higher still, sketching her outline. Mapping every inch like he was memorizing her. His touch grew bolder, one hand traveling up her spine while the other curved possessively around her backside, fingers splaying wide to pull her tighter against him.

For a fleeting heartbeat, there was no danger beyond the ivy. No predators in the woods. Only his breath, her name, their hands claiming each other in the shadows. The moment trembled on the edge of more.

Too much. Too dangerous.

His forehead lowered until she thought, foolishly and desperately, he might close the distance fully. Instead, his hand lifted to her jaw, holding her face firmly in place. He pressed a finger to her lips. Not harsh, but enough to shutter the sounds of her shaking breath.

Be still. Be silent.

And yet even as he warned her, his touch betrayed him. His finger traced her lower lip with aching slowness, pressure igniting every nerve.

Making her want to draw that finger into her mouth, confirming her suspicion that yes, she'd completely lost her mind.

He broke eye contact only to lower his mouth near hers, so close that the stubble on his jaw brushed the corner of her lips. She could feel it in the tension of him, the way his mouth hovered just out of reach.

He wanted to taste her. And she wanted to let him.

The war raging in him was written in every hard line of his body, in the way he held himself perfectly still while shaking with the effort of not taking what he wanted.

Outside, the mercenaries laughed, their voices splitting the growing dusk. But it was nothing compared to the wild, wordless danger straining between them in the shadowed hollow.

Rook moved then, easing past her in a way that felt like a tease. Every inch of contact was a slow drag of heat stamped onto her skin, a brand she'd carry long after it ended.

And then all at once... abrupt and aching absence.

Space yawned cold between them. He had melted backward through the veil of ivy without a sound, becoming one with the shadows that shifted through the trees. Before it fell shut, she glimpsed twin daggers in his hands, drawn as easily as claws unsheathed.

Silent. Lethal.

Where were those?

His eyes remained locked on hers until the ivy swept him from her view. With her heart hammering, she couldn't help but wonder what sort of beast had just slipped out into the forest.

The mercenaries' voices continued to carry, their words painting an awful picture of a world Reny had never seen.

"...Endaria's king wants to go east," one muttered. "Since losing another regiment at Black Pine Bay last month. Sent boys barely grown to hold the line. Damn fool even thinks the Cliffborn will march for him, even after hunting them."

"Aye," another said with a dry laugh. "Because he's a bloody idiot, that's why. The Cliffborn don't march for any crown. Never have."

"Better him than the Drayviens," a third spat. "Rithmor carves out their own in the crypts. At least Endaria pays coin straight. Doesn't care how you catch it, so long as it burns when he calls for it."

"They can keep their war," a fourth grunted. "We'll keep the profit. North or south, doesn't matter. It's whoever lays the heavier purse."

Their laughter broke jagged through the hush, too loud for a Wood that was wild and watching.

Reny pressed her brow to the inner curve of the hollowed trunk, her lungs tight. Through a thin crack in the bark, she searched the shifting gloom for Rook but saw only silhouettes.

Six mercenaries, maybe more. Leaning on spears, thumbing hilts, rolling their shoulders in bored restlessness. One broke away from the group. Tall, lean, with a face weathered as cracked leather.

"Need to piss," he muttered, already moving toward the trees where Sal and the cart were hidden. The last place she'd seen Rook before he melted into the woods.

A shadow shifted through the trees. *And there he was.*

Emerging from the dark, born of it. A measured, lethal advance without hesitation or sound. One hand rose, a dagger catching a faint, final shred of sunlight leaking through the canopy. It flashed once before vanishing again, brief as a predator's eye.

The man never made a sound. Rook's hand closed over his mouth in time with the blade's merciless sweep from one ear to the other. The mercenary's gaze went wide, blood spilling warm and dark down his chest. Reny watched as Rook lowered the man with eerie care, gentle even in brutality.

As if it mattered how the dead hit the ground.

As quickly as he appeared, Rook was gone again. Swallowed by the trees, claimed so completely that the forest made him its own. Silence reigned, heavy and watchful.

Too much time passed after he vanished. Reny's fingers ached where they gripped the bark, her pulse counting out seconds she felt she could no longer afford. Pain pulsed in her ribs with every beat, but still she forced herself to remain still.

He told you to stay here.

Beyond the ivy, the mercenaries began to ripple with unease, their eyes cutting to the shadows where their comrade had vanished.

But what if...

She could not endure the waiting any longer. The dark, the stillness. It gnawed at her, constricting her chest until she thought she might splinter apart.

When their backs were turned, Reny eased through the curtain of ivy out of the trunk's embrace. Every step was a silent battle against roots clutching at her boots, the fire stitching through her ribs. Her breath had gone ragged in her chest, but she didn't care. She had to find him.

Before the forest didn't return him at all.

CHAPTER 26

R ook was already closing in.

One of the mercenaries stood apart, half-turned, his hand never straying far from the knife at his belt. But Rook knew that face. Knew, and regretted, the spring day when their paths had crossed.

That one—*Kreg*—had seen Rook without the glamour spell. Had seen the truth behind the human mask. Even veiled now, some truths refused to be hidden. He needed to die next, before he could say anything that might give Rook away.

Every step was soundless, his blades a shadow's extension. Perfect angle. Absolute cover. He was already leaning into the kill when—

A sound, small and brittle. A twig cracking underfoot. Rook's head snapped toward it, every sense alight with awareness.

Reny. She'd left the hollow, now shuffling through the underbrush with her arm tight around her ribs, pale but jaw set in that same stubborn defiance.

Godsdamn her. All hells.

One mercenary spotted her. He closed the distance in three strides, meaty hand shooting out to fist her hair. He wrenched her head back so hard a gasp tore from her throat, the sound an axe cleaving straight through Rook's chest. Rook clenched his teeth, moving closer. Silent as the encroaching fog.

The men converged on her with wild, easy hunger, forming a tight circle that swallowed her whole. One man viciously forced her wrists behind her back, jerking her arms until her face twisted in pain. She tried to pull free, but his hold only tightened, fingers digging into the delicate bones of her wrists. Another clamped his hand across her mouth as she opened it to yell, his calloused palm grinding against her lips with enough force to split the soft skin inside against her teeth. She tried to bite down, but he only pressed harder, his other hand clutching her shirt collar to keep her still.

Her original captor yanked her head back further, exposing the pale column of her neck. Tears sprang into her eyes from the pain, but she blinked them away, refusing to let them fall.

"Look at that red hair," another sneered, crouching close enough that his sour breath coated her face.

Kreg shoved through the group, smacking the other man's hand away from her mouth. Her lips were smeared with her own blood.

"Hold on here a minute." He seized her jaw, inspecting her like a man appraising livestock, tilting her face side to side.

"I know this one, I do. Sold her name to some Aetherian scum last spring." He drew his knife with a metallic hiss, laying the edge to her throat until it bit just enough that she felt the threat of breaking skin. His grin split wide and ugly, revealing crooked, yellowed teeth. "Now I'll get to siphon her myself. A two-for-one special."

Even with steel kissing her throat and hands pinning her from every angle, Reny wrenched her body enough to draw her head back and take a deep breath. She spat right in Kreg's face, striking him just beneath his eye before it began a wet crawl down his cheek.

The other men broke out in cruel laughter, slapping each other's shoulders at the display. Kreg wiped his cheek with the back of his hand, eyes locked on her. Then, savoring the drawback, he struck her across the face. The impact snapped her head sideways.

"Feisty little bitch," he growled, yanking her upright by her shirt until she was forced to her tiptoes. "Let's see how long that lasts."

Rough hands began tearing at her, fingers fumbling and failing to undo buttons on her pants while another seized the neck of her tunic. Fabric ripped with a sound that made her stomach lurch, baring the curve of her shoulder to the night air. As the cold bit her exposed skin, their fingers dug bruises into her arms.

The hold of men used to restraining prey, eager to leave their mark. Rook watched them turn her over, trying to force her into position with the sickening ease born of habit and repetition.

"Hold her still," Kreg barked, voice thick with anticipation. He fumbled at his own belt, the buckle clinking. "Before we siphon her, let's see how hot she burns, boys."

Laughter rose again as Reny thrashed, refusing to surrender. She threw her weight against the hands holding her, trying to find leverage, but there were too many of them.

Behind their assault, Rook moved. Towering trees, now blackened by shadow, became the stark frame for the predator who'd stepped forward.

No warning. No battle cry. He didn't need any of that—never did. There was only the puncture of steel as it struck home, before any of them had even noticed his approach.

The mercenary who'd been gripping Reny's hair and shirt went still, eyes wide in confusion before rolling back. Rook's daggers had buried themselves deep in his back, angled upward to pierce both lung and heart. Hands released as Rook wrenched the blades free, the man's body folding in on itself, hitting the ground beside Reny.

Before she could turn her head, the second mercenary went rigid, a blade punching through his neck with a sickly sound, wet and terrible. Hot, crimson spray painted her sleeve, soaking through the fabric as his body arced backward and collapsed. Her arms were suddenly her own again, a gasp forcing air into her lungs in a cold rush.

The next man turned too slowly, his reflexes dulled by shock. Rook's fist caught his windpipe with a loud crack that echoed through the silence, cartilage crumpling from the impact. He staggered backward, choking, both hands clawing uselessly at the ruin of his throat. A swift, merciless strike followed, plunging into his belly and twisting deep. The blade withdrew as Rook shoved him away, letting him fall into a twitching heap.

Kreg lunged, eyes lit with a brief flash of recognition, knife raised in a last bid for survival. Rook's hand shot up with an iron grip and caught the man's wrist mid-swing. Fingers clamped down, wrenching the mercenary's arm backward in a single, violent twist. Bone split with a wet crack and a wail as the knife fell into the underbrush.

In the same breath, Rook's dagger punched upward beneath Kreg's jaw, driving deep enough to lift the man off his feet. Kreg's dying image was Rook's face, streaked red with blood from jaw to temple like war paint. The man's body went limp, suspended for a heartbeat on the blade before Rook yanked it free in one savage jerk.

A forbidden twinge of satisfaction knotted in Rook's core.

For the spit still on the bastard's face. For every second she'd refused to break.

Another man had broken from the chaos, panic scattering whatever courage he'd first possessed. He bolted for the brush, crashing through ferns and low branches. Rook gave chase with four long strides that closed the distance.

A crash of bodies. A grunt of impact. Then the squelch of steel punching through flesh.

Once. Twice. A third time for certainty.

Only silence followed Rook back into the clearing, his blades dripping a dark trail in his wake.

There was only one man left, scrabbling backward as he tried to put distance between himself and the malice prowling toward him. Begging pleas and spit spilled uselessly from his mouth, his voice high with terror.

"Please—no, no, please—I didn't touch her, I swear, I didn't—"

Rook did not hurry.

Death incarnate. Each step was measured, inevitable. He bent down and twisted his fist in the mercenary's collar, hauling him partially upright. A dagger came to rest against his exposed neck, its stained edge dimpling skin.

"Please—" the mercenary rasped one final time, heels thrashing, boots scraping for purchase that would never come.

Rook's face never flashed triumph or rage. He merely watched, close and intimate, as he swept the blade once across in a motion of horrific elegance.

Deep. Final.

Blood spilled over his hand, pulsing through his fingers in rhythmic jets as he released the mercenary's shirt and dropped him into the dust.

The clearing held its breath. Bodies sprawled in every direction around her.

Reny tried to stand upright. Her chest heaved as she worked to catch her breath, but the pain was too overwhelming. Her legs wouldn't hold, muscles trembling with exhaustion. She fell forward onto her hands and knees, palms sinking into the cold earth.

Blood pooled beneath the dead, steam rising slowly into the cold air. The metallic scent hung thick, blending with the sickening stench of exposed entrails, until Reny thought she might never draw a clean breath again.

What sort of man could do all this?

Her ribs screamed with every rapid inhale, but she couldn't move, couldn't look away from Rook standing in the center of the carnage.

This was no man.

This was a stranger, a beast, wearing familiar skin. Dangerous, unholy, and utterly unbound by the rules that governed ordinary men.

Gore marred his face in wild streaks. Crimson dripped from blades that hung loose at his sides. He stood there, painted in every glistening shade of violence, breathing steadily. Not winded. Not shaking. Perfectly calm in the aftermath of total slaughter.

Rook moved at last, the only living thing in a field of the dead. He bent, unhurried, wiping his blades on the torn jacket of a corpse until they shimmered clean again. He cleaned each with a craftsman's care before sliding them back into their sheaths.

The forest stretched wide and suffocating in its quiet around her. No twilight birdsong, no insect chirps. Even the wind had stilled, nature itself hushed by what he'd done.

Reny was still staring, her hands flat against cold ground and sharp gravel. Unable to rise, unable to fathom what she'd witnessed. All she could hear was the feral slamming of her heart against her ribs.

Rook's head lifted. His eyes found hers with a clarity that forced her pulse to skip and stumble.

The distance between them shrank as he made his way toward her, each step charging the air with everything he had just done and everything he had not yet allowed himself to do. A predator's hunger lit his gaze, shifting from violence to something far more dangerous.

Her.

In the suspended silence between them, with death bowing at his feet and her heart a relentless war hammer, Reny knew the truth of him in her core with absolute certainty. He had killed for her without hesitation. Would kill again without question if it meant keeping her from harm. He had savored every second of it, finding satisfaction in the destruction he'd wrought on her behalf.

And gods save her. So did she.

That realization alone should have terrified her. Should have sent her scrambling backward away as he—this *thing*—drew near, blood dripping from his fingertips.

But it didn't.

Instead, a primal heat spread through her center, like an answering darkness that somehow recognized itself in someone else. As the gap closed further with his approach, she understood that the storm he'd become was far from over. It had only changed shape.

And was now headed right for her.

CHAPTER 27

B lades loose in his hands and footsteps unbothered by the blood soaking the earth beneath him, Rook casually strolled through the ruin he'd made.

He'd become an unbroken line drawn only to her.

Reny stayed frozen, hands and knees in the dirt, the taste of iron still heavy on her tongue. Every step closed the gap until she could see the blood embedded in the ridges of his knuckles.

When his grip found her, a part of her expected it to be punishing. Expected reprimand and the cold lash of anger for leaving their hiding place. Because she hadn't listened. *Again.*

It wasn't.

Sliding the daggers into his wrist bracers, Rook crouched, wiping his palms down his thighs before taking her elbows to guide her upright. Storm-lit eyes swept her face without accusation or scolding, his touch banked by a bewildering tenderness. She couldn't reconcile it. Couldn't reconcile *him.*

When at last she met his stare, her breath snagged. Those eyes burned, feral and incandescent, with an appetite not yet sated. Beneath the blaze radiating off him lay what Reny knew she was not yet ready to face.

The wild thing she'd fed in the hollow of the tree. *Still hungry.*

Rook gathered her trembling hands into his, turning them over one at a time, inspecting the gravel embedded in her palms. He began removing every fragment with unnerving precision, lacking even the slightest tremble despite the war he'd just waged. She had just watched him move through those mercenaries like a reaper, and now those same hands cradled hers with a reverence that made her chest ache.

When he finished, his attention turned to the blood at the corner of her mouth. His thumb swept it away, slow enough to feel intentional. When her lips parted at the contact, his gaze went dark.

Rook eyed the red bloom on her cheek where the mercenary had slapped her. His knuckles grazed her jaw, following the edge of the forming bruise before letting his hand fall to her side. She flinched when he found the tender skin at her rib cage. He didn't pull away, but went motionless, the world halting along with him.

"I need to see." The words came rough, pulled from the depths of him. "May I?"

The way he asked—not demanded but requested—tightened her entire core, leaving her unable to answer. With no trust left in her voice, she gave him a clipped nod. Lifting her shirt, he skimmed the bruise's border. It sprawled even darker now across her ribs, worsened by what they'd done to her. The touch raked heat over her skin, becoming a maddening mix of pain and yearning.

Rook continued to map the damage with excruciating care, every pass of his hands sending warmth pooling low in her belly. The sensation was winning the war against her battered ribcage, stealing all her damn sense.

She shouldn't want this. Shouldn't crave the feel of his blood-stained hands against her bare skin.

Fog bled into the clearing around them like a dream. His hands drifted over her middle, checking muscle and bone for signs of deeper injury.

She could feel the leashed power in him from fingertips alone. See it in the way his jaw tightened and twitched every time he discovered a new mark. The line of his shoulders tensed as a thumb pressed over one of the uglier marks on her opposite side, forcing her to gasp through her teeth.

"I believe I was quite clear when I told you to stay hidden." Rook's voice breached the quiet. The timbre of his words struck deep, her face flushing with guilt and embarrassment.

A shaky exhale slipped free, her composure cracking.

"I'm sorry... I couldn't see you anymore, and I—"

Rook's brow arched high, cutting her off without a word. A hand remained at her bruised waist, long fingers drifting lazily against bare skin just above her hip. Barely there, but enough to knot her core and reduce her explanation to fragile silence.

"You—what?" His voice was a purr, lips curling with a playful deviance. "Were you coming to *save* me, Reny?"

Her pulse stumbled, lips parting on a breath she couldn't catch. "No, I—" Her voice quivered, cheeks burning. She felt foolish. "I thought you'd been hurt, and—"

"Well, how very sweet of you." He was teasing her. And reveling in it. His hand fell away, gently smoothing her shirt back into place over pebbled skin. When he found her eyes again, they roiled with darkness.

"You don't need to worry about me," he murmured, the words low and velvet.

"Clearly, I don't," she snapped before she could stop herself.

A subtle but victorious smile lit his face for coaxing her into showing her teeth. Her heart slammed against her ribs as the memory of his hands on her in the tree hollow reared up with brutal intensity.

Over the heat still raging inside, she fumbled for a grip on her senses. "You aren't just a tradesman... are you, Rook?"

He canted his head, letting the end of her question hang, his smoldering attention holding her without a single ounce of mercy. Everything about him was unnervingly calm.

"No. But you already knew that, didn't you, Reny?"

A tremor rolled through her at the sound of her name in his mouth, every nerve raw from how close he was, how he seemed to tower over her. The truth, or some part of it, was unfurling just as she had expected.

"Then who are you?" She grasped the emotional armor she'd relied on her entire life. Used it to strengthen her words, to set her expression in steel. "Or rather, what are you?"

Night folded in around them. For a treacherous moment, the only sound was his breath. A measured, hypnotic rhythm that did not belong to someone still painted by the blood of other men.

His eyes dropped to her mouth. Lower, to the wild flutter of her pulse at her throat. He catalogued every detail of her, and without breaking eye contact, unhooked the clasp of his cloak and swept it around her shoulders. As he fastened the clasp, his knuckles grazed her collarbone. The contact was brief but searing. Nearly as overwhelming as the scent that wrapped around her when she took a deep breath. A deep breath of *him.*

Pine and smoke and iron.

And blood. So much of it.

She should recoil. Insist on keeping distance between herself and this man who wore death like a second skin. This man, who had just openly admitted that he'd lied to her about who he was. She forced herself to hold his stare, chin angling up in a fragile kind of fury.

"You can cover and care for me all you like, but that doesn't answer my question."

Ravenous eyes kept her pinned as his hand rose, briefly suspended. Restraint clearly at war with a far more primal part of him.

"A proper response to being saved is to say 'thank you'." Rook caught her jaw, the hold commanding but careful, drawing her into him until she was forced to let her head fall back to keep eye contact. A finger drifted down the column of her neck, tracing over the wild rebellion of her pulse. He looked every bit like a wolf deciding whether to go for the throat or howl his secrets to the sky. With either, she was entirely at his mercy.

He said nothing else. Just watched her like the answer was already there, waiting for her to see it.

"Godsdamnit, Rook. Answer me." A quivering demand.

Rook's body shifted, and his thumb swept along her jawline, slower this time. She watched him hesitate, holding himself back. Saw him losing ground with whatever internal battle he was fighting. His lips parted with the beginning of an answer, but when her focus darted to his mouth—*then, damnit, back up*—he caught it, drawing out that easy, devastating smile.

The look of a man who knew what it did to her. And knew how to use it.

"Does it matter?"

After a few breaths, her eyes softened toward sadness, the fire in them banking enough that the intensity in his own gaze subsided.

"At some point, Rook... it will. It will matter." Reny sighed in weary resignation.

Weary because of how easy it would be to throw herself into his gravity. The terrifying realization that if he decided to close the distance between them right now, she wouldn't stop it. Even with him so lethal and shrouded in lies. He ignited a starving, wild part of her. A force so haunting and magnetic, she found herself craving him, even though he was right in front of her.

It was wrong to find him beautiful like this, all drenched in mayhem. But here she was.

"Fair enough," he murmured, "but perhaps the next time I tell you to do something, you will listen and do as you're told. Yes?" The rumble of his voice rolled through her, the underlying threat making her thighs clench.

"Depends on what that is," Reny answered, defiance unwillingly thinned by want. She tipped her mouth forward just enough that his roaming thumb dipped into her mouth, softly raking over the top of her bottom teeth.

"Mmm. Noted." Rook's eyes nearly went black, and his low hum of satisfaction sent a fresh wave of fire coursing through her veins. Tension rose like a living, pleading thing.

After giving her jaw the faintest squeeze of warning, he released her and stepped back, forcing space between them. His hands lifted, open-palmed in front of him, offering her the choice of walking with his assistance or doing it on her own.

Reny refused his hands, her pride insisting on it. Straightening her spine, one arm curled protectively across her middle, she forced one forward stride. The moment shifting weight rotated her core, pain lanced white-hot and blinding, buckling her with a gasp impossible to choke back.

She would have fallen to her knees had he not been there. His arms caught her against the wall of him, her forehead landing just beneath his collarbone.

They both froze. His pulse found her quickly, reverberating through her brow. Pressed flush to the plane of his body, surrounded by his shadow, she clamped her eyes shut like that could somehow hold back the chaos inside her. She took a deep breath and promptly cursed herself.

Cursed how her chest rose and fell in time with his. Cursed how her body melted into him, chasing heat her mind refused to accept. Her fingers fisted in his blood-soaked shirt, clinging to him even as her thoughts screamed to let go. Rook bent his head, the coarse scrape of his jaw grazing her hair as his mouth found the crown of her head.

Lips settled there, not quite in a kiss, but close. *Dangerously close.*

It sent another bone-deep shiver down her spine. One that had nothing to do with cold.

"I think you like me, Reny. No matter who or what I am." It was only a whisper, but his words roared through her.

"Maybe I'm just scared of you," she whispered back, head shaking against him in denial.

She could feel Rook's smirk spread through her hair where his face rested, his breath fanning warm against her temple. The pace of his heartbeat against her cheek—rapid, insistent—was betraying him.

Not nearly as composed as he wanted her to believe, then.

He dipped his mouth close enough that his lips brushed the shell of her ear. Another whisper slipped free from him, threatening to pull her under. "Maybe you like that, too."

Her breath shuddered, and she felt him smile in her hair again. Felt the satisfaction rolling off him in waves that left her drowning.

Because he knew.

He'd always known.

CHAPTER 28

B y the time they reached Sal and the cart, night devoured the forest. Rook helped Reny onto the narrow bench, his hands guiding and anchoring her movements. The horse nickered anxiously, nostrils flaring, but settled after he murmured a few reassuring words.

Rook climbed up to take the reins, moving with fluid ease. The slaughter he'd wrought slid from him with disturbing grace. Reny watched, realizing the same beast who had mercilessly torn through a group of mercenaries had just gingerly, patiently, walked her back to safety.

But was no less dangerous for it.

They couldn't travel far in the dark. Only enough to put distance between themselves and the ruin he'd left behind, though the air still held hints of iron in the dense fog.

They made camp where the trees grew thick enough to muffle the night.

From the trees behind them came wolves. Not the full-throated harmony of a hunting chorus. Worse.

Snarls. Snaps. Guttural disputes over flesh and bone.

Reny knew what they fought over.

Beside her, Rook stooped and seized a moss-veined log, dropping it onto the fire. The log landed with a hiss, smoke and sparks twisting upward as sap spat into the night. It dulled the wolves' clamor, but echoes continued sweeping into their clearing, haunting the silence between them.

She studied him through the flames, how the light flickered across his face. Traced the hard line of his jaw, the straight bridge of his nose, the furrow carved deep between his brows. Save for the slow rise and fall of his chest, he remained perfectly still.

Some unseen force had caught hold of him, dragging him far away, leaving only the outline of him by the fire.

"Why are you here, Rook?" Her voice cut the night in a way the feasting wolves never could.

The question took time to break through the layers of what held him. His eyes slid toward her, slow to focus. Wherever his mind had gone, she felt an intense urge to haul him back.

For a long time, he didn't answer. Not a silence born of avoidance, but of choice. The pause of a man deciding how much to let her see.

A muscle ticked in his jaw, nearly imperceptible, but she'd learned to watch for it, to read him. He wasn't the only one who knew how to study a face, to catch subtle slips and spot the tells. He was not as unreadable as he wanted to be.

Rook looked right at her then. Firelight split his face in two, shadow cutting one side while flame caught the other, eyes holding an expression she couldn't quite place.

"You weren't really just passing through River's Edge." Her voice held no accusation. Just truth, set bare between them, daring him to deny it.

She waited for the lie. Watched for it in the set of his mouth, the careful arrangement of his brow. He was capable of it. She'd seen him spin words before, bend truth until it fit whatever shape he needed.

But a hairline crack was spidering across the mask he wore. His jaw worked, and the lie—*whatever it would have been*—caught in his throat and died there.

"No." The word rasped free, raw as an open wound. He held her eyes even though it took obvious force to do so. "No, I wasn't just passing through."

The pop of the campfire filled the hollow that followed, sparks scattering off into the night. Reny's nod was small, her stare locked. She asked nothing more, but her stillness was its own kind of demand.

Storm still churned in him. She could feel it pressing on her chest like it was her own. Her body absorbed the dangerous extent of his silence, breathed in the air that thickened when he refused to look away from her.

As if summoned by whatever raged inside him, thunder rolled through the Old Wood, dragging across the hills. Rook's gaze swept skyward. A flash of lightning split the clouds, cold and white, illuminating him for a breath. The second answering rumble wrapped the clearing in warning.

He rose in one fluid motion and crossed to the cart's rear, emerging a moment later with rope and tarp in hand as the first mist of rain broke through the wall of fog. She stirred to rise, to help him with the makeshift shelter, but his hand cut through the air. Not a threat. A command.

Stay there.

In rare form, she obeyed, watching him work in the shifting light. The tarp went up between two trees, angled to deflect wind and divert rain, tied with knots that would hold against the weather. Golden light danced across him in fragments, striking his jaw, his chest. Shadow kept rising to swallow the rest of him.

Fitting.

The charming man who'd arrived in River's Edge, all civility and sly flirtation, had vanished. But neither was he the merciless beast from the clearing. *A thing caught in the between. Something she had no name for.*

His presence felt different now. Whatever had originally brought him into her life, whatever his purpose had been for going to River's Edge, had unraveled somehow. This thing that had evolved between them was consuming it. Consuming him.

And her, more than she wanted to admit.

Her mind warned her that she was being foolish, but her bones whispered a truth she could not outrun.

She was safer with him than without him. Lies and all.

Rook didn't know when the choice had been made.

Perhaps it had always been there, buried deep, waiting for him.

Long before tonight. Long before her eyes caught his through the smoke and refused to let go, his oath had already begun to rot. The vow had been absolute. Palm split open by his own blade, blood spilling at the crown's feet, sealed with ancient ritual and dark magic. He'd sworn to return with the flame to save Rithmor. The weight of it had sat heavily on his shoulders ever since.

None of it was for the crown. He'd done it for his people. For the starving Aetherians, the ageless now losing their war with time and mortality. For the lush landscape turned dead and gray from blight.

He'd been foolish to believe success would make the court embrace him. It no longer felt a worthy prize for such a sacrifice. But he'd done it anyway, because that's what the Rook was ordered to do.

He'd seen nobles swear blood oaths to the king and knew what happened when one was broken. The punishment was agony drawn out across days or weeks. Flesh flayed, bones shattered and mended only to be broken again. What waited for him should have mattered.

But it didn't. Not anymore.

The realization should have sent him reeling. Instead, it descended with the inevitability of rain, steadily washing away everything he'd been until only she remained.

Let them declare treason. Let them hunt him through every shadow and hollow in both realms.

Tareth could send his wolves and his whispers and whatever else the crown could conjure. There would be no more messages inked in secret. No deceitful trail that would lead her to the North Gate. No vipers in royal colors waiting to sink their fangs into her.

He would take her east through the oldest reaches of the Old Wood, to the Veil, to where realms bled together and the Aetherium rose in the mountain range beyond. If he could deliver her there, the dragon sentinels would know what she was and take her to the Master Scribe.

She would be protected. Beyond the reach of men like him.

When they came for her, finding her just beyond their grasp, they would turn on him. Kill him.

And he would face it without regret.

She leaned against him then, not timidly. Her trust, gracefully given, split him open.

Duty, oath, and every chain he'd carried crumbled beneath her weight as she nestled her head against his chest. Mindful of her ribs, he leaned back, pulling a blanket over them as rain started drumming against the tarp.

His arm folded around her, a gentle promise in the way he held her. Not possessive, but protective, as if the world could break apart around them, but she would remain safe in the shadow of him. Reny tucked her head beneath his chin. He felt the moment she let go. The tension bleeding out of her, her breath slowing against his shirt. She'd chosen to trust him even though she knew he was a liar.

A wolf in sheep's clothing.

Her voice was soft against his shirt, more breath than sound. "Don't get any ideas."

Rook didn't look down, but his mouth quirked up, fully unguarded. Even as need threatened to devour him from the inside. "I don't know what you're talking about."

She gave a small huff of laughter, a flicker of warmth before it faded. Sleep took her in pieces. The rain, the fire, the rhythm of his heartbeat pulling her under.

Her body against him had become both solace and sentence. A tether he would not sever, allowing it to become wound so tight it had become part of him.

He'd become a man undone.

This woman, nestled against him with her trust given so carefully, was worth more to him than any vow he'd ever made. Every sacrifice in the name of duty.

Worth his life. Even if he'd die a traitor.

In the end, it wasn't blade or chain. Wasn't the cruel brother or the resentful father. None of them had managed to break the Rithmor king's Rook.

Only her, sleeping peacefully against his chest beneath the sound of pouring rain.

CHAPTER 29

The storm had claimed the night.

Not a passing drizzle, but a relentless, bone-soaking siege that stripped leaves from their branches and turned the earth to mud. By dawn, the forest hung in sodden drapes, pine branches drooping from the weight. What remained of their camp was a circle of soaked, scorched ground and a sagging tarp.

Rook had hardly moved all night. He'd kept Reny close, only adjusting when she did. She'd felt the heat of him, the unspoken watchfulness even in sleep. It had been the first night in countless days she'd woken without the cold biting at her bones, without nightmares plaguing her thoughts.

But the rain was too heavy for too long. They wouldn't stay dry much longer.

A warm hand on her shoulder pulled her from her comfortable state of half-sleep. She stirred reluctantly, the ache in her body protesting with each shift, but she rose. They broke camp together in silence, their hands quick and practiced in the dreary gray. It wasn't long until Sal was hitched and pulling them back onto the trail.

Or trying to, at least.

The road had turned to mire, deep trenches of mud sucking at the wagon wheels and Sal's hooves with every step. Reny drew her cloak tighter, the cold seeping into her skin anyway.

Somewhere ahead, the Veil waited. No longer a distant idea, but a fixed point drawing closer with every mile. And with it would come an end, or a change, to whatever this dangerous thing was that kept growing between them.

She'd told herself she was ready for that. The heaviness in her chest said otherwise.

Rook was quiet company, staring through the sheets of rain with a locked jaw, his focus intense from beneath the hood of his cloak.

"I know an inn near here," he spoke to her over his shoulder, the roar of rain burying the subtle reluctance living in the suggestion. "Keeper owes me a favor."

She didn't want to know why, pitying whatever poor bastard who'd put himself into debt with the man beside her.

Through the gray wall of rain and forest, a shape emerged at last. A looming silhouette, tall and jagged, its roof knifing upward into the sky. Walls of mottled stone rose beneath timber framing warped and blackened with age and moss. It was the kind of place that had never once needed permission to exist, persisting through time and nature with its spiteful, relentless spires.

The Black Dragon. Its sign swung on a chain, the carved dragon mid-roar, wings spread wide in welcome.

Or warning.

Rook led Sal to the lean-to stable, unhitching her in the smell of wet hay and old wood. Reny leaned against a post, watching him rub the mare down, murmuring words she couldn't hear. Her attention kept drifting to the inn looming nearby, to the amber light glowing from within.

Warmth wrapped around her as they stepped inside, the air heavy with the smell of woodsmoke, old wine, and older books. A massive stone hearth dominated the room's center, its surface covered in carvings of dragons and sigils she didn't recognize. Fire burned high inside, orange glow casting restless shadows along the arched, smoke-stained beams overhead.

It was flanked by uneven shelves of tomes, a few worn scrolls, and haphazardly placed, dusty knick-knacks meant to pass as décor.

The innkeeper looked up from behind the bar, mouth parting in greeting. Only to freeze when his focus landed on Rook just over her shoulder. Recognition shifted his expression, subtle but undeniable.

Whatever welcome he'd meant to offer vanished unspoken. The man's silence left her feeling oddly misplaced, like she'd walked into a conversation that had ended too quickly.

One she didn't belong in.

She moved closer to the hearth's welcoming heat as Rook exchanged quiet words with the man, conversation too low for her to catch.

When he returned, they climbed the stairs together, boots leaving wet prints on the worn boards. At the last door in the hall, Reny stopped beside him, the storm dimming to a distant roar outside.

"Which room is mine?"

His mouth twitched, shoulders a tight line. "We're lucky to have this at all. Seems the storm's pulled half the realm off the road. There's only one room left."

Reny's brows rose, that familiar, underlying anger sparking in her expression. A skeptical little wildfire. "You can't be serious."

"Swear it on the gods." The words carried a hint of playfulness, but she could feel the lurking, unspoken dare beneath.

She wanted to smack him for it.

"There are none." Reny folded her arms. "So that means nothing."

He only grinned and turned the key, the door easing open on smooth hinges. Heat spilled out to greet them from the small fire dancing in the hearth. Light glanced over a table, two mismatched chairs, a foggy pair of narrow windows, and one bed piled high with fresh coverlets and white pillows.

Comfort—the sheer sight of it—hit her harder than she expected, stirring the ache of how long it had been since she'd felt anything resembling home.

She stepped inside, the storm still rattling the windowpanes, and let her satchel drop into one of the chairs. Firelight spilled across the floor, catching on the drops of water falling from the soaked hem of her cloak. She adjusted her stance, shoulders angling in her growing discomfort as she heard the latch click. Felt Rook looming there, leaning against the door.

Her thoughts were racing.

He had been sent for something, arriving in River's Edge with hidden intentions, and lied to stay close to her. He was, or had been, bound to an ulterior motive. As silly as it felt, she wanted to believe the bone-deep intuition telling her he would not see it through.

That for her, whatever oath had bound him had been broken.

That she was safe.

There it was again.

That undeniable pull, alive and restless between them. It wasn't the storm or the miles ahead or behind them, but the echo of a truth he'd let slip the night before.

He should have kept them off the main road, found different shelter. But the storm was its own beast, and they were running out of time and options. If he'd kept going, the cart or Sal—or both—would have been lost to the mud. Still, unease grew at the base of Rook's spine. A gut-deep warning that this was a decision he might come to regret.

But the innkeeper knew who he was. Knew what he could do.

Perhaps that would be enough.

Rook remained at the door, studying her. She'd shifted her weight from one leg to the other, eyes repeatedly sweeping over the neatly made bed.

Poor little doe.

He'd thought that of her before, when he'd cornered her in the cramped chicken coop behind the barn. All bristling and wild-eyed, her jaw clenched, every muscle resistant to his presence. She'd measured him then, too aware of every exit, eyes never resting on him for more than a breath. He'd taken a dark satisfaction in seeing himself reflected in the bright defiance of her gaze. In testing how close she'd let him get before she bolted.

In her fear of him.

Seeing that same wariness ripple through her now struck him differently. The urge to test and push her until she met him with fire continued to live in him. But more so, unexpectedly, was the pull to shield her, to coax her to relax. Not so she would yield to him, or so he could exploit the vulnerability.

But because she deserved at least some time without the internal debate on when to run.

Deserved one damn moment of peace.

Rook pushed off the doorframe at last, crossing the room with unhurried intent. He set his bag beside the second chair, near enough to reach but far enough to leave her space to breathe, to think without him casting her in his shadow.

The air between them still smoldered. Hers, a wildfire, barely controlled. His, a low, relentless ember that, to his own amusement, seemed to keep her burning.

He could see her caught between wanting to flee and wanting to stay, the inevitability of the closeness in this room pulling at her like a tide. She made no attempt to hide the lines of growing unease in her frame.

Rook let the silence drag on until his mouth tugged into the barest flicker of a smile. A sad one.

"I'll sleep on the floor," he said evenly. Like it cost him nothing.

"No." The word sprang from her before she could stop it. Sharper and louder than she must've intended, because they both nearly jumped. His brows rose, unable to hide his surprise.

She scrambled to fill the rift she'd torn open, her flush visible even in the low light. "It'll be... that's fine. It'll be fine."

The words fell thin and unconvincing.

And adorable, if he was honest about it.

Rook wasn't used to seeing her like this. Totally frayed, her resolve brittle and worn through. Instead of striking at the weakness, he felt the unwelcome ache of soft admiration. She was strong even now, brave enough to hold ground when everything was falling away beneath her feet.

He studied her, turning over every blade she'd ever raised against him. She glanced over her shoulder, and he knew she caught it—the temptation he wasn't willing to hide. The half-curve of a mouth ready to push, to prod and tease her, just to see what might break loose if he did.

But he only let out a slow, measured breath, allowing the moment to slip away. His presence hovered behind her for one hesitant beat before he stepped away.

"Get yourself a hot bath, Reny. And dry clothes." His voice came out far gentler than he intended as he tipped his head toward the door. "I'll give you some privacy."

He turned away and gripped the latch, but he couldn't stop himself from looking back.

She stood where he'd left her, watching him go. The breath that left her didn't look anything close to relief.

And the look on her face—

He smiled weakly as he stepped into the hall, pulling the door shut behind him before he could do something foolish. Something he couldn't take back.

But the image of her followed him anyway.

That unmistakable flicker of disappointment as he left.

CHAPTER 30

F or Rook, the descent felt like walking to his own execution.

Each stair dragged him farther from her, from the warmth of that room, and deeper into the leaden ache gnawing at his chest. Every floorboard creaked like a bell's toll, marking another step into a future he was choosing against every oath, every duty, every blood-bound promise he'd ever made.

By the time he reached the bottom, his jaw was clamped tight, a stillness barely containing the storm he held inside.

The common room sprawled before him, vast and dim. Shadows pooled across the empty floorboards like spilled ink, stretching from the corners where the firelight couldn't reach. The air hung with the familiar scent of old smoke, damp wood, and sour wine, clinging to all the places where secrets were bought and sold. A place built for the crown's darker work.

And he'd chosen it himself.

He couldn't escape the irony. This very inn—the Black Dragon—was where he'd first heard her name. Where, months ago, he'd sat across from a mercenary in a dark corner, listening to rumors of a young woman in River's Edge who could light fires with her bare hands.

A woman who didn't burn.

He'd left that night skeptical, his coin pouch gone and carrying a name he wished he'd never learned. Had ridden south in human guise until he'd found exactly what had been given to him.

A woman with fire in her eyes, defiance and fury in her heart, working a simple job in a simple village.

But nothing about her was simple. Here he stood in the same inn, in a different season, with her upstairs and the blood of the man who'd given him her name buried under his fingernails.

From the dimness behind the bar, movement stirred. The innkeeper emerged—a man whose name Rook had never learned nor cared to—his gait slow with hesitation that came from years tip-toeing around secrecy and threat.

A slip of parchment hung between two of his fingers. Thin, curled at the edges, the telltale deep ivory color meant for whisper ink. Enchanted and untraceable, used only for messages that could destroy kingdoms.

Or condemn brothers.

The note landed on the counter between them. Neither man spoke, but the parchment's presence demanded an answer.

Rook didn't touch it.

Behind him, murmurs drifted from the far corner, slurred with drink. He'd noticed the two men hunched over a table near the hearth when they'd first arrived, their faces obscured by haze and cheap ale. Merchants, perhaps, or travelers smart enough to keep their heads down and their mouths busy. His focus latched onto their words.

"—heard it from a peddler come through Black Creek," one said, voice rough with drink. "Said the whole forest went mad. Knocked over trees on its way to swallow folks whole."

"Hollowmire's a ghost story," the other muttered, dismissive.

Rook's fingers curled against the bar, knuckles turning white.

"I'm telling you what I heard. Peddler swore on his mother's grave." A pause, then the sound of sloshing in a mug. "Says it was real. Says something woke up out there."

The second man scoffed. "And I say it sounds like a good way to look too damn mad to be taken into Endaria's regiment. They're not asking for men anymore. They're taking them."

Rook's pulse hammered in his ears, louder than the crackling fire, louder than the voices behind him. He steadied, keeping his expression unreadable even as every muscle tensed.

Endaria's desperation to grow their ranks was troubling. Rumors of the Hollowmire stirring in the Old Wood were much worse.

The innkeeper's gaze flicked toward the men, then back to Rook, expectation sharpening. He'd been paid well to keep this checkpoint quiet, to pass messages without question, to look the other way when Drayviens darkened his door.

"What's the latest, traveler?" the innkeeper asked, his voice carefully neutral. He gestured toward the parchment with a slight tilt of his head, never quite meeting Rook's eyes.

Rook stared at the slip of paper. It would be easy now. He had come so close. A few words in whisper ink, simple and expected.

"On schedule. Delivering the ember to the North Gate as instructed."

Duty, and the memory of sunken-eyed Aetherians in the streets of Rithmor, sat heavily on his shoulders.

On his heart, if he even had one.

"No message." The words left his mouth, quiet but final. A blade cutting through the last thread that bound him to that damned crown.

The innkeeper's salt and pepper brows knitted in confusion. "Pardon?"

Rook leaned in, frost coating his words. "I said, no messages. Not from me. Not from you. Do you understand?"

For a breath, the room itself tightened around them. The slip of parchment hung there, an expectation neither man could ignore. The fire cracked once—sudden, violent, throwing sparks in all directions. In the corner, the merchants had gone silent, their conversation dying as if they too felt the shift.

The same way prey goes still when a predator passes too close.

The parchment vanished, tucked back into the innkeeper's apron with trembling fingers. His eyes pinned Rook, filled with suspicion too shrewd to dismiss. Fear, too. Or the calculation of a man deciding how to protect his own neck when the crown's sword finally fell.

Rook didn't flinch. He held the innkeeper's stare with the weight of every kill, every throat he'd opened in service to the crown, his eyes promising only ruin.

The innkeeper looked away first, his fingers twitching at his side. Submission and survival. The only smart choice when facing a man who was not only a predator but now a rogue one.

"Good," Rook murmured. He straightened, rolling his shoulders once as if shedding the last shreds of the man he used to be. "Whiskey. Strongest shit you've got."

The innkeeper moved quickly, grateful for an excuse to put distance between them. Amber liquid splashed into a glass. Too much, his hands still shaking. He slid it across the bar without a word.

Rook lifted it and drained it in one long pull. The burn tore through his gut and flared hot in his veins, but it did nothing to loosen the knot in his chest. If anything, it settled deeper, like a stone sinking to the bottom of black water.

He set the empty glass down with a soft clink, the sound impossibly loud in the silence.

"Send food up to the room," Rook said, his voice gravelly. "Whatever you have that's hot. For two."

The innkeeper nodded quickly, eager for practical tasks. Anything that didn't involve a Drayvien's cold glare. He disappeared into the kitchen without a word.

And just like that, it was done.

Rook had made his choice. He would not deliver her to the crown. Would not hand her fire over to Tareth, to his father's husk, to the twisted god they'd sworn themselves to in blood and shadow.

He wouldn't allow her to be used, broken, forged into a weapon for a kingdom that, perhaps, deserved to fall. Deserved the death and ruin that was consuming it.

Consuming him.

Whatever storm followed now would be his to weather. There was no pulling this thread back through the weave.

Yes, he would fight to live through what he could. Would guard her, protect the strange, unbreakable tie that had formed between them. A tether of torment he could feel even now, thrumming inside him, pulling him back toward the room where she waited.

But grim knowing sat deep in his marrow, heavy as iron chains.

For him, this road ran only one way. The bitter truth was inescapable. And terribly, perfectly ironic.

He, of all creatures, caught in this sacred, undeniable pull to a mortal. The mortal woman somehow carrying the very power he had been sent to collect. The woman he could never fully claim in the way his blood demanded.

Not when he was what he was, and she was what she was, and the world had no place for a connection like theirs.

Maybe he'd always been cursed. Bound to failure from the moment he drew his first breath as his mother drew her last. Punishment for every drop of blood he'd spilled in the crown's name, for every sin he'd committed, convincing himself it was duty and not damnation.

Rook bowed his head into his hands, elbows braced on the bar, the reality of what he'd done settling into every line of him. Duty, loyalty, obedience. All of it had bled out of him tonight, leaving only the harsh clarity of what would come next.

Above him, up the stairs and down the hall, the reason for his torture waited. One he would continue to choose. Over crown, over homeland, over blood.

Over the foolish, fallen gods themselves until there was nothing left of him to give.

The innkeeper moved quietly behind the bar, filling Rook's glass again before retreating into the kitchen. He left Rook alone with the rest of the whiskey bottle. With all his questions, his demons, his treason.

Rook turned, gaze finding the dying fire across the room, embers glowing beneath ash and coal. So much like her eyes when the flames rose in her, when the power she didn't understand or fully control burned through her veins and spilled from her skin.

Terrifying. And beautiful.

His. He wanted to make her his.

The thought came unbidden, primal, and he didn't fight it this time. Couldn't, even if he'd wanted to. Whatever had formed between them had become too strong, too real for him to overlook. It lived behind his ribs like a second heartbeat, pulsing in time with hers.

He pushed away from the bar and sank into one of the chairs by the hearth, elbows on his knees, head bowed. Restless. Full glass in one hand, the bottle in the other. The merchants had slipped upstairs, leaving the common room to the storm and his misery.

Wind rattled the windows, rain hammering against the glass as if trying to get in. Or maybe trying to warn him of what was already on its way.

Go on, then. Rage. He'd weathered worse.

And he would weather whatever came next. For her.

The fire hissed and sank even lower. Rook closed his eyes for just a moment. Just long enough to gather himself before climbing those stairs. Before facing her again with the full truth of what he'd become written across his face.

A traitor, a brother condemned. A man unsure if he was choosing damnation or salvation. He didn't care about any of it.

Only about her.

CHAPTER 31

He gave her more than enough time. Long enough for her to wash away the rough travel, long enough for her to fade from his senses. *For both their sakes.*

When he returned, two glasses of whiskey were already hot in his blood, and a third sat full and cool in his hand. He knocked on the door. A soft, patient rap of his knuckles.

No answer.

An unwelcome surge of worry urged him to try the handle. The latch gave without resistance, and the door yawned open.

She was sprawled the wrong way across the still-made bed, one arm trailing toward the floor, hair damp and loose where it spilled over the mattress edge and into the firelight. The wide collar of her sweater had slipped from one shoulder, exposing pale skin to the hearth's warmth. Her breathing was low in a peaceful sleep.

He sank into a chair by the fire with the glass balanced on his knee and let himself watch her. The guarded lines of her face had eased in rest, leaving her almost unrecognizable. Softer, unburdened.

The sight struck him deep in his core.

She stirred, lashes fluttering open, as if the twist in his gut bore sound and disturbed her.

Her eyes pinned him instantly. Recognition caught on the amber in his hand, the way he occupied the chair as if it had been waiting for him.

"Where were you?" For just waking, her voice carried no softness.

He paused before answering, the drag of whiskey slowing his gaze. "Bar. Ordered dinner." His words were raspy, husked by liquor. He didn't try to hide it. "Figured you'd want space."

"Is that all?" Her head tipped to one side, damp strands sliding off her shoulder.

The fire snapped, sparks biting into the quiet he let stretch. She carefully eased herself upright. Flame washed across her face, sharpening the line of her mouth. And the conviction there.

"I didn't realize this was an interrogation," Rook drawled, rolling the whiskey glass in one hand, attention drifting to the bare curve of her shoulder.

"You didn't think I'd let this go, did you?" She fully straightened, arms folding in her lap, legs tucking beneath her on the bed. The motion brought them both abruptly back to the fact of it—*this one bed*—waiting.

His focus darkened as it tracked the shift of her body. He drank deep, never breaking eye contact over the rim. She managed to hold his stare even as her throat worked, visible even from where he sat. When he lowered the glass, his tongue swept across his lips.

He saw the way her breath caught, the subtle clench of her jaw.

Reveled in it.

"No," he said, danger lurking. "You're too stubborn for that, aren't you?"

"Maybe." She forced strength into her answer, her back straightening. "But I deserve some answers."

He leaned back in the chair, posture slack in appearance only, before tipping another swallow. He lowered the glass just enough to reveal the smirk that was already there.

"Ask me, then. Ask me your questions." Invitation veiled as indifference.

Her eyes narrowed against the firelight. "Were you sent to kill me?"

Rook's laugh rolled warm into his glass. He made no effort to hide the way he studied her again, frank and unapologetic over where he let his focus roam.

"If I were," he murmured, words unspooling like thread, "you'd already be dead."

Her breath stuttered. He caught the flash of unease beneath her rallied courage. The shock over the utter certainty in his answer. He'd always been so confident in the dealings of life and death.

She shifted in place, and he tracked every movement, letting his gaze drag paths over her skin that he wished belonged to his hands.

The doe was about to bolt.

Rook watched her swing her legs over the side of the bed, bare feet brushing the cool floorboards as she rose. She crossed to the window, each step removing her from the bed's gravity. But the space did nothing to ease the pull of his.

He traced the line of her from heel to shoulder, drinking in every detail. The damp ends of her hair, the curve of her hips, the elegant sweep of one shoulder exposed from the loose fall of her sweater. The firelight dancing over her like an offering.

The reverence surging in him caught him wholly off guard. His hand twitched with the urge to raise his glass in a silent toast. To her defiance, her beauty, every impossible way she was destroying him.

Her brow furrowed, arms crossing over her chest. The last remaining wall relentlessly defended. "Why, then? I want to know. I deserve to know."

"Fair enough." Amusement touched Rook's face as he tipped back, draining the last of the amber in a single tilt. Clinking the empty glass down on the table, he pushed up from the chair and, in three slow strides, was nearly on her.

He was still road-worn and half-damp, streaked with mud, soot, and blood in places that not even the heavy rain could wash away. He loomed over her, studying her with a devouring look.

"Well, get on with it." She stood firm, tilting her chin up.

Gods, he wanted to seize it. To claim and consume that mouth so masterfully skilled at scowling at him.

He bit the inside of his cheek before he spoke. "A power like yours is... coveted."

She glared at him, rain pelting the thin windowpane at her back. "All this, for fire magic? That's all you want?"

He nearly rolled his eyes at the tide threatening to break him. He leaned in, jaw locked, one hand bracing on the wall beside her. The other hung, clenching and flexing at his side. "I think you know better than that."

Her lips parted to reply—

Three knocks. Three fast raps at the door.

The sound cleaved the moment straight through, and despite her resilience, her stubborn restraint, he caught the frustrated sigh that escaped her.

And his grin curved too damn close to her mouth.

Rook turned away, throwing a smirk over his shoulder as he strolled, entirely pleased, across the room to open the door.

A slender wisp of a barmaid slipped in with a tray balanced in her hands, filled with bread, cheese, a pot of stew still steaming, and a bottle of whiskey with two fresh glasses. She moved quickly, setting the tray on the small table. A hasty curtsy before she disappeared back into the hall, the latch clicking shut behind her.

Rook stood by the door with his back to Reny, fighting like all hells to rally his self-control before turning toward her again. The tie between them still seared, invisible but no less agonizing.

At last, he tipped his head toward the table. This time, he didn't look at her. His voice was an even command despite the inferno roaring in him. "Sit, Reny. Settle down and eat. I'm going to wash up."

He didn't wait for her reply, desperate to blast himself with cold water before he boiled over. The bathing room door shut behind him, muffled by the rush of the rain against the windows.

Reny's pulse was still racing.

With effort, she crossed to the table and lowered herself into one of the mismatched chairs. Her hands trembled faintly as she reached for the bread, the simple act grounding her against the storm inside her chest.

Settle down. She drew a breath, failing to fight off the tremors shaking through her. Cursing herself, she put the bread back on the tray.

The ghost of his proximity clung to her skin. Woodsmoke and iron, copper and storm, the bite of high mountain air and too much whiskey. In any other circumstance, from any other man, she would have been repulsed. Knew she should recoil from the man still drenched in memories of violence.

Instead, she'd found it intoxicating.

Her eyes scanned the tray of food he must have ordered for them while she napped. Shot a pointed glance at the full bottle of whiskey the barmaid brought up too, and swore that off immediately.

That was the last thing she needed.

She left everything as it was and sat dutifully in the chair, deliberately ignoring his order to eat. Instead, she listened to the rush of water coming from behind the bathing room door, ignoring how eager she was for him to come out.

When Rook emerged from the bathing room, steam trailing after him, every trace of dried blood and mud had been scoured from his body. He had changed into loose black pants and a dark, V-necked tunic, the sleeves rolled to bare his forearms. His hair was damp, unruly from a brisk towel dry. He'd avoided the mirror but knew the unshaven shadow along his jaw had grown darker since he'd seen himself last.

Reny was exactly where he'd left her, the tray of food untouched and waiting on the table. Instead of eating, she'd waited. Posture poised, hands folded neatly in her lap.

It was either another small act of defiance—intentionally going against his instruction to eat—or she wanted to share the meal with him.

Rook smirked at the thought of both.

Without a word, he unwrapped the bread, passed her a bowl of roasted meat and stewed greens, and poured a glass of whiskey for each of them.

They ate in silence by the fire. It wasn't tense or strained, but rather the kind of quiet that settled too easily, familiar and serene, where her questions should have still burned. He could feel her holding back. Could see the questions still smoldering behind her eyes that she, for whatever reason, kept banked.

He didn't push his luck.

Exhaustion crept visibly into her frame, her usual defiance softening into tempered resignation. By the time their plates were empty, and the hearth had burned down to the grate, the hour was late enough that even their shadows seemed sluggish. Two more glasses of whiskey sat empty before Rook, but hers remained nearly untouched aside from the smallest sip.

Smart woman.

The bed loomed. He watched her shoulders constrict, her mind churning as she shot it a quick glance.

Rook slapped his thighs as he rose, stretching long limbs as the last of the firelight caught the crooked smirk already on his face. "Come on, Reny. I won't bite." His eyes danced, all mischief, as he strolled over and dropped onto the mattress. Propping himself up on an elbow, his grin widened with whiskey. "I mean... unless you want me to."

Her glare was a clear warning as she crossed the room and eased under the covers, avoiding his trailing eyes. She pulled a folded stack of extra linens between them, forming a pitiful but very intentional barrier. He eyed her quick, efficient motions and the growing barricade of blankets, suppressing a chuckle.

Charmed by the sheer effort she was investing into maintaining distance.

For a long moment, the only sounds were shuffling fabric and the rain slapping at the glass panes. Reny, finally satisfied with the makeshift defense, sank deeply into her pillow with her back to him. But her posture—the tense bunch of her shoulders—betrayed the awareness very much awake in every inch of her.

"You're good at building walls and all, but..." He shifted, lowering himself until his words nearly brushed the curve of her shoulder. A hushed, unmistakably velvet threat. "...if I wanted to have my way with you, do you really think this would stop me?"

He watched as the question rolled through her. A visible shiver.

"Rook." Her voice came out thin.

Adorable.

He grinned before claiming his side of the mattress in one giant, heavy flop. His presence radiated through the linen divide, but he didn't push the line. He lay back, honoring the boundary she'd set.

Even when every part of him longed to cross it.

She was too still on her side of the bed, too tense. So he waited.

With a loud, annoyed huff, she frantically rolled, snatching the barrier in one large handful before tossing it all onto the floor. He eyed her as she grumbled to herself, scooting closer to him between the sheets. Like the night before, she nestled herself tight against his side, her cheek finding the measured rise and fall of his chest.

"Can't resist me?" He chuckled before his arm curved around her, drawing her in until she settled directly over the rhythmic thrum of his heart.

"This is only so I can sleep," she mumbled, eyes already drifting closed. "So don't get any ideas, you miserable drunk."

Rook lowered his head until his exhale stirred her hair, words a deep, vibrating current echoing the night before. "I don't know what you're talking about."

He swore he felt the curve of her smile against his shirt.

Time passed, counted by the sound of rain falling and fire popping and dying in the hearth. He felt the tension bleed out of her almost immediately, her body melting into his like it belonged there.

The feel of her, the smell of her, lulled him quickly into deep sleep. A gentler oblivion than he would ever deserve.

But his dreams were waiting, and they were not kind.

He was in the Old Wood again, the creek running like black tar at his feet. A colossal beast of shadow and raw muscle rose from the depths, its form a churning mosaic of his failures. It lunged for Reny, hands reaching for her throat.

The closer it got, the more its face twisted, the bones reshaping, features contorting until a familiar face was staring back at him.

Tareth, as a young boy. With eyes too old for his face, the boy's form giggled as the beast continued its charge toward them.

She would have loved you, Ric.

Another phantom appeared from the mist, an older version of his brother. Youthful but arrogant and cruel, with a familiar, vicious smirk. He watched as his brother raised a hand, a stream of black shadow pouring from his fingertips to tear at Reny. Rook tried to move, to intervene, but his limbs had turned to stone, locking him in place.

You'll be the death of her, too.

The visions shattered and reformed as panic seized him. He stood on a battlefield shrouded in fog. Tareth, a brutal warrior well-versed in the art of war, stood atop a hill of bodies, the Drayvien black banners whipping in the wind.

He threw back his head and laughed, a hollowed sound that roared, fracturing the earth beneath his feet. A terrible darkness bled from his eyes, seeping over the bodies, into the ground, onto a pedestal in the distance where Reny's silhouette lay crumpled, motionless, bloodless.

From the edges of his vision, black wings—feathered and thrashing violently—blocked out the light. They didn't belong to Tareth, or to anything Rook had ever known, though they moved like a bird's wings twisted beyond natural law. Yet with a final, guttural cry, his brother commanded them. And they obeyed.

The bodyless wings spread wide into a terrible eclipse as the world went silent, the shadowed feathers swallowing all remaining light.

For a moment, Rook hung suspended in the vacant abyss before he began plunging into the void, haunted by the image of the light draining from Reny's eyes.

She would have loved you, Ric.

Rook surfaced with a start, sweat clinging to his skin. He lay in bed frozen, pulse hammering, lungs tight with the echo of the nightmare. He took a deep breath, willing himself back to the present.

Reny was clinging to him in sleep, cheek nestled in the hollow of his shoulder, her breathing even and untroubled. His hand drifted down her back, anchoring himself in the warm reality of her, but it wasn't enough. With mindful care, he drew her sleeping body closer and wrapped his other arm around her.

She didn't wake, her body only melting further into him. He sighed.

Outside, rain still battered the windows without mercy. They'd be here another day at least, maybe two. Rook wasn't upset about it. If anything, relief bloomed. Another day tucked away, another day before the world came for them.

For him.

He watched the gray light of dawn edge along the ceiling. The room felt suspended, caught between the nightmare and this false, fragile reality he'd spun lies to keep. For the space of a few breaths, he let himself believe this was all there was.

The storm, her body against his, the comforting cadence of her breath. He counted every inhale, every soft exhale against his neck, as if they might provide the solace he needed to hold back the dark consuming his mind.

But for him, peace did not come. It was always just out of his reach.

CHAPTER 32

W hen Rook eventually rose for the day, Reny knew something was wrong.

She could see it in the tight set of his shoulders, the way his eyes swept the room like he was still searching for something that had followed him out of sleep. Dark circles ringed his eyes, and his hands weren't quite steady.

Whatever it was, he carried it throughout the rest of the day. She watched the unease in his gait, the way his head turned at every sound, every shift in light. She could feel his agitation as they ate a simple breakfast in the room. He was restless and withdrawn, snapping the bread loaf in half with unnecessary force.

They hardly spoke.

Her eyes studied the slight tremor in his hand as he lifted his cup to drink. His usual cool composure had fractured overnight. She dismissed the signs, unwilling to lean into the intimacy of understanding emotions he didn't outright share. It was likely nothing more than the venomous bite of too much whiskey and a night of unfulfilled desires warring with his carefully constructed mask of control.

But when she finally met his eyes across the table, she held them. Whatever he saw in her gaze made his jaw tighten.

She was choosing distance. Let him wonder what she was thinking for once.

The storm showed no signs of relenting, so later, they drifted down into the inn's main room, each finding their own way to fill the passing hours of the dreary day.

Rook claimed a seat at a corner table where he could watch both entry and exit, scanning every face that came and went. Vigilance, she assumed. Habit. But there was a restlessness in him today that had nothing to do with survival.

Reny curled into a battered leather chair near the hearth, legs tucked beneath her, a book open across her knees. The shelves nearby, lined with countless forgotten spines, had drawn her instantly. Histories gone yellow with time, bardic epics gathering dust. A book of poetry so faded the title had nearly vanished.

She felt his attention more than she saw it. Every time she glanced up, his eyes were already there. Once or twice, she offered a small smile. Fleeting things that she pulled back before he could give her one in return.

When her fingers paused on another book's title—*The Tales of Aurelia*—a strange weight settled over her. She pulled the volume free, a small cloud of dust exhaling from its vacant place on the shelf. The leather cover was split, its gilded lettering worn to nearly nothing. She settled back down in the chair, opening it with the utmost care, the binding cracking in protest.

The first few pages were intact, at least. A painted illustration opened the text, time-worn but breathtaking. A woman's figure surrounded by flame, arms spread wide as if summoning the dawn itself. Beneath the image, a single line remained legible.

From Her fire, the first light. From Her flame, all becoming.

Reny turned the page.

A patchwork of beauty and ruin followed. Some sections were intact, quill script flowing in elegant curves across parchment that had survived its years against all odds. Others were torn, stained at the margins, or missing entirely. Ragged remnants clung to the binding like broken teeth where someone had ripped other sections free.

Her fingers traced a passage near the beginning, and she read silently.

In the time before time, when the world was only shadow and void, the Four rose from the sacred Seam. First among them was Aurelia, the Dawn-Bearer, whose flame gave birth to—

The rest of the sentence was gone. Someone had torn the page away diagonally, leaving only a partial fragment. Reny's brow furrowed. The next page, she hoped, would continue the thought. Instead, she found half a page that spoke of war.

—and the realms bled. Brother turned against brother, light against shadow, and the Seam itself began to fray. In her sacred rage, Aurelia—

A brutal tear cut the text short. The next three pages were missing entirely, leaving only the tattered spine. Frustration slipped from her in a breath, and she skipped ahead with newfound urgency, scanning for anything complete.

A few pages later, another section had survived. Faded, but mostly intact.

The Queen of Dream and Memory, who'd once walked between the living and the dead, keeper of the Eye through which all futures trembled. She alone saw what was to come, the unraveling that would consume—

The text cut off, the next several pages missing.

Reny leaned back, the book still open on her lap. None of the damage appeared accidental. It looked deliberate. Someone had gutted this volume, removing entire sections with precision. Or violence. She flipped through the remaining pages, cataloguing the damage.

Whole chapters stripped from the binding. Fragments of poetry left behind like ghosts. References to "the Four Pillars" appeared repeatedly, but never with enough context to understand who they all were or what they'd done.

One passage in particular caught her eye. It was written in different ink, in a different script, as if added later by a reader's hand.

Let it be known that the North has forgotten its mother. They worship the shadow in her stead, calling prison righteousness and undoing eternal. But the ember remains. It waits in the South, patient as stone, bright as—

Fire had claimed the page's bottom half, reducing it to bits of ash gathered in the book's center. Reny caught the ghosting smell of lamp oil. Staring at the blackened parchment, a strange cold settled in her chest.

The ember remains.

A familiar weight pressed against her thoughts, and she looked up, meeting Rook's eyes. He sat motionless across the room, his focus fixed on her. Or rather, on the book in her hands. His expression gave nothing away, but his posture had gone rigid, fingers curled too tightly around his empty tankard. Rook was the first to look away, his jaw working as he turned his attention back to the rain battering the window.

Reny returned to the volume, more unsettled than before. More pages revealed only scraps of text, the rest scratched out beyond recognition by a quill's sharp, ink-soaked point.

—betrayal in the house of gods—

—the Veil rose to hold back—

—one remained, a ghost of silver pine—

Nothing complete. Nothing clear. Beautiful, aching fragments. The final pages held only illustrations. Or what was left of them.

A mountain split by lightning. A figure wreathed in darkness with antlers rising from its skull that felt horrifically familiar. A woman holding a mirror that reflected not her face, but a sky full of stars. And on the very last page, barely visible beneath layers of spilled ale and age, a single phrase.

When the Four rise again, the realms shall be remade. A new Seam to be sewn.

Reny closed the book and sat with it in her lap, staring into the hearth fire. She understood why bards had written songs about this.

Whatever this was.

The language felt too grand, too sacred to be mere fiction. Gods and wars, betrayal and sacrifice. A story carved into the bones of the world itself.

But the truth of it? Nearly all of that had been ripped away.

And Reny now found herself starving for it.

For the truth.

By the time dusk painted the windows in bruised light, the inn had filled with voices and warmth. Travelers crowded in, shaking off the rain, the air thick with woodsmoke and wet wool. The scent pulled Rook back to dark, familiar places. Monstrous memories that clung to the walls.

He ordered another ale near the dinner hour, the barmaid's practiced smile sliding off him like water. Her face was already forgotten. He was too distracted by sneaking glances at Reny and the conversations around him.

When he turned to look at her again, drink in hand, she was no longer reading. Her eyes were locked on him. The unflinching, level look she gave him sparked low in his ribs. It flared hotter when she flagged down the same barmaid, pointing toward his table with a few words he couldn't catch from where he sat.

He watched her rise from the old leather chair, shamelessly tracing the movement of her frame as she wove around strangers and tables with ease. The firelight caught behind her, illuminating her like hot coals until she claimed the seat across from him and settled back, stretching her legs, fully occupying the space.

It was a posture he knew well. One he'd used often enough himself.

"You've been quiet today."

He took a slow sip, meeting her eyes over the rim. Clear, incisive green. Unyielding, even when the barmaid appeared and set a glass of water in front of her. Reny lifted it, casual and fluid, confidence folding around her like a cloak. She didn't look away from him, either. The rattled, flighty energy of the previous days was gone.

There was a new curiosity in her stare, tempered by the confidence of some silent decision that was entirely her own.

The corner of her mouth curved, not coy, but certain. Especially after she saw his expression darken at the sight of it. Up to this point, he had firmly held the reins of control, always finding a way to drag her into his current.

But now, the tides were turning.

He cleared his throat, setting his drink down with deliberate care. "Just the boredom of a rainy day."

"You strike me as a man who could find many ways to prevent boredom." Her voice dipped honey-sweet, tone echoing the way he so often teased her. But it was warmer.

More dangerous.

Heat spread beneath his skin, sparks catching in every vein. His brows lifted. "What are you up to, Red?"

"Reny," she corrected. He recognized the echo immediately. The night they met. But now, it landed more like a dare than a venomous warning.

"It's a good nickname," he defended, drawn to the dark auburn waves spilling over her shoulders.

She didn't waver at the compliment. Settling deeper into her chair, she claimed the whole table with her presence, letting the quiet stretch until it was his turn to shift uncomfortably under her unrelenting focus.

"I think it's time to answer my questions."

His heart kicked hard, a furious beat he fought to soothe. She sipped her drink like nothing in the room could touch her. He tried to mirror her impenetrable calm, clinging to the coldest edges of discipline he'd honed all his life. "And what is it you'd like to know?" His voice was carefully neutral, though they both knew exactly what she wanted.

"The truth."

Rook exhaled through his nose, feigning calm despite the rising tension inside him. Before he could speak, Reny caught the barmaid's eye and waved her over, leaning in to murmur words meant only for women. He couldn't make out a single syllable over the flurry of conversation around them.

Moments later, the barmaid returned with a sly smile and two small shot glasses, both full of dark liquid that flashed a rich, coppery gleam in the firelight.

Reny slid one across the table, her gaze locked entirely on his. "Hard truths call for harder spirits."

She raised the glass and swallowed its contents in a single, unbroken motion. Her head fell back, exposing the delicate column of her throat long enough to hold him captive. The drink's viciousness showed only in the slightest parting of her lips, though her expression remained unnervingly still. She set the glass down slowly.

This was a challenge, he realized. *An invitation to his undoing that he could not refuse.*

Rook hesitated, savoring the tension across the table before emptying his glass with a fierce tilt. The spirit slammed home, an instant searing heat. Harder than anything he'd tasted in either realm's taverns. He was already fraying as he set it down with cautious precision, willing the burn to settle.

"What the hells did you order?"

The corner of her mouth curved, so faint he might have missed it had he not been staring at her. She caught the barmaid's attention, holding up two fingers, then turned back to him with dark satisfaction in her eyes. "Any decent tavern keeps at least one bottle tucked away for those who can handle it."

When the woman returned and set down two more glasses of the same copper-dark drink, Rook lifted his, studying it in the firelight. "Does it have a name?"

"Widow's Bite."

He paused, brow lifting. "Why?"

Reny swirled hers once, watching it catch the light, before tilting her head back and draining it in one smooth motion. When she set the glass down, her eyes locked on his, unflinching.

"Because the men who drink too much of it don't make it home."

The silence that followed rose between them like a living thing. She was studying him in a way that felt different from before. Like she was comparing him to words on a page, measuring him against knowledge she hadn't possessed that morning. Her fingers drummed against the scarred wood of the table.

A lethal reflection of himself, sitting right across the table.

He felt the shift. The way her questions would no longer go unanswered, one way or another.

"Why, exactly, did you come to River's Edge?" Her voice was stripped of all its previous warmth.

He catalogued the room, assessing every shadow, every face turned away in laughter or bent over their own secrets. Only when he was sure their words would vanish into the rest of the noise did he lean in to answer her.

"To find a woman rumored not to burn." His eyes landed squarely, searching hers for any sign of retreat. His fingertip traced the rim of his glass, the motion subtle, meant to distract her. To demand a wandering glance.

She conceded nothing.

"One who carries a power called the flame of becoming." He braced for the expected explosion of temper, for the immediate blaze. Instead, he met only perfect, chilling calm. The slightest tightening of her jaw betrayed what seethed beneath the surface.

Anger choked down beneath a mask of serene indifference.

She gave a single, terse nod. As the barmaid passed, Reny lifted two fingers without breaking eye contact with him. Four more shot glasses arrived soon after, brimming with the same dark liquor. Two she slid toward him, two she kept within her reach, as if laying markers between them.

"Why?" Her voice was reduced to a cold, clean blade.

A chasm ripped open inside him. The longer this unfolded, the more his mastery fell away. Over her, over the course they were on, over himself. *If he had ever even held it at all.*

It felt like standing on a precipice, knowing the next step would be the fatal fall. A reckless leap into his own demise. He searched her face, starving for any shred of kindness or the flirtatious play he'd indulged in before. All he found was resilience. Determination had cast her features in stone.

"It's the key to saving Rithmor." His voice dropped, eyes sweeping the room again, habitual vigilance never loosening. "Or so they believe."

For an instant, her mask cracked. A quick ghost of pain and bewilderment flashed before she sealed herself off again. Her lashes lowered, fingers white-knuckled on her glass before she downed its contents. He did the same, letting the burn anchor him to this pinpoint on which everything was about to turn.

"Why would you be working to help Rithmor?" She held his gaze, hand closing around the next drink as though bracing for his answer.

He finished the final drink, the liquor delivering the confession he could not bring himself to voice. Emptied, it met the table with a hollow clunk. The lines of his face strained, heavy with a truth he couldn't articulate. But he didn't need to, anyway. She read him too easily, had always possessed the cruel insight to see it laid bare as fate between them.

Her lips parted for a word that died unspoken. She took the final drink in one quick tilt, expression hardening before she stood, the chair scraping back across the floorboards. She had no words left. Only the cold fire of her intent as she turned away. Each step she took through the room and up the stairs fell like a verdict, carrying her out of his sight.

Rook sat still, staring at the void she had created, her fury swallowing the liquor's lasting warmth. At last, he slid a few gold coins toward the edge of the table, his fingers steady as stone despite the collapse in his chest.

Then he rose, following the ghost of her.

Chasing the very end of everything he had ever been.

CHAPTER 33

S he was just about to leave when the door swung open behind her.

Inside, the hearth blazed with savage light, flames throwing wild shadows across the walls. She had already packed her satchel, her cloak flung across the table in preparation for travel. Rook slid the lock-bar across the moment the latch snapped shut behind him.

A final, heavy sound, barring them inside.

"Don't you dare lock me in." She'd broken from the earlier veil of calm, her words razor-sharp. "I'm going back to River's Edge."

"The hells you are." Rook spoke it plainly, without force or sneer. He didn't need to. The words alone propelled her closer to the door. To him.

"Every step of this entire journey—every bullshit backstory—you were never taking me to the Aetherium, were you?"

She watched the words land. *Watched him go hollow.*

"Listen to me." He tilted his head, words rolling smoothly across the room. It only stoked her rage further. She felt the fuse light inside her, felt the fire answer.

There would be no listening.

She laughed, but the sound was humorless. A cold, short thing that twisted her mouth into a snarl. Her breath came ragged, the anger bleeding into panic. "Gods, I *knew* better. Knew you were all wrong the moment I laid eyes on you. I was a fool to think otherwise."

Reny snatched her bag, jerked her cloak off the table, and stormed toward the door again. Rook stepped sideways into her path, his jaw set. Nearby, the flames clawed higher in the narrow grate, answering her wrath.

She barely paused before shoving his chest with both hands. "Get out of my way."

"Reny—" But she slammed into him again. And again. The force knocked the cloak and satchel from her hands, but did little to move him. She drew back with clenched fists, ready to swing with all her strength.

The bruise to her ribs, still a lingering plague, seized her middle, the pain checking her momentum just enough.

Enough that he caught her wrist before her well-aimed fist could land. He grabbed her other arm, holding her tight in his grip. She twisted against him, chest heaving, eyes and breath gone frantic.

"Let me go!" She wrenched against his hold. "You're no different than the mercenaries!"

A muscle in his jaw ticked, his voice rising like iron. "I'm not like the rest of them. I've protected you. Fought off every damn threat since River's Edge."

She paused, but it was only to rally more force. Heat danced vengeful in the hearth, in her eyes, in her core. "You only did it for Rithmor! You protected your own motives!"

He ground his teeth. His gaze flashed, dark and dangerous, as she saw his own anger rise to meet hers.

"You think this is still just about Rithmor?" The question ripped out of him as a raw shout. He yanked her closer to his body. "You are my only motive now, Aurenya."

"You don't get to call me that!" Heat erupted from her, ribbons of fire spilling down her arms, circling her wrists. The flames leapt for him, but when they struck him, they guttered, harmless over his skin. Just like before.

A furious gasp clawed free from her, defiance trembling as she watched her fire recede, sparing him.

Even now. Even in her fury, the flames refused to hurt him. How?

"Now is when it matters, Rook. Right now." Her voice cracked like lightning. "Who are you, really? *What* are you?"

He squeezed his eyes shut for a beat, then opened them. The glamour shattered, its spell slipping from his skin like released smoke. The truth of him rose violently to the surface.

Gold burned molten through the storm-gray of his eyes, the angles of his face sharpened, becoming otherworldly, like cheekbones carved straight from mountain stone. At his ears, faint points emerged, and when his lips parted, she saw the glint of his teeth—the canines lengthening, resembling fangs.

Fully unveiled, he was a pure predator. A cruel creature of shadow that had been at her side all along.

Beautiful. Terrible. Entirely Aetherian fae.

"No more hiding, Reny."

Terror surged through her, dredging up the ghosts of her past. She could still see it—*see them*—all with piercing clarity.

The Aetherian legion that stole her family and childhood in one burning, blood-soaked afternoon. The swing of their swords and the flash of fangs as they laughed in the face of utter devastation. Her mother's screams. Her father's blood on the floor. The smell of smoke and copper that had never fully left her.

The same pointed ears. The same golden eyes. The same terrible beauty that haunted her nightmares.

And now one of them held her pinned tight to his body.

"No." This time, a growl, not a gasp, ripped from her lips. "No, no!"

Fire answered her denial. A flame lashed from the hearth like a whip, but instead of landing, it recoiled back to the grate, leaving the air trembling around them. She turned her head away, unwilling to meet the illuminated stare drilling through her.

"Yes. This is who I am. What I am. Look at me, Reny," he demanded.

"No!" Her cry tore through the room, pained and unguarded.

What followed was no dance, but wild, desperate combat. Her driving madly for the door with all her might, him countering and holding the line. She thrashed harder, heat bursting from her skin, only to fail when it met him.

She fought to free her arms, to drive her knees up against him, anything she could recall from Garron's lessons to break free. But Rook held fast, blocking her strikes each time. Step by step, he forced her backward into the room. Reny twisted and shoved, burning through every motion until her shoulders struck the wall. In his true form, he was a pure beast. Fierce angles, golden eyes ignited, teeth bared.

"It isn't safe out there for you," he snarled, his shadow now towering over her.

"It isn't safe out there. It isn't safe here with you. What's the fucking difference?"

"I'm not a good man," he ground out like the words inflicted pain, "but I'm not going to hurt you. I swear it."

Her breath hitched, betrayal and fear bound together. "You aren't a man," she hissed. "You're a monster, and your words mean nothing. Now let me go!"

Her words were claws tearing through him. She could see it in his face. That miserable tether between them pulled taut, and she felt it too. A wrenching pull. His grip loosened for just a moment.

But he was too quick to change his mind, his hands tightening again, pressing her wrists into the wall above her head. Denying any chance of escape.

"Maybe," Rook rasped like the truth was a blade at his throat. "Maybe I am a monster. But I can try to make things right."

"I said, let me go, Rook!" She shook her head frantically, fighting him and herself both.

"I can't do that," he breathed, voice breaking as she arched again, straining to push him away. "Godsdamn you, Reny, I can't let you go."

Her shoulders slumped, the fracture in his voice strangling the fight out of her. The fire died back into her entirely, smothered by the wall of him. Panting, Reny let her head fall against the wall.

"Why?" The word was threaded with pain, tears glinting in her green eyes. "Why can't you let me go?"

His eyes closed, shoulders rising with a shuddering breath. When he opened them, the gold blazed through the gray, a restless sea of everything unspoken. She sucked in a breath as if she might drown in them.

Their hearts pounded in tandem, flush together, the air charged with an all-consuming, magnetic draw. A connection that made no sense to her, defying every rule she made. Every wall she'd built around herself.

"You know why." It came out torn, not by anger, but want.

Need. She felt it like an arrow in the chest.

For a suspended moment, the world went still. The inn below, the nearly unbearable heat of the hearth. Everything faded until only the fever-bright space between their mouths remained, the crackle of magic alive across her skin.

She should hate him. Should recoil from the creature wearing the same face as the ones who destroyed everything she loved.

But it was still Rook. The man who'd pulled her from the darkest depths. Fought for her. Killed for her. The man who allowed the mask to crack open to show her what was real. Who looked at her like she was the only light left in his world.

Monster and man. Both of them, tangled together.

And gods help her, she wanted them both.

All thought fell away. Heat split her from the inside as she surged upward on her tiptoes and claimed his lips.

The kiss struck him like lightning.

A desperate clash of two forces, neither one of them gentle. Rook groaned into her mouth at the feel of her, the sound vibrating through them both. The last of his restraint shattered, hunger flooding in to fill the wreckage of him.

Her body arced into his with the same primal ferocity that had driven her fists moments before. Releasing her wrists, he seized her hips and dragged her closer.

She was fire and paradise, mayhem and salvation. The one truth in a life of lies he could no longer deny.

Even if she didn't know all of it. The full weight of his betrayal. Who he really was.

He should tell her. Should rip the rest of the mask off and let her decide with all of it laid bare. But he was a selfish creature.

A monster.

And right now, he wanted her more than he wanted to be worthy of her.

In one swift motion, he lifted her, her legs locking around his waist as her back hit the wall. The hard length of him ground into her center, and he swallowed her gasp. Her arms wound tight around his neck, fingers buried in his hair.

Rook's mouth left hers, charting a maddening path down her jaw to the hollow of her throat, where her pulse raced wild. There he hovered, breathing her in like she was the only thing keeping him alive.

When he spoke, the words frayed against her skin. "Tell me what you want."

Her answer, a demand and confession in one, tore out of her. "The rest of you."

The rest of you.

She hadn't said it in seduction or desperation, but with honesty so pure it destroyed him. Because she had seen the monster in him again and again and still, even when it bordered on madness, she chose the man.

Chose him. Or who she thought he was.

The thought should have stopped him. It didn't. A guttural sound escaped as he claimed her lips again, collision more than kiss. When Rook tore away enough to look at her, heat searing in the center of his chest, the truth struck him with violent finality.

No. This, between them. It was never really a choice.

It was an inevitable part of him, of her, like blood and bone. *Even if he refused to name what it truly was.*

She met his look—fury, defiance, want—nothing hidden, nothing soft about any of it. And it only drove him further off the edge. Still holding her, he crossed the room in three long strides and dropped her onto the bed, the mattress jolting beneath her.

Rook stood between her knees, chest heaving as though he'd just been through battle. And in a way, he had. Each step toward her had been a war with himself, one he knew he would eventually lose. Waiting and wanting, she drew him in with nothing but her eyes.

Off came the shirt, firelight spilling across the scars and every hard line of him. Her hands froze on a boot, attention dragging over his bare chest. He caught her leg and stripped her boots and socks away, tossing them to the floor.

"I had it," she muttered, almost to herself, and shot him a cutting glare.

The corner of his mouth lifted. "You were taking too long." Then he was on her again, hot and insistent, peeling away the rest of her clothing until nothing stood between them but firelight and want.

Reny fell back, hair a feral halo of embers across the sheets, her chest rising fast. The war played across her face—logic against want—and want clearly won.

Holding her stare, his belt slid free with a rasp, buckle and strap hitting the floor with a heavy thud. The rest of his clothing dropped until he stood bare before her. Man and myth, beast and shadow in equal measure. Her eyes dragged over him, taking in the hard, undeniable proof of his need. She bit her lip in raw invitation.

That look alone pulled a deep, broken curse from his throat. He snatched her legs and jerked her toward the edge of the bed, studying her body in agonizing slowness before he kneeled.

Intent to worship at the altar he had, until this moment, been denied.

Until her thighs tensed beneath his palms. He stilled.

"Shy, Reny?" One brow arched, amusement tugging at his mouth.

"Maybe." Her answer was soft, guarded.

"You shouldn't be." He pressed a slow kiss to the inside of her knee, then her thigh, letting her exhale, letting her soften. "Do you know how often I've thought about this?"

Then he bit the soft flesh of her inner thigh. *Hard.*

"Rook!" A breathy cry escaped with a rolling arch of her spine.

A low chuckle rumbled against her skin as he scooped his arms under her hips and forced her closer. He sank between her legs, devouring her. If divinity existed, he found it here—between her thighs, in every sound she made for him.

His mouth and fingers worked in tandem, every movement mindful. Listening for every gasp, noting every time she writhed beneath his touch. To each reaction, he offered more.

Relentless, Rook didn't stop, forcing her to break again and again until she was trembling and breathless. Completely at his mercy.

"Rook—" His name came out wrecked, half-plea, half-warning. "I can't—"

He lifted his head just enough to take in her flushed face. Just enough to meet her desperate gaze. "You can. And you will, Reny."

Her head fell back as he dove back down, returning to what he knew drove her mad. Whimpers escaped her, and then she tensed, shattering again. Only then did he relent. Crawling up over her, he trailed kisses over her ribcage, lingering on the fading bruises there. Bruises earned from the danger he'd led her into with his lies.

He didn't deserve the gift of her surrender. But took it anyway.

Rising above her, kneeling between her thighs, Rook's thoughts had narrowed to a tangled labyrinth of need and vicious reverence. No words necessary—his eyes spoke for him.

Tell me to stop. Or let me have you completely.

She arched her hips up to meet his, giving him the only permission he needed.

With one guiding hand, he slid into her in a single slow thrust. Not for gentleness, but for depth. For the soul-deep possession he had sacrificed everything to have. The sound that ripped free was raw—relief and ruin tangled into one—as he framed her head with his fists.

"Reny. Gods."

Her head tipped back, lips parting, spine curving into him with unrestrained abandon. She gave herself to the moment, lashes fluttering shut as though the force of him was too much to face head-on.

"Don't close your eyes." Low, edged in possession. One hand caught her jaw, not to force, but to anchor, pulling her attention back to him. "Look at me."

He needed her to see what she had made of him.

The pace was blissfully brutal, every thrust a vow, each heavy breath its own retribution. When her lips met his, it was with heat and teeth that nearly split his lip, forcing another rough sound from his chest. He lost himself in the rhythm of their bodies, her cries cutting through the blaze.

In one fluid shift, Rook swept his arms under her and drew her with him as he sat back against the headboard, never leaving her.

"Why are you looking at me like that?" Reny fought to catch a breath as she straddled his lap, firelight gilding along every curve.

"How can I not?" He was looking at her like a man starved, drinking her in as if he could carve her into his soul.

His hands roamed her back, her hips, her spine in a drawn-out frenzy—an effort to memorize the shape of the woman he had chosen above everything. Above duty. Above the blood oath.

Let him come. Let them all come. He'd kill every last one of them before getting to her.

She moved over him, each rise and fall driven by the need to feel all of him. Torment and salvation intertwined until control became agony.

Her head dropped forward, lips flushed and swollen, stray hair clinging to damp skin. He brushed them away with a gentle hand.

"Rook." A whisper.

"I know." He didn't know anything anymore, but the word left him anyway.

All he could do was watch, letting her take what she wanted, letting her strip him down to pure need until it threatened to tear him open. He answered her relentlessly with every upward thrust.

One hand slid up her body, tenderly closing over her throat, thumb brushing the wild flutter of her pulse. The other traced the inside of her thigh until that thumb found her center, working her with torturous circles. He held her eyes as if watching her come undone was the only absolution he had left.

Her breath hitched, rhythm faltering as the pressure built. Her head dipped, focus dropping.

"That's it." Low as a prayer. "Right here, Reny. Eyes on me."

She fought to obey, lashes fluttering, a soundless plea on her lips. Her cheek tilted into his palm, and he let his hand cup her face fully. Air caught in his throat as her eyes locked on his, and this time, refused to drift.

"There you are." He held back a smile, his thumb circling slower, drawing out the motion. Savoring every tremble and gasp she gave. "Beautiful. Now let go. Keep your eyes on me."

A broken sound escaped her, nails digging into his shoulders.

Watching her like this undid him. The full length of him inside her, the merciless rhythm of his thumb between her legs, his eyes consuming every second of her surrender. When she came around him this time, head thrown back, calling his name to the ceiling, it pulled him under with her. Her name ripped from somewhere deep, a near unholy sound as he spilled into her, succumbing to the wildfire that had taken hold of him. He had fully stepped into the flames of her more than once, knowing it might burn him to ash.

But chose it anyway. Would keep choosing it, choosing her, until he no longer could.

Reny collapsed against his bare chest, sweat-slick and panting, her heartbeat thundering with his. He held her there, one hand pressed to the small of her back, letting himself have this.

Just for another minute. The illusion that he could keep her. That she wouldn't hate him if she ever learned the rest.

The confession sat heavy on his tongue. He swallowed it down.

She let out a shaky breath before slowly pushing upright, eyes fierce even in ruin.

"This isn't forgiveness," she whispered.

His thumb brushed along her jawline. That smirk returned—the slightest uptick at the corner of his mouth that had repeatedly left her undone.

His reply was carved from iron and stone. Simple, final.

"I wasn't asking for it."

Chapter 34

The silence of dawn was a new, fragile sound. The total absence of rain.

When Reny woke, the quiet jarred her. The storm's thunderous, consuming rhythm had been so constant that the sudden lack of it felt unnatural, like a missing limb. For days, the downpour had battered the windows and roof above them, sealing them within a false perception of safety.

Now, there was nothing.

No rain, no wind. Only the slow pulse of two hearts.

Realization settled in her chest, cold and absolute. Whatever reprieve the storm had granted them was over. With it went their perfect seclusion and the reckless surrender it had allowed.

She had no clear vision of what came next. Lying on her side, knees drawn close, she faced him in the gray-blue hush of pre-dawn. Time felt irrelevant. She refused to acknowledge it.

Rook slept still, one arm tucked beneath the pillow, the other loose beside her. The slow rise and fall of his chest lent him an almost mortal peace. His breath was soft. Warm.

Maddeningly human.

Yet the man sleeping inches away was no longer cloaked in illusion—in spellwork she hadn't known existed until he'd shed it.

Her gaze traced the unnerving details that daylight no longer allowed her to deny. The elegant cut of his cheekbones, the subtle taper at the top of each ear. Lips parted in sleep, concealing what she now knew lay behind them—elongated, pointed canines. Fangs. The unmistakable mark of a race Reny had only ever known as executioners.

The Aetherian fae.

She had seen their kind only once before. From the cowering pose of a child as her village burned all around her. The glint of blades in the smoke. The thunder of hooves. The gleam of fangs in the firelight as they laughed.

Everything human had burned or bled that day.

Everything but her.

And now, one of them lay just within reach, his soft exhales stirring the spill of her hair across the pillows.

In the pale light that seeped through the fogged window, he looked deceptively unchanged from the man who'd first walked into the tavern. And maybe that was the most dangerous thing about him. That even unmasked, the truth of him right in front of her, he still looked so peaceful.

Made her feel peaceful, too.

Her thoughts spiraled. The journey he had led her on. The stories he'd told, the promises of sanctuary—all threads spun of half-truths or outright lies. The story of the Aetherium stretched before her like a chasm, and she was already falling.

What fate had he been leading her toward? How far were they from whatever safety he claimed to seek on her behalf?

Her racing pulse must have betrayed her. His eyes shot open.

The change in him happened in an instant. One heartbeat, he was lost in sleep. The next, awareness flooded him, tightening the narrow space between them. Gold ignited in his unveiled eyes, seizing what scant light leaked into the room. There was no haze of waking, no slowness to him. Only the alert, watchful intensity of a creature honed by pure instinct. A predator waking to threat.

Or to loss.

He searched her face—for hate, perhaps. For fear. But Reny only looked back, calm beneath his scrutiny. The reality of him no longer felt like a haunting nightmare from her past, but a reckoning she refused to flinch away from.

"What happens now?" she asked, the question gentle. Stripped of accusation, leaving only quiet, genuine curiosity.

He didn't answer at first. Suspicion and wonder warred across his expression, as though he, too, were unsure of the stillness between them.

"For now," he said at last, voice barely above a whisper, "we rest."

Rook shifted beneath the tangle of sheets and drew her closer, sweeping her into his arms, pulling her body against his.

An invitation to chase away reality for a little while longer.

She went willingly but couldn't hide her hesitation. Not with the tension in her spine, the furrow in her brow. Her expression alone was a demand.

A long sigh escaped him, more resignation than weariness. "I'm going to take you to the Aetherium."

"How can I believe that?" She studied his face, not bothering to hide her hunt for any hint of deception. All while her heart knocked a frantic beat against her ribs.

"Look at me, Reny. Tell me I'm lying." His challenge hung in the air. A gauntlet thrown down between them.

"What about your original plan? What's the cost of betraying whoever sent you?" She held him with unyielding expectation, watching him absorb the question. Watching the shadow pass behind his eyes.

A single shake of his head, dismissing it all. The hand resting on his bicep squeezed in unspoken command.

Answer me.

"Don't worry about it." Low, meant to soothe. But it didn't.

His refusal cut like a fresh betrayal. Her brows knit together, mouth hardening into a thin line. He dipped toward her jawline, letting his lips begin to roam while his hands slid down her body until his fingertips traced the curve of her hip.

"That's not an answer, Rook." Need and aggravation laced through her words, her body betraying her as her head tipped back to expose her neck, spine arching into him. His mouth found the curve of her throat, placing kisses where her pulse raced and tumbled.

"I mean it, Rook." Reny tried to pull back, to create space, failing miserably. "Were you hired by the crown? Won't they be looking—"

"Stop, Reny." He pulled away then, bringing her up with him. In one swift motion, he rolled them to the center of the mattress, ending up on his back with her atop him. His hands settled on her hips as he guided her into a straddle across him. "When we get to the Aetherium, I'll tell you everything."

Her lids grew weighted, the angry, demanding fire banking and dissolving into flowing, molten want. She silently cursed herself as the need for him began to outweigh her quest for answers.

"Please." She tried to sharpen her voice, but it emerged as a broken whisper. "Tell me."

He saw it. The moment she stopped fighting. *The moment he'd bought himself a little more time.*

"I will, Reny." His gaze swept over her. "When we get there. When you're safe."

Her hands explored, discovering him ready, and a groan rumbled through his chest before he could stop it. Now the one in control, she moved, lowering until he slid fully inside her. Their hips locked with a shuddering jolt, her gasp at the stretch nearly undoing him.

She straightened, sitting tall, body adjusting to the fullness with an instinctive roll of her hips. The last twist of white linen slipped from her shoulders, leaving her bare to him in the faint blue light of the morning's earliest hours.

Rook inhaled deeply, letting the scent of her fill his lungs. Eyes closed, he committed the moment to memory like a brand on his soul.

If such a thing remained.

The growing ache in his chest convinced him that perhaps he did possess one after all.

"Look at me," Reny commanded in a whisper, drawing his focus—and a smile—instantly.

He didn't rush her. Made no demands of her on top of him. Instead, he let her lead, hands anchored to her waist, thumbs pressing into her hips with smoldering heat.

With an intensity wholly distinct from the night before, he watched her. No longer predatory, but something closer to intoxicated admiration. Stunned reverence, written plain across his face when her eyes fluttered shut and her chin tipped toward the ceiling.

"No, don't do that." Hips drove up to meet her even as she tried to escape, to get lost in the rhythm of their bodies. "Look at me, Reny." One hand caught her jaw—not hard, but insistent—and brought her back to him. When her eyes met his, the last of her resistance, the last of his restraint, fell away.

She was rocking him into madness. He took her hand and pressed it flat against his chest, letting her feel the wild, frantic beat beneath her palm. The words he wanted to say were locked inside, trapped behind his own lies.

For you. This is for you.

Her head dropped forward, surrendering. But he kept her hand at his heart, held it there for the confession he couldn't speak aloud. Hoping it would be enough when it was all over. Tell her what he couldn't find the words for.

Dawn light filtered through the window, painting her in soft shades of gold, illuminating the dust motes dancing around them. He wondered what she saw when she looked at him now. Monster or man. *Probably both.*

In her face, he saw salvation. *Entirely undeserved.*

His hands mapped her body like borrowed time. Every roll of her hips lured him closer to ruin. One he chased willingly. She leaned forward, chest to chest with him, and his fingers tangled deep into her hair.

Not to guide. Just to hold on to what was his.

For now.

She arched back again, throat bared to the dawn, and rode them toward their inevitable shatter.

CHAPTER 35

A raven perched in the eaves of a massive silver oak, its branches draped heavily above and around the Black Dragon Inn. The bird remained motionless, save for the occasional tilt of its head, each movement unnaturally precise. It strained to listen, catching the muffled sounds from within the inn that only its supernatural hearing could discern.

At first, nothing.

The ordinary shuffle of the morning.

A few pairs of boots on floorboards, the creak of ancient timber settling, the distant clatter of dishes being stacked in the modest kitchen below. Black eyes swept the facade. Searching.

Then, from within the ordinary noise... something else.

Soft. Rhythmic. Unmistakable.

The creature's head snapped toward the source, fixating on a second-story window. A sound easily ignored in places like this. But today, it was intrusive.

Damning.

The bird hopped a few paces down the branch, claws scraping against bark as it secured the exact angle needed to peer through one of the narrow windowpanes.

A woman, bare and bathed in pale morning light, rode atop a man. Her head tipped back, spine arched, hair spilling like embers down her back and shoulders. The man beneath her, hands gripping her waist, his face stripped of everything but worship, was utterly undone.

This was not just any woman. This was the Flame-Bearer. And the man beneath her was the Rook.

Deep within the creature's mind, beneath the dark grip that held her, Korva's true voice screamed.

Run. Gods, girl, run while you still can.

The thought blazed through her. Bright, desperate, and immediately smothered. Her master's presence coiled tighter, crushing the air from her lungs. The compulsion to report, to betray, to deliver pressed down like iron.

No. Please, no.

Through the window, the woman's hand pressed flat against the man's chest. Even from this distance, Korva could see the devotion written across his face. The surrender.

Korva's heart—her true heart, the one that still remembered wind and cliff and freedom—wrenched.

Brenn. Brenn, I need help. Can you come get me? Can you hear me?

His name rose unbidden, a lifeline cast into drowning darkness. She could almost feel the salt spray of the Cliffs, hear Orwyn's laughter echoing through the stone halls. The weight of Brenn's hand on her shoulder the day she left returned to her. The way his evergreen eyes had searched hers with concern she'd been too proud to acknowledge. To rely on.

I should never have left. I should have stayed. Please help me.

Regret lodged like a blade between her ribs. Orwyn would be so disappointed in what she'd become. How easily she'd been used. The Bear and Wolf had raised her better than this. Taught her that duty meant protecting the flock, not hunting them. Not delivering them to slaughter.

I have to warn her. I have to—

The thought snapped like a twig under a boot. Pain lanced through Korva's skull, white-hot and absolute. That cold voice slithered through her mind, crushing every fragment of rebellion.

You will watch. You will remember. You will report back to me alone.

Korva's talons dug deeper into the branch, splinters of bark flaking away. Inside, she was screaming. A soundless cry no one would ever hear. Her wings trembled with the effort to stay still. Every fiber of her being ached to hurl herself at the window—to scratch and claw and screech through the glass until the woman understood.

Even if her fragile, avian neck snapped in the process.

But she couldn't move. *Couldn't disobey.*

Through the glass, the woman leaned forward, chest brushing against the man beneath her, and his hands tangled in her hair.

Traitor. The voice hissed through her. *He has betrayed me. And you will help deliver his reckoning.*

Korva longed to weep. To rage. To fly north to the Cliffs and throw herself at Brenn's feet and beg forgiveness for walking away, for thinking she was strong enough to go alone. But those thoughts, those frantic, clawing hopes, his will snuffed out one by one. Candle flames in a windstorm. Only his command remained. It left no room for mercy, no space for the girl she used to be.

The location burned into her mind. The Black Dragon Inn. Second-story window facing east.

No. Please. Don't make me do this.

But even as she begged, even as her true self thrashed and fought against invisible chains, her body obeyed. With a violent push, the creature launched from the branch and swept through the canopy made thinner by autumn's ruthless rain. Korva's mind broke into a war.

I need to go back. I need to warn her of what's coming. Orwyn, I'm sorry. Brenn, I'm so sorry—

But that consuming presence was cold and unrelenting.

Fly. Report. Obey.

She beat her wings faster, each stroke a betrayal of everything she'd once been. The forest blurred beneath her as she pushed harder, faster, even as her soul protested. Part of her still reached for the Cliffs. For home, for the family she'd abandoned, for the life she'd thrown away because she'd been too proud to stay. She could almost see Brenn's face, could almost hear him calling her back.

But it was too late. Too late for warnings. Too late for redemption. She was nothing now but the instrument of his will.

The Rook had failed. Betrayed the blood oath. The flame of becoming would not be delivered as promised.

But Korva knew. Against every prayer, every frantic wish to simply forget, she knew exactly where he could find the power that belonged to him. And she was going to tell him. Even if she didn't want to.

The raven disappeared into the gray morning sky, a streak of darkness against fading storm clouds. Inside that small, feathered body, a girl who had once soared free above the Cliffs was drowning in shadow, her voice swallowed by a will far stronger than her own.

Leaving the inn behind her, Korva flew on, carrying the weight of doom on wings that no longer belonged to her.

CHAPTER 36

One of Rithmor's hour bells was still ringing when black wings cut through the darkness. Its shriek split the air like a wound tore open.

Down the corridor, every torch guttered low. The High Priest moved quickly, his black velvet robes whispering across the floor. He knocked once upon the prince's chamber door, head already bowed.

Locks scraped, and a bolt slid. The door opened wide to darkness.

Tareth stood within it, the shine in his eyes feverish and thin. Behind him, incense had burned too long. Its bitterness clung to the air, sour in all four corners.

"A messenger has arrived," the priest whispered, his frame looming cautiously just beyond the threshold. "Shall I fetch the king?"

"No." The word struck clean. Tareth's jaw tightened, the muscle at his temple flickering. "It is my private messenger. Leave, priest, and tell no one. That is a royal order."

The priest hesitated only long enough to turn pale before disappearing into the shadows of the hall. He did not pause near the king's door. He could feel vicious eyes boring into his back until he vanished around a bend in the corridor.

Tareth stepped from his chamber still clad in royal leathers, rest long forgotten. He crossed the hall and unbarred the double doors that opened to the eastern balcony. Night met him, cold and waiting. Below, the city lay in uneasy silence, its lamps dimming to dying embers. Mist shrouded the spires, the royal banners on the ramparts sagging under decay and a thick coat of dew.

The cold crept up through the flagstones until it met his bones. The balcony drank what little light the moon gave, returning only a gray wash across his black and gold armor. Whispers came without performing the ritual now and hadn't left him for days. A tide that filled the hollows of his skull.

Where is she? Where is the fire that belongs to me? What of the oath you swore, child of men?

The dissonant chorus wove through his mind, distorting each of his senses. He couldn't recall the last time he'd slept through the night. Tareth shoved the heel of his palm flush to his brow. Behind his eyes, the darkness writhed, alive and restless.

Begging for release.

"Quiet," he hissed out loud, though he knew they would not. "You'll have it. You'll have your flame. I'll have my crown."

You swore with your soul. With your father's soul. The words came smooth as oil.

The Rook promised in blood to you. Do not think the One Eternal forgets what is promised.

Pain bloomed behind his temples, his thoughts scattering like shattered glass.

A flicker of shadow swept the balcony's edge. The raven dove, and when it touched stone, it was no longer a bird but a young woman clad head-to-toe in black leather. Korva knelt where she landed, feathers unspooling into long black hair. The air bent around her, reforming her shape as though the night itself delivered her. Her knees met the cold slab, head bowed before him. When she raised her face, her eyes looked hollow. Solid black drowned over them, fathomless mirrors that reflected nothing back.

Tareth's hand moved before thought could stop it. He snatched her by the jaw, forcing her face up until the moonlight broke across it. She didn't resist, only shivered. A small, broken movement. The reflex of a creature that once knew freedom but was starting to forget.

"Tell me," Tareth spoke down to her, his tone almost courteous for all its cruelty. "Where is the Flame?"

The whispers pressed close, their words lacing beneath his own breath.

Answer. Answer now. What has been done with what is mine?

Tareth jerked his head as if to shake off the voices, but the movement carried through his grip, snapping her jaw in his hold. The tremor in his hand betrayed him. The balcony swam, the horizon skewing at strange angles. He grimaced and leaned closer, words rough through clenched teeth.

"Answer me, damn you."

Korva flinched. When she spoke, her words carried a strange duality. Two cold, flat tones sharing one breath. Whatever free will she once possessed had been remade.

Unmade.

"The Rook," she said at last.

Tareth's expression stilled, but his gaze hardened.

"I followed their trail," Korva continued, the rhythm of her speech broken, uneven. "The Flame. At the Black Dragon Inn. Before dawn." She swallowed, the motion visible. "They are lovers."

One of the torches along the outer wall popped and guttered.

"He broke the blood oath he made to the crown." Her tone tightened, as if the words were forcefully twisted from her throat. "He will not bring her to the North Gate. He has chosen her over the crown. Over you."

The whispers surged in unison.

He betrays you. He betrays me. He takes what is mine and believes it is mercy!

Korva's mouth moved still, the words not entirely her own. "He will not deliver. I saw his hands on her. Her head was thrown back in the morning light—" Her breath hitched. "He loves—"

Tareth's control splintered, his hand striking her cheek before he realized it. Korva's head snapped to one side, but she didn't cry out. Her palm pressed to where he'd hit her, and she remained kneeling, shoulders heaving.

Tareth towered above her, his breath wild and desperate. The veins in his jaw jumped as the whispers swelled into a fevered shout.

Strike again. Tear out her tongue! Find the brother. Break the oath from his bones!

He sucked air through his teeth, and the world tilted, the balcony seeming to sway beneath his boots. Korva lifted her face. Blood had gathered at the corner of her mouth, crimson beneath the moonlight, the twin voids of her eyes devouring his reflection whole.

His fingers twitched in reflex, reaching for a weapon that wasn't there. Or a lifeline. The noise inside him became a continuous roar.

They will seek sanctuary. I need what is mine!

Tareth remained frozen, shoulders slumped.

She only grows stronger. Bring me what I have been promised, or you'll never wear the crown.

The crown prince shook his head in wordless refusal and held his hand out to the woman still kneeling before him. Korva's lashes fluttered as she set her palm to his and rose to her feet, blood dark across her bottom lip. With terrifying gentleness, he brushed it away, the crimson smearing across his thumb.

Before rational thought could slow him, he slid it across his tongue. Tasting her blood. Tasting the treason she'd witnessed.

"You are only a messenger," he murmured, the violence melting into a soft caress. "A mere servant." His hand ghosted over her face, tracing her cheekbone, the hollow beneath it, barely touching. The long black hair, the ethereal stillness, the eyes that were nothing but infinite shadow.

A thought rose through him, slick and dark, winding around the edges of his mind. The whispers shifted, becoming vile. Indulgent.

You are clever, Tareth. That is why you are chosen. Take the shifter. Make her your consort and your spy. Your eyes, your knife. Send her back to the Cliffs. That's where the Eye waits...

The idea clicked into place. The ache behind his eyes loosened. Not gone, but leashed. *Sated.*

Tareth tipped her chin higher with a single finger, noting the way the moon lay a silver stripe down her nose and mouth. "You hear him as I do," he whispered.

Not a question. Recognition.

"Good. Then you understand."

Korva stood motionless. The only proof of life was the pulse dancing wild at her throat. Tareth tilted his head, studying the movement of it, before dropping his hand. He began to circle her in slow, measured steps.

Prey, already caught.

"Tell me." His tone had turned intimate. "How did he creep into your mind, feathered one?" He stepped closer, gaze narrowing. "Was it grief that made you weak?" A faint, cruel smile bent the corners of his mouth. "Your brother's death broke your heart and left the door wide open?"

Visions forced themselves into Korva's mind, the memory of Orwyn's scream tearing through her consciousness. Pain followed, but it drowned beneath the darker current consuming her. Another whisper unfurled, lies threading through her thoughts until they became cold and clear as truth.

It was Rhedda who killed him. The witch who gave the order. The Rook obeyed it. This is truth. This is what you believe.

Korva's body jerked as if struck through the chest, her breath catching. When she spoke, her tone carried borrowed fury. "I want revenge for my brother," she said, each word shaking. "I want to make them pay for Orwyn's death."

Tareth's eyebrows lifted. A child's wonder, wrong and eerie, upon a monster's face. He studied her like a craftsman admiring his greatest creation. "Make who pay, little bird?"

Her brow knit, confusion and conviction wrapping together as her head tilted to one side, listening to voices only she could hear. A horrific new reality had been revealed to her, and she believed it completely.

"The witch, Rhedda." Her words were thick with the certainty of betrayal. "And the one they call the Rook."

Tareth's smile crept into a grin. The whispers in his mind quieted, pleased.

"That's a good girl," he murmured, admiring the icy expression she wore as she glared out into the darkness sweeping over the mountains.

He ended his prowl and closed the distance between them. Near enough that his breath touched her face. Molten gold traced the sharpness of her cheekbones, the hard-set line of her mouth. He leaned in, inhaling like an animal cataloguing scent, and she went rigid.

"You are quite exquisite for a half-breed." Tareth's tone had dropped, obscene in its intimacy. "You'll serve me well, won't you?"

He pressed closer still, breath against her temple, lips brushing her brow.

Korva stared past him, over his shoulder. Toward the horizon, toward the edges of the world. She dipped her chin. "Yes, master."

Tareth hummed, a rumble of approval in his chest. He moved around her again, his presence a cage she couldn't escape. Close enough now that she could feel him against her back. Looming, possessive, breathing down her neck.

Deep inside her, a woman's voice—her own voice, once—was screaming and sobbing.

"If you want to avenge your brother," Tareth said as he leaned in, lips brushing against the shell of her ear, "you will walk among your people as they knew you. You will find the Eye and bring a piece to me. And if you come across the Rook, you will kill him. Do you understand?"

Korva continued to stand tall, her back unnaturally straight, gaze cast out to nothing. "Yes, master."

Tareth lingered there, the tower of him suffocating. A low chuckle escaped him as he stepped away. The sudden absence left her swaying.

"Who do you serve, feathered one?" He circled back to face her, his grin satisfied.

"Only you." Korva's reply was breathless. Weak.

Tareth's smile unfurled into sick satisfaction. He stepped past her and struck the parapet with his fist, a sharp crack that scattered the whispers from his skull.

Her entire body jolted in place.

Tareth turned back, feverish gaze pinning her. "You know your task, and you know the cost of failure. Now go. Bring me a piece of the Eye."

Korva nodded and tipped up her chin. "It will be done, master."

The woman dissolved, leaving the raven in her place. It launched itself from the rail before he could turn away—a dark blur against the fading moon—and vanished into the mist swallowing the castle spires.

Tareth remained on the balcony, elbows braced against cold stone. The faint scent of iron and ash clung to the air where she had stood. He pressed the heel of his palm to his brow, and the ruinous choir in his skull rose again. He let them come. Let them flood his mind. All that mattered was the crown.

Not just of Rithmor, but of both realms.
Because soon, it would all be his.

CHAPTER 37

T he halls of the Cliffs no longer echoed with the chorus of those who lived within them. They swallowed the sound whole. Since Korva learned of her brother's fate and fled, a silence more suffocating than any storm had settled over sea and stone. It pressed into Brenn's chest like granite, heavier with every passing hour.

He saw the mark of her absence clearly on their leader. Rhedda had not spoken a word, nor had she consulted the Eye. She'd become a figure carved from unyielding rock, answering no pleas from the witches or searching glances from the other Cliffborn. Whatever she knew from vision or dream, she had buried it deep and sealed the earth behind her.

The others moved through the chambers like ghosts. What shifters remained clustered in small, uneasy knots, hollowed by sleeplessness, exchanging grim whispers. The Whisperfolk, the most fragile wards of the sanctuary, kept to their shadows and corners, guarded by witches who offered wordless, warm embraces.

Brenn passed among them, the air shifting subtly in his wake. Everything left unspoken followed him like a rising tide. Failing to protect Orwyn and the others cut deep. Shame he bore willingly.

Outside, the wind tore at sparse shrub and scattered grit across the ledge. The sea below hurled itself endlessly against the rock, a chorus of fury that matched the one inside his own chest. He turned the bend in the narrow path and nearly collided with Aric.

The fox-shifter looked markedly better after his days among the healers, though the glint in his amber eyes had not dulled. He blocked Brenn's path, words already forming.

"Do you have any idea where Korva might have gone?" Direct as always, but far from accusatory.

Brenn shook his head. The motion felt impossibly heavy, as though his entire frame might bow under its weight.

Aric's expression softened as he closed the distance between them, resting a hand briefly on Brenn's shoulder. "You can't take this on alone. You did your best."

A half-cynical laugh, half growl escaped him. "My best was wrong. It wasn't enough."

Aric turned toward the horizon. The breeze caught his hair, teasing auburn strands across his jaw, salt air leaving a pale crust along the stubble there. He searched the endless gray for any sign, but the sky offered nothing. Only gulls wheeled far out over the surf, their white bodies flickering above the churning water, cries lost to the crash of waves below.

"We're no strangers to loss," Brenn acknowledged, his voice carrying over the gale. "But it's starting to feel... pointless."

Aric folded his arms and leaned against the weathered cliff at their backs. Narrower than Brenn, but just as firm against the wind. His crimson cloak snapped at his heels, sea spray brightening the dark weave until it gleamed in the overcast light.

When he finally spoke, it came after a long, uncertain silence. "Do you think the Eye of Nytheris can be trusted? Do you think we're being misled?"

A measured shrug. "The gods have slept so long that maybe their relics remember only how to whisper wishes, not truth. Not prophecy."

Aric frowned, studying him. Brenn could feel the weight of his scrutiny—the fox reading the quiet ruin beneath his solid composure. He held Aric's look, then turned back toward the tireless assault of waves far below.

"I think what's left," Brenn murmured, "are godless men doing godless things. And we're caught in their ruins, as we always have been."

Aric sighed, leaning back against the rock wall. He tipped his head to the sky, rust-red hair wild in the salt air. "So, what happens now?"

Brenn shifted beside him, thick arms folding across his chest. His dark, pine-green eyes were fixed on the sea. Another huff of breath escaped him, closer to a growl than anything else. "I think we go back to minding our own damn business. If the Aetherians and the humans want to tear each other apart again, let them. I doubt this time will be any different than the last." He paused. "We only take care of our own."

Movement caught his eye. Another presence rounding the narrow bend. A woman, the hem of her dark green cloak drawn close against the relentless wind. Long, russet-brown hair spilled loose from her hood, dark waves catching in the sea air. Her footfalls found the uneven ground with quiet certainty, concern creasing her warm brown features as she made her way toward them.

Both men straightened, pulling away from the rock wall as Elenna approached.

Light of frame and fine-boned, even in human form, she moved with the same fluid grace as her wild self. Quick, watchful, silent. She nodded her greeting to Aric first, and Brenn caught the warmth that passed between them in the brief meeting of their eyes. Then she turned toward him, chin raised, the wind forcing her hood flat against the thick coils of hair gathered at her nape. Her amber irises, sharp as autumn leaves, held his.

Brenn spotted it almost immediately—instinct reading what words wouldn't reveal.

The quiver of fear beneath composure.

Aric shifted his weight, unconsciously placing himself at her side, angled between her and the open rock that dropped away to the sea. Two creatures cut from nature's same cloth, despite the differences in their human forms. Elenna gave him a small, grateful smile and brushed her fingers against his arm. Light and fleeting, acknowledging what he'd done without making it more than it was.

"Brenn," she began, her voice steadfast, "I know you told us to stay within the Cliffs. But I needed to clear my head."

His brow darkened, a rumble starting in his chest. Aric tensed, but Elenna cut in before either of them could speak.

"You can be upset with me if you want." She kept her head high. "But I'm glad I went into the Old Wood. It was peaceful until it became the wrong kind of quiet. That's when I heard it."

"Heard what?" Every trace of ease vanished from Aric.

Elenna swallowed and drew a deep, grounding breath. "The unmistakable roar of death, Brenn. A thousand cries woven into one."

"Only one creature makes such a sound." Aric exchanged a grim look with Brenn.

"A Hollowmire." Elenna forced out the name like a curse. "It's hunting again, through the Old Wood. I saw it heading toward the Veil's border."

Brenn's focus went distant, lost to dark memories. For a heartbeat, he stood wholly vacant. He blinked hard, fighting off the images, before dropping his broad, calloused palms on her shoulders.

"Elenna, are you certain it didn't sense you? Didn't turn back and follow you home toward the Cliffs?"

Her head snapped to the side, locks of hair thrown by the wind. "No. I would never risk that, Brenn. I stayed in my animal form and waited long after it passed before heading home."

Brenn scanned Elenna for the slightest hint of self-doubt, keeping his own expression unreadable.

"It never came back around," she insisted, solid as the ground they stood upon. "It kept to its course. Nose to the ground, headed toward the Veil border, toward that old inn with the pitch-black roof. The one beyond the silver pines."

"Have you told anyone?" Careful, as he let his grip fall from her shoulders.

Her focus flicked between them before she shook her head. "I came straight to you. I haven't even stopped by my chambers."

Aric gave Brenn the slightest shake of his head, the unspoken warning passing between them. Brenn caught the look, gave a small nod, and softened his tone, but the command in it remained.

"I need you to keep this to yourself, Elenna. Can you do that for me?"

"Yes, of course. I won't speak a word of it to anyone." She held his look, her demeanor easing.

He forced ease into his shoulders and gave a nod of approval, reaching out to pat her arm. "Thank you, Elenna. Go rest. And for the love of the sea, woman, stay within the Cliffs as I've asked."

Her mouth curved into a weary smile as she nodded. Her slender fingers fell over his, feather-light against the breadth of his palm. "We believe in you, Brenn. I need you to know that."

His throat worked. He couldn't quite manage to return the smile, but she seemed to understand. She patted his knuckles a final time before pulling away.

Turning, she nearly bumped into Aric, who'd settled in especially close without seeming to realize it. Their eyes met and held a beat too long before they both looked away, laughing softly under their breath.

Brenn watched the exchange. *Noted it. Filed it away.*

"Be careful," Aric murmured, dipping his head.

"I will." Elenna's fingers grazed his arm as she moved past him, lingering just a fraction longer than necessary.

The fox watched her until she disappeared around the bend in the path. Brenn watched him. The gale rose to claim the silence she left behind, sweeping through the cliff's edge like an unspoken warning.

"You love her." No question in it. Despite the weight pressing down on him, the slightest flicker of warmth bloomed in Brenn's chest.

Aric settled his fists on his hips, exhaling through his nose as he stared at the space where she'd vanished. "I care for her deeply, yes."

Brenn started walking, heading down the trail toward the cliff's main cave entrance. Aric fell into step beside him.

"Aye, fox. Just say it outright. You've been dancing around that truth for the better part of the year. You're quiet, but you aren't invisible."

Aric stayed silent, unreadable as they walked.

"It doesn't matter now," he finally said. "Everyone's grieving who we've lost, and now a Hollowmire's on the move. Nothing about our lives is certain enough for such declarations."

Brenn stopped, his massive form filling the narrow path. "That's the very reason why you make them," he insisted over the chaos of the sea raging below. "Nothing is certain. We only have what we grasp in our own two hands."

He clapped a palm the size of a dinner plate onto Aric's shoulder—an anchor and comfort all at once—and waited for him to meet his eyes.

"Tell her. You could end up regretting it more if you don't."

A half smile, then Brenn let his grip fall and started toward the sanctuary entrance. Behind him, he heard Aric draw a long breath of salt and air before following.

Whatever was coming, they would face it together.

CHAPTER 38

R ook felt the judgment of the trees in the set of his shoulders, their wordless verdict thrumming through the tension in his spine. The unease beneath his skin had little to do with the mare's gait.

They had fled the Black Dragon hours ago. After making it only a mile, they were forced to abandon the wagon, half-swallowed by deep mud left from the storm. With the supplies divided between Sal's saddlebags, they'd traded burden for speed, but the road remained a maze of sucking earth. Every stride was a weary pull.

Reny's presence—the heat of her at his back—was the only thing keeping him grounded. Her arms made a loose anchor around his waist, her cheek resting against the coarse wool of his tunic. He felt the quiet pulse of her breathing and the subtle effort she made to calm his rigid frame. He didn't need her words to know she sensed what plagued him.

The brace for a blow that had not yet fallen.

He tightened his grip on the reins as the woods around them became increasingly strange. This deep into the Old Wood, the air should have carried the soft sigh of wind through pines, the musk of wet earth and decaying leaves. Instead, the world had gone too still. As if time itself had stopped trying.

Every leaf hung motionless, oddly vivid, clinging to lush colors though the season should already have bled them dry and torn them down to the forest floor. A hush that belonged not to peace, but to another world entirely.

Behind him, Reny shifted. Her warmth fell away from his back, and he could feel her attention on him. The hard line of his shoulders, the near-constant swivel of his head as he scanned the trees.

"Who are you expecting to see leap out at us, then?" Her words sliced through the unnatural quiet, sharp over his shoulder.

Rook exhaled slowly, the sound caught somewhere between sigh and curse. Sal's pace faltered, her hooves sucking at the mud with a weary rhythm. The mare's patience was thinning with every step.

When his only answer was silence, she withdrew her arms from his waist. He felt the loss immediately. The deliberate space she'd carved between them on the single horse's back.

"You can't just bed me and then expect me to stop asking questions."

Rook glanced skyward, a crooked smirk tugging at his mouth as he looked back at her over his shoulder. "Could I try again to see if that works?"

"Rook." His name landed flat but with enough warning. He didn't need to fully meet her look to feel its severity.

Sal tossed her head and snorted in protest, refusing another stride through the muck. Rook murmured a few low words to coax her along, but the horse was having none of it. He guided her toward a cluster of tall pines.

Reny swung down first, boots sinking into the earth. Rook followed, reins loose in his hand. Her eyes pinned him even as he sauntered forward, lazily looping the straps over a low branch.

"I told you not to worry about it." His shadow shifted as he finally turned to meet her stare.

She planted her hands firmly on her hips, accusation narrowing the space between her brows.

He gave a faint, humorless huff. "But I suppose it would be very unlike you to just do as you're told."

"If you're working for Rithmor, you must've been hired by the Drayviens." No waver in her tone. "They're butchers, Rook. If they're coming for you, I want to know."

His heart knocked hard against his ribs as she moved closer, her words tying a knot in his chest. He held her in full focus, studying the details of her face. The anger carved there, and worse—

Her fear. Not of him, but for him.

The stark reality of his lies stood right in front of him. She'd given him everything, and in return, he'd offered breadcrumbs. Half-truths or no answers at all. The right words, the whole truth of who he was and why he'd come, had long since turned to bitter ash in his mouth.

How could he even begin to tell her now?

Behind him, Sal shifted with an impatient snort, hooves squelching as if she, too, demanded answers. Rook let out another resigned exhale, folding his arms across his chest.

"Yes." The admission scraped out of him at last, forcing himself to hold her eyes. Another partial truth. "They sent me."

She grimaced and closed the gap between them.

"What was their plan?" Her hand lifted to rest lightly on his arm. Too lightly. The contact unraveled him, his folded stance giving way beneath her touch. Everything about her was warm, comforting him in a way he didn't deserve.

He let himself trace the planes of her face before answering. "To weaponize the flame of becoming. Said to be the greatest power of the old gods. Strong enough to sunder the Veil, to regain all Aetherian magic, and immortalize the crown."

She swallowed visibly at the look he gave her, though she fought to keep steady. "They can't cross the Veil, right? Once we get through—into the Aetherium—we'll have sanctuary. Somewhere they can't go?"

"You will have sanctuary," he said softly. The silence between them grew heavy as confession.

She didn't miss his choice of wording. Her expression hardened. "We'll have sanctuary."

"You will have sanctuary," he repeated, too gently this time. He met her in the truth of it, allowing himself to be trapped in the fierce green of her gaze.

She shook her head as disbelief curdled into fury. He watched understanding dawn, the memory of what he'd said at the inn surfacing behind her eyes.

I'll tell you everything when we get to the Aetherium.

She turned away, spine drawn tight as a bowstring. "You son of a bitch."

The distance between them became unbearable, so he closed it, letting her words cut where they must. When he reached for her elbow, she yanked away and spun to face him.

"You never had passage through the Veil, did you?"

Rook flinched—the smallest tell—his hand falling uselessly to his side.

Before he could respond, she smirked. Humorless. Heartbreaking. "I suppose not, if you weren't even planning to take me to the Aetherium to begin with."

She began pacing the forest floor, boots whispering over the dense bed of fallen needles. Each pass grew shorter, more agitated. Rook let her move. Even Sal backed off a few paces, lowering her head to nose through the damp grass.

"So, what do we do?" Reny's words came faster now, her careful control beginning to fray. "If you don't have passage across the Veil, how will I get across? Will they just let me in? Can I ask them to—"

Her tone pitched upward, the first threads of panic weaving through. Rook watched her, a wave of self-disgust rising at the sight. She was tearing herself apart trying to find some way to save him.

He didn't deserve it. Any of it.

He shook his head, glancing toward Sal before turning back to Reny, now a gathering storm of frustration and fear in the middle of the wood.

"I'll take you to the edge of the Veil at the mountain pass. The Sentinels will sense what's inside you and let you through. They would stop me if I tried to cross that close to the Aetherium."

She stared at him, disbelief stark across her features. "Drop me off? What's a Sentinel?"

The corner of his mouth twitched—unbidden, involuntary. The smallest, saddest excuse for a smile.

She caught it instantly. "This isn't funny, Rook."

He shook his head in quiet protest. *None of it was funny.* But gods help him, he couldn't stop admiring her relentless refusal to surrender. "The Sentinels are the guards of the Veil. You'll know it's them when you see them." He sighed. "What matters is, you'll be—"

"I'm so tired of people—*you*, mainly—making decisions about my life without my input." Her interruption came sudden and fierce, laced with heat he could feel radiating from her. "What's going to happen to you?"

Rook closed what distance remained in two long strides. The instant their breath met, fire leapt to life. Ribbons of flame raced down her arms, crashing into his chest. He caught her wrists before her hands could push him back, holding her there. The flames swept into his skin and vanished, the energy melting into him on contact. His breath caught in a low groan, thumbs brushing the underside of her wrists.

Gentle, despite the inferno that met him.

"I failed my mission. And in Rithmor, failure is punished." The confession threatened to break him, but he smoothed it away with a half-smile. "If they can catch me. But you'll be safe, out of their reach. I've accepted whatever fate brings me."

"But I don't accept it," Reny growled through clenched teeth, straining against his hold. The flames still rolled, restless and utterly useless against him.

He watched her fighting. Not with him, but for him.

For a future that wasn't theirs. *Certainly not his.*

And the sight broke him wide open. Rook tilted his head, unable to hide the aching tenderness bleeding through. "I know you don't, but you must."

"I don't accept it, Rook."

His silence was raw as he drew her against him. Though tendrils of flame still curled down her forearms, she didn't resist him this time. She yielded completely when he bent his head and let his mouth rest just above her temple. He folded his arms around her until he could feel the heat fade into the depths of him.

"This was my choice, Reny." The whisper disappeared into her hair. "And I would choose it again."

She shook her head in reply, her face buried against him as the last of the flames died out. A heartbeat passed before Reny pulled back just enough to look up at him. "Are they going to kill you?"

"They can try." He studied her, knowing both the truth and what she wanted to hear. *Knowing he could not give her either.*

The air between them ached. Her lips parted, caught between anger and grief, trembling on the edge of words half-formed.

But the surrounding woods had changed.

Silence—absolute and consuming—swept through the trees. Rook froze, lifting his attention over her shoulder, scanning the growing shadows beyond them. Over to where Sal grazed...

Had been grazing.

Only emptiness. The mare was nowhere in sight. What little birdsong had been chiming through the late afternoon stilled into abrupt, unnatural nothing.

As though the forest itself had drawn its final breath.

They needed to find Sal. Needed to leave.

Now.

CHAPTER 39

Reny fell into step beside Rook as they moved quietly toward the stand of pines where Sal had been grazing. The ground still held her tracks, deep impressions in the mud pointing them forward through the trees and the mist that had gathered.

Rook lifted a finger to his lips in silent warning as he took the lead. He kept their bodies low and close to the trees, moving in and out of shadow as the light waned. The sun had already begun its slow retreat beyond the mountains, leaving the forest washed in the thin, spectral gray of late autumn's afternoon.

A tangle of underbrush caught at Reny's boots, damp leaves whispering underfoot, until the thicket gave way to reveal a narrow deer trail. The air hung heavy with the smell of moss, every measured breath cold and earthy.

Up ahead, Sal stood in the center of the path, her head lowered, tugging at the last scraps of green the forest floor had left to offer. Rook's exhalation came in a shudder, the tension bleeding from his shoulders as his back straightened. He took a cautious step forward, one hand lifting slightly in reassurance. Relief unfurled through Reny's chest, loosening the tightness she hadn't realized had coiled there.

Sal's ears flicked forward, her whole body drawing tight.

The forest exploded.

A massive form, fast as shadow, tore through the tree line. Reny's mind registered the claws first—curved like sickles, black as pitch—raking through Sal's flank with terrible precision. Flesh parted, muscle split, the wet and fatal give of a body torn open.

The mare's scream split the world apart.

A sound Reny would carry forever. High and shrill and utterly broken, the kind of agony that had no language, only raw animal terror as death found its mark. Her mind could not keep pace with what followed.

The burst of movement, the copper-iron stench of blood flooding the air thick enough to taste. Rook's arm hooked her waist, dragging her back as thin branches struck her face. They stumbled down into the underbrush, her knees slamming into earth behind a heap of fallen trunks, chunks of bark digging into her palms.

Sal's cries grew weaker, wetter, each one shorter than the last.

Then came the roar.

Not just noise, but a thousand tortured throats at once. Human and animal, all twisted into one unholy wail that clawed its way up from some lightless place beneath the world. The sheer wrongness of it struck bone-deep, reverberating in Reny's teeth and chest and skull. She clapped her hands over her ears, her own scream lost within its madness.

Rook had gone utterly still beside her, his focus locked forward on the clearing, every line of him frozen and barely breathing.

The shape lumbered into view.

Impossible. Blasphemous.

A bear, or what might once have been one, its body warped beyond recognition into what should never exist. Blackened hide sloughed from its frame in strips, revealing jutting ribs and glistening veins of rot that pulsed with sickly luminescence. Exposed, decaying muscle, gray and fibrous, clung to bone in wet ribbons where fur should have been.

One eye had filmed over with milky white, blind and weeping, while the other burned like coal inside a furnace of ruin. An ember of malice that saw everything, consumed everything. Its jaw hung open at an unnatural angle, the lower mandible torn half away, leaving shreds of flesh like cobwebs between yellowed fangs. The teeth themselves were too long, serrated, nothing that belonged in any living creature's mouth.

Its front legs bent wrong, joints reversed, claws scraping against stone. Every step released a thick squelch, as if the creature's own body was rotting from within even as it walked. A being hollowed out by death, and yet it lived. It hunted.

The Hollowmire.

Sal had stopped screaming.

Everything tilted. Edges blurred. All sound warped into a distant, unreal hum as Reny's vision tunneled. Time stretched, though she could not tell minutes from seconds.

Rook turned toward her slowly, as if he'd been pulled from the depths of a nightmare and wasn't certain yet which world he inhabited. His face had drained of all color, the shadows beneath his eyes stark as bruises against his skin. He swallowed hard, the movement sharp in his throat, his jaw working as if testing whether he could still form words.

Then his hands were on her face—warm, calloused palms pressing firm against her cheeks—forcing her to look at him, to stay grounded in him and not the horror unraveling just beyond their hiding place.

"Do not call your power." The words barely scraped past his lips. "Do everything you can to suppress it. Do you understand?"

Reny nodded, quick and desperate, her stomach heaving as wet, tearing sounds filtered through the trees. *It was feeding.*

Bone cracked, followed by the sickening pop of organs giving way. Reny bit down on the inside of her cheek until she tasted iron, fighting back the bile.

Rook's grip on her face stayed steady, but his thumbs trembled faintly against her skin. His chest rose and fell too quickly, each inhale shallow and insufficient. His expression fell in a somber collapse, something that looked horribly like acceptance.

She knew what he felt before he said it. The underlying pulse beginning to rise beneath her skin despite everything, the spark she couldn't fully bury, responding to her terror like a cornered animal desperate for survival, even as she screamed for it to stay locked away.

"Rook—" Her voice broke, strangled thin. "I'm fighting it, I'm not calling it, I swear, I'm trying—"

He silenced her with just a touch, carrying the look of a man who had already walked this moment in his mind and knew how it ended.

"Reny." He spoke her name like it might shatter. "Listen to me. When I tell you, you run. Head north, follow the ancient silver pines. They'll lead you straight to the Veil, to the mountain pass. It's only a few hours from here."

She shook her head, wild and disbelieving. "What are you saying?"

"It hunts magic and consumes it," Rook whispered low, calm in a way that cleaved through her chest like an axe. "It never stops hunting once it's woken, but it can't cross the Veil. You must get there. I'll buy you time."

"No." She shook her head hard. Instant refusal of the words and the world that demanded them. The feeding had dulled to a muffled blur behind her racing thoughts. "You're not doing that."

Rook's stare didn't waver. "This isn't a choice."

The Hollowmire's movements were changing, the guttural sounds of consumption giving way to low huffs as it lifted its ruined muzzle, tasting the air. It was growing restless, its massive form swaying as it turned in a slow circle.

Searching.

"Come with me." Reny's plea trembled, barely making any sound at all.

Rook shook his head.

"Come with me," she repeated, her whisper cracking with desperation. Tears welled, blurring her vision until all she could see was the shape of him.

Still. Resolute. Unbearably calm in the face of horrific, impending death.

He reached out and brushed a single tear from her cheek with his thumb, his frame sagging in a weary, broken way that made him look smaller than she'd ever seen him. Mortal. "Maybe this is how I make it right."

Let me try to make it right.

The words rose between them like a ghost. The same words that had broken through every wall she'd ever built just the night before. During confessions and surrenders, when the lies and every defense she'd ever forged around herself had come crumbling down for him.

This couldn't be it. This couldn't be the redemption he meant.

He leaned in and brushed his mouth against hers. Not a kiss of passion or longing, only the tender kind meant to last in memory. Meant to say what words could not. When he drew back, his exhale was warm against her lips, carrying the taste of salt and sorrow.

"Let me do this to right my wrongs." The whisper disappeared into the space between them. "If this is the price for falling in love with you, I'll pay it."

"You're not a monster." The words flew out of her, tasting like guilt as she recalled what she'd thrown at him when anger had been easier than everything else she felt.

"Yes, I am." Rook gave her another lopsided smirk, but it didn't reach anywhere near his eyes. Hollow, a ghost of bravado worn too thin. "Takes one monster to face another."

She opened her mouth to speak, to argue, to beg, to scream—

Movement.

The Hollowmire had gone still, that massive skull jerking up as its single burning eye fixed on nothing. On everything. Steam hissed through its teeth as it turned, drawn by the scent threading through the air on an invisible current.

Her. The spark of magic beneath her skin, a beacon to the thing that hungered to feed on it.

"Reny. Run." Rook's hand caught her shoulder one last time, guiding her focus back to him, anchoring her in the reality of what came next. He kissed her again, harder, more desperate this time, before he spun her around and shoved her away with both hands. "Go!"

Reny stumbled forward, catching herself against a tree, spinning back just in time to see him step out from behind the fallen trunks and underbrush, out from the fragile safety of their cover and into the creature's line of sight.

The Hollowmire's skull snapped toward him with unnatural speed. For one suspended moment, everything stopped. The forest held its breath.

And then it charged.

The last thing she heard before she ran—before the forest swallowed her whole and her own sobbing breath drowned out everything else—was the sound of it finding him. A roar that shook the earth, layered and endless, a symphony of the damned as the Hollowmire closed the distance in thundering strides.

And behind it, barely audible beneath the terrible cacophony—

Rook's voice. Steady. Defiant. Drawing its attention, buying her time.

Trying to make it right.

CHAPTER 40

The forest had all but devoured light.

What little remained sifted down in thin, stubborn bands between the silver pines, just enough to turn the ground into a quilt of ash and fading amber.

Reny ran as fast as she could, hearing only her boots striking the earth and the wild, drumming roar of her pulse in her ears. Her frantic thoughts had narrowed to a single command.

Run.

Pain came like a hook driven under her breastbone. It jerked her mid-stride, ripping the air from her lungs. She caught herself on a fallen trunk pitched across the game path, bile scorching the back of her throat from the agony of it. Doubled over, she could only hear the ragged rasp of her own breath and the now far-off sounds of ruin.

Tree branches breaking and that awful, haunting cry echoing in the distance.

"No," she told no one. The word barely formed, more breath than voice.

The hook tugged at her again, harder this time. An ache that called her back to him. It had always been there, that quiet pull beneath her ribs. A presence she'd forced herself to ignore out of necessity.

But the thought of him lingered like the shore's weary yearning for the tide. Now, the tether between them drew cruelly taut, her bones humming with a note she could not bear.

Bracing her forearms on the fallen log, she pressed her brow to the rough wood until the sting in her eyes lessened. Through the trees, the horizon smoldered the color of old copper before collapsing into darkness. Somewhere beyond that, the Veil waited. Safety waited.

He told her to run.

Her head snapped up as a branch cracked to her left. Only a squirrel, frantic and mindless, skittering across the trunk before vanishing into a darker slope of branches. She swallowed, willing her thundering heart to slow.

Past the ordinary stirrings of a forest nearing nightfall, the distant melee stuttered and surged with the unmistakable crash of a force too large and too wrong for the world it moved through.

A searing twinge behind her sternum again, forcing her to wince.

Rook.

"Damn you," she whispered, the words shaking as flashes of him blurred in her mind.

This isn't a choice.

Reny swung one leg over the log, then the other, landing on the rutted path with her hands braced on her knees. Heading toward the Veil, like he'd told her. One foot dragging in front of the other in a gruelling march forward.

Run, Reny.

Toward the north. Just a few hours.

Come with me.

The silver pines grew ancient and straight along this path like he said they would, their trunks like the pillars in a sacred temple. She pushed herself forward, every step uneasy as the ground tilted and dipped beneath her feet.

Go.

Her legs trembled with exhaustion, muscles burning from the sprint and the terror that had fueled it.

Maybe this is how I make it right.

Another step. Then another. The path blurred out of focus from the tears welling in her eyes.

If this is the price for falling in love with you, I'll pay it.

The tether thrummed, winding through her pulse until it became impossible to tell where her heartbeat ended, and his began. Every few strides, it gave a violent yank at her center, sharp and painful enough to make her stumble.

He'd made his choice before pushing her away, suppressed fear falling to grim resolve right before her eyes. The end of the line. He would make it costly, but it was the final stand.

I'll pay it.

Reny stopped moving, her hands finding the rough bark of a nearby pine to hold herself upright, legs nearly giving out beneath her.

She could go. Had every reason to. Could leave him to this noble end that he'd brought upon himself. The Veil offered safety, a wall to keep her separate from danger. From the invisible thread unspooling inside her. That strange, almost living thing connecting her to him that she could not explain.

Her fingers dug into the bark. The thought of crossing the next threshold without him, of stepping into sanctuary while he bled out somewhere in the deep, wild dark alone...

The air in her lungs turned to glass.

Movement in the mist to her right forced her attention upward.

A spectral shape emerged through the vapor between two black columns of trees. Antlers caught one of the final rays of dying light, gleaming like burnished bone. Massive and intricate, branching toward the darkening sky like the limbs of an ancient tree. Familiar.

The stag.

He stepped into a small clearing of silvered ground, hooves silent over the carpet of fallen needles. His coat shimmered, rippling between frost and shadow like an apparition half-born of the wild, half of a dream. Steam rose from his nostrils in long, ghostly ribbons that curled and dissipated into the collapsing twilight.

The forest held its breath. Their eyes met, and Reny forgot to take her own.

The stag's gaze was endless and timeworn, weighted with old wisdom. Older than the trees, than the mountains, than the sea. But those dark, fathomless depths held more than wisdom.

Grief.

Worn smooth by centuries of carrying it on the breadth of his back.

I know what lives in you.

The thought arrived without words, settling into her mind with stunning clarity. Not her own voice. Not any voice at all. Only grand understanding echoing in her ears.

I have always known you.

A different kind of ember, one that had been waiting deep within her, stirred and flared in answer. Power unfurled hot through her veins, quiet and luminous. Not the wild, destructive flames that burned through her when fear or fury took hold. This felt different. Older.

The stag did not move, but his bearing shifted, watching closely as Reny clenched and relaxed her fists, allowing the power to flow through. The ancient sorrow in his gaze deepened, and for one breathless moment, Reny felt the heaviness of it in her own chest.

Like bearing witness to a loss so vast it had shaped the very bones of the world.

Do not fail as I have.

Words still unspoken. But she felt them like a hand against her heart, urgent and gentle at the same time. A tremor passed through the clearing, a subtle whisper, the air quivering in its wake. The earth beneath her boots seemed to pulse with a great, slow heartbeat matching the rhythm thrumming through her bones.

She understood then.

This wasn't just a deer, if it ever had been at all. It was her omen. A calling.

The wild does not abandon its own.

The stag held her in its stare, long enough for the truth to settle into her marrow, long enough for her to feel the echo of his ancient vigil, before dipping his antlered crown. He turned then, the mist swallowing him whole just as the forest exhaled the breath it had held for them.

For her.

Time crashed back into her lungs. Violent, cold, and real.

Her hands fell away from the tree.

She had to go back.

The flame in her chest demanded it. This strange, terrible gift she'd spent so long trying to suppress wasn't meant to be run from. It was meant to be faced.

To be claimed.

And of all the divine forces rising with and against them, Reny knew in that moment she could not let Rook face any of them alone.

Rook gauged time by pain and by breath. Reny's breath in exchange for his pain.

He could accept that bargain.

If only to help him focus a while longer, he worked to suppress that relentless tether that bound him to her. The cruel stretching of it wrecked him more than what the Hollowmire had already done.

The smell of blood—Sal's and his—had grown oppressive. He needed to give her just a bit more time, needed to hang on a little longer.

Needed to get to his sword to do that.

The Hollowmire had the forest's colors matted in its pelt, carved from the very root and rot and the black water of the western swamps. The beast hit the undergrowth and shouldered through with its many-jointed limbs, reeking of carrion and caves.

Of everything that had ever died in pain and darkness.

Rook waited until the last possible heartbeat before rolling out of its path, his body knowing this dance like a perfectly balanced blade. The earth came up gritty and cold, but he was on his feet in a single motion, sprinting toward the ruin of leather and horse where the sword had to be.

He uttered no prayers to find it.

Didn't have the audacity to ask old gods he'd never cared to know for favors now.

His allotment of divine grace had run out years ago. But some small part of him, the long-lost, half-forgotten child of royal halls and ritual blood oaths, cataloged the scene before him with unspoken hope. The ghost of a plea to the skies above foolishly held between his teeth as he surveyed the chaos in front of him.

The stink of burst gut over wet earth, the torn girth straps half-buried in gore. And then... a shimmer.

There. Steel, half-hidden under saddle and torn flesh.

The long blade came free with the song of metal leaving the scabbard, familiar weight settling into his arm and shoulder like an old friend. He rose and turned with his feet in a wide, ready stance.

The Hollowmire faltered mid-lunge, banking with a low, guttural hiss, as if remembering an element it hadn't accounted for. It drew in the air through jagged teeth, tasting what lingered there. The scent forced it to pause.

The sword was beyond old, born of an age when the world itself had still burned with creation's fire. With the way its focus changed, the creature must have recognized the blade. Sensed the ancient power woven through the steel. Its pace slowed, becoming almost cautious.

"So," Rook let the weight of his voice steady his hands. "Here we are, again."

He braced. The magic in him had dwindled down to embers over the years, but even embers could catch and burn if the right wind found them. He let what remained of his power flare through his eyes, baring his teeth without smiling. The monster's head canted, drawn to the flicker like a moth to flame.

"Come on, you son of a bitch." His grip tightened on the hilt. "Hope you choke on it."

It obliged.

The Hollowmire lunged, an avalanche of rot tearing through the undergrowth. The forest floor broke under its force, earth and needles flung skyward as if the woods themselves tried to spit it out. Rook didn't give an inch, shifting just as it came, the blade meeting decay in a flare of silver light.

Steel bit deep into its shoulder, the impact ringing up his arm and into his jaw. For a moment, the world was nothing but sound. Metal grinding bone, the wet rasp of flesh that wouldn't bleed. Motes of pale light burst from the wound, scattering like fireflies trapped in a smoke cloud.

The Hollowmire's scream followed, its layered, grinding wail clawing its thousand voices to the sky. Its stench rolled over him in horrible waves. Swamp water, mass graves, and centuries of death compressed into a single, suffocating assault.

Then it struck.

A limb the size of a fallen oak caught Rook along the ribs. Agony cracked through him, bright and blinding, as the rest of the world fell away. He hit the ground hard but turned with the motion, letting it carry him along. He slid, rolled, and came up on one knee, every inhale torn loose and raw.

The sword remained in his hand, muscle memory refusing to let go even through the impact. The Hollowmire lunged after him, closing the distance with terrifying speed. Rook didn't have time to stand. He twisted from his knees and swung upward as the creature reared over him, the blade catching its underside in a desperate arc.

Steel sliced a long, shallow seam in the creature's belly. The air hissed where the wound yawned open, black ichor spilling thick and steaming. The blade shuddered in his grip, alive for a heartbeat. *Drinking.*

The Hollowmire reared backward, more in surprise than suffering, its gnarled limbs clawing for balance. Another rumble followed. Low, seething, and hungry.

Rook braced himself, one hand clamped over ribs he knew were broken. Each inhale tore through him, but his gaze burned as bright as the runes now pulsing along the blade in his hand.

He'd struck the damn thing. Not deep enough to kill—there was no such thing for a creature like this. But deep enough to draw its fury and keep it looking at him instead of hunting for her.

Beneath the rush of battle and the pain, he could still feel her. The impossible thread pulled tight, headed north. It had been a constant hum in his chest, but was finally starting to dull. He told himself it was because she'd gotten far enough away.

Not because of the weakness threatening to drag him down. Not because he was running out of time.

The Hollowmire's head tipped back, tasting the air to the north, tasting the magic it wanted to consume.

"Not her, you big, ugly bastard." Rook's growl carried the vicious command of a man who had once trained legions. "Me."

I'm right here. Come take your fill.

The Hollowmire answered his words, his thoughts, without hesitation.

It came for him again. A low lunge that twisted mid-strike, a forelimb whipping toward his waist meant to throw him. Rook swung to intercept.

The blade bit, then skated, the impact tearing him from his feet. He hit the forest floor rolling, pine needles sticking to his cheek, copper flooding his mouth.

He moved again on instinct alone.

The monster plowed through the space he had just occupied and slammed into an old oak. Bark exploded, the tree groaning like an old ship in a storm as it tumbled over. Rook's breathing sawed, not from fear, but from the demands of his body pushing every limit. He set his stance, adjusted his hold on the hilt, and let thought return only long enough to anchor him.

Keep it facing you. Give her minutes, as if minutes were coin and you were rich.

He was not rich. But he could still spend.

The Hollowmire turned, deliberate and terrible, its eyes wet pits of starlight. It lowered its head, and the air turned colder for it.

Rook's fingers tightened on the hilt. The last of the magic in him came forward, just enough to wake the blade's glyphs, the old runes tasting him in the open air. He promised the sword more if it behaved.

He promised his body nothing.

"You and I aren't so different, you know," Rook admitted, the words almost conversational over the rasp in his throat. "Both hollow. Both hungry. Both too fucking stubborn to die when we should."

The creature's head tilted, listening.

"But I have one thing you don't." Rook shifted his weight, feeling the broken ribs grind and pop, feeling the thread to Reny grow fainter still. "Something worth paying for."

The Hollowmire charged, the forest floor shuddering beneath it. Rook stepped in to meet it, blade angled, his body firmly planted.

This was the only truth he'd ever known besides her.

Violence with violence, blood for blood, time bought with flesh. He was ready.

Ready to pay, and pay, and pay.

They hadn't told Rhedda.

Brenn knew that would cost them later, but later was a luxury the Cliffs did not have if a Hollowmire was awake and hunting. The choice had been made before Elenna walked away. If a Hollowmire stalked this part of the Old Wood, it could not be allowed to nose its way back toward the Cliffs.

Not with the salted scent of their kin thick on the wind and the pulse of old magic thrumming through every stone, not with the Whisperfolk and the young ones sleeping unguarded in chambers carved into the open rock.

When he told Aric he'd go alone, the fox threatened to scream his plans to the sky. They left together shortly after, the last light bleeding from the horizon.

They wasted no time, running in their animal bones through the Old Wood until oak and birch gave way to silver pines, the change in the trees like a passage between worlds. Ancient trunks narrowed and stretched toward the darkening canopy, their bark pale as bone in the failing light. The undergrowth thinned, replaced by a carpet of fallen needles that muffled the world to rushed whispers.

In the bear's body, Brenn felt every shift of root and slope through the pads of his paws and points of his claws, the earth speaking in tremors up his spine. This form knew the forest as intimately as he knew the cliffs, reading the language written in soil and stone.

Aric flickered ahead in bursts of russet and shadow, soundless despite the speed, his tail a living flame cutting through the silvered dark. The fox's smaller frame granted him what the bear could not. Silence in motion, the ability to slip through spaces that didn't seem to exist until he'd already passed through them.

They ran without words, the old rhythm between shifters needing none. Decades of partnership had worn grooves into their movements, each anticipating the other's turns and pauses without conscious thought.

But the silence stretched too thin, their steps striking louder than they should even with the bed of needles beneath them.

Even the air tasted wrong.

Storm and char and copper had been forced together and left to rot. Not the clean sharpness of lightning-split wood or the mineral bite of rain on stone.

Corruption. Decay with a pulse.

The deeper they went, the more the smell pressed down on Brenn's chest until even his lungs rebelled at drawing another breath of the tainted air.

He slowed. A heartbeat later, Aric did the same.

Brenn's bulk shifted and halted at the edge of a shallow ravine where the pines grew wider apart, their roots exposed and gnarled across the slope. The scent hit them fully then. Blood, fresh and obscene, sprawled across the wind like an open wound. Not the simple tang of a hunter's kill or predator's feast, not the honest work of fang and claw claiming sustenance.

Slaughter. Desecration.

As if the earth itself had soured, decomposition turned inside out and left to fester.

Brenn lifted his muzzle, nostrils flaring wide, and turned toward the source. Aric had gone utterly still, belly low to the ground with every hair along his spine standing upright. The fox tested the air in short, careful inhales, amber eyes catching what little dying light still threaded between the pines.

Their gazes met without words. Only that shared, heavy understanding. *The Hollowmire was near. Too close to home.*

A low rumble built in Brenn's chest, resonating through the massive cavity of his frame. The Hollowmire did not belong anywhere, but certainly never here. These were the trees close to the cliff's edge, where the salt wind whispered through the branches and the magic of their people pooled thick in the soil. Not the putrid marshlands of the northwest, where things died and refused to stay that way. For a creature born of black water and blacker magic to come this far east, either it had been driven here by a greater threat, or it hunted a specific target.

Neither possibility offered comfort.

Brenn swung his massive head once toward the east, where the cliffs lay hidden beyond a few miles of forest and mist, where Rhedda waited in her private chamber unknowing, where the others slept, trusting him to keep the darkness at bay. Then he turned back to face what came from the west. There was no question about which way to go.

He would not, could not, allow it this close to home.

Aric fell in beside him, tail low, ears swiveling to catch the faintest disturbance in the suffocating quiet.

A tremor pulsed through the earth. A heavy weight advancing, slow but immense, each footfall registering like distant thunder. Brenn felt it in every joint, in the empty ache in his chest. The fox glanced up, muzzle flecked with frost from his own rapid breathing, and gave a small jerk toward the source. The bear answered with a single grunt.

Agreement. Acknowledgment. Promise.

Together, they moved. Through more silver trunks and air that smoked with their breath in the plummeting cold, they followed the scent of ruin threading deeper into the forest's heart.

Ahead, the wind shifted as a roar split the twilight. Not human, not beast, but a sound woven from agony and fury and ages older than both. The kind of sound that made Brenn's bones twist and his hackles rise instinctively. The sound of someone fighting for their life against a force that had no right to draw breath.

The Hollowmire had found its prey. And that prey still lived.

They both broke into a run, the bear's thundering gait and the fox's silent sprint converging on the source of that terrible roar.

CHAPTER 41

Reny kept to the narrow game trail, no longer running from fear but from the voice that lived in her chest. The one that sounded like him.

Run, Reny.

She could almost hear the bite of his tone, the one he used when trying to protect her, even from herself. Perhaps she would have obeyed if her heart hadn't rebelled against reason. If the fire in her hadn't already answered to a summons older than thought, older than fear.

And she was not known for following his instructions anyway.

Branches tore at her sleeves, needles grazing her face. The silver pines loomed higher, roots like bones clawing up through frosted ground. She dodged around them, vaulting over fallen timber, letting instinct lead.

Though she couldn't explain how, she could feel Rook weakening. The tether had thinned to a hollow tug at her core.

He was faltering. Reny's pace quickened, pushing her body to the brink.

"Hold on," she whispered. An order and plea.

The roar came again. More layered, deeper, folding in on itself until bark shivered on the trunks. She didn't cover her ears this time, using the sound to find him instead. And then she smelled the unmistakable copper stench of blood, the heavier rot beneath. The Hollowmire's breath carried on the wind. Her stomach lurched, but she clamped down until her teeth ached.

Finally, the forest broke open, forcing her to see it all at once.

The earth was slick, every root blackened with gore where Sal had fallen. Beyond that ruin, Rook was dragging himself upright, a long sword glinting oddly in his hand. His cloak had been torn off, blood darkening his tunic at his middle. He turned as the Hollowmire drew back to charge.

Reny's breath hitched, but she didn't cry out. She stood frozen among the trees, cold biting at her skin, watching it all unfold in brutal clarity.

The creature's next charge. The arc of its limbs. The exact place where his body would fall.

A horrific glimpse of a future she could not allow.

Rot and bone reared back as the Hollowmire readied to strike. In that instant, Reny called to the fire. Not with voice or even thought, but with the raw knowing, the part of her that had always been there. Her power answered, swift and merciless, rushing in until her body could barely hold it. Light seared white behind her eyes, through every vein.

Then came the flames.

They tore free from her hands in a violent burst, heat unfurling through the silver pines in flashes of gold and amber. Bark hissed and peeled away, needles reduced to ash, and the Hollowmire's stench was lost to smoke as it wheeled toward the blast.

Through the blaze, their eyes met.

Rage sharpened to a point as the creature turned away from Rook, its focus now on her alone.

The devastation on his face gutted her, the forest roaring with them both. Rook's voice was the last thing she heard before the Hollowmire surged forward.

Her name. Fury and heartbreak bound in one shattering cry that cleaved the world in two. But she stepped into the open anyway.

As he'd done for her.

Everything narrowed to that single step. Her boots crunching into dirt and stone. A hiss of breath she didn't realize she'd drawn.

Gods, no. She came back.

"Reny, no!" Rook lurched forward, hand outstretched as if he could push her back by will alone. "Get out of here!"

The Hollowmire's limbs moved like smoke through the underbrush, its black hide rippling. Its hellish eye fixed on her alone, glowing with unimaginable hunger.

Twin lashes formed from the light and fire in Reny's palms. Whips of molten gold snapped free, cracking through the air, striking the Hollowmire across the chest. It let out a raw, splintering cry—countless agonizing notes layered into one. Murders of crows burst in black clouds from the canopy, scattering in every direction above their heads.

Blazing, amber light cast every branch and trunk of the forest into an infernal silhouette. The Hollowmire stumbled and rolled, crashing through saplings and old logs, clawing at its own burning hide.

Rook dragged himself forward, vision swimming with red and gold and pain. He watched her burn bright enough to render the night into dawn. The sight broke and remade him.

Her eyes were gone, replaced by orbs of white light. Hers, but wholly other. Her face was expressionless, focus unyielding, as if she had become nothing but the fire itself.

The Hollowmire charged again, faster this time. A desperate blur of teeth and hungry darkness. Reny's flames snapped before lashing forward, but the arcs struck too wild, too wide, shattering against the ground directly behind the beast, scattering embers across the earth.

Rook moved before thought could catch him. He lunged with a hoarse shout, his sword igniting, runes flaring along the blade like liquid fire. As the creature barreled past him, he swung with every ragged ounce his body still held. The blade bit into the Hollowmire's flank, ripping loose a shriek that shattered the air.

It reeled and thrashed, screaming its tortured symphony. Still, Rook pressed on, as though his battered frame alone could be the wall between them. The Hollowmire reared, its limbs unfurling like black banners beneath the burning sky. With one cataclysmic sweep, it struck both ways, the blow of a storm made flesh. Reny was flung one direction, Rook the other. The world dissolved into smoke and soundless light.

But it was Reny who rose first.

Rook's breath came shallow, each inhale a blade drawn straight through him. As the haze bled from his sight and he came to his senses, he made out the Hollowmire towering above him. Vast and unholy, its shape blotting out her firelight. Its maw yawned slick and wide, the promise of demise inches from his face. The sword lay too far to reach. He flinched beneath the Hollowmire's shadow but didn't try to escape.

Not this time.

A strange calm washed over him instead. Warm, quiet acceptance. He turned his head, searching for her.

Wanting to see her just one more time.

Their eyes met through the heat-warped air, and for a heartbeat, time gifted them that small, final mercy.

Then Reny charged forward, her breath wild, face contorted in fury and focus. Desperate to master the magic that raged against her. The whips of fire writhed and gathered, their molten light twisting into shapes that refused to obey.

They flared brighter. Shrunk back. Grew larger.

Too much. Not fast enough.

The Hollowmire's layered shrieks lowered, dropping into a chorus of softer voices, all of them whispering promises of death only Rook could hear. Its open jaws began their descent over his throat.

A fitting end, he thought. *One monster ending another.*

Reny screamed. *The last sound he'd ever hear.*

But then the world erupted above him.

A massive shape collided into the Hollowmire's side. In an explosion of motion and sound, the beast was thrown from its place, rolling across the scorched forest floor in a charred cloud of ash. Rook lifted his head just enough to see what led the assault.

Another bear, smaller than the Hollowmire but still monstrous, had thrown it off him.

Air cracked, deeper than thunder, like stone splitting in the heart of the world. Heat poured from Reny in a rush that turned ground frost to steaming vapor. The twin lashes that had whipped and flailed moments before stilled and hovered, coiled like serpents awaiting a strike.

Rook couldn't look away. The white in her eyes wasn't light anymore. It was all fire, immense and divine, a furnace barely caged in flesh. Her skin looked thin as parchment held to flame, glowing amber beneath, every inch of vein threaded gold. The air around her bent, rippled, refusing to hold its shape. When she moved, she didn't rush. Each step was now unhurried, like time itself had learned to wait for her. The lashes rose, no longer desperate or wild. Executioners' blades.

Striking as one.

The first cinched around the Hollowmire's middle, searing through its rotten hide, thick smoke pouring from the wound. The creature convulsed, its thousand-voiced scream rising in a different kind of agony. Before the sound could crest, the second lash snapped forward, seizing it by the throat.

Forcing devastating silence.

Rook pushed himself upright on weak elbows. Night itself bowed to her, every shadow retreating through the trees to make room for her light. He could feel her power in his chest. Not just heat, but immense gravity, like standing too close to a cliff's edge.

Reny stopped, her expression carved from stone. Her fire tightened at her unspoken will, dragging the Hollowmire inch by terrible inch toward her. The creature thrashed, its limbs wildly clawing air, reaching for her, for anything. Her fire only constricted further, searing deeper into its decay. After another step forward, Reny's head tilted, studying the beast suspended before her. The Hollowmire convulsed once more in a final spasm of defiance. The flaming lash around its throat pulled impossibly taut.

Bone snapped.

The sound rolled through the clearing and echoed off the silver pines. The beast went limp, hanging in the fire's grip for one slow breath before her flames lowered it to earth. But instead of releasing it, Reny stepped closer, raising her palms skyward. Force gathered there like water building behind a dam about to break.

Her light shifted, no longer burning outward but pulling inward. Drinking liquid shadow from the corpse in threads that unspooled in the clearing like living night. A thousand sighs released at once from the Hollowmire's remains. The collective exhale of souls finally cut loose from their rot-bound prison. It filled the air, carried on winds that hadn't been there before.

Thread by thread, its dark essence flowed toward her palms. As it drew near, the black burned to gray, gray washed to silver, silver brightened to gold just as it vanished into her skin.

Rook pressed a hand to his side, squinting against her light. Along the tree line, the bear stepped back, one paw lifting as though to ward off a blow. The fox was impossibly still, amber eyes fixed and wild. Pupils blown wide, whites showing at the edges.

Reny drew in the last of the darkness in a single, blinding flash of gold. Her spine bowed, head tilting back as the power flooded through her, as if she might tear apart.

Too much force crammed into too fragile a vessel.

Gold and flame faded, seeping back into bone and blood and marrow. Her flames flickered, softened from blinding white to a warm, faint amber. When the last light guttered out, the forest surrendered to silence. Evening's shadows crept in, reclaiming what her light had stolen.

The white brilliance in Reny's eyes faded, allowing emerald, bright and familiar, to return. Before her, the Hollowmire was nothing but a pile of ash and chunks of bone.

Rook looked at the two animals still clinging to the edge of the small clearing, at the charred ground, at her still standing in the center of everything. Reny was swaying when their eyes met through the hanging smoke. Hers were unfocused, glazed with exhaustion, struggling to find him.

He saw her face the moment recognition landed. A brief, fragile spark of relief and peace. Her eyes rolled back, and she collapsed–the whole world along with her. Time stopped.

Rook moved.

He couldn't stand, but he could crawl, dragging himself through ash and mud and excruciating pain with a feral desperation. His elbows gouged trenches in the earth as he went, every inch a punishment. The world had narrowed to her alone, motionless in the dirt just ahead.

Nothing else existed.

Only her.

Whatever she'd done, whatever she'd become for those few moments, had drained her. Taken too much.

He reached her and dragged himself upright, pulling her into his arms the way he had that night in the tavern. Desperate, starved. Blood-slick fingers pressed to the hollow by her throat.

There. The faintest flutter beneath his touch. *Barely there.*

A sound tore from his chest. "Don't you dare. Don't you fucking dare. Reny."

Rook turned inward, clawing for any scrap of power left in his Aetherian blood, searching for anything he could give her.

Nothing. Only echoes of everything he'd already spent.

He drew her against him. For all the fire she'd commanded, her body was ice now, skin leeched of color. He folded forward, forehead resting against hers. Ash and smoke clung to her hair. He searched for the thread that connected them, the quiet pulse that had woven through his soul the day they met.

It was there, but fading like a candle flame caught in a heavy draft. He clung to it, begged it, willed it to hold as the wind stirred up ashes around them.

Heavy footsteps, men's boots across the clearing, broke the quiet behind him.

"Does she live?" The voice was a low, familiar boom, overriding the ringing in his ears.

Rook lifted his head toward where the animals had just been. His vision swam before the shapes resolved into two men. One tall, narrow-faced with hair like rusty iron. The other towering, broad, forest-eyed and furious, his presence filling the space like a mountain taking root.

Rook's voice was gravel. "She lives..."

A beat passed. He swallowed hard, the name landing bitter on his tongue.

"... Brenn of the Cliffs."

CHAPTER 42

T he ground was still hissing.

Brenn stood over them, over the ruin of the clearing. His gaze swept the aftermath. Smoke coiled from the earth in thin, spectral ribbons, carrying the mingled scents of blood, ash, and old magic.

He loomed in human form, his massive frame casting a long shadow across them. The moon hung high and cold at his back.

Reny's head rested limply in the crook of Rook's arm, her hair tangled and streaked with ash, her lips pale and bloodless. She might have been sleeping, if not for the wrong kind of stillness clinging to her like a shroud.

Rook drew her closer, his body folding protectively around her. Every breath rattled from his broken ribs.

"Does she know you as I do?" Brenn's voice was low, dangerous in how soft it was. A threat dulled only by careful restraint. A muscle twitched in his jaw.

Rook's breath hitched.

Brenn's cold pine-green eyes did not waver. "... *Vaelric* of Rithmor."

The name landed like a killing blow, worse than anything the Hollowmire had done to him. Rook's jaw clenched, his eyes falling to the blackened ground. He gave a single, weary shake of his head.

"No," he conceded, the admission a raw whisper. "She doesn't."

Brenn scoffed, the sound humorless, his expression carved from granite. "Your lies have no bounds, do they? What name do you wear this time, deceiver?"

Beside him, Aric stood rigid, jaw working, his focus fixed on Reny's still form. He looked like a man caught between reverence and terror.

Rook ignored the question, finally letting his eyes meet Brenn's. "She needs to be taken to the Veil."

"We take her to the Cliffs," Brenn growled. He adjusted the sheathed blade at his hip. "The Sentinels won't let you cross with a half-dead girl thrown over your shoulder. If you can even lift her in the piss-poor state you're in." His chin jerked toward Rook's side, where blood had soaked through and was now a slow, steady drip into the dirt.

Rook's teeth bared. "What can your kind even do for her?"

Aric broke from his stillness. He stepped forward, words sharp as any blade. "More than you can, Aetherian. We have healers, and more magic than you cursed bastards will ever understand."

Brenn extended an arm, a grounding hand settling on the fox shifter's shoulder. "Don't waste your breath. He's not worth it."

Aric jerked free of the touch, his fury too strong to contain. He stalked toward the charred edge of the clearing, boots crunching over the dark, brittle remains.

Rook watched him go, tension thick as the lingering smoke. When Brenn looked down again, his gaze found its mark like an axe blade.

"Your brother killed three of our kin recently. Including a leader in our ranks. A mentor. A man who outsmarted even *you* more than once." He paused. "Orwyn. The owl."

Owl.

Rook's stomach turned, bile rising in his throat.

"Aric was the only one to escape. The others were siphoned. Slaughtered." Brenn's stare offered no mercy. "All to feed your failing bloodline."

Rook's lips twisted into a faint smirk, defiance masking his despair. "Then why did you intervene? You could've let the Hollowmire end me right here."

"And let you get off that easily?" Brenn jerked his chin at Reny. "You're only alive because, for some godsdamn reason, she wanted you to be. Nearly burnt herself to death trying to keep you from your well-earned fate."

Rook's hold on her grew tighter, more possessive. "I told her to run."

"How noble of you," Brenn sneered.

The air between them hummed with their hate, but neither man moved, both too bound by what they couldn't undo. By the blood and history that stretched between their peoples like an uncrossable chasm.

Rook looked back down at Reny. With bloodied fingers, he gently tried to brush away black soot from her brow, but the effort only smeared crimson across her skin. He grimaced.

Brenn watched, something unreadable flickering across his face before it hardened again. He cleared his throat. "Let me take her."

"I'll be damned." Rook recoiled, the reaction instant, visceral, primal. A flash of canines, a flicker of gold beneath his lashes.

"You already are." A warning rumble answered from Brenn's chest, the sound more bear than man. "Don't be stupid, you Aetherian prick."

Rook's posture shifted, grudging acceptance bleeding through. He adjusted Reny in his arms one final time before Brenn stepped forward and knelt, scooping her up with surprising care. The breadth of him made her seem impossibly small, impossibly fragile, as he stood and let her settle against the fur of his vest.

Brenn gave a curt nod. "You're coming, too. She needs to hear the truth from your own tongue when she wakes, and the Cliff Mother seems to think you're worth talking to. Though I'll never understand why."

Without a word, Aric retrieved a sturdy branch from the forest floor and stalked over, planting it between him and where Rook knelt like a dare. Rook eyed it, his gaze narrowing despite the haze of exhaustion.

Brenn's snarl rolled through the clearing. "It's more kindness than we should give you. Now take it and get up."

Rook seized the branch and forced himself upright, every muscle screaming. His breath caught sharply, face draining of color, until he stood between the two men. It took everything in him to tear his focus from the sight of Reny cradled in Brenn's arms. Every blood-born instinct screamed at the sight of another man holding her.

They trudged forward, an unlikely trio bearing precious cargo through the rows of silver pines. Rook limped behind Brenn, weight balanced precariously between the walking stick and the stubborn pride that kept him moving. Every step sent white-hot pain through his broken ribs, threatening to buckle his knees.

He refused to let it show.

Reny's unbound hair no longer caught the wind like the defiant banner it had in the late-summer sun of River's Edge. Now, silvered by moonlight and ash, it hung like a white flag of surrender. Soft, defeated, beautiful in its ruin.

She didn't wake or stir. But she breathed—the smallest proof of her resilience. For Rook—and the humming tether buried inside him—that was enough.

Hours passed, marked by the moon's descent and the eerie dark just before dawn. Rook had slowed them considerably.

At some point, Aric grew too restless and took to his fox form, padding silently at Brenn's flank. His amber eyes caught stray threads of moonlight, watchful and wary as they wound through the forest trails. Brenn moved ahead, still carrying Reny against his chest. He paused now and then to check her pulse, to gently shift her weight, but he never faltered. His stride remained steady, the set of his jaw unyielding.

He never put her down. Never traded duties with Aric. None of them spoke as they moved through the evergreen giants toward the coast.

Until Rook stumbled. A misstep on the uneven trail jarred his ribs, sending pain ripping through him like fire. He caught himself between the walking stick and a nearby tree trunk, breath tearing from his chest in a guttural gasp.

When his eyes lifted, Brenn and the fox were both watching with a look that held no mockery. Only grim acknowledgment of weakness, of mortality, of the limits even pride couldn't overcome.

Rook straightened despite the agony, said nothing, and kept moving forward.

The air changed as the silver pines began to dwindle, outnumbered now by the occasional ancient oak or birch. The scent of sap faded, replaced by sea salt and woodsmoke. When the trees finally broke open in full, the world fell away to wind, water, and sky.

The Eastern Cliffs stretched vast and white along the edge of dawn. Far below, the sea clawed at the rock in bursts of foam and thunder, a sound both magnificent and monstrous. But it wasn't the ocean that caught Rook's breath and held it captive.

It was the light.

The cliffs themselves were alive with it. Torches burned along ledges and walkways, flickers of flame tucked into carved-out dwellings and narrow windows that dotted the rock face like stars. Ropes and ladders swung from ledge to ledge, an intricate labyrinth of bridges and hidden paths spiraling down toward the roaring surf.

A world he had never known existed. Never been close enough to see. A sanctuary hidden in plain sight, protected by magic and secrecy and the sheer audacity of its construction.

The horizon fractured with the first strike of day, bleeding red, pink, and indigo across the sea until they painted over the rock face. The sight blurred at the edges as bone-deep exhaustion sank its claws into him. His breath shuddered once, twice, catching on both pain and wonder.

The taste of salt touched his lips. Whether from the sea or his own tears, he couldn't tell.

The world tilted.

And then went black.

CHAPTER 43

T he Cliff Council chamber was quiet, save for the low crackle of
torches. Their light cast the stone walls in a warm amber glow,
chasing shadows across the tapestries that lined the room.

Each told a story older than the cliffs themselves. Woven depictions of
gods and monsters, of the forging of wind and earth, and the birth of the
first wild kin who walked between them.

Brenn sat at the round table of carved sandstone, elbows braced against
its edge. His attention traced the tapestry nearest his seat. The Lord of Air
and Stone, haloed in light and mountain range, surrounded by stags and
bears, foxes and ravens. The sacred kin of the old world. The scene came
to life in the torchlight with its intricate threads of moss-green and gold.

Across from him, Aric's fingers drummed an uneven rhythm on the
tabletop. One knee bounced beneath the table. Restless energy the fox
couldn't quite contain.

When the heavy door opened, both men looked up. Rhedda entered
with poise, her shadow stretching long behind her before the torches
claimed it. She stopped a few paces from the table, her eyes anything but
soft on the pair before her.

"The healers will be able to help them," she said, her tone certain. "Both
will survive."

Brenn huffed—half disbelief, half exhaustion—but didn't bother to
speak.

Rhedda's stare sharpened, the lines of her face deeply set in reprimand.
She folded her arms across her chest. "You did not tell me you were
leaving the Cliffs."

"There was no time." Brenn's words were clipped. "We heard a Hollowmire hunted nearby and needed to drive it from the borders. Found
those two in the process."

He leaned back in his chair, wood creaking beneath his weight. Rhedda
regarded him, tired blue eyes scanning his face. The stern lines around her
mouth softened a fraction, just enough to betray deeper thought behind
her disapproval.

Aric's restraint broke. He struck his fist against the tabletop. "Do you realize what we've done by bringing that Drayvien monster here?"

Brenn's gaze dropped to the table.

Rhedda turned to Aric, shaking her head. "Only the three of us in this room know what the second-born looks like. Have either of you told anyone?"

Brenn grunted. "We came straight here after leaving them with the healers."

She held his stare, the question unspoken.

He scowled, arms folded tight across his chest. "I didn't give their identities. But he can't stay here, Rhedda. Let him recover for one day, then we cast him back to the Old Wood."

Rhedda's chin lifted, her authority clear in every word. "We do no such thing. He stays. That's an order, bear."

Both reprimand and reminder of rank landed heavily on his chest.

"Neither of you will speak his real name within these stone halls." Her attention swept between them. Expectant. "Do I make myself clear?"

Aric's composure was gone, his focus fixed on Rhedda's face with unforgiving judgment. Cliff Mother or not. "What are you thinking?" His words trembled beneath a sharpened edge. "The man has killed our own, Rhedda. We are giving sanctuary to one of our greatest enemies."

Brenn felt the same anger and all that lay beneath it. Pain and grief, wounds too fresh for any of them. The muscle in his jaw pulled tight. He didn't speak, unable to find it in himself to defend her decision as he would normally do. The silence he held was a reluctant offering. A space for her to give the explanation and justification that he could not. *Would not.*

Rhedda's expression didn't waver. "The answers will come in time, Fox. What he's done cannot be undone, but he may be the key to our future. He is not his brother."

Aric let out a shocked, humorless chuckle. "Do you hear yourself? Have you lost your mind to the mirror at last?"

Brenn shifted in his chair, uneasy, but held his tongue.

Rhedda slammed her fist against the table, her patience gone. "You will watch your mouth, Aric." Leashed thunder caught in every word. "I know your heart breaks, but you will not disrespect me in this chamber or any other."

Aric rose, amber eyes flashing as he looked between them. "I will keep this to myself for now. But I will not hesitate to put him down myself if I think any of us are threatened."

Brenn met his friend's eyes, trying to say with his gaze what he could not speak. Aric held the look.

"And still, Korva remains missing, and you've hardly said a word of her." Aric's attention burned across to Rhedda again. "This is not disrespect, Rhedda. This is truth. Your priorities aren't in the right order." With that, he stormed from the chamber, the stone hall devouring the sound of his footsteps.

Rhedda stood unmoved, watching his exit with a face that gave nothing away. She turned to one of the ancient tapestries, silence stretching between them long after Aric's anger faded from the corridor.

"Brenn." His name broke the hush, weighted with unspoken questions.

"He won't do anything. But he has every right to be upset with you." Brenn rose to his full height and crossed the room, stopping at her side. He leaned close, tone hushed but honed by defiance. "But I am with him. If I suspect a threat, I will kill the Aetherian while smiling."

A beat passed. He released the words he'd been holding for too long. "Prophecies be damned."

Rhedda did not answer. She stared ahead, shoulders rigid, refusing to acknowledge his declaration. Brenn let the words hang a moment more, then turned and left the council chamber. His footfalls echoed away, every step a quiet, deliberate rebellion.

The tapestries of the old gods watched on in their woven, solemn silence.

Rook had no sense of how much time had passed.

His mind had been a churn of shadows and half-heard voices. Echoes above him, words he could not decipher. Between them, fever dreams. Violent flashes of memory he would have given anything to forget. When consciousness finally returned, the pain in his body had dulled to a distant throb.

The world around him was suffocatingly quiet.

He lay on a narrow cot, a coarse blanket drawn over him. A single torch burned beside the door, its light flickering with a strange, ethereal hue. Not quite fire but warm all the same.

The walls, all smooth stone, seemed to drink in sound. No footsteps reached him. No murmured voices from beyond. Not even the faintest echo, though his Aetherian hearing strained for it. His thoughts regained clarity on one thing only.

Reny. Where was she?

Rook pushed himself upright, a hand braced against his bandaged side. The movement sent a pulse of pain through his ribs, made tolerable by what he assumed was healers' work. No longer the searing agony he remembered.

Someone had bathed and redressed him. A plain tunic, loose trousers, dry socks. All clinging to skin that still felt feverish. His boots sat neatly by the cot's corner, cleaned and ready. He took his time lacing them, every tug of the leather sending dull aches rippling through his torso.

When he finally stood, the room tilted before he righted himself.

The door loomed across the chamber, an arch of stone around thick, dark wood reinforced with iron at the seams. He expected it to resist him.

But when he reached for the handle, it turned. The door creaked open to reveal a vacant corridor beyond. Long, silent, carved in the same pale, seaside rock. Torches lined the walls at even intervals, their glow strangely alive.

No guards. No footsteps. Nothing but the echo of his own breath.

The corridor was thick with the scent of salt, incense, and woodsmoke. Rook stepped from the threshold, shadows folding over his shoulders like a cloak. Cool air brushed his skin, carrying the ghost of sea wind from somewhere beyond. He moved without sound, passing doors carved into the stone. Each one marked another space he couldn't see, another possibility of where she might be.

If she was here at all.

He reached inward, searching for that thread between them. It was there, but muffled. *Distant.*

Turning a corner, he glanced one way and then the other, just before cold steel brushed the base of his spine. Rook stilled and lifted his hands. A glance over his shoulder confirmed what instinct already knew.

Brenn stood behind him, dagger drawn, torchlight igniting his gaze.

"Where the hells do you think you're going?"

Rook's mouth twitched into a half-smirk, more threat than charm. "I have no idea where I'm going. Is this how you treat all your guests?"

"You're not a guest." Brenn sheathed his blade, though his fingers hovered near the hilt. "You're a problem I haven't decided how to solve."

Rook let his hands fall, turning to face him fully. "Where is she?"

For a long moment, the only answer was the wind's faint howl through the corridor.

"In one of the healers' chambers," Brenn said at last. "She lives. But she hasn't yet opened her eyes."

Whatever air Rook had drawn left him slowly, his expression faltering despite every effort to hold it in check. Something flashed in Brenn's face—recognition, perhaps, or reluctant understanding—before it hardened again.

"How long?" Rook's voice had quieted, its earlier edge lost to weariness.

"Three days."

"Take me to her."

Brenn's frown deepened. "The healers prefer space when they work." The shifter's reply was far gentler than Rook expected.

Rook's jaw flexed, the muscle fluttering beneath the dim light. His hands curled into fists, his grip on control a fragile, failing thing.

"I can respect that," he ground out, forcing civility. "But I ask this of you, Brenn." The words threatened to fray, no longer armor or knife but plea. "Please. Take me to see her."

Brenn hesitated only a heartbeat longer before exhaling sharply through his nose. "Fine. But stay close."

He led the way down the opposing corridor, his gait heavy and sure. Rook followed, matching the bear's stride the best his body could allow. The passage wound deeper into the cliffs until the stone walls gave way to an open courtyard.

Light struck him first. Bright and unfiltered after the dark hallway, the sun hung high, throwing gold on the faces of the cliffs where the sea wind whipped through. It carried salt and chill, biting clean through its warmth.

Brenn didn't slow. They crossed the yard and stepped back into the rock. The walls in this passage were broader, airier, veined with sunlight filtering through narrow slits.

Everything was softer here. Sweet herbs and dried flowers and burning incense. Bundles of greenery hung from wooden beams overhead, leaves rustling whenever the breeze stirred. Stone pots lined the corridor's base, each one spilling color and fragrance. A vivid rebellion against endless white and gray.

Rook's pace slowed despite himself, the unfamiliar gentleness unsettling after so much blood and destruction.

As they rounded a corner, movement caught his attention.

A child hiding along the wall, crouched between pots of greenery. A narrow shaft of sunlight fell through a carved opening in the ceiling, painting her in gold.

Rook saw the ears first. Too large, too pointed for any Aetherian child. Her skin was pale cream, her gaze wide and bright as spring leaves. She looked almost unreal. A creature shaped from pure sunlight and curiosity. She lifted her head as they approached, her smile flashing quick and unafraid. First to Brenn, then to him.

Rook froze mid-step, her ethereal stare wholly disarming. It felt older than it should have been, despite the innocence of the face that carried it. Rook managed a nod, awkward and uncertain under her study.

Brenn slowed when the child sprang upright. She wore simple linens the color of sage, her feet bare, toes and soles smudged with dirt.

For a heartbeat, light shimmered behind her—an almost-invisible flicker of wings, so thin and delicate it might have been a trick of the eye. But when she stepped through the shaft of sunlight, they caught the beam and glimmered before vanishing again.

Rook blinked, wondering if he'd hallucinated.

She smiled widely and started toward him with comfortable ease, blissfully unafraid. Her fingers wrapped around his pointer finger—warm, startling for how gentle.

Brenn huffed with immediate disapproval, but even that softened into a reluctant smile when she took his massive finger in her other hand.

The sight left Rook baffled. These two figures who couldn't stand one another, carved of shadow and legend, held together by the delicate grip of a girl no taller than their knees.

Brenn rolled his eyes. "Whisperfolk orphan," he muttered. "No one knows her true name, so we just call her Edie."

Whisperfolk?

An echo from another age. Rook's wonder broke through the weary lines of his face. He had thought they were long gone. Hunted to extinction for their gifts, the ancient art of bending thought and memory, and for their blood.

The same blood the Drayviens had used to make whisperink for centuries.

He looked down at her, unable to hide the awe that rose unbidden. And the underlying guilt.

Brenn sighed and started forward again. Edie held fast to both men, her small shuffling steps leading them through the corridor.

"She's taken a shine to the flame-touched girl," Brenn offered over his shoulder. "Spent most of her time by her bedside. I keep shooing her off, but she keeps going back."

The child tilted her chin up to Rook, the spring green of her eyes catching the light. She held the look for a heartbeat, then flashed a wide, toothy grin—mischievous, unguarded.

Impossibly, wonderfully alive.

He felt the answering curve of his own mouth before he could tamp it down. Brenn glanced at the exchange but said nothing, his silence a small allowance.

Edie led them onward, her bare feet whispering over the stone, her little hands swinging theirs as they walked. They stopped before a large wooden door carved with curling vine work and old sigils worn smooth by salt air and time.

Before Brenn could lift a hand to knock, the girl raised her tiny foot and pressed her bare toes against it.

The door swung open. Not forced, but gently guided. Warm light spilled out to meet them, rich and golden, carrying the scent of flowers, herbs, and fresh spring water. The chamber was alive with color and daylight. Ferns spilled from stone alcoves, pale vines reaching toward the sunlit ceiling. A slender waterfall traced down one wall into a shallow basin, its trickling music filling the space.

Two women stood near the basin at a narrow table, sleeves rolled to the elbow, hands busy mixing crushed herbs with oil. They glanced up when the group entered, faces softening into knowing smiles before returning to their work. Edie released the men's fingers and ran toward them, her laughter brightening the room.

At the chamber's center, surrounded by light and life, lay a bed draped in white linens. Reny rested there. Still, but not lifeless.

Her hair fanned around her like spilled flame, her face touched by the sunlight pooling across the bed. She was propped slightly upright on a stack of pillows, her chest rising and falling in soft, even breath.

Brenn's jaw tightened when his gaze found her. He shoved his hands deep into his pockets and gave the healers a brief nod. They paused their mixing, exchanged pointed looks, and slipped to the far corner.

Rook didn't move.

He stood rooted near the threshold, his shadow stretching long across the sunlit floor. The sight of her stole all his strength, hollowing the air in his chest until every breath felt heavier than the last.

A soft giggle broke the hush. Edie slipped between the healers and darted toward the bed, clambering up with a bounce big enough to stir the linens. One of the healers chided her gently in a language Rook didn't know. Even her words faltered into a smile when the child's laughter rang out again as she flopped down against Reny's side and snuggled in.

Brenn exhaled through his nose. Equal parts irritation and affection. He crossed the room in a few strides, the motion easy and practiced.

"Come on, little pixie," he grumbled. He slid massive hands beneath Edie's arms and lifted her free, earning a squeal of protest that turned to delighted giggles when he placed her on his shoulder. Her toes wiggled at his chest, sunlight catching in the stray wisps of her light brown hair.

She looked down at Rook, grinning widely, but the sadness in his face dimmed the reflection of her joy. Brenn adjusted the girl's weight and stepped close, his expression serious even as her fingers worked to muss his thick sweep of pepper-black hair.

"I'll give you one minute," he said beneath Edie's laughter, edged with warning. "I'll be right out there."

Rook inclined his head, the motion sincere.

Brenn ducked through the doorway with Edie still perched on his shoulder, her laughter echoing until it faded into the hum of the cliffs.

The healers hesitated by the corner. One murmured something soft—blessing or comfort, he couldn't tell—and both women offered smiles too kind for the weight in his chest. Then they, too, slipped from the room, closing the door behind them.

Silence claimed the chamber, gentle as Reny's sleeping breath. Rook's eyes found her where she lay beneath the spill of sunlight. With forced effort, he crossed the space. One step after another, each one loosening the despair clenched too long inside him.

There was a sudden jolt in his chest. That thread pulling cruel and taut between them once again. A pain he now welcomed, even when it seared. It meant she was still there, still tied to him in a way he didn't fully understand but craved. He sank onto the edge of the bed, the mattress dipping beneath him.

"There you are." The words escaped him like an exhale.

His hand hovered, suspended between hesitation and need, before finally surrendering. He reached out and brushed the side of her face with his fingertips.

She was warmer than she'd been the last time he saw her. The pallor was gone, color and life returned to her skin. Relief struck him hard and caught in his throat—a half cry, half breathless laugh—before he forced it back down into stoic silence.

He found her hand beneath the sheets and gathered it into his own. Turning it over, he traced the inside of her wrist, following the blue rivers beneath her skin until he reached her palm.

There, a scar pale as moonlight. A perfect circle where that power had emerged. He stared at it, thoughts and memories pressing heavy behind his ribs.

Was this to be the price, then? To love a woman who might never wake?

Before his thoughts could drown him, a soft knock sounded against the doorframe.

"She will wake, second-born. I have seen it."

Rook's head snapped toward the doorway.

A woman stood in the open doorway, tall and still, wrapped in a shawl marked with silver sigils that shimmered in the sunlight. Jewels winked from the white braids that fell across her shoulders, each one etched with runes of its own. Her gaze, pale blue and terribly wise, held him with a knowing that made the air between them shift.

The Cliff Mother had come to speak with him.

CHAPTER 44

T he Cliff Mother approached, her steps soundless over the pale stone floor. Her hands were clasped before her. She stopped on the far side of Reny's bed, gazing down in quiet reverence.

She looked at Rook. He kept his expression still, willing to endure whatever allowed him to remain by Reny's side. *No matter what that meant.*

"I suppose you know who I am," she said softly.

He inclined his head. "I know you're called Cliff Mother, but I assume you have another name."

A faint smile touched her lips. Her eyes moved over him slowly, assessing.

"My name is Rhedda," she said at last. "You may call me what you wish." Her tone was patient, almost amused. "And what is it that I shall call you?"

"Rook." His focus drifted back to Reny, to the rise and fall of her breath. "But you know my other name, don't you, Seer?"

Quiet stretched between them, filled only by the trickle of water into the basin. He met her eyes again over Reny's still form.

Rhedda's smile deepened. It was unexpectedly warm, given the centuries of violence between their kinds.

"I know exactly who you are. I have for a very long time."

Storm-filled eyes returned to the bed, tracing the familiar lines of Reny's face, willing her to wake. "What have you seen, then? Do you know how this ends?"

A low laugh slipped through Rhedda's composure. "No one knows how this ends, not even me. Not even the oldest windows into the world could show us such things."

Rook huffed a sound that might have been a chuckle, if it weren't so tired. "Then what kind of Seer are you?"

Rhedda laughed outright, the sound unrestrained. "The kind of Seer who knew a girl somewhere in the Southlands carried the Flame of Becoming. And the kind who knew better than to have you beheaded at our highest cliff edge upon your arrival here three days ago."

Rook regarded her with one hesitant, sidelong glance. "The Drayviens slaughtered your kind," he said. "Me being one of them. For a time."

"Yes, until you had a change of heart. Then you began to find reasons to avoid it, did you not?" Her pale eyes held his, openly curious.

Rook said nothing. Instead, he pressed a kiss to Reny's knuckles and tucked her hand beneath the blanket. Slowly, he rose from the mattress.

"Perhaps I did. It doesn't change the lives I stole, though." He held her stare across the bed. "So why order my safekeeping?"

"Well." Rhedda folded her hands behind her back as she strolled to the foot of Reny's bed. "Much to my second-in-command's dismay, you play an important role in all this."

"All this?" Rook's brow arched.

"The prophecy." Rhedda nodded as if he should already know. When he offered only a blank stare, her face softened into something like exasperated sadness. "Of the Flame's true reason for return. To remake the world and unite the realms?"

Rook shook his head.

She drew a breath, letting it settle into the silence. "You truly don't know, do you, prince? I hadn't realized just how far the Aetherians have fallen into madness." Her hands clasped and unclasped as she began a slow pace across the floor. "Or how much the Drayvien monarchy altered history, erased the most sacred of the divine teachings to serve their own ends. How much was lost."

Rook's jaw tightened. "I never paid mind to the tales of supposed gods who abandoned us. I served the crown. I served my people."

Rhedda's eyes darkened, her previous warmth fading to grave resignation. "The same people your father chose to starve. Not only of food, but of magic too. That's what happens when you make bargains with the god of undoing."

His head shook as though trying to dislodge the words. "What are you talking about?"

"When the gods fell silent, you were taught it was abandonment." Each word fell carefully. "But silence was never abandonment. It was a consequence."

Rook's brow furrowed deeper.

"Your magic and immortality waned." Rhedda paced along the foot of the bed. "Your crops withered. The Aetherian lands began to rot from the inside out. It did not happen by fate or famine. Or by any ill will from Endaria or the Cliffs, Rook. It happened by choice."

"Choice?" His throat felt unnaturally dry.

Rhedda stopped, facing him fully. "Your father and his firstborn turned your realm, and its souls, over to Malorith, the god of death and undoing. Through ritual."

Rook's face paled. His hands gripped the footboard of Reny's bed until his knuckles went white.

Rhedda's voice softened, but she did not relent. "They fed him your strength, your magic. They let him drink from the veins of your people and land, all to buy what they were promised. Immortality without limit, dominion, the power of gods when he rose again."

"That's not possible." He shook his head. "The tales said Malorith was imprisoned—bound in stone—"

"Yes." Rhedda's interruption was soft but immovable. "And they were deceived into giving him a path to freedom. A way to shatter the prison from within, using magic and lifeblood as the key to undo the lock. Every decay that spread through your land was not a curse, Rook. It was merely the cost of your father's bargain."

She paused, her attention shifting toward Reny.

"Malorith seeks to walk the world again. To become what he calls the One Eternal. Divine command over the living and the dead. And to do that, he needs the Flame of Becoming." Another pause. "The last ember of Aurelia. The first of the Four Pillars."

Rook's attention snapped to Reny. To her, still and peaceful in sleep.

"Her." His throat worked, pulse hammering beneath his skin. "The ember is hers."

Rhedda's tone eased, though the sadness beneath it was vast. "You were used, and you were lied to, second-born. If he breaks free from his prison and walks this world again, he will come for her. One way or another, he has always been coming for her."

"I won't allow it." Words tore from him before he could temper them.

She smiled at him. "It's not up to you. It's up to her."

Rook looked from Reny to Rhedda, a fierce spark lighting his eyes. "What does that even mean? She's human—how could she possibly—?"

"Is she?" Rhedda tilted her head, mischief flickering over her face.

Rook's mouth opened, but no words came.

Amusement tugged at her lips. "Was it not you, Vaelric Drayvien of Rithmor—full-blooded Aetherian—who walked in a human's form for over a year in Endaria? Just a trick of simple spell work."

Rook pressed a hand to his temple, the throbbing there relentless. Everything he'd known was crumbling.

"I have not seen what she chooses or what she becomes." Rhedda's sigh carried unbearable weight. "But within her lies the key to either our salvation or our unmaking. A new world, or the end of it."

The hush that followed fell heavy between them.

"What does this have to do with me?" Rook finally managed.

Rhedda crossed to the window, where sunlight streamed through in golden shafts.

"Tell me, Rook," she said at last, not turning to face him. "What do you know of the Four Pillars?"

He frowned, searching through fragmented memories and half-forgotten lessons and bard songs. "Creation myths. Aurelia was the first, the Flame of Becoming. And Malorith, of course. There were the others, but..." He trailed off, the rest lost to time and his family's deliberate assault on history.

"The Lord of Air and Stone," Rhedda said, her words taking on the cadence of stories told by firelight. "The Keeper of the Wild. Aurelia's chosen mate." She turned to face him. "The one who gave breath to the sky and roots to the mountains. Who taught the first kin to shift between forms—to walk as both beast and being." She held his gaze. "Do you know what became of him?"

Rook gave no answer.

"The texts say he gave himself to the world when the Veil was forged. Poured his essence into the boundary between realms so it would hold." She stepped closer. "But the ancient songs say something different. They say he would return when the Flame did. Embers cannot burn without the breath to kindle them, without stone to ground them."

"Ancient songs," Rook said quietly.

"The Flame needs the earth," Rhedda insisted, passion igniting her words. "Air to kindle it. Stone to shelter it. The wild heart to guard it, inspire it." She paused, letting each phrase find its place in him like prayer. "The ember cannot burn alone, Rook. It never could. That was always the lie your family told. That power could be seized, hoarded, bent to someone's will."

Rook's jaw worked, every muscle tight. "What are you saying, Seer?"

"I'm saying," Rhedda replied, "that the gods did not simply vanish. They became fragments scattered like seeds, waiting for the right soil, the right season. Echoes through time, just waiting for someone to listen." She came to stand across from him, Reny sleeping between them. "I'm saying that when you chose her over everything else, even if it meant your death, perhaps it wasn't truly a choice at all. Perhaps it was simply... remembering."

"Remembering." Rook looked down at Reny, at the way the sunlight caught in her hair and made it shine like captured flame. His hand reached for her without conscious thought.

"Are you trying to say," he managed, voice rough, "that I'm the echo of Aurelia's mate, then?" Rook scoffed. "The fates wouldn't give that to a darkness like me."

"Do storms not bring black clouds that carry the rain to nourish the land?" Rhedda's look bore into him, unrelenting. "There is darkness in all of us, Rook. The question is not whether you've walked through shadow. It's whether you emerged still carrying light."

Stillness settled between them, heavier now.

Rook shook his head, unwilling to accept it. "I can't believe that."

A new sound broke through. Raspy with sleep, but strong enough to cut through everything.

"Believe what?"

Both swung toward the bed. Reny had pushed herself farther upright against the pillows, one hand against her temple, her face tight with pain. Her eyes struggled to focus as they shifted between Rook and the stranger standing across from him.

Reny was awake.

CHAPTER 45

T he chamber erupted with movement.

Rook sank down next to Reny's bedside as Rhedda swept toward the door, summoning the healers with calm command. Brenn followed close behind, coiled tight. Aric had joined him but kept to the room's farthest edge, every line of him rigid as the healers surrounded the bed.

Reny tried to surface through the blur. Voices overlapped, hands brushed over her, a dozen unfamiliar words traded between the women tending her. The language was foreign, melodic in her ears. Rook reached for her, but one of the healers pressed him back with gentle hands. Their eyes met only in fleeting intervals, when shifting bodies allowed.

In the commotion, a small figure slipped closer. Edie, barefoot and curious, crept from the doorway until she stood at the end of the bed. Wide green eyes found Reny's. The girl smiled, and Reny, despite all the confusion and pain in her head, found herself smiling faintly in return. It was the only approval Edie needed. She climbed onto the bed and curled herself neatly at Reny's feet like she belonged there.

Rhedda murmured to the healers in their tongue. They answered with firm shakes of their heads, words clipped but respectful as they gestured to the bowls of crushed herbs. Their expressions made clear: the work was not finished.

The Cliff Mother's mouth pressed into a thin line, but she nodded her acceptance. A tip of her chin directed the men toward the door. Brenn caught Aric's eye, an unspoken agreement passing between them before both went single file into the corridor.

Rook didn't move.

Rhedda's gaze settled on him as a gentle hand landed on his shoulder. "We'll see her soon. Let's give them time to finish their work."

His frown deepened as he watched the healers speak softly to Edie, who obediently slid aside. They eased the blankets away and coaxed Reny upright. Her limbs trembled, motions fragile after such a long sleep. One healer supported her back while another checked her pulse, murmuring observations.

He hesitated, every instinct a tether refusing to break. At last, with a rough exhale, Rook stepped back and followed the others into the hall.

Rhedda closed the door behind her, sealing off the healers' voices. When she faced them, three pairs of eyes were waiting. Rook's, shadowed and fierce. A few feet beyond him, Brenn and Aric stood shoulder to shoulder, their faces hard as drawn blades.

Aric's fingers drummed once against his thigh. Brenn's jaw was set, shoulders squared as though bracing for impact.

Rhedda motioned for them to follow, her pace brisk as she led them down the corridor. None of the men spoke, boots on stone the only sounds between them. She reached the last door at the hall's end and pushed it open without pause.

The chamber beyond was modest but warm. A small sitting room lined with worn plush chairs and a deep couch, a table strewn with books and half-spent candles melting into their trays. Bundles of dried sage hung from the ceiling beams, their scent mingling with old leather and beeswax.

"Sit." By Rhedda's tone, it was no suggestion.

Each man obeyed. Brenn and Aric claimed the couch. Rook remained apart, lowering himself into a high-backed chair on the far side of the room. He rested an elbow on the armrest, fingers brushing his jaw in restless thought.

The quiet stretched.

Aric broke it first. His amber gaze traveled between Rhedda and Rook before landing on the man across from him. "So," he drawled, the casual tone sharpened to a point, "when are you going to tell her?"

Rook looked up. Brenn and Aric were both watching him now.

"You're fucking joking," Rook bit out. His hand dropped from his jaw, body tensing in the chair. "She just opened her eyes."

Rhedda looked between them, brow lifting.

Brenn caught the look and answered it with grim clarity. "He needs to tell her who he really is."

Rook's entire frame went rigid, the casual lean transforming into something dangerous.

"And what," Rook said, each word sharp, "would be the proper timing for that particular revelation, in your expert opinion? Before or after she's recovered from nearly dying?"

"Before she falls into a lie any deeper than she already has," Aric shot back. "Before she wakes up one day and realizes the man she's trusted is—"

"Is what?" Rook leaned forward, a predator straining against its leash, every muscle singing with threat. "Say it, fox. Finish that sentence."

Aric held his ground, amber eyes blazing. "A Drayvien. The second-born prince of the very kingdom that's been hunting her. The brother of the man who wants her power. Or worse."

Power rippled off Rook, a tangible threat.

"You think I don't know that?" he asked. "You think I haven't carried that every single day since I met her? That I don't see my family's sins written everywhere?"

"Then tell her," Brenn rumbled, the words like stones grinding together. "Stop hiding behind your excuses and tell her the truth."

Rhedda's voice cut through. "And what exactly would that accomplish right now?"

Both shifters turned toward her, disbelief flashing across their faces. Aric's composure faltered, his mouth parting, for once left speechless. A sound tore from Brenn. Deep, animal, the growl of a creature forced to sit still when every bone urged action.

Rhedda didn't flinch. She met their stares, shoulders drawn back.

Aric let out a short, cold laugh. "Seers are supposed to be carriers of wisdom and truth. And you're standing here defending his lies."

"I'm defending strategy," Rhedda corrected. "There's a difference between lies and the timing of truth."

"Timing," Aric repeated, the word bitter on his tongue.

The change in Rook was inevitable. Any hint of warmth bled away until only the merciless shadow of him remained. The same one that had cut through the mercenaries in the woods. Molten gold flared in his Aetherian eyes. One hand curled around the armrest, knuckles white against the dark leather.

"How and when I tell her," he said, voice gone cold, "is none of your business."

"When you're within my Cliffs and among my people, your deceit is absolutely my fucking business." Brenn's voice thundered, nearly shaking the candles in their trays.

"Whose Cliffs, Brenn?" Rhedda's voice fell like a hammer from across the room.

Brenn didn't answer, but the wound showed on his face despite every effort to hide it.

"Whose people, Brenn?" she pushed, softer now but no less pointed as she crossed her arms.

No one spoke.

"As long as I am Cliff Mother," Rhedda continued, "these cliffs, these people, and these decisions are mine to make."

The challenge was laid bare. Not cruel, but absolute.

Aric's snarl tore through the air before anyone could respond. "Then maybe you shouldn't be." The words landed like a stone in still water.

Rhedda's gaze fell on the fox, her face unreadable. Quiet in assessment, as though looking at a problem that had finally revealed its shape.

Across from them, Rook's temper unwound. The storm in him banked as he watched the discord play out, guilt seeping into his chest. This division, this break in their unity, was the fault of his presence.

His secrets and lies.

He sighed and leaned forward, elbows resting on his knees, the motion heavy with fatigue. "Stop this."

Three faces turned toward him.

"She deserves to know," Rook admitted, the words costing him. "She will know. All I ask is that she has some time to recover from what happened. From what we saw her do." He paused, gaze distant. "I knew of the fire. But never in my years, and I'd wager not in any of yours, has anyone, least of all one in a human's body, siphoned and transformed a Hollowmire's power."

The admission shifted the room. Aric and Brenn's anger didn't disappear, but it receded. Aric's eyes dropped first, the fight draining from his frame. Brenn followed, both men suddenly lost to the memory of that moment in the clearing.

"She... what?" Surprise carved across Rhedda's features. She looked between her men, then back to Rook, brows drawing together.

Rook nodded, settling back until the leather creaked. He propped his chin in his hand, the exhaustion of the last three days finally showing. "She drew it out," he recounted. "Pulled the corruption from the creature like black thread from a wound. Absorbed it into herself. Purified it, somehow." He shook his head, disbelief in his words. "Until it was only ash and bone."

Rhedda's gaze dropped to the floor, searching for answers she could not find. She shook her head, drawing her shawl tighter around herself.

"She... unmade it?" The words came slowly, testing the shape of them. "That isn't how—" She stopped, started again. "Hollowmires are Malorith's corruption given physical form. They can be banished, sealed away. But to unravel one in purity?" Her hushed voice trailed off. "How fascinating..."

She was about to continue when the door behind her creaked open.

A small figure peeked through first, knee-high and crowned with pointed ears. It was Edie, blinking against the dim light of the sitting room, her wide eyes searching the faces of Rhedda and the men inside. They twinkled with mischief before a muffled giggle slipped free. She pushed the door wider with one hand.

Clutched in the other was Reny's.

Reny stood in the doorway of her own accord, dressed in a simple white linen gown that hung loose on her frame. The healers stepped into view just behind her, faces creased with concern.

Reny was... different.

During her days of sleep, she had lost some weight, but that wasn't what had altered her. Wasn't what lent her face a new and striking, eerie grace. Delicate points rose at the tips of her ears, visible since her hair had been brushed and braided by the healers' careful hands. Her eyes found Rook across the room. Still green, still hers, but woven now with unmistakable strands of living gold.

The tether between them snapped tight, violent in its demand. His hand flew to his chest as if struck, body bowing forward, breath torn from him. He couldn't rise right away. The connection between them, no longer muted by her unconsciousness, made itself painfully, undeniably clear.

Brenn and Aric froze, transfixed by the woman in the doorway, all argument forgotten.

Rhedda stepped aside, her features softening. A glimmer of recognition crossed her face, as though a question she'd held for days had been answered. Edie broke the hush with a bright, bell-like giggle, tilting her face up toward Reny in total wonder.

Brenn started to speak, voice rough with shock. "She's—"

Rook had managed to stand, though the movement cost him, hand still clutched to his sternum. The word left him before he realized he'd even spoken.

"Aetherian."

CHAPTER 46

T he stunned silence that followed was absolute.

Every man in the room had gone still, every breath held. The only sound was the soft, distant rush of the sea against the cliffs far below. Reny's gaze found Rook and held, stealing the breath from his lungs.

Rhedda was the first to move, motioning to the little girl by the doorway still grasping Reny's fingers. "Come, little one."

Edie released her grip and ran, laughter spilling as she leapt into Rhedda's waiting arms. The Cliff Mother caught her easily, balancing the girl on one hip with effortless, maternal grace. Without a word, she turned to Brenn and Aric.

She didn't need to speak. Both men rose at once, crossed the room, bowing to Reny as they passed before taking position near the door.

Reny was studying them both, taking in the weathered lines of Brenn's face, the heaviness in Aric's amber eyes. For a heartbeat, none of them moved.

"Thank you." Her voice was rough and broken, enough that she had to clear her throat before continuing. "For helping."

Brenn straightened, visibly unsure what to do with himself. "It was our... Yes, you're welcome. Of course."

Aric said nothing, face tight with stunned reverence.

"I didn't—hurt any of your people, or...?" Reny's brow creased, searching.

Aric shook his head, but Brenn was the one to answer her. "No. No, you saved us all."

A sad smile ghosted over her lips.

Rhedda gave a subtle gesture, and the three of them withdrew with Edie in tow, their footsteps fading into the corridor's hush. The healers clung to the corners a moment longer, uncertain whether to stay or follow.

When Reny moved forward on her own, they seemed to exhale in unison. Slowly, she crossed to the couch opposite Rook and lowered herself onto it. The cushions were warm from where Brenn and Aric had been sitting.

One healer slipped away without a word, the door sighing shut behind her. The last to remain was a narrow, silver-haired woman with light, porcelain features and clouded glass eyes. Rook had no idea if she was human, shifter, or something else entirely. She bowed once in greeting.

"My name is Maela. I am the master healer." Each word lilted, elegant as old scripture. An accent Rook couldn't place.

"In our assessment for injury, we noted a sacred sigil hidden within the hairline." Maela's slender fingers gestured toward the back of Reny's skull as she moved closer. Her steps made no sound, her body seeming to float rather than walk.

"It took two nights of intensive study to identify its meaning and undo the cloaking spell. Very old magic. Aetherian in origin, the most complicated I've encountered." She paused. "Once we administered the correct tincture, she was revealed to us. Quite an alarming discovery."

Reny sat perfectly straight, her face touched by a distant calm, like someone half-awake, lost in a dream.

"The purification and absorption of such ancient corruption required extensive rest. The human shell was certainly ready to be shed."

Rook heard the words, none of them seeming to land. They drifted past him, meaningless against the single, impossible truth before him.

Reny was alive. She was Aetherian. Like him.

Reny's gaze had wandered across the table, to the tray of mismatched pillar candles dripping wax in slow, colorful rivulets, their flames low and dancing in the room's draft.

"Performing such acts of divinity inside a mortal glamour would have likely killed her," Maela continued, wonder woven through her words. "But as her mate, the tether between you kept her heart beating long enough for us to—"

Rook blanched, but it was Reny who cut through first, attention snapping back to the conversation happening around her. "What did you just say?"

Maela froze, eyes darting between their rigid postures and pale faces. "Oh, dear child, I thought that perhaps..." She wrung her fingers together, embarrassment coloring her cheeks.

Rook shook his head slightly to spare the woman further discomfort, though he never looked away from Reny.

"Mate," Maela repeated gently. "The two of you. Your pairing is fate-driven. Natural, though quite sacred, for Aetherian lineages." She cleared her throat. "We added stabilizing herbs to a healing tonic to ease her through the transition. Full Aetherian senses and instincts at once, in addition to the bond, would be too overwhelming. She must regain her strength gradually."

Reny stared at the woman, her face unreadable.

Maela managed a wavering smile before glancing back at Rook. "If the connection to her feels strange or distant, that is why. It will take a day or two for her to settle into her immortal state."

Immortal.

Rook nodded once, though his pulse thundered in his ears. He tracked Maela as she retreated, her murmurs fading beyond his hearing in the hall. The door clicked behind her.

Mate.

The word echoed through him, settling into the hollow spaces between his ribs. That was what this pull had been all along. This relentless, undeniable gravity between them. A part of him had known but desperately tried to deny it.

Reny was staring at him, unblinking. Yet somehow still far away.

Rook drew on years of hard-won discipline, forcing down the instincts already screaming in his blood. He could feel her imbalance, the way her senses were cloaked and only half-formed. He managed a weak, lopsided smirk. Turning inward, he reached for her, testing that thread between them.

Yes, there. In his mind. She was there. Present but distant, like standing outside a cottage with no door, watching her through one narrow window. Close enough to see the light, brief movements through the glass, but barred from entering.

For now.

Reny's fingertips drifted upward, grazing the refined planes of her face. She traced the unfamiliar shape of her ear, brow furrowing as she found the subtle point there.

A sharp inhale tore from her as she slid lower, brushing over her lips until she found the edge of her top teeth. Canines, now elongated, unmistakably sharper, pressing against her fingertips.

Fangs.

Self-awareness hit her like a shockwave. Her heartbeat turned frantic, wild and alive, and somewhere distant, she felt an echo of it that wasn't her own.

"Hey, hey..." Rook closed the space between them on the couch, his grip finding her wrists as he guided them down from where they hovered by her face. "Look at me."

Look at me.

The words, familiar and commanding, struck through the fog of her thoughts. Memory stirred by the other times he'd said them, her heart stumbling in reply. When she finally met his eyes, his expression had changed. He was drinking in the sight of her. She could feel it through the muted bond. *Fascinated. Aching.*

"All this time." His thumbs brushed her wrists where her pulse fluttered.

Her words became too small and fragile to be hers. "I didn't know."

"You weren't supposed to." He exhaled, caught between sorrow and wonder.

For a while, neither of them moved. She felt his attention on her, cataloguing the changes, the new shape of her ears, the lines of her face. Hunger, plain and clear, flared in his eyes. Restrained, but barely.

He forced himself to stay still, letting her breathe. *Letting her be.*

"Who did this to me?" The horror in her own voice surprised her.

Rook steadied himself, folding her palms in his, lowering them to rest in the small space between them on the couch. "This is who you really are," he said softly. "Someone, or something, must have cloaked you... to keep you safe. Hidden."

She winced, searching for anything to hold onto. "But my parents, I—"

A helpless shake of his head was all he could offer.

Reny blinked several times. And then the world, in alarming, crushing clarity, hit her all at once. A torrent of sensation struck her—sound, scent, memory—each one colliding with the next until she could hardly tell where one ended and another began. Air caught, then deepened, and she realized it was him she was breathing into her lungs.

The scent of Rook wrapped around her, weaving through every vein.

Silver pine sap and crisp mountain air, cedar and storm and smoke. It flooded her senses, fierce and intoxicating, every note unraveling in her chest.

Memories followed. Not just hers, but flashes of images that did not belong. Fragments of laughter and battle, wind howling over stone, the echo of a name half-swallowed by time. All of them were too jumbled to truly identify.

Impossible.

Reny squeezed her eyes shut, shaking her head as if she could throw them off, but voices rushed in. A chorus, rising and layered, filled every corner of her mind. Too many of them, too loud, too real. All of them trying to tell her everything at the same time.

Through the chaos, she felt him reach for her. His arms pulled her close, holding her as if his strength alone could keep her from vanishing into the flood in her mind. She fought him at first, lost in the swell of it, limbs straining. He held fast, grounding her the only way he knew how.

Her resistance broke slowly. Knees drawing up, body curling into him, her face buried against the line of his throat. He turned and pressed his mouth to her temple, murmuring words she couldn't make out through the rest of them.

All she heard was his deep tones, the low hum she followed through the chaotic noises in her head. The one sound against the thousand that threatened to drown her. The storm in her ebbed, the other voices fading away until stillness returned and darkness rose to meet her. She slipped beneath it, surrendering again.

This time, she was held fast in his arms, the echo of his heartbeat the last sound she carried with her into the dark.

CHAPTER 47

The great hall of Rithmor had grown as hollow as the kingdom it ruled.

Courtiers no longer filled its galleries. There were no lords or ladies to fan the air with fine silk and lies. The braziers smoked low, their light dulled to a sickly orange that painted the dark marble in bruised tones.

There was only the sound of Tareth's breathing. Unsteady. Uneven.

Several sleepless days had passed since he'd sent the raven to the Cliffs. He sat below the throne on the dais floor, one elbow resting against his knee, fingers pressed to his temple to quiet what no one else could hear. The prince's crown lay discarded at his feet, its black metal dull, edges streaked with dried blood where his nails had dug in.

The double doors opened.

Rithmor's general entered first, helm beneath his arm, the weight of sleepless nights dragging at his shoulders. Behind him came two priests, the High Priest of Rithmor and his silent apprentice, their faces drawn and bleak.

"Speak," Tareth demanded without lifting his gaze.

The general hesitated. "Your Grace... our forces remain at station. But the men are failing. They're hungry. We've lost a dozen more to sickness this week. If Endaria marches on the North Gate, I fear we cannot hold the line."

Tareth looked up, pupils blown wide as though his mind lived elsewhere. "Then find more men."

"From where, your highness?" The general's exhaustion bled through, too worn to hide his desperation. "The farms are barren and the forges cold. What Aetherians remain can scarcely lift a fork, let alone a sword."

"Then you will make them. Sanction any Aetherian man or boy still breathing in this city. If they can stand, they can fight."

The priests shifted, the apprentice drawing a quiet breath of protest.

"My prince," the High Priest murmured. "Our people will not survive war waged in this way."

"They will not survive me if they fail to report."

The general swallowed, a muscle ticking in his jaw. "And what of the new weapon you promised? The power you said would turn the tide in our favor? Will the Rook return in time to lead the charge if the Gate falls?"

The words struck like lightning.

Tareth's expression went distant, then blazed. "Do not speak that name in my presence! He will not return. Nor do we need him!"

Whispers curled in the back of his mind, low and venomous.

He betrayed you. He lies with her now.

Tareth's palm twitched, flexing at his side.

"My lord—"

"Enough! Leave me!" The command boomed through the hall.

The general bowed, the priests following suit. They did not meet his stare, nor one another's, as they withdrew, but the glances exchanged between them said enough.

Rithmor was falling.

When the doors closed, the quiet that swallowed Tareth became unbearable.

Another presence filled it. Familiar, old, but still jagged enough to cut.

"I wondered how long it would take before I found you here again." King Maelor stepped from the shadowed corridor, his entrance like rolling thunder. His robes, though frayed, still bore the glimmer of gold thread. His eyes, bleary and wrinkle-framed, were fixed on his son with grim appraisal. "Every day, it seems, you become as disappointing as your brother."

Tareth's jaw shifted, the faintest twitch at the corner of his mouth. "You should be resting, old man."

"I should be ruling." The king's tone was acid. "But each time I wake, I find my heir sitting in my place, giving orders he has no right to give. Tell me, boy, do you think me blind?"

"Someone must act." Tareth rose slowly, descending the dais steps. "You've done little else but drink and decay since mother died."

Maelor's expression flickered, rage and disbelief warring there. "You've been giving orders without my consent. How many, Tareth? How many orders have you given?"

A cold smile. "As many as I please."

"You arrogant twit." Maelor's words came out as a growl. "Do you think this crown is already yours?"

It should be.

An icy hiss slid through his skull.

His jaw clenched, at war with his own anger and the presence threading through his mind. "Does it matter? Have you not already abandoned it?"

He will have your head. You know this.

Maelor's lip curled. "You ungrateful wretch. You think you're the chosen one? It is I who struck the bargain, boy. You're merely sick, just like the rest of this cursed land, until I get what's mine."

Chosen one. The whisper breathed silk and fire.

You are the chosen one. My heir.

Tareth blinked, the internal words drowning out everything else.

It's not his. It's yours.

Tareth's voice went smooth as a drawn blade. "Your bargain, perhaps. But you wear my crown. You're too old, too weak, too out of your mind most of the time to make any sense, let alone lead. You're merely keeping it warm for me."

Even the shadows in the corners seemed to hold their breath.

Maelor's palm trembled as it rose, his face a ruin of wounded pride and fury. "You dare speak to your king that way—"

Do it.

The slap cracked through the chamber, a bitter chord that sang off the marble and left a bloom of heat along Tareth's cheek. He felt the strike down to his bones, hot and shameful. For a breath, he was seven again. Curled in his mother's lap after his father's first blow, her cool fingers brushing the sting from his face.

"Hush now, my star. You are more than he will ever see." She smelled of night-blooming jasmine. Her hands had been the only gentle thing in Rithmor.

For a pulse, the world narrowed to the small, burning ache.

Do it now.

When he looked up, there was no pleading, no regret, no hesitation. Only an awful, cold clarity that had not been his own for some time.

Take your rightful place.

"You should not have done that."

The dagger was a flash of silver, pulled before his own thoughts could object. It drove up beneath the king's sternum with swift, terrible grace. King Maelor's breath left him in one astonished gurgle, his crown slipping from gray hair. It toppled to the floor, the only sounds its clatter against dark marble and the king's wet rasps for air.

Yes.

He held his father there by the blade's hilt, feeling the subtle quiver of life ebb at the other end. Tareth's free arm slid around Maelor's shoulders and drew him closer, tender enough to resemble affection. From a distance, it might have passed as a son's apologetic embrace.

"It's me," he murmured against the king's ear. "It was always meant to be me."

Tareth jerked the blade free, and the king slumped to the ground, the floor awash in spreading crimson. He simply stood over him, chest heaving, the dagger loose in his grip. The whisper came again, louder and closer than before.

Below.

He broke from his trance.

The chamber, my heir. You know the way.

Tareth barely felt the dagger slip from his grasp, barely heard it clatter against the floor. His gaze caught instead on his father's fallen crown, its iron dull with age and tarnish. Red flecked its rim where it lay in the spreading pool.

Bending, he lifted it from the floor. Streaks of scarlet smeared across its cold surface, marks of lineage and ruin. When he settled it atop his skull, it slipped slightly to one side, ill-fitting and too heavy. He didn't bother to fix it.

You are a king now. And kings must answer the god who made them.

A strange calm settled over him, though his hands still trembled. A haze softened the world around him until only sound and shadow remained. He turned from the king's body and descended the steps that led to the ritual chamber. Each footstep he took left a damning stain.

Come, my son. The altar waits.

The chamber opened into a wide hollow beneath the throne room, where the voidstone pedestal waited, pulsing faintly with an inner darkness. Torchlight wavered against the walls as he approached, the floor black and slick where old rituals had burned themselves into it.

Tareth's palms were still wet when he placed them on the pedestal. The voidstone hissed, drinking deep, its surface rippling where blood touched. The carved runes flared to life one by one, pale gold shifting to red that throbbed like a second heartbeat beneath his touch. The chamber itself stirred as if to shake off the centuries, dust falling from the vaulted ceiling as a sound rose from below. Low and guttural, waking within the earth's most primal depths.

He did it first. Your father traded his soul and his people for power, but he was never strong enough to finish what he began.

The runes brightened, the voidstone beginning to tremble beneath his palms.

"But I am," Tareth whispered.

Yes.

A crack split through the pedestal's center. The sound echoed through the chamber. A deep, ringing fracture that splintered down and crawled across the floor. The stone beneath his boots groaned before giving way.

Tareth staggered back, heart hammering. The pedestal sundered into two pieces, and from the widening seam in the floor, light poured. Not white, but black, with a radiance that devoured itself as it rose. The earth yawned wider, revealing a jagged wound.

You have released me.

The air went hot, heavy with the smell of smoke, sulfur, and rot. Dark, sentient mist curled from the chasm, billowing to meet fresh air and freedom. It coiled around Tareth's boots, winding higher, brushing along his legs like a lover's touch.

He had the urge to run, but the film over his sight wrapped him in that strange, weightless calm. For the first time in months, the whispers in his skull were completely silent. The pressure eased, allowing the room to steady around him. Tareth stared down at his palms as if they belonged to someone else, his father's blood drying dark against pale skin. The crown sat crooked atop his head, stained at its edges. Only now, in a state of cruel clarity, did he understand the enormity of what he'd done.

"What—" The word cracked. "What have I—"

I needed a dark enough vessel to carry me. And I waited long enough.

"No, I—"

You're the perfect fit.

Another memory surfaced, haunting and unwanted.

Sunlight through the rose garden, gold, red, and pink petals drifting on the summer wind. Vaelric beside him, both of them only boys, wooden swords crossed in mock battle. His brother's rare laugh. The way Tareth had sworn, even then, that he would protect him. That they would rule together, side by side, when they were grown.

The memory shattered like glass. Before Tareth could draw another lungful of air, the shadows surged upward. They hit him like a storm breaking, a rush of impossible cold that plunged into his eyes, his nose, his mouth, choking out the sound of his screams. The blackness threaded through every part of him, filling the hollows of his bones, every chamber of his heart. His veins darkened, frame convulsing with a force it could barely contain.

All at once, he stilled like a marionette suspended mid-air.

The last of the light guttered out of the runes. The lock that had kept him contained. Tareth's form jerked upright in broken, stuttering movements. His head snapped sharply to one side, then the other. Terrible silence swelled, the entire space bent inward, wary of the thing that now stood breathing where a ruined prince had been.

Fingers twitched first.

One by one, they curled and flexed as he reacquainted himself with muscle and bone. He straightened fully, joints cracking like breaking ice as he rolled his stolen shoulders. His gaze turned toward the shattered pedestal, lips parting in a blissful sigh. When he spoke, the sound came out in dueling echoes.

One Tareth's, one far older.

"It's been a long while." He looked down at the dark stains on his palms, turning them over, and smiled. "But this will do."

Malorith, god of death and undoing, breaker of vows, shifted in his new shell, settling easily into the shape of his host. The movement was disturbingly casual, like a man slipping on a familiar coat. He drew air into lungs new to him, tasting the living world for the first time in ages. The sound□ echoed through the hollow chamber.

Deep, cold, endless as the void that had birthed him.

He raised his gaze toward the ceiling above, toward the world he'd been denied too long. A content hum rolled in his throat as Malorith began his slow ascent up the slick stairs, leaving the wreckage of his cage, and the memory of Tareth Drayvien, behind him.

CHAPTER 48

Rook sat silently in Reny's chamber. He'd lost track of the hours he'd been waiting for her to wake.

The moonlight through the carved window slits painted her in silver and shadow, her flame-red hair spilled dark across the pillow. She looked fragile in sleep. Mortal, almost, if not for the new points of her ears and the way the light seemed to gather around her like it couldn't bear to leave.

He sat in the far corner, one arm resting along the chair's armrest, chin propped against his knuckles. Close enough to reach her. Far enough to pretend he had any restraint left.

The healers' tonic still muted the bond between them, but he could feel her now more than before. Present but still distant. Which meant her thoughts were still her own.

And so were his. For now.

It bought him some time. Time before she could step inside his mind and see the entire, horrible truth of him and learn the name that hung there like a blade above his head. One he'd shamefully wished had killed him already.

Vaelric Drayvien. Second-born prince of Rithmor. Brother to the monster who wanted her power. Son of the king who had sold his people to a death god for the promise of eternal rule.

She didn't know. She couldn't know. And every hour he spent at her side without telling her was another lie added to the pile, another weight he would eventually have to answer for.

But not yet. Not tonight.

Tonight, he would simply watch her breathe and pretend that was enough. A soft sound broke through the silence. Reny stirred, her brow creasing, fingers twitching against the sheets. Her breath quickened, lips parting around words he couldn't hear. Rook straightened, a tense knot forming in his center. He knew a nightmare when he saw one. Her head turned sharply on the pillow, a small, broken sound escaping her throat. Whatever hunted her in sleep was gaining ground.

Just as he considered rising from the chair, her eyes shot open.

Darkness had split the world in two.

A realm deprived of life, gray and barren, tore apart at the very seams, castle spires crumbling, its streets devoured by black veins that pulsed outward like rot beneath glass. The ground itself groaned, splitting open to reveal an endless maw. From the cracks bled lightless mist, thick and hungry, creeping up the broken stones to swallow everything it touched.

A figure moved through the ruin. A man, gracefully unhurried, his stride unbothered by the collapse around him. Not merely unbothered. Eerily delighted. The way he carried himself felt painfully familiar—the liquid, predatory cant of his head, the line of his shoulders—but his face refused to come clear.

All around him, the blackness teemed. Shadows with teeth and claws tore toward the sky, raking the mountains, gnawing upon the very fabric of the world, unraveling, ripping along its seams. Everything fell away until nothing remained but the void.

And her.

The rim of the world crumbled beneath her feet, threatening to pull her into the looming abyss. She screamed inward, calling to the light, to the fire that had once answered her, but found only bleak, endless cold.

Far stronger and more violent than the mimic in the creek had been, the shadows surged and seized her by the throat, dragging her down off the ledge. She tried to scream, but her breath had been stolen, lost to the chasm of the shattered world that swallowed her whole.

Reny's eyes flew open.

Only the distant, muffled hush of the sea somewhere beyond, and the steady rhythm of someone breathing. She blinked hard, letting her sight adjust to the room's blue-dark stillness. The carved window slits in the stone walls revealed silver moonlight.

She was back in the same room where she'd first woken. *Wherever that was.*

In the far corner, Rook was sitting upright in a chair. Pale light spilled over one side of him, leaving the other lost to shadow. Rough stubble darkened the lines of his face. He hadn't spoken, his attention clearly fixed on her.

Reny pushed herself upright, every muscle stiff. "How long have I been asleep?"

Rook studied her for a moment, his face unreadable aside from a soft haunting beneath the surface. A shadow she recognized. He eased back in the chair, more at ease now that she was awake. "Hours. Not days this time."

She paused, listening to the wind shift outside the carved window, carrying whispers of salt and rain.

"It's the middle of the night," he added.

Reny sat up more, pulse quickening with a sudden, inexplicable awareness. She could see him clearly, too clearly, for a room barely lit by the moon alone. Every line of him stood out in sharp contrast against the low light.

She had become too aware of everything. Of the cool air against her skin, the distant sound of the sea, the ruffling slide of the sheets she lay upon.

But mostly of him.

He'd washed since she'd seen him last. His hair was still damp where he'd swept it away from his face. He was dressed in black from throat to boot, every line of him severe and unyielding against the pale glow that blanketed the room. Her heart hammered, wild and uneven. Rook rose from the chair as if drawn by the sound of it, stepping free of the shadows until the moonlight caught him fully. Her gaze swept over the length of him, clocking the graceful ease in his stride, the familiar gait she knew.

All felt painfully magnified.

He stopped at the foot of the bed, lips twitching into a smirk that barely softened the steel she knew lay beneath it. Sensation surged through her in an unforgiving rush.

Restlessness. Thirst. Hunger. Want.

All of them struck at once without warning, fierce enough that she almost reached for him without realizing it. Rook turned before she could speak, movements so fluid it startled her. He reached for the small cup on the bedside table, holding it beneath the carved spring in the wall until water filled it to the brim. He passed it over, watching her closely.

She eyed it warily, glancing toward the window. To the distant call of the sea. "Isn't that salt water?"

He shrugged, the corner of his mouth lifting. "You tell me."

Inhaling near the rim, she was immediately struck by the crisp, clean scent of a mountain spring, so pure that it burned. She tossed the cup back and drank, the cold of it shocking her throat, doing little to quench the underlying thirst.

He watched her with quiet pride, undercut by awe and need. All of them woven together in a single, unguarded look. She set the cup aside and pushed the blankets off her legs, eager to move. He stepped back, giving her room. She swung her legs over the side of the bed and rose.

Too quickly. Black spots threatened the corners of her vision as her body swayed, her balance faltering for the briefest moment before he was there to catch her.

She huffed, gripping his forearms to return to balance. The muscles beneath her fingers tightened as he adjusted his hold, his strength coiled and warm beneath her touch. The feeling of him this close was its own kind of vertigo, a heat blooming in her chest that made her pulse stutter.

"It's... a lot to adjust to, I'm sure." His words and smile were gentle. Too gentle for what she could already sense building in him. Waiting for her.

She peered up at him, drawn closer without realizing it, the space between them collapsing until her cheek brushed his chest. "Is it like this for you all the time?"

His smile held, but sorrow was quick to shadow his face around it. "Not quite. Not since Rithmor and every Aetherian that side of the Veil started declining."

A sudden sensation swept over her, stealing her focus. A newfound presence in her own mind, like a hand reaching for hers through a dense fog. It felt like Rook, but she couldn't see him. The bond pulsed softly between them, there but guarded.

Strange. If she could just focus on it long enough to...

"Hey." Rook's tone was coaxing. He brushed the curve of her jaw with his fingers, tilting her chin back toward him. The touch felt deliberate, perhaps to ground her. She let the internal curiosity subside.

"I'm pretty sure," he murmured with velvet intent, "I told you to run that day. To run and not come back."

"You said yourself it would be unlike me to do as I'm told." Her reply cut like a blade wrapped in silk. A beat passed, her lips curling slightly. "How lucky for you."

Her wit had always been quick, but now it lashed with a newfound precision. Sharp, alluring, dangerous in how it reared up at him. She searched his face, defiance resurrecting in her eyes.

"I couldn't leave you, Rook. I would not let that be the price you pay." Her tone softened, falling from playful banter into raw vulnerability.

His breath left him in a quiet shudder. Hers met in tandem, as though drawn from the same air. He leaned in, dipping to kiss her. Reny rose into him, molding to his body as if she'd been made for it.

Because she had been.

A sound caught deep in his throat. Low, visceral. She pressed in, urgency rekindling into the same desperate need that had flared the moment he'd offered his life so she might keep hers.

The need to keep him, no matter the cost.

She broke from his mouth but didn't pull away, her breath a fragile tremble along his jaw. "I never thought I'd see you again."

He caught her in an instant, arms sweeping around her, pulling her hard against him. Her fingers clutched his arms with desperate force. The bond between them blazed despite the healers' dampening spell, threads of gold and flame weaving through vein and marrow. It pulsed once, violent, ready to tear down every wall still holding them apart.

Groaning against her, she felt the war in him. Restraint fighting something deeper, more volatile. His palm found the small of her back, dragging her in until there was no space left between them.

But just as the world fell away...

A knock rattled through the chamber door.

Rook exhaled an uneven, frustrated sigh, giving her a forlorn smirk. The kind that carried both an apology and an ache. He stepped toward the door and drew it open.

Brenn filled the entire threshold, torchlight from the corridor spilling over his wide build. The warm glow caught the hard angles of his face. First, revealing a brief shock, then clear irritation. Reny could see it from where she stood in the chamber. The line of Rook's shoulders went rigid, tension building visibly down his spine as he lifted an arm, bracing himself within the door frame.

Blocking the bear out.

Brenn's gaze flicked past him, landing on Reny where she stood illuminated by the moon, her form wrapped in the dusky blue of the chamber. His jaw worked once.

Rook shifted subtly, stepping back into his line of sight, eyes narrowing. "What do you want?"

Brenn huffed, the sound equal parts annoyance and disbelief. His scowl deepened. "Thought I'd find you here."

Rook's brow arched, tone sharp. "Where else would I be?"

Brenn's reply dropped, all pretense stripped from it. "Your own chamber."

Reny moved to the window, locating a light robe on a hook. She shrugged it over her shoulders, tying it at her waist before stepping into the space just behind Rook.

Brenn regarded her, something flickering in his eyes—there and gone before she could name it. Whatever it was, he forced it away, dipping his chin with a half smile. "My apologies, my lady."

Rook's mouth curved, his features twisting with dark amusement as he eyed Brenn. They held each other's stare for a fraction too long. Brenn's eyes flashed, catching the storm light in Rook's.

"I hoped to have a word with you," Brenn said finally, glancing toward Reny, then back again. "Privately."

Before Rook could answer, Reny's palm rose, resting lightly on the arm he'd braced against the doorframe. Rook exhaled and lowered his arm, casting a brief glance back at her.

"I think I've slept enough," she said, clearing her throat. "Please, come in."

Reny turned and drifted back into the room. Her grace had returned, her steps easy and sure as she crossed to the far side of the chamber. She moved to the clustered candles gathered in their uneven towers of color, trays of wax half-melted from use. With a few soft murmurs and a flick of her wrist, she coaxed the wicks alight with new ease, one tray after another. Warm amber light spilled through the room, pushing back the chill. Brenn watched her closely, saying nothing as the glow deepened and steadied, chasing away every shadow.

All but one. The one that stood off to Reny's right, arms folded tight across his chest. For all the newfound light in the room, Rook was still a towering pillar of night.

Reny turned, finally facing the two forces divided across the chamber. Even spaced far apart, the men were still too close. She studied them with wary curiosity, attention sweeping back and forth until it settled on Brenn. He had taken up a broad stance along the wall beside the window, candlelight gilding the planes of his Cliffborn armor.

"So, what is this about?" She regarded them with quiet authority, her chin lifting.

Brenn cleared his throat, dipping his chin before his eyes cut to Rook. "We received correspondence." His tone was a careful, diplomatic calm. "Endaria's forces have left the capital city. They have a full regiment marching toward the North Gate."

Reny's brows lifted, alarm breaking through her composure. "Outright waging war? Now?"

Brenn paused, but his focus on Rook was unrelenting. "I was wondering if you might have information on how Rithmor might respond under such circumstances."

Rook didn't move. Reny turned toward him, expectant, waiting. He rolled his shoulders once, shifting his weight as he chose his words.

"I haven't been inside Rithmor in over a year. I'm not sure what their response could be."

Brenn's glare darkened.

Rook met the challenge head-on, threat simmering in the air of the chamber. Something unspoken passed between them. Reny couldn't read it even as her eyes swept back and forth over both men.

Brenn nodded, calculating, weighing every word before releasing it. "I thought that perhaps, with your affiliations, you might have insight that would be useful."

Rook's jaw ticked. "I wasn't aware the Cliffs had allied with Endaria."

Brenn's reply was immediate. "The Cliffs only care to know for the sake of the Cliffs. We are our own allies."

Reny intentionally stepped forward, placing herself between them. Neither man acknowledged her, too distracted in their silent war. She fixed her gaze sharply on Rook, Brenn now at her back.

"Well," she asked, "what could it be? Based on what you do know about the Drayviens?"

Brenn shifted in the space behind her, but she did not acknowledge him. Her focus was locked on Rook, unrelenting.

"Rook."

He tore his stare away from Brenn, thunder of his own gathering beneath the furrow of his brow as he met her instead. "With the ongoing blight weakening Rithmor's magic," he explained, "the legions are far less capable than anyone realizes. It was the crown's hope to get your power before Endaria could launch an offensive. To manipulate its properties, forge it into weaponry, and reinvigorate their abilities to invade and conquer Endaria."

Reny's breath caught. "So, they hired you to track me down. And they told you this directly, or are you assuming?"

Brenn folded his arms, dark amusement crossing his features. "Work for hire? I hadn't realized they actually started paying you, Rook."

The glare Rook shot him was enough to take down mountains. Brenn smiled in return.

Reny felt the tension rising as immense pressure in her lungs, forcing an exhale to rip from her. The candle flames in the room leapt high on their wicks in response, light flooding outward, gilding every corner in sudden brightness.

"Alright." She snapped, hands finding home on her hips. "What's going on here?"

Neither man spoke.

"Someone *better* start talking."

CHAPTER 49

"Out with it." Reny's words cracked through the chamber like a whip. "What the hells is wrong with you two?"

Rook and Brenn had closed the distance despite her anger. Reny held her ground in the narrow space between them as the immovable line neither would dare cross.

She looked between them, eyes searching. "I don't know what kind of territorial male pissing contest is happening here, but there are more pressing matters at hand if Endaria and Rithmor are going to war."

Rook glared at Brenn over her head, barely acknowledging her words. "You have a lot of fucking nerve coming here in the middle of—"

Brenn barked over him. "My nerve? When you're standing here in the heart of the Cliffs, after the blood your line spilled to—?"

Rook's face went black with fury, his lips parting with his next attack.

"Enough!" The force of Reny's voice wasn't sound alone. A pulse of magic rippled through the air, through both men. The candle flames bent toward her briefly before steadying with her annoyed exhale.

Brenn and Rook breathed hard, the old war between them seething, threatening to break. Sweat shone on Rook's temple. Brenn's jaw worked, a feral glint in his eyes.

"Stop behaving like fools," Reny snapped. She pressed her palm against Brenn's chest and reached toward Rook with the other. The instant her fingers brushed Rook's sternum, the tether between them pulsed with a jolt of heat that rolled through all three.

Rook swallowed hard. "Rithmor's forces can't cross the Veil without significant cost. Not even at the North Gate, where it's thinnest." He paused. "It's too draining. Aetherians have weakened to the point of mortality."

"Good to know." Brenn smirked, almost amused.

Reny lifted her hand from the bear-shifter's chest, unafraid of the mass looming above her. One finger rose in warning. "Watch your mouth."

Brenn yielded, back straightening as he stared at Rook. "I want to know where your alliances lie, Aetherian. Considering."

"What's that supposed to mean?" Rook growled.

"It means Endaria may think Rithmor is a level playing field, but that sounds a lot like bait to me. Perhaps that's what Rithmor just wants us to believe."

Rook took a half step forward, closing the distance until Reny's hand was all that held him back. "You think I'm lying?"

"I think," Brenn said, closing the distance into Reny's other hand, "that either Rithmor's gone utterly mad, or suddenly the crown's found something that'll let them walk through the Veil unharmed."

Reny's brow furrowed, pushing both hands outward to force each man back. "What are you suggesting?"

His jaw tightened. "I'm suggesting Rithmor's not as weak as it claims. They're all liars, so I'll wager they've drawn power from somewhere they shouldn't. That maybe they've aligned with the wrong kind of god."

Rook's tone went ice-cold. "You don't know what you're talking about."

"Don't I?" Brenn shot back, the growl in his throat deepening. "I've seen the ruin your kind leaves when it lusts for power. The lengths you'll go to get what you want, no matter who or what you destroy in the process." He glanced briefly at Reny, then back again.

Darkness flooded Rook's features. "I'll kill you myself."

Reny's hand shot up, finger stabbing toward Rook's face this time. "You will do no such thing. Don't forget this man helped save your life."

Holding her stance, Reny refused to move until both men finally exhaled in reluctant surrender. They pivoted from one another in unison.

"If Rithmor forces have weakened like Rook says," Reny said evenly, cautiously lowering her hands, "and they don't have my magic or any other at their disposal, Endaria could defeat them, right?"

Rook looked up at her, weary. "That doesn't mean they all deserve to die. There are good men, young boys, in those ranks..."

Brenn's mutter slid in like a blade. "We clearly differ on what makes a good man."

Rook's temper broke. He lunged forward, teeth bared. Brenn didn't flinch, that grim smile holding as Reny's hands pushed out again, forcing Rook backward. The only barrier between two storms ready to collide.

Brenn held Rook's stare. "Your crown may have finally released Malorith from his voidstone tomb, giving Rithmor an advantage it will never deserve. Endaria could be walking into a trap. With King Maelor's death—"

Rook's body went terribly still. "What did you say?"

Reny's breath caught. One of the names Brenn uttered was totally foreign to her, yet still felt like a familiar poison in her veins. A once-known ash in her mouth. "...Malorith?"

Rook took a half step forward. "What are you talking about, Brenn?"

The bear-shifter's anger faltered, his shoulders dropping.

"I have intel of a murder," Brenn murmured. "A coup, of sorts. King Maelor is dead. Tareth presides over the throne now, and there are rumors of a great chasm splitting open beneath the castle. A whole spire crumbled down the hillside with the force of it."

Malorith...

Their voices around her had become indiscernible. Reny's body felt frozen over, her focus cast off, fixed on nothing. She turned inward, desperately trying to claw her attention back into the room. Back to the men in front of her. But part of her mind had been stolen away by that terrible name, thrusting her memory into darkness.

Her eerie stillness drew Rook's attention first, then Brenn's. Reny had gone pale, color leeched from her skin.

Rook rushed to her, his hand brushing gently across her arm. "Reny..."

When she didn't respond, he took her elbow and drew her into him, his touch far too gentle for the bedlam behind his eyes when he lifted them back to Brenn. "I don't know what you think you were doing tonight. She still hasn't fully recovered."

"Didn't stop you from coming to sniff around in the dark," Brenn snarled, though he glanced toward Reny with genuine worry. When he looked back at Rook, every bit of venom returned. "I'm doing what I must to keep my people safe. Doing what's right. Not that you'd know a godsdamn thing about that."

Rook scoffed, tightening his hold. He looked over Reny, still vacant, then fixed on Brenn. "Does your cliff mother know that you're here tonight? Does she know her pet has come to play commander?"

Brenn didn't miss the sting, nor did he spare one in return. "What do you suppose your mother would think about what you've done?" His head tilted with cruel intent. "Would she be proud of the crown's rabid lap dog?"

The wound struck true. Pain, grief, fury. They gutted any shred of light from Rook's face in one breath. "You'll regret that."

"Watch it, Aetherian," Brenn warned, taking a wide step toward the door. "I'll have your head on a pike."

"Try."

"I'll fetch the healers." Brenn ignored the threat, shouldering his way out the door.

The moment Brenn crossed the threshold into the hall, he nearly collided with Aric, who came barreling around the bend of the stone corridor. Winded, wide-eyed, and pale beneath the torchlight. The chamber door swung inward, Brenn never having the chance to pull it shut behind him.

Inside, Rook had eased Reny into a chair. She was coming back to herself, still pale, but awareness lit her eyes like dawn emerging through thick fog. Rook turned at the sound, drawn toward the commotion at the doorway.

Brenn caught Aric by both shoulders. "Brother, what's wrong?"

Aric tried to speak, his lungs heaving beneath Brenn's grip.

"Korva... Korva's back." He swallowed hard, catching more breath, amber gaze distraught. "But something's wrong. She's asking to be taken to the Eye."

Brenn and Aric left Rook and Reny with the healers, footsteps echoing quick against the stone as they ran through winding halls toward the far end of the cliffs.

The great doors loomed before them. Towering ancient driftwood banded in dark iron. Brenn pushed them open, hinges groaning beneath his strength.

The chamber beyond was dim, lit by a few oil sconces and the shimmer of moonlight filtering through fissures in the wall. Maela hovered off to one side of the room, face drawn tight. At the center of the room, Korva sat alone in a high-backed chair. Rhedda leaned nearby, somber and unreadable.

Brenn took in the silence, the unease, the scent of brine and herbs. His instincts prickled as he stepped closer.

Korva appeared smaller. Frailer. The hollows of her face had deepened, carved with new, weary lines. She seemed far older. Haunted.

"Korva..." His voice softened. "What happened to you? Where have you been?"

At the sound of his voice, the girl lifted her chin, meeting him with a winter-blue stare. Familiar, but far too cold. Behind him, Aric settled against the wall, still trying to steady his breath.

Brenn knelt before her, folding his height until they were eye level. Her hair was wild and tangled, matted with dirt and twigs. His throat tightened at the sight of her.

"Come on, baby bird," he murmured, the endearment breaking on his tongue. "Talk to me."

The girl moved, the motion stiff and halting, as though her own body had become foreign. She swallowed hard, gaze dropping. "I was captured by the Aetherians. Taken to Rithmor."

The words struck him like a landslide.

But Rhedda barely moved. She remained at her post against the table, silent and watchful. Brenn had expected her to have already wrapped Korva in her arms, offering the comfort of their kin, but she hadn't moved. Even Maela, hovering along the room's outer edge, seemed frozen in quiet assessment.

"The Drayvien prince," Korva added meekly. Barely more than a rasp.

A low growl built in Brenn's throat. Soft, but filled with violence all the same.

Korva's words trembled. "Vaelric, the second-born. He's the one. He killed Orwyn." Her accusation hung in the air, fragile and poisonous.

Aric stirred with obvious discomfort, taking a few steps forward. "Korva... that isn't true. I was there."

Her head snapped in his direction, eyes cold and glassy. "I saw it. They are deceivers, playing tricks on your vision. I know he killed him."

Brenn glanced between them, his jaw tightening. "She's confused. You've seen what the Drayviens are capable of. What they can twist and manipulate."

Aric's frown deepened, but he said nothing more.

Korva shuddered, her hands clenching and flexing, working over one another in her lap. "The Eye. I need to see the Eye."

Brenn blinked, his face twisting with confusion. "Why, Korva? What do you think it will show you?"

She looked up at him. "The Flame Bearer. I know how to find her. The Eye will confirm it. I can lead you right to her." Silence swallowed the room, Brenn's own breath stalling. Aric went rigid against the wall.

Rhedda's voice came low and terrible. "And where do you believe the Flame Bearer to be, child?"

Korva's chin lifted, certainty sharpening her tone. "Rithmor's been hunting her. I know where she's hiding. The Eye will show you I'm right. Then we can finally end this."

No one spoke.

Brenn's hands had curled to fists at his sides, his knuckles white. He glanced toward Rhedda, then Aric, the same horrified recognition passing between all three.

"Korva, she's—" Aric stepped forward, voice tight.

Rhedda raised a hand in Aric's direction, cutting him off. She drew closer to where Korva sat, too straight and still. "Something's got hold of you, child. Something old. Something that sent you back to us with a purpose all its own."

Korva's head tilted. Wrong, too far, like a puppet dangling loose on its strings. "I don't know what you mean. I escaped. I came home."

"Malorith," Rhedda said flatly, staring directly at her. Into her.

Korva didn't flinch. Didn't blink. Her face remained perfectly, eerily still.

Brenn shook his head, trying to drive off his own spiraling thoughts. "This is nonsense. She's traumatized, Rhedda. Gods know what they did to her, what she's seen. She needs our support."

Rhedda faced him, unyielding and calm. "And you believe she escaped Rithmor, scared and shaken? That she simply walked away?"

Brenn flung his hand toward Aric. "He escaped. It's not that surprising."

Aric's reply came from behind him, thick with grief. "I escaped during the ambush on the Endarian side, Brenn. They didn't take me into Rithmor."

"She's alive, she's here, because she fought. She outsmarted them!" Brenn's shout had become a desperate roar through the council chamber, echoing off the sandstone. "Because she's strong. Because she's ours."

Rhedda shot a look at Korva before taking a step closer to Brenn, holding her shawl tight at her middle. "And if she isn't ours anymore?"

Brenn froze, fury roiling beneath his skin. He rose to full height, a tower above the rest. "Then take her to the Eye. Let her see it, let it see her. That'll tell us what we need to know, won't it?"

"Please... take me to the Eye, Cliff Mother." Korva's slow breathing was the only sound between them. She looked up at Rhedda innocently.

Rhedda's head tilted, carefully guarded suspicion flaring anew. "Why, child? Why does it matter so much?"

Korva blinked with eyes too empty. "Because it's the only thing that will make this right. For Orwyn. For all of us. Please believe me."

The words should have been grief-stricken. Should have been desperate, broken.

They weren't. *Too flat, too hollow.*

Maela shifted uneasily as Rhedda shook her head.

Brenn rounded on their leader, cracks forming in his bellow. "You hear her! She's begging you. We owe her that."

Rhedda's jaw set. "We owe the truth more than we owe our guilt, bear. We owe our actions to the prophecy."

"Fuck the prophecy!" Brenn roared now, the sound shaking the chamber. "Can't you see you're failing her? You're failing all of us!"

For the first time, Rhedda flinched when his temper broke free. Aric came forward, weary and pained, a hand reaching out to ground his friend. "Brenn, please—"

Brenn wasn't listening anymore, the fracture in his chest widening. "She's lost her brother, been captured and likely tortured for us. She comes back in obvious distress, and you stand there doubting why she's here?" The strength in his voice threatened to break. "She needs us. Needs you, now more than ever."

Rhedda met him head-on with a look full of sorrow. "No, Brenn. She needs saving. From whatever came to the Cliffs tonight wearing her face."

Brenn's breath caught. He turned away, unable to face her a second longer.

From where she sat, Korva spoke again, her tone soft and sweet as decay. Easy and so very wrong. "Take me to the Eye, now."

"I will not, child." Rhedda folded her arms, her mouth set in a narrow line, unmoved by Brenn's mounting fury.

Korva let her head hang forward, shoulders slumping as if the weight of exhaustion had finally caught her, long strands of black hair veiling her face.

Rhedda nodded toward Maela, who finally stepped forward. The healer crossed the chamber and helped Korva rise, one hand at her forearm, the other steadying her waist. Together, they moved toward the infirmary. The council doors closed with a dense thud, the echo swallowed by silence.

Brenn's eyes were already fixed on Rhedda from across the table. "Take her to see the Eye."

The Cliff Mother shook her head again. "Not until she's been fully examined. The healers will assess her, and she'll have rest. I will turn inward, see what my visions give me. Then we'll decide."

Brenn's deep growl rumbled. "We don't have the luxury of waiting for one of your ridiculous dreams to lead us down another wrong path."

Rhedda's hand lifted, a wordless warning louder than any shout. "I know you love her, swore to protect her. But I am not taking her to the Eye."

Brenn held her gaze, unblinking. "If you don't, I will."

"You will not," Rhedda bit out, her composure visibly breaking for the first time. "And that is an order, Brenn of the Cliffs." The words, the title, struck like a blade.

Brenn's lungs heaved, the bear in his skin fighting to free itself. He braced against the table with both hands, fingers digging into its stone edge as his body trembled with the effort to hold back the shift. When he finally spoke, his words drew more snarl than speech.

"I'm done following your orders." Every syllable came bitten through his teeth. "She rests for the night. And in the morning..."

Brenn leaned farther forward, burning through the dim. "I'm taking her myself. And there will be nothing you can do to stop me. You're finished making decisions for the Cliffborn."

Aric's head jerked up in shock from his place along the wall.

"I'm calling a leadership vote." The words detonated. "Tomorrow morning."

"You overstep," Rhedda said softly, not as a threat. As someone speaking to a man already lost. "But I suppose you feel you must."

Brenn didn't answer. He pivoted from her, the movement raw and animal. The heavy doors shuddered against their hinges as he shoved them open and vanished into the corridor beyond, his retreat echoing down the hollow stone halls until the sound was swallowed by the sea.

Aric remained frozen for a heartbeat longer. Reluctantly, he trailed after Brenn, pausing in the threshold to glance back at Rhedda. A wordless look passed between them, carrying too much.

Apology, pity, dread, regret.

Then he, too, was gone.

The council chamber fell utterly silent. The whisper of wind through the fissures in the rock was all that remained.

Rhedda remained by the sandstone table, her shoulders finally sinking beneath the weight of what she'd seen coming for weeks. What she'd hoped would not come to fruition.

But the Eye was never wrong.

She looked toward the great doors Brenn and Aric had left swinging on their hinges, and though sorrow deepened the lines in her face, she was not surprised.

Not anymore.

CHAPTER 50

T ime passed, allowing Reny to shake herself free of the trance, its fading fog too familiar. Like waking from one of her worst nightmares.

Rook stood near the doorway, arms folded tight across his chest, watching her. Low lamplight carved shadows across his face, catching the hard line of his jaw. He hadn't moved since Brenn and Aric rushed off, though the tension in his shoulders had eased the moment they'd disappeared.

Reny sat where he'd placed her in the chair, elbows on her knees. Her fingers still rubbed her temples as she looked up at him, the shock lifting with each breath.

"What is it between you and Brenn? What's the story?"

"It's... complex." Passing, grim amusement crossed his face.

"How enlightening." She rose carefully, steadying herself on the chair's arm before he could move. When he reached out, she waved him off. "No, I'm fine."

She crossed the chamber to one of the narrow windows carved into the cliff wall, bare feet soundless over the stone. The moon had begun its descent toward dawn, silver bleeding into the room's darkness. The pale light caught her face as she peered out, cool against skin that still burned. His attention on her back felt like a physical weight.

When she turned to lean on the wall, she was grateful for the cold stone at her spine and the relief it offered against the constant wildfire beneath her skin since she'd woken up. "So, what are you not telling me?"

A muscle in Rook's jaw twitched. He slid his hands into his pockets. "Nothing you'd want to know before dawn."

"That's not an answer, Rook." She shook her head, arms folding over her chest. An odd glimmer passed over her eyes, catching the eerie blend of fading moonlight and candle flame.

The air between them had changed. Reny felt it before she understood it—a hint of presence brushing against the edges of her mind. Not intrusive. But *there*, hovering at the threshold like a hand against a frosted glass window. The effect of the healers' tonic had been fading for hours. She'd felt the walls inside her growing more translucent. And now, standing across the room from him, she realized how little remained between them.

A veil. Thin as breath. The last fragile divide.

He was testing it. She could feel him there, curious and hungry, his awareness pressing against that gossamer barrier. Searching for a way in. Then his touch slipped through. From the opposite side of the chamber, Reny inhaled sharply as invisible, feather-light fingers traced the line of her throat and slid lower.

She froze. "What did you just do?"

A sinful darkness swallowed the slate of Rook's eyes. With a languid, arrogant lean against the door, he studied her, mischief glinting beneath the hood of his brow.

Heat smoldered in the air around her.

"Did you feel me?" He smirked, wholly unguarded, when she didn't answer.

Inside her mind, he leaned closer, breath ghosting against the curve of her throat, hovering above the pulse hammering beneath her skin.

Can you feel me here?

Reny gasped out loud at the sensation, at the unspoken words she heard too clearly. Her spine bowed in an involuntary arc away from the stone wall, her body responding to the insistent pull from deep within. She answered his summons before her thoughts could catch up.

Predatory triumph crossed Rook's face as he pushed off the door, the soft click of the lock bar nearly lost beneath her uneven breath. He prowled toward her, the air shrinking around his approach.

Reny recognized the predator for what he was and, for the first time, fully understood the instincts that drove him. Her heart thundered against her ribs, the draw toward him fierce and unforgiving. He stepped fully into her space, looming over her. She was caught between him and the cold stone wall.

A pleased, purring hum rose from his chest. The resonance traveled through her bones, vibrating through both of them. "This is such a familiar place for you, Reny."

"Between a rock and a hard place?" She tilted her chin up in defiant amusement, flashing him that familiar steel resolve.

"Something like that." A wolfish grin spread across his face. One arm lifted to brace on the wall beside her head. The other hung loose at his side, fingers flexing with restless need.

Reny held his stare and mentally reached back. Her own awareness brushed against the bond, searching for clarity beyond the sheer divide. She couldn't fully make out his form, but she knew he was there. And felt something in him *give*.

She lifted one hand, pushing into the strange, thin barrier. It found his chest on the other side, her fingertips trailing down the plane of his torso, over his center and waist—

Lower.

A soft, involuntary sound escaped Rook, echoing both in the chamber and in her head. This time, she was the one smiling, newfound understanding in her green-and-gold eyes.

Lightning struck in the glowing gray of his. "Clever girl."

Pressing her hand to the force and heat of him beyond the divide, she mirrored the movement in the room's hush. His head dipped forward, face lost to darkness as the moon slipped beyond the window.

"You should know bedding me doesn't stop me from asking questions." She looked up at him, heavy-lidded. Challenge and invitation.

"Oh, I know." His chuckle was dark, intoxicating. Still braced against the wall, he let his free hand rest on her hip, holding her there. "But this time is different, Reny."

"How so?" She tilted her head, her touch intentionally torturous now. Teasing.

"You're Aetherian," he said. His expression shifted, guarded reverence cutting through desire. "And you're my mate. What happens next isn't just want or love. It's claiming. An eternal binding."

"Is that something you want?" Reny arched a brow, studying him despite her relentless touch.

He leaned in, his body brazen as sin against hers now. The stone wall was ice on her spine. Rook was the fire consuming her front.

"I want nothing else," he murmured, the confession thick in the air. His free hand, once resting at her hip, slid up with unbearable softness to trace the curve of her ribs, then the swell of her breast. "It's all that I want."

Every touch inside the tether mirrored their movements in the room. In the unseen chamber of their thoughts, she closed her hand around the hard length of him, teasing him through the fragile divide.

His hand slid down the wall, dragging with the wicked weight of his remaining restraint. A groan tore from within, and when he caught her chin and tipped her mouth up to his, his voice was raw. "But this isn't about me. I need to know what you really want."

Her lashes fluttered. "The rest of you."

Something inside him broke over her words. She felt it through the bond—a violent surge of memory and longing. He seized her jaw and kissed her hard, forcing her to meet him in a collision of tongue and want.

Rook wrenched himself away first, but his grip on her jaw didn't loosen. "You don't know what that means," he said, resting his forehead on hers.

"I don't care what it means," she answered back, twisting both fists into his shirt. His mouth trailed down her neck, each breath scalding as his tongue traced over the wild rhythm of her pulse.

"You called me a monster once." His voice was a low rasp against her neck.

"I didn't mean it, Rook." Her words fractured, split between an exasperated laugh and apology.

"Yes, you did," he said, lips brushing the curve of her shoulder.

"You're not a monster."

Their bodies converged, too committed to unraveling, becoming a tangle of grabs and pulls and jerks, tearing at the fabric between them until every barrier lay discarded across the stone floor.

Rook caught Reny by the waist, the heat of his hands branding into her skin as he guided her backward toward the bed. He lowered her into the soft folds of the duvet, his weight following as he settled between her thighs. His teeth grazed her shoulder, and she responded with a hiss, pain and pleasure fused in the same breath.

She traced the tense line of his spine as her gaze pinned his. The gold flecks in his gray eyes were glowing, the thread between them burning hotter. The last thin veil that separated their souls was smoldering, its edges curling inward to ash.

"What if I am, Reny?" he murmured, mapping her curves with calloused hands. "What if I'm the last thing you'd ever want bound to you for your long, Aetherian life?"

"Whatever you are, whatever you've done, you're still mine." Her nails dug in, sinking crescent moons into his back. A warning growl tore out of him.

Mine. Her voice was a haunting echo through every part of him.

Still mine.

"You don't know what you're saying." His face twisted with ache and despair, the war in him visible.

She arched again, her body obeying only instinct and blood and heat. Her legs wrapped around his waist, forcing him lower. Closer. To a breaking point neither could stop.

Too close. The rigid length of him brushed over her center. The slightest dip into the slick heat waiting for him.

He sucked in air between his teeth with a muffled curse. She writhed, clutching his shoulders, trying to pull him down again. His fists seized the duvet on either side of her head, every muscle locked in resistance.

"I want all of you," Reny said, all triumph and desperation. She hooked a heel behind his knee, forcing him to drop until their hips aligned. "Let the monster claim me, then, Rook. If this is the price for falling in love with you, I'll pay it."

If this is the price...

She felt the moment he broke. Through the bond, his willpower shattered. Thought and reason burned away, leaving only the wild, ungoverned pulse of what he was. Gold flared through his eyes, pupils blowing black and wide, as he claimed what had always been his.

He drove deep. Reny cried out in both shock and relief, the sound swallowed by his descending mouth. The rush of him wrecked her completely.

Until the tether detonated, eclipsing everything else. Reny's mind split open to let him in, light and sound folding in on themselves as the veil between them dissolved in a blinding flash of white.

You're mine. He said it through her mind, the thread between their souls igniting.

"Mine." Then out loud. "You're mine."

The bond didn't open gently for her. It tore.

Mine.

Rook's soul crashed into Reny's consciousness like a raging sea bursting through a cracked dam. She gasped, nearly choking on the psychic onslaught threatening to drown her. Visions of memory and emotion slammed through her mind in rapid succession.

A golden-eyed little boy, sad and motherless, standing in a grand hall. Vaulted ceilings carved from dark stone. Figures in fine silks moving past him like he wasn't there.

Rook's mouth met hers again, drinking every sound as his hips found a relentless, consuming rhythm.

Training yards. Blood on boots, pools of it in the dirt. The satisfying crack of bone beneath knuckles. Power learned through violence.

Reny felt the ache of his loneliness, but the faces in each memory were blurry, details muffled before she could try to understand them. She could sense his own resistance like a desperate swim against the raging current he'd unleashed.

A garden, sun-drenched and quiet. An older boy with similar features—dark hair, golden eyes—kneeling among roses. He looked up with an innocent smile, full of life. "She would have loved you, Ric."

The nickname echoed through her, warm and aching.

A brother. A mother they'd both lost. But him... Who are you?

Rook's forehead pushed against hers, his movements slowing as if the release of memory came at a substantial cost to him. The bond's pull to reveal more was merciless, and she could feel him warring with it.

Dark forests. Dead ends. More failure. Tracking, hunting. The scent of magic on the wind, leading him closer. Closer to... A break in the trees.

River's Edge. Lantern light on the twin bridges. And then—her own face. From across the tavern.

The moment everything changed.

The memories weren't just flashing images, but sound. Scent. Feeling. Each one bled into her, becoming overwhelmingly unified.

Cold determination to save Rithmor's starving people. That's what had driven him south. That's what justified every Cliffborn death. But then doubt...

She pressed lips and tongue and teeth against his shoulder, the rhythm of his thrusts returning.

Doubt when he saw her with the stag. When he'd pulled her from the mimic. When the mercenaries captured her. And then painful, corrosive guilt, until finally all that remained was the all-consuming love that had broken every oath he'd ever sworn to...

Darkness. Before the memory could be revealed to her, it was ripped away.

Sworn an oath to whom?

Their bodies moved, not by will alone, but by something older. Hungrier. Her hips rose to meet his, her body insatiable, craving everything he would and wouldn't give her.

"I can feel you holding back, Rook," she breathed against the corner of his mouth. Her fingers threaded into his hair, gripping tight. "Why won't you let me see you?"

Rook, please.

A tortured sound tore from him at the sound of his name. One of them. His rhythm faltered, slowing, arms trembling on either side of her.

"Once I show you, there's no going back," he warned, rough and wrecked.

"I'm already yours." She pulled her head away just enough to meet his eyes. "Whatever it is, I'm yours. Let me in."

His head dropped to the curve of her throat, breath hot and ragged against her thundering pulse. She felt the pointed graze of his canines against her neck, the silent question in his hesitation as he hovered there. Her hand slid to the back of his head, holding him as she tilted her chin up, instinctively baring the column of her throat in wordless offering.

Yes.

He groaned into her, into his own demise, and dove in—sharp canines sinking into her skin.

But the bite was not violence. It was communion.

Reny's back arched off the bed in strange, overwhelming relief. A bone-deep satisfaction in the way he trembled, in how his sounds burned through her veins.

Her blood flooded his tongue, surging into him like liquid flame, searing through the hollow places where Rithmor's blight had weakened him. Long-silenced magic roared awake, igniting an inferno in every corner of his soul. And hers.

Oh gods.

Power—raw and ancient—flowed back into him like a river finding its course after decades of drought. She felt it as if it were her own, felt the staggering force of what her blood unlocked. It rushed through the bond in a torrent of heat and light, filling the dark, starved places inside him until he was blazing. Whole in a way he hadn't been in years.

And she had done that. Her blood. Her flame.

Rook released her throat with a sharp inhale, pulling back just enough for her to see his face. His eyes were no longer storm and slate, flecked with illuminated thread. They burned solid gold, lit like twin suns. The predator she'd always sensed in him had fully awakened, called to the surface by her blood rushing through his veins.

Before she could speak, he moved.

He withdrew, the loss a sudden, cold shock, before he stood. In one fluid motion, the world tilted. He turned her, guiding her down until she was on her hands and knees, breathless and exposed.

Before she could anchor herself, his hands seized her hips, dragging her back against the solid wall of his body. There was no hesitation, nothing wasted in his motions. He thrust back into her in one heavy, claiming stroke, filling her completely, creating a sudden and beautiful ruin of her breath.

He held still. *A predator savoring the trap.* She felt his satisfaction through the bond—dark and possessive—as her body tightened around him, her fire-and-embers hair spilling forward to curtain her face.

His hand slid up her spine, a ghost of heat tracing the line of it, until his fingers splayed against the back of her head. With bewildering gentleness, he gathered her hair, letting the strands slip through his fingers before his fist closed tight.

"Look at you," he murmured, all dark revelry. He wrapped the silken length of her hair around his fist. Tethering her to him like this, too. "Perfect."

The low roll of his voice reduced her to a single, trembling whimper. Desperate, aching, she tried to rock back against him. Anything to appease the need for movement, for friction.

But he wrenched her head back. The sharp pull forced a broken, blissful cry from her throat, baring her neck to the cool air. The sting bloomed bright across her scalp.

"Patience, Reny." His voice was gravel and smoke. "You'll take what I give you."

He moved then. A slow, torturous rhythm that was cruel in its restraint. Wildfire spread through her veins. He was savoring this, taking his time as if he meant to dismantle her just to enjoy the wreckage. But through the haze of pleasure, Reny sharpened her focus on the bond.

Hunting. *If he would not give her the truth, she would take it.*

She pushed past the physical bliss, sinking her claws into the mental link between them. Fragments of memory began bleeding through the cracks in his armor, pulsing in time with his thrusts.

Cold stone halls. The weight of a sword too heavy for small hands. A faceless, ruthless king.

His grip in her hair tightened to a painful, grounding point. His hips bucked forward, harder than he intended. *Control beginning to fray.* She felt it—the way her will had yanked the motion out of him.

No. Not yet. The command lashed through the bond back at her, sharp with desperation.

But she was not known for obeying him.

I'll take what I want.

Reny closed her eyes and sank deeper into that golden thread lit between them, wrapping her presence around his mind in a suffocating embrace. She felt the cracks in his resolve, the war between a predator's hunger and the dread coiled tight beneath it.

The terror of what she would find when it all fell.

In body and mind, she clenched. Pulled.

"What are you—" His entire body jolted, breath hitching in his chest. The hand in her hair released, sliding down to grip her hip with bruising force. The torturous rhythm he'd taunted her with snapped.

A dark castle built at the foot of darker mountains. And the banners, black and—

Rook drove into her without mercy now, all previous pretense of control and power over her gone. Her body rocked back to meet him with the same frenzy, the inevitable end building like a savage storm.

She shattered around him, the force of it nearly dropping her to her elbows. But the pleasure brought no peace. It demanded more. More memories. More truth.

Black banners with a royal crest that she knew from every nightmare. The coiled serpent devouring its own tail.

Rook groaned, a guttural sound torn from his chest with every brutal snap of his hips.

No, it can't be...

He tried to seize command over the bond in a final, desperate grab, but Reny breathed flame and fury against his resistance, denying his ability to choke back the memories.

He wouldn't give her to Rithmor. Let them come for him instead. Redemption purchased with his own death. That way, he'd never have to tell her.

The thoughts poured into her, tasting like ash and shame.

Terrified she would reject him for what he was. She had every reason to.

His movements became a relentless, fevered worship. Her nails clawed at the sheets, trying to anchor herself to the beast he'd become. Magic—pure and whole, untainted by the decades of rot—hummed in his blood, in hers, like a siren's song calling him home.

"All of it," she moaned, finding him over her shoulder. *There was no going back.* She needed the truth, and she needed him, with the same necessity as the air she kept trying to catch.

The air he kept stealing from her.

"Fuck, Reny." He sucked in a harsh breath, tightening his grip on her hips until she was anchored against him.

And he yielded to her, the command severing the final thread of his resolve.

The dam broke.

A throne room. A king seated on obsidian, ancient and cold. "You will bring her back, Vaelric. Alive. You swore with your own blood at my feet. Do not fail me."

The brother from the garden, older now. Beautiful, poisonous. "She's the key, brother. The key to everything."

Vaelric.

The name landed like a lethal blow, forcing the air from her lungs.

Vaelric Drayvien. The infamous second son of Rithmor. The king's Rook. The monster sent to find her, track her, deliver her to a crown that would bleed her dry for power.

...The monster that was buried inside of her. He tried to summon her through the spiraling of her thoughts, his voice in her mind a broken prayer.

Aurenya.

It wasn't just a revelation. It was devastation.

No.

The light threading through them pulsed, filling Reny with crushing heaviness. He was pleading with her, begging her to understand the awful, undeniable truth.

I love you. I loved you while lying to you. Loved you enough to betray my own blood, my crown, my homeland.

Her own cold thoughts swept through the bond, cutting over his pleas like a cruel, winter wind.

But not enough to reveal the whole truth before eternally binding me. Not enough to give me a choice.

Rook's head tipped back. He was unable to hold on any longer. A man destroyed. He came wholly undone inside her with a hoarse cry of her name into the room. Into her mind.

Aurenya, please...

But it was done. She had been claimed in the way the old gods had written, in the way their kind was first bound. Their souls were fused, immortalized. What had been forged could not be undone. Even if she hated him now.

He slumped forward, planting an infuriatingly soft kiss on the back of her shoulder before he withdrew. Heavy silence filled the space between them. Wrapping both arms around her, he pulled them down to the mattress, turning her until they faced one another in the tangle of sheets.

Her eyes opened, and she saw him. Truly saw him. The man, the monster, the whole truth of him. The one terrible, beautiful thing revealed to her at last.

From the moment he'd arrived at the tavern in River's Edge, every shrieking instinct she had was right. As drawn to him as she'd been, as alluring as he was, some part of her had known all along. Deep in her bones, in her very soul, she had known. But ignored it anyway.

For all the fire she carried, she'd still been the moth.

And he, the unforgivable, lethal pyre.

Unable to meet his unrelenting stare a second more, she rolled to her back, fixing her gaze on the ceiling. Through the bond and her body, she could feel his power. The terrifying scope of the secret he'd kept from her.

"You're... Vaelric Drayvien." The name broke from her lips, tasting like forbidden scripture. Like tears and poison and truth.

Rook stiffened. He started to speak, but the words died in his throat. Through the bond, she felt the final piece lock into place. Irrevocable, permanent, eternal. And felt the grief that nearly tore him apart. Her head turned toward him on the pillow.

"I meant it when I told you before," he murmured, swallowing hard as he lifted on an elbow to hover above her. He searched her haunted eyes. "I'm not a good man."

Reny said nothing. The truth was out. She knew everything.

And the dawn was still hours away.

CHAPTER 51

From across the Veil, he felt them.

The sensation struck without warning. A divine jolt that tore through the barrier between realms like lightning through parchment. No amount of distance, no veiling magic wrought by gods or realm dwellers, could stifle the unmistakable resonance of an ancient bond forging itself permanently.

The ember of Aurelia had been claimed. He was sure of it.

It stopped Malorith mid-stride across the throne room, the impact like a molten dagger driven between his shoulder blades. His borrowed body went rigid, the mask of Crown Prince Tareth's beautiful face twisting, grim amusement curdling into a thing far darker. More primal.

Hunger. Rage.

And beneath it all, a delicious, vindictive satisfaction.

For a moment, Tareth's broad shoulders remained locked, every muscle straining with malice barely contained. The throne room itself seemed to hold its breath, shadows deepening in the corners where the torchlight couldn't reach, the very stones recognizing the presence of a thing that should not be.

Then, easily, he forced the tension away. It rolled from him like oil sliding off water, grace returning to every fluid movement. The practiced, princely elegance that Tareth had spent years perfecting was now his to wield. His hand lifted, long fingers adjusting the jagged crown upon his brow. The iron bit into skin that was not his own, but he felt no pain.

He had not felt pain in eons. Had forgotten what it meant to suffer in any way that mattered. Pain was for creatures who could die. For things that ended.

He was eternal. He was the end itself.

And soon, he would also be every beginning.

Silence reigned in the empty hall, broken only by the distant groan of dying foundations and the whisper of wind through shattered windows.

"Hmm." The sound was thoughtful, almost amused. "No matter."

He resumed his measured pace, boots echoing against cracked marble as he crossed to the vast balcony that overlooked the broken lands of Rithmor. What had once been fertile valleys and prosperous towns now stretched beneath him in ruin. Blackened soil, veined with the slow rot of his blight, extended toward distant mountains shrouded in perpetual gray. Narrow plumes of smoke rose from scattered fires where the remnants of Rithmor's legion huddled for warmth against the unnatural cold that had seeped into the land.

They waited.

For command. For mercy. For death.

For anything beyond the suffering they'd endured since the curse had begun its slow consumption of their homeland. Of them.

Since he had begun his glorious work of undoing.

Malorith placed both palms upon the balcony railing. It gleamed with an oily sheen beneath his touch, as though the stone itself recoiled from what wore a prince's skin.

His eyes, Tareth's eyes, once a warm amber, now burned with hate, dark and frigid. Twin voids fixed on the distant encampment below. On the hundreds, perhaps thousands, of Aetherian men, all of them deliciously desperate, clinging to the last threads of loyalty to a crown that had never cared whether they lived or died.

Perfect.

He had watched civilizations rise and crumble to dust. Had seen empires span continents only to be swallowed by the earth they'd claimed. Mortals built their little kingdoms, fought their little wars, loved their little loves. And in the end, all of it fed the same hungry dark. All of it returned to him.

This kingdom would be no different. These men would be no different.

They simply didn't know it yet.

"The bond did not matter before," Malorith murmured to the empty air, to no one, his voice carrying the weight of millennia. Memory flickered across his face. Distant, aching.

A garden burning beneath a black sun. A goddess on her knees. The taste of her tears as his banishment tore nearly all of her from existence.

"He failed her then, when it mattered most." His lips curved, the expression wrong on Tareth's face. Too knowing. Too cruel. Too old for any mortal mouth.

"And he will fail her again."

He had waited centuries for this. Had rotted in his prison of voidstone while most of the world forgot his name. A relic of a darker age best left buried.

Power gathered at his fingertips, eager to consume. He swept one hand across the railing in a languid arc, as if conducting an orchestra only he could hear. The air shimmered and pulsed, bending around his will.

Below, the first tendrils of merciless shadow began to rise. It came not from the ground but from the spaces between, the cracks in time and space where his presence had weakened the very fabric of the world. Darkness bled into the wind like ink through water, churning and billowing as it built into a vast, terrible storm.

A storm with consciousness. With its own desire and intent.

His desire. His intent. An extension of the void that had birthed him before the first mortal ever drew breath, before the gods themselves took names.

It spilled over the encampment in a wave of liquid night, blanketing every living being below with his will.

The men looked up, just in time to see the darkness descend. Some tried to run. But most simply stood, transfixed, as it poured into them through their open mouths and wide, horrified eyes. Like drowning, it filled their lungs. Like poison, it flooded their veins, carving out their hearts and everything that made them men.

Leaving only hollow obedience in its wake.

He felt each one as they fell. Thousands of small flames snuffed out, their consciousness collapsing into his own like drops of rain into an endless sea. Their fear tasted sweet. Their final, desperate prayers tasted sweeter.

No god would answer them. Not anymore.

When the void finally settled, having soaked through mind and marrow, they rose. All of them black-eyed and soulless.

Just like him.

They moved immediately. Not with the confused stumbling of the newly possessed, but with a singular, terrible purpose. Their armor was donned, their weapons gathered. Formations assembled with the precision of a hive mind, every soldier a single cell in a body that answered to him alone.

"Yes," Malorith breathed, pleasure and satisfaction warming the words as he watched his new legion fall into deadly, beautiful lines.

All at his command.

The ember of Aurelia had found her mate. Let her have this small happiness. Let her believe, for these brief mortal moments, that love could protect her from what was coming.

He had shattered greater things than love.

The cold white of the moon had not yet surrendered to dawn when Korva slipped from her bedchamber.

A shifter had been stationed outside her door. For her protection, Brenn claimed.

In the still of night, her guard had drifted into sleep, succumbing to exhaustion and the soft, relentless drumming of the tide against the rockface.

She had spent the entire night perched on the edge of her bed, waiting for such a moment. Korva paused as she pulled her door closed behind her without making a sound. She tilted her head, studying his face. Only a sliver of the young woman she'd once been, buried deep within the corrupted labyrinth of her mind, recognized him.

The polecat. In his human form, he was long-limbed and just as lean. Naïve and careless with youth.

Like her once.

Her fingers tightened around the dagger she'd retrieved from its hiding place inside her bedframe. The one placed there at Orwyn's urging. The brother who'd always watched over her, always protected her, always given her advice.

"Never find yourself unarmed, no matter where you are."

Never to be found unarmed again, now that she herself had become the weapon.

Kill him. Kill him before he wakes and stops you.

The blade rose, catching a flicker of the low torchlight as the master's whispers swam in her ears, but her arm froze mid-air.

Please... I don't want to. He won't wake, I swear it.

The faintest thread of her true self whispered her pleas from the darkest corner of her consciousness. From within the mental cell where she'd been locked away, kept conscious just enough to witness what her body did in his name. Just enough strength left to keep the blade from falling.

Please spare him.

Her jaw tensed, body twitching with uneven movement, raised arm trembling. Malorith's anger gripped around her frail voice like two fists, annoyed by her resistance.

You're pathetic. Just go and get me my Eye.

Her arm fell slowly, her shoulders rolling before she turned away. Korva moved through the corridors on soundless feet, turning corner after corner, descending a narrow flight of stairs.

Toward Rhedda's chamber.

Her hand closed over the latch and turned. Her lips curved into a smile that wasn't hers as it gave way without resistance. No lock to keep her out. The Cliff Mother never locked her door in case one of the Cliffborn came seeking her in the night. Came seeking her help.

But no one could help her now.

Korva slipped inside the room and shut the door behind her, unseen in the black hush before dawn. Concealed, even from the seer herself, as she crossed the threshold and hovered near the bedside.

With both hands, she gripped the dagger's handle, raising it high.

Rhedda's eyes opened. Not with the jolt of the startled, but with the quiet resignation of one who had been waiting.

She'd seen this. Of course she'd seen this. She had known exactly how her story would end. And had done nothing to stop it.

Their stares locked, recognition passing between them. Sorrow, and a heartbreaking sense of understanding. Rhedda's lips parted, and for one breath, Korva thought the Cliff Mother might speak. Might offer her absolution.

Might say *"I forgive you,"* or *"It's not your fault,"* or *"I'm sorry I couldn't save you."*

But Rhedda said nothing, the old woman choosing only to close her eyes against her inevitable end.

And the blade came down.

The first strike was the worst.

Not for the blood, though it came, hot and immediate, flooding over Korva's knuckles. Not for the sound, though she would never forget the wet, tearing give of flesh beneath steel.

It was the worst because the last remaining part of her felt it. Locked inside the prison of her own skull, Korva still felt the dagger sink into the woman who had only ever shown her kindness. And could do absolutely nothing to stop it.

No no no no no—

Her body folded into the motion, grace and madness entwined, as silver met flesh again. And again.

STOP PLEASE STOP—

The blade rose and fell.

Rose and fell.

Rose and fell.

Inside her own mind, Korva screamed until her voice shredded to nothing. Her hands kept moving, controlled by an ancient, wicked hunger that insisted she witness every moment through eyes that were no longer hers.

She did not stop until her breathing came ragged and her pale skin and long black hair had been painted red. Until the room reeked of iron and salt and death. Until the woman on the bed no longer resembled the Cliff Mother at all.

And then—unexpectedly, horribly—Rhedda's memories began to overwhelm her.

They flooded into Korva's mind like an incoming tide. Violent, drowning, relentless. The visions the seer had witnessed. The prophecy she'd based every decision on. Her own awful, bloody death.

The Eye of Nytheris. The location revealed itself as clearly as if she'd walked the path herself hundreds of times. The words to undo the wards protecting it were as familiar as if she'd written them herself.

Chest heaving, heart thundering, Korva released the blade, letting it clatter beside her on the sandstone floor, crimson dripping from steel and hilt and hand. Thin rivers of blood streaked down her face, tracing the hollow planes where mercy and innocence had once lived.

In the cold, dark depths of her former self, the true Korva sobbed.

But her body stood calm, satisfied with its work, soaked in the proof of it. Without looking back, she turned and slipped into the hallway as quietly as she'd come, moving through the corridor with terrible certainty.

To the Eye.

And with every step, the true Korva screamed into the void of her mental cell, unheard and unheeded, while she carried out the will of the One Eternal.

The sheets were a tangled ruin around his legs.

Brenn had spent the night at war with the mattress, finding no truce in sleep. He rose at the first gray bleed of dawn, watching the sun drag itself up from the sea.

Forcing a breath into his lungs, he willed the restlessness in him to settle. Deep in the cage of his chest, the bear paced, agitated and snarling, before finally curling down into a sullen wait. Into acceptance.

He owed her an apology. And he would give her one.

The Cliff Mother had been the stone against which his anger broke, time and time again. She never crumbled, simply offering him the quiet grace of her presence until he could rebuild the fragments of himself whenever he fell apart.

He splashed his face with water from the basin, the glacial cold shocking the heat from his skin. He rolled the tension from his shoulders and pulled on a clean tunic, layering a heavy fur vest over it. His fingers found the iron brooch at his lapel.

A wave curling over a mountain peak.

He pressed his palm against the cold metal, the heartbeat beneath finding a steady rhythm.

Breathe.

They would find a solution. They always did.

Stepping out into the hushed dim of the cliffs, he let the morning wind scour the lingering exhaustion from his mind. He moved through the stone halls with purpose, boots silent on the rock, heading toward Rhedda's chamber. She would be awake. She always rose before the sun.

But when he rapped his knuckles against the wood, only a hollow silence answered. So he knocked again.

Nothing.

As he leaned in to press an ear to the door, to listen, he smelled it.

The unmistakable tang of copper hit the back of his throat, triggering a violent, primal alarm through his entire body. His hand closed around the handle.

Slipped.

Brenn pulled his hand back and looked down. His entire palm was slick with it. Dark and tacky.

No.

Brenn threw his shoulder against the wood as he grabbed the handle again and wrenched it open, left frozen in the threshold. His mind stuttered, refusing to process the sight.

The red splashed across the walls. The chaotic spray across the bed furs. The wrecked, awful stillness in the center of it all.

For a heartbeat, the world stopped. Until the floor dropped out from under him.

A roar, raw and all animal, tore from his throat. Brenn staggered back, gripping the doorframe as if it were the only thing keeping him upright. His vision swam, black spots dancing at the edges. He stumbled into the hall, his legs heavy, unmoored from his will.

At some point, he roared a second time. Voices answered. Footsteps. Motions blurring past him.

Rhedda.

His gaze fell, snagged on the floor. Faint, dark smears marked the sandstone. The clear, damning impressions of boot prints in a trail leading away, down a path that was a secret shared only between him and the Cliff Mother.

Brenn's chest constricted, the air turning to broken glass in his lungs. He didn't need to follow the tracks to know whose boots had made them.

Already knew. The heartbreak fractured into a blinding, white-hot rage.

He ran. Ran faster than a man should be able to move, feet thundering against the rock as other Cliffborn ran by him toward Rhedda's chamber. Fighting every instinct to shift, Brenn raced through the twisting corridors, down the winding stairs, tearing through the hollowed veins of the cliffs. Ran until the salt air burned his throat like acid. Until human thought dissolved into the singular, desperate instinct of the predator.

He had to get to the Eye.

CHAPTER 52

Reny wasn't sure how much time had passed before she slipped from the bed.

She retreated into the private alcove just off the chamber. A narrow, modest bathing space where the spring water ran fast and clear. She scrubbed until her skin burned.

As if she could scour him away. As if she could scrub herself back into a reality where none of it was true. Where he'd never stepped foot in River's Edge.

When she emerged at last in a billow of steam, she found him exactly where she'd left him. Rook had moved only enough to pull on his black pants, leaving them unbuttoned at the waist. He lay sprawled across the bed in the earliest lavender of pre-dawn, propped up on one elbow, watching her.

His darkened eyes tracked her through the haze, cataloging every detail. She'd dressed. Clean boots, black pants, and the crimson top the healers had left behind. His jaw tightened. She cut him one cold look as she crossed the chamber, heading toward the door.

"Are you done having a tantrum so that we might talk about this?"

"Oh, fuck off, *Vaelric.*" She spat the name at his feet like poison. "The time for discussion has passed."

His brows lifted. Not in amusement, but something more clinical. As if gauging exactly how deep the wound went. "It's still just Rook."

"Is it?" She finally faced him, the hatred there enough to flay him open. Her right hand lifted, the gesture born of thoughtless instinct and rage.

Rook sat up slowly, making no move to retreat. "Don't."

Without hesitation, a white orb bloomed in her palm, a thin lash of fire unfurling from it. The flame arced toward him, lethal and wicked, but his hand rose with otherworldly speed. Fingers closed around the searing light, seizing it mid-air before she could blink.

He didn't recoil, holding her flame with a new, unsettling ease as it sizzled harmlessly against the palm of his hand.

"You're much stronger now," he observed, his voice thick and dark with approval. "Such control."

Half-snarling, teeth gritted, she willed the blaze to hurt him. Willed it to hurt him as much as what was cleaving through her chest.

It didn't.

"But you see, Reny—" He pushed off the bed and stalked forward, the fire-whip shrinking between them as he reeled it in. The heat curling in his voice had become its own sin. "You can't hurt me this way. You never could, no matter how mad you were."

He closed the distance, one step for every word, until he had walked her back into the wall. As he'd done so many times before. She held her ground, nowhere left to go, her face twisting in despair as the tower of his frame became a cage.

"And now... You know why."

Fire kept bleeding from her hand, the lash shortened but still reckless. His easy acceptance waited on the other end of it, absorbing her flame wherever it touched him.

"You lied to me, Rook." The fury in her voice burned where her flames could not.

"No." He met her unflinchingly, the word landing like a blade. "I didn't."

"You hid it from me intentionally," she seethed. "You used me."

Her left hand, trembling, rose in a sharp sweep toward his jaw. Before she could connect, he snatched her wrist.

"You kept it from me until it was too late." She yanked at both arms, trying to break his hold. "Fucking coward."

"Reny." He spoke low, unbearably calm.

"Was this just to get your power back?" Her emerald eyes narrowed, laced with Aetherian gold and bitter accusation.

"No, Reny." The sigh that left him was ragged, fraying. "Though that was, admittedly, a pleasant surprise."

The arrogance he wore as armor threatened to tear her in half. Heat flickered at her fingertips again, but an answering storm rolled in his eyes. His grip tightened on her arm and her magic before the light could emerge, forcing the spark to gutter and die.

Stop it, Reny. Just stop.

"Your family killed mine," she breathed, the unspoken words he slipped down the bond only stoking the rage. "The Drayviens took everything from me."

"Not everything," he snapped. But his eyes shifted, briefly softening like a wound reopening. There and gone, lost to the storm of him.

His body pressed into her until she could feel the heat rolling off him. Reny moved in one furious wrench against his hold, a desperate attempt to break away and reach the door. Her mind raced. Spiraled.

Maybe if I yell for Brenn...

Rook growled, turning inward to the bond and seizing it. Seizing her.

His magic surged full force, sweeping her resistance and her control completely away. Her body became a temporary prison.

"Would you just fucking listen?" His words were rough steel, nearly shouting. "I've killed. For a time, that was all I did. What I was made to do. But that wasn't me that day, Reny. I swear it. I never killed Endarian people for sport."

"Why should I believe you?" Despite his iron grip, she fought him, eyelashes fluttering to keep the stinging tears at bay.

"If you'd just stop and think for one damn second," Rook grumbled, the timbre vibrating in her ribs, "you can see for yourself. See everything."

"No, I don't want—"

"See me!" He pressed his forehead to hers. *See me.*

It wasn't a demand or offering.

It was a flood.

Rook's power forced the bond open, forced her mind open, and in one broken gasp, her grip on the world dissolved into a montage of memory.

The copper tang of blood. The weight of a cruel father's silence. A silence that told a young boy he was the reason his mother died. A brother, once an ally, who eventually believed that, too.

"Stop, Rook." She tried to sever the link, but he wrapped himself tighter around her mind. The same way she'd done to him. His hands gripped her arms, keeping her pinned against the stone wall.

A man molded into a monster in a cold, dark barracks. Black royal banners snapping in the wind over his shoulder. Steel meeting bone in the mud of Rithmor. Of Endaria. The scars on his back burning under a healer's touch, only to be reopened by another whipping.

"Please, Rook, stop!" She clawed for her power, but his horror drowned it. His guilt suffocated it.

The sickening realization that his brother's campaigns were slaughter for pleasure, not war for peace. The blood oath he took at the feet of unforgiving men. The lies he told Tareth to buy more time with her. To stay human just a little longer. The quiet acceptance of his own death if it meant she had a chance to live.

Reny's scream split the air, split their minds, raw and unmade. "Stop! Gods, please, stop!"

The hold over her snapped. Rook staggered back a half-step, disoriented by the force of her. Her heart thundered like a war drum, his own answering in the same brutal rhythm.

If I can just get to the door...

Reny stumbled to the side a few paces. Rook regained his footing and lunged for her just as she made for the door handle.

"I'm only trying to make it right," he said, the words torn down to almost nothing as he caught her forearm, jerking her back into the wall of his body. "The only way I know how."

"By forcing your way into my head? By making me watch what you're too chicken shit to say?" She wriggled, tried to surge forward as he wrapped his arms around her and drew her farther back into the chamber.

"By letting you see what no one else has ever seen." His jaw worked as he spun her, pinning her to the far wall. "I've never—"

His voice trailed off, shoulders falling in a weary line as his eyes met hers.

She was fighting to catch her breath, trapped yet again between him and the unyielding stone. Tears fell unbidden despite every stubborn effort to prevent them. "You could've told me first. You could have given me a choice."

"You've always had a choice." His jaw tightened, the beast in him rising to the surface. The slate of his eyes had surrendered to a simmering, solid gold. "And every damn time, you leaned into the worst of me. You *chose* this. Me."

"You didn't trust me to know this, though." Reny's voice broke on the words, and she hated herself for it. Hated herself for wanting to lean into him, even now. "I will never forgive you."

"Then don't," Rook shouted, the force of it traveling down his arms, shaking her shoulders. "I never asked for forgiveness."

"Maybe that's what's wrong with you."

Her words struck home. Body heaving with feral breath, he forced himself to let her go. To take a step back. She could see the war in him, every muscle trembling as the predator fought its leash.

"They were *your* words, Reny, not mine. You wanted the monster to claim you," he snarled, his voice breaking over her like dark water. "If *that* was the price."

She didn't move, only stared at him as her own words rose up to haunt her. To remind her how right he was, how she had chosen the darkest parts of him time and time again.

He burned in the half-light of morning as he jabbed a finger toward his own chest, the movement so sharp she felt the impact in her ribs.

"This is the price, Aurenya."

CHAPTER 53

T he air still shivered between them when the walls themselves began to tremble. A deep, resonant sound rolled through the cliffs. A long, mournful tone that seemed to rise from the sea's very bones.

Reny froze, confusion flickering across her face. She didn't know what it meant.

But Rook did.

He went still in front of her, head turning toward the narrow window cut into the rock. He'd heard it before. Once, distantly, when he'd come near the cliffs to parley with Brenn.

The sea-horn.

A warning. Someone—or something—had breached their wards.

His gaze returned to her, lingering a heartbeat too long. As if he were searing her image into his memory before he finally stepped away. Without a word, he buttoned his pants, grabbed his discarded shirt, and dragged it over his head before making quick work of his boots.

Reny pushed free of the wall, the seething heat between them collapsing to ice. The unbreakable thread between them settled into grim, patient silence.

"What is that?" she demanded, following him as the horn sounded again, louder and longer. "What's going on?"

Rook unlocked the chamber door with a rough twist and jerked it open. The sea-horn bellowed a third time, its echo careening down the corridor. His jaw worked as he tipped his head, a wordless summons for her to follow.

They moved fast through the winding halls, down several flights of steps, until the air grew thick with salt and the din of shouting. Torchlight threw shadows along the walls as voices rose in unified alarm.

Aric rounded a corner at full stride and collided with the breadth of Rook's chest. Both men staggered, catching their balance.

Rook took him in with a swift, sweeping glance. "What's going on?"

Aric's amber eyes were wide, red-rimmed. "The Cliff Mother—" He swallowed hard. "The Cliff Mother has been killed. And we can't find Brenn."

Rook hissed a curse, spinning toward Reny. Her face was tight with alarm, focus darting between the two men.

"And Korva—she's missing too." Aric's voice cracked. "I think... I think they might be with the Eye. I don't know."

Rook's gaze sharpened. "With what?"

Aric grimaced, like realizing he'd said too much but was too desperate to stop himself.

"The Eye of Nytheris." He pressed a hand to his chest, fighting to steady his breath. "One of ours was missing. She came back last night, but she acted... off. Claimed she was imprisoned by Tareth Drayvien. Kept asking the Cliff Mother and Brenn to take her to the Eye, said it could reveal what she knew. She was rambling lies. About you."

Rook's throat bobbed. Behind him, Reny had gone still. He didn't need to turn around to know the look on her face. He could feel the power radiating off her like a violent, underlying current, vibrating through the stone beneath their feet.

Aric swallowed, his voice a jagged whisper. "Only Brenn and the Cliff Mother knew where the Eye was kept. Hidden deep within the Cliffs. But there's—"

He stopped, the fox's amber gaze meeting their faces. "A blood trail."

Rook and Reny finally locked eyes, the same sense of dread a rising tide between them.

Brenn barreled down the last set of stairs and burst through the hidden door into the chamber beyond, already whispering the words to drop the final ward.

Dawn had broken over the horizon, spilling pale gold into the cavern that opened to the sea. Soft light bled across the walls, over the Eye.

Over the girl.

Korva stood in front of the mirror, half-hunched, drenched in the blood of their Cliff Mother. Brenn's stomach lurched. His hands rose without thinking, bile climbing his throat. He took one wide, cautious step forward, but she did not react to his presence. As if she existed outside of time, in a different space, suspended between one heartbeat and the next.

Then, the smallest flicker. A twitch in her arm.

Her whole body jerked toward him in disjointed movements, every motion wrong. Her eyes—solid black, like her raven form—were gutted of warmth and awareness. Something else stared back at him.

Not her. Through her.

Brenn's lungs seized, refusing the breath he tried to draw.

"Korva..." He spoke gently, calm despite the despair and fear raging inside him. He took another step.

Her head snapped up, and her hand shot out. Then wrenched back, fingers clawing at her own throat as if trying to strangle away the words before they escaped.

"Get back, Brenn." Voices ripped from her in layers. Hers, desperate and terrified. A man's, cold and commanding, booming above it. "Stay away!"

"Please..." Korva's voice broke through solo, frail and drowning. "Don't come any closer, Brenn."

"I'm not leaving you, baby bird." The tremor in his voice betrayed him. He forced his fear down, refusing the cold truth gnawing at his gut.

Rhedda had been right all along. A darkness had come to the Cliffs inside Korva. A primordial force that was now waging war against her. Inside her.

And he'd condemned the Cliff Mother for it. His doubt in her, his threat to her leadership. Those were the last things she ever heard from him.

Korva folded inward with a strangled cry, her hands frantically slapping and clawing at her own arms, leaving red welts in their wake. As if she could tear away what tortured her with her bare hands.

"I didn't mean to, Brenn..." A sob, only hers again, cracked through. "I'm so sorry..."

"No, no, it's okay," he murmured, words barely carrying above the thunder of the tide.

"It's not." Her cry splintered and divided. One tone human, the other warping deep beneath it. She shook her head, bending forward until the ends of her blood-matted hair brushed the pool of salt water before the Eye, sending ripples across its surface. "It's not going to be okay. I killed her, Brenn."

"That wasn't you." Brenn fought to keep himself steady, his heart pounding louder than the sea-horn still calling from atop the cliffs. "That wasn't your fault."

Korva's body convulsed, spine abruptly arching backward at an angle that no form should bend. Her mouth opened in a silent scream before snapping back shut, teeth cracking together. Tears rolled down her face, every line of her frame shaking under the strain of what had taken root inside her.

"Stay with me," Brenn urged, fighting off tears of his own. "You're stronger than that thing. You hear me?"

Her head jerked violently side to side, teeth bared, face twisted in agony.

"I'm trying—" Her teeth clenched so hard that Brenn heard them grind. One hand flew to her skull, nails digging into her scalp, drawing blood. Strands of black hair came away slick with it. "I'm trying, I'm trying, I'm—"

The deeper voice tore free from her mouth. "The Eye!"

She screamed over it, raw and defiant, clutching her head at the temples.

"Korva!" Brenn shouted, rushing toward her, but a sudden flare from the Eye stopped him mid-stride.

The mirror blazed, its radiance bending, twisting on itself as the air went molten with old magic. Responding to presence.

Footsteps thundered into the chamber from behind Brenn. He turned as they spilled from the stairwell entrance. Aric first, breath ragged and wide-eyed, Reny and Rook close behind.

The Eye of Nytheris flared again, brighter this time, its light stretching and writhing like it had come to life.

A cry tore from Korva, raw and uncontained.

Malorith's voice erupted from her, booming across the realms, across the Veil, across time itself. Reny lurched forward as if struck, moving toward the possessed girl before anyone could stop her.

Korva's head angled far to one side, turning toward Reny with deliberate precision. A tormented puppet, its strings pulled too tight by its master. That black stare fixed on her, unblinking. The thing inside the young shifter smiled with her mouth.

"There you are." It was too tender. Ancient and wrong. "I've been waiting so long, little ember."

Reny did not waver, holding that black stare without flinching. Korva's eyes canted, as if what wore her was drinking in the sight of its prey.

"I can see you now. I can see where you are."

Brenn's heart dropped. *The Cliffs were no longer safe.*

"Shall I go to the Cliffs to retrieve you? Or go to River's Edge and force you to come to me? Yes, I shall travel to the Southlands... It's been... quite a long time since I've seen it with my own eyes..."

River's Edge. The threat landed like a blow.

Reny shoved past Rook, light blooming in both palms, fury written across every line of her.

But she froze mid-stride, as if seized by an invisible hand. Rook's focus had locked onto her, his jaw tight. Whatever passed between them somehow managed to hold her in place. Her hands trembled, light still crackling between her fingers.

Brenn lunged toward Korva. Rook's hand shot out, catching the bear shifter by the arm, yanking him back before he could take another step.

"Don't," Rook hissed, his hold unyielding. Brenn fought him, muscles straining, but Rook's strength was iron.

Korva's veins darkened, ink spreading beneath her skin like cracks through porcelain. She twisted at an unnatural angle, valiantly fighting whatever writhed inside her one final time. But her arm drew back against her will and thrust forward in a brutal strike against the Eye.

The chamber erupted.

The mirror exploded with light that burst outward in a concussive wave, slamming into the walls and sending ripples through the rock. The impact shook the sea cave, sand and fragments of stone raining down from above.

The glass split into four separate shards, each piece glowing from within, bleeding a thin fog of bluish light that crept along the floor like a living mist. The air hissed with it, the sound seeping through blood and bone.

Korva let out a broken cry that warped to pure screaming as her body seized and crumpled. A raven tore free from the woman in a collapse of feather and shadow. The great black bird snatched one of the mirror's shards in her talons before launching herself through the cavern's opening and up into the ocean air.

Brenn's voice shattered. Man first, then bear, the roar ripping from him as he wrenched free of Rook. He bolted toward the cliff ledge, one hand outstretched as if he could drag her back from the sky by his will alone. Aric was close behind, if only to grab his friend by the waist to prevent him from throwing himself into the sea. The two arrived at the rock ledge just in time to watch helplessly as the raven swept out over the water, the mirror's shard catching the newborn light like a blade fresh from a forge.

The sound that erupted from Brenn was not a roar. It was grief. Pure and raw and animal and utterly, impossibly human.

Rook and Reny moved further into the chamber, the air still quivering with the aftershock of the broken relic. The three remaining fragments of the Eye lay strewn across the ground at their feet, each one humming with a high, almost imperceptible pitch.

They gleamed in the shallow pools of seawater that held them, casting ripples of iridescent light that crawled up the cave walls like living blue fire.

Brenn stood at the ledge, staring at the sky long after the raven's silhouette had vanished toward Rithmor. At last, he turned, his expression hollowed by disbelief. Aric followed close behind, his face ashen in the strange, shifting glow.

From high above the cliffs, the sea-horn still sounded, its mournful note echoing through the rock.

Through Brenn's chest.

His devastated stare drifted between Rook and Reny as he drew closer, lungs filling with one long, heavy breath. The air between them had changed. He could feel it, even though he didn't want to. The quiet charge humming there, invisible yet undeniable.

Grim recognition settled over him as he sensed the current between them. He studied Reny's face, the defeat in his chest deepening. Reny only bit the inside of her cheek, refusing to meet or acknowledge the recognition Brenn held in his eyes. She looked instead to the fractured glass on the floor.

To the shadow standing rigid at her side.

"What does this mean?" she whispered, watching the pooling seawater embrace the remaining pieces.

Rook looked at Brenn, deferring for once. The disbelief on his face was plain. A man who'd clearly dismissed the Eye as myth, confronted with its shattered remains.

The bear's jaw worked, his hollow gaze falling to the wreckage at their feet. The Eye of Nytheris. The sacred scrying glass of a goddess, guarded by shifters for generations.

Broken.

One fragment was already winging its way toward Rithmor in Korva's talons.

He'd failed. *Failed everything and everyone he'd sworn to protect.*

"It means our sanctuary is gone," Brenn said, dragging a hand down his face. "Malorith has a piece of the Eye. A part of Nytheris herself." He lifted his head, meeting Reny's stare with the weight of a man who had watched his world crumble before the sun had even fully risen.

"And he'll be coming."

CHAPTER 54

T he raven had flown for hours.

When she finally fell from the sky, her descent was graceless. Wings faltered, feathers scattering against the wind. Her talons struck the stone balcony hard, scraping across it, the shard's broken edge slicing deep until blood ran from the bird's feet. Feathers burst and scattered, surrendering to flesh and trembling muscle and bone.

From the archway's darkness, Malorith emerged. Hands clasped behind his back, unhurried, draped in the Drayvien crown's regalia. He paused beside the balustrade, his gaze lowering to the woman crumpled on the ground.

Korva lay curled on her side, breathing heavily, one arm wrapped tight around her knees.

"Do you have it?"

With a quivering hand, she drew the shard from beneath her body. Rhedda's blood had dried in her hair, matting it into thick, knotted ropes.

Malorith stooped, plucked the fragment from her palm, and straightened, his lips curling at the edges.

"You look terrible, girl." The words dripped with mock tenderness. "Now get up."

She pushed herself upright, both hands braced against the stone. When she finally stood and lifted her head, she managed the strength and defiance to meet his stare. Something flickered across his face—amusement, perhaps, or the cold interest of a collector studying a butterfly pinned beneath glass. The corner of his mouth twitched.

"Do you want to know how I took control of you?" Malorith tilted his head, the crown upon it glinting despite the gray, dying light. He let the question hang there. An offering she hadn't asked for.

Korva shook her head faintly, attention fixed on the man before her. The crown prince Tareth, and yet not.

Worse, somehow.

"Because you were already coming undone." He began to circle her with eerie grace. "And I... am the god of undoing."

He moved with a predator's pace around doomed prey, voice smooth as black glass. Every word precise. Unhurried.

"The creek, that day. You were in the wrong place at the right time when my power bled through the ground into the water. Your grief, your resentment... those were an open door for a force like me."

Her bottom lip quivered despite her best effort to still it. He smiled faintly and raised a hand, brushing his thumb across it in a cruel mockery of compassion.

"Human or otherwise, you lesser creatures are all the same." Dramatic disgust twisted his features. "I have watched your kind for millennia. You will do unspeakable things once your weak, pathetic heart is broken."

Her mind became a harrowing sea. Memories broke the surface only to drown again. What he had made her do, what he had made her believe, and the truth itself, all tearing through one another like waves in a storm of blood and salt.

"Your brother's great power, once it was siphoned, didn't last long. The prince I now wear managed to burn through every drop of it in a single day." He paused, savoring the way her face crumpled. The way her tears smelled. "He enjoyed using the owl's wings. Soaring over the mountains your brother will never see again."

Korva's focus flared. She lunged, body before thought.

He caught her by the throat in an instant. His hand clenched tight, yet the rest of his body remained utterly still.

"Ah, ah, now." Malorith's tongue clicked softly. He cocked his head and squeezed harder, pupils swallowing all color as her breath faltered in his palm. Her slender fingers dug at his wrist. He watched her struggle, nearly smiling.

"You could have been something remarkable, you know." His tone was conversational, as if she weren't dying an arm's length away. "A god's weapon, forged from grief and fury. But you fought. Tried to resist me." His grip tightened. "I'd be impressed by your resilience if it weren't so pathetically mortal."

Malorith regarded her in silence as she gasped for air. A fish out of water. The mirror shard turned between his fingers in his free hand. Light broke along its surface, ghostly hues of blue shifting within, like trapped souls searching for escape.

He hummed, almost contemplative. "What shall I do with you?"

His hand loosened. Korva dropped, knees crumpling as she struck the stone. She stayed where she landed, each breath a ragged fight.

His attention swept over her once more before shifting to the shard in his grip. Its surface caught the rising moonlight, rippling like a bottomless pool.

He tilted it, searching the depths. "Show me," he murmured to the glass. "The Veil. The pathway to the Aetherium. The wards." His focus darted across the surface, hunting. "Show me the Flame of Becoming and my traitorous brother."

The scrying glass resisted. Its wavering light dimmed, unwilling to reveal anything to him.

A slow smile spread across his face. "I have cracked minds before," he said, almost to himself, turning the shard in the dying light. "Planted seeds of deceit and decay. Used vessels like you to manipulate and corrupt." His smile sharpened. "I cannot create life anew like Aurelia. Not yet." His stare narrowed. "When the Eye broke, how many pieces were there?"

Korva didn't answer, still desperately chasing breath. Her lips parted, but no sound escaped.

Tareth's voice, but Malorith's command, cracked like iron struck in a forge.

"How many?!"

The question echoed off the dark fortress walls. From behind his silhouette, Rithmor's skies had darkened. Clouds rolled in from the Veil's border to join the coming nightfall, the distant mountains, and the sea, all converging into one wall of black across the sky.

Korva coughed, her throat razored and raw, as she dragged herself along the floor in her last attempt to retreat.

If she could shift, if she could spread her wings and fly back...

Malorith stalked after her until his shadow eclipsed her entirely. His boot slammed into the center of her back, forcing the air from her lungs.

"I asked you a question!" He leaned in with his full weight, the grind of his heel against her spine drawing a strained whimper from her chest.

"Four," she cried out. "There were four."

"Four pieces," he echoed softly, the words rolling from his tongue like a revelation he already knew. He tilted his head, cold amusement gleaming in the dark. "Like the Four Pillars." A deep, velvet chuckle broke from him, devoid of warmth, reverberating like thunder in the hollow air. "How fucking quaint."

He turned the shard over once more. "I bound that bitch Nytheris to this glass a thousand years before your ancestors crawled to the sea. Perhaps I can draw enough of her out to be useful until I collect the others."

Malorith looked down at Korva, still struggling beneath his boot. His smile widened, touched with revelation.

"And if I undo your soul..." He pressed down just enough to make her choke again, delighting in the sound. "With the half-breed magic in your blood, I should be able to bind her to you instead. A perfectly controllable vessel."

Korva looked up at him from over her shoulder, trapped between his boot and the ground. She had fought herself to exhaustion, limbs burning, muffled cries spilling helplessly into the stone.

"Yes, my pet." A dark satisfaction curled through his voice. "I believe you will still be of use to me after all."

Another broken sound tore from her, catching between gasps as she tried to form words.

"What's that, dear? I can't hear you." Malorith's tone was sweetly venomous. Indulgent in her suffering.

She drew from the last, fading depths of herself, clinging to ghosts of memory. To a place she no longer knew how to find.

Please, she thought. *Let Orwyn already be waiting for me. I just want to go home.*

Her voice came thin, trembling, but clear enough to cut through the gathering darkness rolling over the castle. "Why... why are you doing this?"

Malorith stilled. His attention drifted down to her, slow as falling ash, his expression empty. His gaze was lost to the void, the whites consumed until nothing remained but endless black.

"Why?" he repeated softly, the single word dripping with incredulous amusement.

He lifted his boot from her spine and crouched beside her, bringing his face close to hers. When he spoke, his voice deepened, resonating with power that shook the space between them.

"Because I deserve to be the One Eternal. To reign not only over death, but life." His voice rose, every word thunder's bellow. "I have waited millennia for this. I will not simply undo. I will remake. The Seam. The realms here and beyond. Every crawling, breathing thing that dares to exist without my permission."

He grinned, wide and fevered. "All will be rewritten in my image. As it always should have been."

The ground shook beneath them. A low hum built in his chest, growing, swelling, until it became a roar that split the sky above him. A plume of black light erupted from him, liquid shadow spilling outward and binding to the shard still clutched in his grip. The glass screamed as it absorbed him, or he it. Light and darkness twisted together until they became one fused abomination.

The power he had summoned devoured the remaining air around them. Swallowed her sobs, her breath.

Consumed her until nothing remained of Korva but empty obedience, and the promise of a goddess remade to serve him.

CHAPTER 55

In the hours since Korva had flown from the cliffs, the Cliffborn had rallied together in confusion and grief. They scrubbed blood from the halls, prepared their Cliff Mother's body for the sacred rites, and tended to one another.

They laid Rhedda upon a stone dais in the largest of the common rooms, candles encircling her like a vigil of stars. Their flames quivered in the damp salt air, but they held, burning through the evening as kin gathered to mourn.

Reny kept to the shadows along the back wall, her focus locked on the body cocooned in white. The silence of the room was a physical weight. One that she could not find the words to break.

Not even for Edie, who had wandered in to hold her hand with quiet, childish gravity before Elenna scooped her up for bed.

Guilt gnawed at her relentlessly. Every time she closed her eyes, the white-shrouded form in front of her vanished, replaced by the rolling greens of the Southlands and the towering giants of the Oakwoods. Her thoughts drifted home. To Garron's steady presence, to Maren's playfulness, and to Flinn's rolling laughter.

Gods, she just wanted to go home.

But Malorith's voice still echoed in the marrow of her bones, a cold promise whispered through Korva's stolen mouth. *River's Edge.* He didn't just name it. He'd marked her home with lethal intent.

She'd been reluctant to follow Rook's plan from the beginning—reluctant to leave, reluctant to trust him—but she had understood that leaving was an act of protection. Reny had willingly traded her presence for their security so that her absence might shield them from threat.

Instead, she had only drawn death to a new doorstep. Brought blood to the Cliffs in her desperate and now failed attempt to spare River's Edge.

Now, those she held dear were more threatened than ever.

She hadn't been a shield. Her absence hadn't either. She had become a beacon, and the fire she carried had lit the way for another monster to find everyone she loved.

A quiet sob broke from somewhere nearby, pulling her back to the room.

Near the front of the hall, Brenn stood before Rhedda's body. He had been there longer than anyone, his height casting a long shadow over those who stepped forward to lay flowers or bow their heads in prayers that Reny had never heard before. She watched the fallen curve of his shoulders, as if the cliffs themselves had collapsed upon him.

And she supposed, in a way, they had.

A few candles around the dais guttered, spitting in the damp drafts, threatening to burn out. Reny narrowed her focus on them. The flames steadied on their wicks, resuming their quiet vigil.

If she couldn't protect anyone, at least she could do this.

Brenn felt hollow, gutted by everything.

He'd placed the three broken shards of the Eye upon the council table himself, covering them carefully before posting a guard. Then he returned to the hall where Rhedda lay.

He stood before her body until his legs ached, watching the Cliffborn cycle through. Laying flowers, murmuring the old prayers, weeping quietly before slipping away. The weight of it pressed down on him until he thought the stone beneath his feet might crack.

When he finally turned, his eyes found Reny instantly. She stood alone in the shadows at the back of the room, arms folded tight across her chest, as though she could bar the world away.

Even though it had clearly already gotten to her.

Dark pine met her gold-lined emerald and held, the air between them compressing to that single, silent exchange. She was the first to look away, forcing a faint smile toward a pair of shifters as they left the hall.

When her gaze lifted again, Brenn was already standing there.

He took in the line of her jaw, the exhaustion carved into her face. Her attention darted to the front of the room, quick and fleeting.

That's when he noticed the candles, their flames no longer guttering in the drafts. He followed her focus and realized what she had been doing for hours, back here alone in the dark.

Keeping watch over flames that were not hers to tend.

A knot formed in his chest, sudden and tight.

"Are you standing back here blaming yourself, fire-born?" He stepped aside for a few of his people as they passed, nodding to them before settling into her orbit, leaning on the wall beside her.

"Is it that obvious?" Reny cast him a sidelong glance.

"It's not your fault," he said softly.

"But it is, though, isn't it?" Reny leaned her head back against the stone, still commanding the army of candles at the front of the room. "It all comes back to me somehow. I don't even know what I'm supposed to do. Or why."

Brenn's attention lingered on her a little too long. He cleared his throat. Shifted his stance. "She had been waiting for you," he offered after a pause. "Waiting for you so long that some began to doubt her. I doubted her."

Reny turned her head, studying him. "I wish I could have asked her why."

Brenn found he could not meet her eyes and turned back to the dais instead. He sighed, the memory of his last words to Rhedda tightening in his chest. He replayed the night before—his anger, his pride—and clung to the fragile hope that with Rhedda's power of sight, maybe she knew he didn't mean the awful things he'd said. That she might have foreseen the apology meant for the morning.

A morning the seer never saw.

"She was convinced the ember of Aurelia had returned in you. That the Four Pillars would rise again, divine wrongs would be righted, and the realms would be reforged. A new dawn." He watched confusion flicker across Reny's face, the weight of prophecy settling on shoulders that had never asked for it.

Reny frowned. "I grew up thinking they were only bard songs."

The bear shifter huffed, a sound more weary than dismissive. Shadows rolled off the broad width of his shoulders as he shifted forward into the chamber's soft, amber light.

"They're far more than that," he said. "While Rithmor and Endaria were busy fighting over scraps of dying magic, coin, and land, we kept to our cliffs and our roots. Kept to the truth of our beginnings."

Her eyes lifted to him, something like surprise flickering there.

Brenn sighed again, voice dropping to a murmur beneath the surrounding whispers of prayer. "You need to get to the Aetherium. The Master Scribe there is the most powerful seer still living. Understanding of the world before the Veil. He will be able to give you guidance no one else can."

She nodded, exhaustion plain on her face. "I never truly had a chance to thank you."

"For?" Brenn tilted his head.

"For charging the Hollowmire," Reny said. "For throwing it off Rook. For buying me enough time to do... whatever it is I did."

He gave a wry half-laugh, shaking his head. "Don't thank me. I only did it so that I could be the bear to kill him later."

A breath of honest laughter escaped her, her attention drifting back to the candles again. Their flames wavered, then rallied strength, reflected in the gold of her eyes.

He allowed the moment to stretch, studying the light and lines of her face. The subtle, primordial glow that lived just beneath the surface. Brenn pushed his thoughts aside, knowing better than entertaining any of them.

"You made that ugly, hateful, shadow-bastard come undone," he said quietly, shrugging with reluctant admiration. "And you killed the Hollowmire, too."

A pause. Long enough for the joke to land.

When it did, she smiled up at him, fully unguarded. He returned it, eyes holding a newfound light.

"You just may save us all yet, fire-born."

Rook loomed in the corridor outside the great hall where they had laid Rhedda's body. He did not have the audacity to step inside, placing himself in the middle of their mourning.

Even if they didn't know exactly who and what he was.

It gnawed at him that Reny noticed his discomfort, that she had seen his hesitation when they carried the Cliff Mother's body through the hall and up to the dais.

But she had gone in anyway. And stayed there for hours, somehow dismissing every call he had made to her through the bond.

He paced the length of the long hallway, his boots whispering over the cold stone. The torchlight crawled across him each time he passed, every flicker throwing his shadow long and restless along the walls.

Cliffborn moved past him in their quiet procession, faces hollow, some with hands faintly stained with the work of death rites. Rook didn't meet their eyes.

His thoughts narrowed to a single point.

Rhedda's voice the previous morning, calm and certain as she unraveled everything he thought he knew. The way she'd looked at him with kindness despite knowing who he was and everything he'd done.

His heart knocked off rhythm once, twice. A spark unfurled in his chest, sudden and unmistakable. Too familiar to be anything but her.

Reny?

The bond was a simmering line between them, though more ache than warmth. Something had kindled a brief light in her again. Light he could feel but not take credit for providing.

He turned toward the archway just as Brenn appeared. Every predator instinct in him flared.

Though his face was still carved in grief, the bear looked lighter than he had earlier. Rook could sense her on him. Echoes of her nearness, her voice, ghosting through the space between them.

Rook leaned back against the stone wall, trying for ease, forcing his most savage edges to smooth into a false veneer of calm.

Brenn saw right through him. A brow lifted, unimpressed. "Don't have the balls to go in there, Drayvien?"

"I'm being respectful," Rook drawled, folding his arms across his chest, bracing one boot against the wall.

"A first for you." Brenn moved to shoulder past him, but Rook pushed free from the stone, stepping directly in his path.

The air in the narrow corridor buzzed.

Rook's eyes burned with veins of gold beneath the gray. Brenn's green brightened into a lush forest to welcome the storm. The power between them threatened to crack like a fault line, nearly giving way beneath the weight of two predators testing their own restraint.

"What were you talking to her about?"

Brenn's jaw set. "That's none of your business."

"It is my business." Rook's reply came too fast, venomous. "She is my business."

"Does she agree with you on that?"

"That's not your concern." The words came through gritted teeth.

Brenn's hand shot out and grabbed Rook's shoulder, slamming him back into the wall. Rook's snarl was more beast than man, his canines flashing like razors in the low light. Brenn only leaned into him harder, iron answering steel.

"Don't pull that territorial Aetherian shit with me, you miserable prick," Brenn growled, the bear in him clawing toward the surface. "I don't care if she's supposedly your *mate*."

"Supposedly?" Rook held still, not out of fear, but because one wrong breath would invite absolute mayhem. Rage prowled restlessly behind his ribs, begging for the cage to open. Brenn's grip tightened, muscle and bone locked in raw defiance.

"You don't deserve her," Brenn answered. "Never will. Would not surprise me if this bond is some shadowed, Drayvien mind trick, and if it is..." He leaned close enough that Rook caught the edge of his breath. "I'll tear you limb from limb."

Rook's mouth curved to a lethal smile mere inches from his face. "Now who's being territorial, you fucking animal? Jealousy doesn't suit you, Brenn."

The smug grin landed just as he intended. A roar threatened to tear from Brenn's throat, deep and vengeful, the air pulsing with power barely contained.

But their heads turned in unison as all gravity shifted, collapsed, with her arrival.

Reny.

She was already there, watching them, framed in the archway with her arms folded. The scathing verdict on her face made Brenn's hand drop from Rook's shoulder. Rook straightened immediately, rolling the ache from the joint as he smoothed his face into a cold mask of indifference.

The tension didn't break. It only changed shape to match the disappointment alive on her face.

"Are you two done?" Her question was fully stripped of warmth.

Brenn looked down first. He stepped aside, creating distance.

Rook pushed his hands into his pockets, forcing himself to be still. She felt cold to him. Hardened in a way he didn't recognize.

He absolutely hated it.

Reny? He reached for her in the bond instinctively, needing to feel the thread of her reserved only for him in his heart, in his head.

Only to hit a solid wall of iron.

As if she'd spent the last several hours forging it around herself using only fire and spite. The lit cord of his mental reach recoiled hard, folding in on itself, leaving him hollowed and alone in darkness.

Reny! Come on. Please don't do this. His mind struck the iron wall like a clenched fist, the impact reverberating back through his bones.

Impossible. She had blocked him out. Put a wall over the bond.

RENY!

Unbothered by his efforts, her presence confined inside the walls of her mental fortress, Reny stepped free from the archway and moved through the corridor. They both followed without a single glance in each other's direction. Brenn to her left, Rook to her right, the three of them slipping through stone and shadow.

Around the next turn, far enough from the mourners to speak freely, she stopped and whirled on them, her focus landing on Brenn first.

"I want to see the three remaining pieces of the Eye," she said, strong and clear.

"I don't think that's a good idea." Rook took half a step toward her, his brows drawn tight, hand flexing in his pocket.

Reny's eyes cut over him in brief passing. "I didn't ask for your thoughts."

She'd already dismissed him before the words finished leaving her mouth. Rook caught Brenn's brows lift, fleeting. *The bastard had noticed.*

Reny turned back to Brenn. "Right now, if possible. I don't think we have the luxury of time."

With a nod, Brenn pivoted, a flash of a grin ghosting across his mouth as he caught Rook's eye. Then he moved past her to lead them down the winding passage toward the council chamber.

Rook followed with his teeth clenched, falling in step with the shadows behind them. In the muted space of their joined minds, he loomed. A dark, silent sentinel on his side of her iron wall.

Waiting. She couldn't keep the wall there—couldn't keep him out—forever.

CHAPTER 56

A ric stood stationed beside the towering council-chamber doors, one hand resting on the hilt of his long blade. At Brenn's approach, he dipped his head and swung the massive doors open, stepping aside as Rook and Reny followed the bear inside.

The doors boomed shut, their deep echo rolling through the chamber's stone ribs.

At the head of the long table, the three remaining shards of the Eye lay beneath a dark linen cloth. Brenn advanced and, without touching the relics, drew the cloth back.

The chandelier above burned dim, its wax tapers shrunken, flames guttering in the salty draft. Yet they burned just bright enough for the glass shards beneath to catch light. Their fractured faces scattered it across the chamber walls in strange, restless patterns.

Brenn exhaled heavily as Reny stepped forward, her gaze sweeping over the broken remains. "Can you explain what this is to me, exactly?"

Rook positioned himself just behind her shoulder, watching how the shards' glow rippled over her features. He risked a careful press down the bond, only to meet the same solid iron locking him out.

Godsdamned stubborn, infuriating woman.

"The Eye of Nytheris," Brenn began, his words carrying the weight of old memory. "It was the scrying glass of Nytheris herself. One of the Four Pillars. Divine sister of Aurelia, goddess of time, memory, dreams, souls. She saw over the unseen and all that dwells between. She could walk through the realms of the living and the dead without consequence."

Rook moved closer, aligning himself with Reny's side. Across the table, Aric held himself rigid, his focus never straying far from the shards. Or from her.

"She tried to warn Aurelia that Malorith meant to seize her power. To become all-powerful, the One Eternal." Brenn's focus went distant as he recited the sacred history. "But at Malorith's hand, Nytheris was undone and cast into the glass. Her essence has been bound to it ever since."

Color drained from Reny's face, the shadows beneath her tired eyes deepening. The implications were settling over her like a shroud, and Rook could do nothing but watch.

"Only the most powerful seers can use the Eye," Brenn said, gesturing toward the table. "With it, Rhedda learned of the Pillars' return and of the ember's rebirth. Of you."

"What could Malorith do with one piece?" Her voice wavered between fear and disbelief.

Rook said nothing. The hard lines of his face served as their own omen.

"Nothing good," Brenn answered, clearing his throat. "He might try to scry with it. To look for you. Or worse, bind part of Nytheris to himself. Twist her gift. Manipulate dreams, memories..."

Rook swore under his breath, bowing his head until it hung between his braced forearms on the back of the chair. The curse was savage, barely more than a growl. Every revelation carved another line of dread into his chest.

"You keep mentioning Four Pillars," Reny said, eyeing Brenn carefully. "I've only ever heard of three—Aurelia, Malorith, and Nytheris. Who's the fourth?"

Brenn hesitated. When he finally spoke, his words were dry as ash. "Kaelor. Lord of Air and Stone. Creator of seasons and the physical world. He raised the mountains and carved the rivers and seas. He is the origin of all that's wild—the animals, the shifters, the elementals."

From his post at the door, Aric cast a cold, sidelong glare toward Rook. "We were never half-breeds. Just a different divine bloodline your monarchy tried to erase and blame for your sins."

Rook met the glare but didn't rise to it. *Not yet.*

Brenn forced his expression to soften. "Kaelor was Malorith's brother." A pause that hung too long. "And Aurelia's chosen mate. The first bonding."

The words hit Rook like a blade between the ribs. He watched Reny go still—watched her bite the inside of her cheek, her focus locking onto Brenn with deliberate, painful precision.

He willed her his way with every ounce of mental power, but she still refused to look at him.

"So Malorith walks," she said carefully, measuring every word. "I carry the ember of Aurelia. And Nytheris can be pulled from the glass." A pause, the words catching before she forced them through. "Where, or who, is Kaelor, then?"

"Up for debate," Aric muttered from the wall, arms folded.

"Unclear," Brenn cut over him, tipping his chin toward Rook. "Rhedda believed it might be him, but the Eye never gave her a clear answer."

"Because it could never be a fucking Drayvien, that's why," Aric spat.

Rook's shoulders flared, but he didn't dignify it with a response. His attention stayed fixed on Reny. On the careful way she held herself, on the walls she'd built to keep him out.

"Who else could it be?" she asked, her voice falling away before she could finish. "If the bond—"

"It would be a shifter, for starters," Aric cut in.

Rook turned on him then, storm and impatience breaking together. "That's enough from the fools in the gallery, don't you think?"

Aric's glare could have drawn blood, but Brenn's warning growl rippled through the air, deep enough to vibrate through the rock beneath their feet and silence them both.

"Aetherian bonds are biological," Brenn continued, calm in his authority. "Aetherians are descendants of Aurelia, made in her image. It's a matter of lineage or compatibility." He paused, words almost dismissive. "For... mating purposes, mainly, so—"

"Mating bonds are rare and sacred." Rook stepped toward Brenn, his composure fraying. "It's fate. Don't stand there and reduce them to—"

Brenn lifted his hand, interrupting. "Don't. Not now. It's not about you."

He pointed toward Reny, who stared at the glass shards gleaming on the table, refusing the intensity of their faces. "This is about her. She's the one who can change the tides for all of us, but she needs to know how. We need to get her to the Aetherium."

Rook scoffed, the sound thick and bitter. "We? Who's we?"

Brenn held firm. "We as in you, me, and Aric. We will all escort her to the mountain pass."

The muscles in Rook's hand went white-knuckled where he gripped the chair's back. "I can take her myself."

Brenn's reply came low, with underlying threat. "Because you did such an amazing job escorting her the first time?"

The accusation landed like a blow. Rook's jaw clenched, rage simmering just beneath the surface, but he held his tongue.

There was nothing to say. The bastard was right.

Reny's head swam.

She gripped the chair before her, steadying herself as the room tilted. Exhaustion and revelation warred for dominance, each trying to drag her under.

"What about Endaria? And Rithmor?" She forced the words out. "Endarian troops are already marching. How much time do we have?"

Brenn shook his head, brow furrowing. "Depends on how winter rolls in. A week, maybe two, before the Endarian legion reaches the North Gate. I sent a message to Endaria's crown, but I don't know if it will arrive in time."

Aric stepped forward, words falling like heavy frost. "Malorith will want war. He feeds on undoing and rules over the dead. After a battle, he'll consume the souls. It could give him enough power to fully sunder the Veil that Kaelor raised when Aurelia fell."

She finally looked up, watching as Rook wiped a hand down his face and then pressed his fingers against his temples.

"If the Veil falls...?" she asked quietly, scanning their faces for an answer she wasn't sure she wanted.

Aric shifted his weight first, unease radiating from him as he looked to Brenn.

The bear's face was grim. "Then we all do."

The silence that followed was crushing. Reny shut her eyes, forcing the world beneath her feet to steady. Her breathing slowed, controlled, as she pulled herself back from panic's edge.

River's Edge. Garron. Maren. Flinn.

The names moved through her like prayer. Like a compass finding true north.

When she opened them again, her voice was clear. "How far to the mountain pass from here? To the Aetherium?"

Rook was the first to answer. "Two days, if we travel hard and make minimal stops."

Reny lifted her chin, something sharp and quiet settling behind her eyes. A flame repurposed from fear into resolve. "Then we leave at first light."

She tested the iron wall in her mind. It held, impenetrable.

Good.

"Wrap the shards. We'll take them with us."

Brenn and Rook exchanged glances, wordless tension crackling between them. Neither moved. Aric side-stepped toward the chamber doors, his hand hesitating over the handle as though waiting for someone to contradict the order.

"What are you all waiting for?" Reny's voice cut through the standoff, molten and final. "Move it."

CHAPTER 57

T hey had scattered from the council chamber with purpose.

Brenn to see to the rest of Rhedda's rites and their travel rations, Aric to guard duties and steel. Rook had vanished into shadow, leaving Reny to a quieter kind of preparation.

She sat in the chamber where she'd first been laid to recover, the bed she and Rook had undone remade, the sea-worn window latched against the howling wind.

Nothing remained for her to pack. The Hollowmire had taken Sal and, with her, destroyed everything Reny had owned.

She let herself think of the mare for a breath. More than just a horse. Her long-time companion that Garron had saved up to buy her when she turned ten. A stubborn soul, just like her, who had carried them both farther from River's Edge than they ever should have gone. Grief rose, quick and sharp, but Reny willed it down. Tucked it away, like everything else.

The threshold to her room became a flurry of motion. Cliffborn clan members came and went. Quiet-eyed women with measuring cords and chalk, a pair of young shifters with crates of buckles and leather straps, an old, hunched woman with strong hands and a seam ripper between her teeth.

They murmured in the soft cadence of their people, talk skipping from seam to strap to weather. The warm, steady rhythm of those who had buried their dead and kept working anyway.

It reminded her of Garron instantly.

Work is the kinder companion. Asks nothing of the heart.

Maela arrived last, a smile warming her narrow face. She carried a stack of folded garments and a sweep of thin leather armor draped over one arm—fur-edged, sea-stone studs blue as the water, stitching precise enough to have been done by enchantment.

"Stand up, love," Maela said, setting the stack at the end of the bed. "Brenn's orders. You'll be fitted for armor before you head for the mountain pass."

Reny's jaw tightened, though she kept her face still. *Brenn's orders.* Another part of her path that had been decided for her.

She rose. The new leathers smelled warm and earthy, of craftsmanship and salt air. They were neutral enough, but the cut and accents were unmistakably Cliffborn. Built for endurance, for protection, for movement through harsh, unforgiving places.

A long-sleeved black shirt came first, soft but tight over her skin. Maela straightened the hem and tucked it into fitted fighting leathers before adding a vest and bracers banded with thin straps. She cinched and double-knotted each one with brisk hands.

"Breathe," Maela murmured, sliding the chest plate down over Reny's head. "Again." She eased it to settle along her sternum, centered and straight across her shoulders. The stone accents caught the dim light, framed by the fur lapels.

Reny obeyed, air pressing against the tightness in her ribs. She took another breath. The armor hugged her without pinching, its weight distributed evenly across her body.

"Too snug?" Maela asked from behind, peering over her shoulder.

"It's... good, honestly." Reny twisted slightly, testing the fit, rolling her shoulders beneath the thin plates.

"We always keep extra on hand, but this looks like it was made for you." Maela's fingers worked sure and quick, sliding leather tongue through buckle, pulling each strap tight, and tying off the ends. Her breath warmed the nape of Reny's neck as she spoke. A strange comfort Reny could not quite place.

"Brenn has a good eye for sizing. He picked this set himself. I may give him a new job when he returns."

Reny's throat tightened, but she smiled faintly. "Thank you."

Maela smiled back and reached for the utility belt, swinging it around Reny's waist and fastening the buckle behind her. The belt was adorned with dagger sheaths, reinforced spaces for knives and other tools, and a buckled side loop large enough for securing a long blade.

"There," Maela said, giving the strap a final tug before stepping back. "You'll do."

Taking Reny gently by the shoulders, Maela guided her toward the corner where a full-length mirror leaned against the wall.

Reny stopped. Her new Aetherian reflection stared back at her for the first time since she'd changed. Her features were sharper, honed with an otherworldly grace and beauty. The tops of her ears now carried the faint, unmistakable points of the ancient fae she had spent most of her life fearing.

And hating.

Her green eyes had become brighter, more vibrant. And laced with gold, as if the ember she carried had become a constant, controlled burn.

The leathers really did fit as though they'd been made for her. Black and deep brown, a soft sheen of oil catching the lantern light. Sea-stone accents gleamed as she turned to check her profile, each flash echoing the cliffs beyond the walls.

Behind her, Maela's reflection caught her attention. "Aye," the older woman murmured, pride woven through the sound. "That's how our kind look when they've decided to fight back instead of sitting and waiting at the edges of the world."

Reny held her own reflected stare. A silent confirmation.

Fight back.

A firm knock broke the moment.

"Stay put, dear." Maela turned toward the sound, skirts whispering against the stone floor as she crossed the room and drew back the latch.

Aric and Brenn stood beyond the threshold. Both men had donned the same Cliffborn leathers, though theirs were heavier, made for men's battle and bulk. Their chest plates were reinforced by smooth scales of steel, their belts already heavily lined with their chosen weaponry.

Brenn held two arms full of steel—swords of varying length and weight—while Aric's hands held a fabric roll full of daggers and knives, their deadly edges tucked safely inside the cloth.

"Come in, then." Maela nodded and stepped aside.

They entered, their attention drawn immediately to the far side of the room where Reny stood before the mirror. Lanternlight gilded over her, every curve of leather and gleam of sea-stone catching like the gold-threaded green of her eyes.

For a rare, unguarded moment, both men went silent. Reny caught the way Brenn's step faltered, the way Aric's brows lifted before he could school his expression.

She realized how different she must look to them since they'd first seen her. No longer the frail stranger Brenn had carried through the silver pines and up the cliffside.

She'd been reforged. *Reborn.*

Aric cleared his throat, breaking the silence. He shifted the weight of the daggers in his arms and nodded toward the array of weapons they held. "Not sure if you know how to use any of these, so we brought a few options for you. Figure you might want to travel armed."

Reny's attention flicked between the amber of Aric's gaze and the deep pine of Brenn's. The corner of her mouth lifted, betraying a smirk she didn't bother to hide.

They meant well enough. All of them.

"I meant no offense," Aric added quickly when he noticed she let the silence stretch too long. He crossed to a small side table, setting down the fabric roll, unfurling it with care. Rows of knives and daggers gleamed within, each sheathed in soft leather or bound with a cloth tie.

Reny shook her head, a small laugh escaping. His humbled embarrassment was too endearing to let him suffer. "I know my way around."

Brenn remained near the door, arms full, staring. Aric jabbed an elbow into his ribs just as Reny leaned over the array of blades. She inspected them with comfortable ease, choosing one, then another, testing their balance before sliding them into the empty sheaths at her hips. Intentionally ignoring their nervous shuffling.

"I—" Brenn blurted, straightening as Aric's elbow struck again. "I have swords."

He stepped forward in two long strides and let the steel clatter across the bed.

Reny, unbothered, chose one final dagger, tucking it into the leather band around her right thigh. She crossed to the bed, studying the blades Brenn had laid out. Their lengths, their weight, the different hilts. Her fingertips brushed along the polished steel, pausing now and then to test the balance of one before setting it back down to try another.

"Were these all forged here?" she asked without looking up.

Brenn cleared his throat. "Here. Yes. I—well, I thought you grew up in the southlands. In a fishing village?"

Reny's mouth curved faintly as she lifted one of the swords, its hilt wrapped in dark leather worn smooth by time. She stepped back to test its balance, letting the blade turn fluidly in her grip.

"My father," she said, her focus on the steel. *And on the man she spoke so fondly of.* "The man who raised me. He was an Endarian soldier. Saw to it I knew of bows and blades since I was a little girl."

"Good man," Brenn murmured, nodding once.

"He is," Reny agreed with quiet reverence, taking a step back. She lifted her arm, moving through measured arcs. Half swings and slow, controlled turns. The kind born of long practice rather than vanity. The blade caught the light, throwing silver ribbons across the ceiling.

"You're good with a sword, then?" Brenn asked, a half-smile finally pulling at his mouth.

"Impeccable with a bow." A voice came from the doorway. Smooth, rich, and unmistakable.

Rook.

The sound rolled through the chamber like smoke, chasing a chill down Reny's spine. She froze mid-arc, the sword still raised and angled toward him.

He stood framed in the archway, shadows coiling around him like a second skin. She looked him over in a quick drag. The Cliffborn armor suited him.

As did everything.

Dark leather fitted close, trimmed in sea-stone and salt-worn steel. He looked fresh from a forge himself, every edge polished and dangerous.

The easy air in the room vanished. Aric's almost boyish amusement dissolved, his brow knitting as he folded his arms across his chest.

"I need my sword back." Rook leaned against the doorframe, attention locking on Brenn. "When I woke up here, it wasn't in my chamber."

"We weren't about to leave you armed," Aric shot back, taking a step forward.

Rook's reply was a controlled threat. "I wouldn't need to be armed to end you, fox." His unforgiving gaze cut between them. "But now, I'd like it back."

Brenn let the silence carry, expression settling like a stone in water. He broke eye contact and moved to gather the swords Reny hadn't chosen, stacking them with deliberate calm.

"You'll have the sword for the journey."

Aric's brows rose.

"Under one condition," Brenn added quickly.

Rook shifted free from the doorway, unamused as he stepped into the chamber. "What condition?"

"That when we reach the Aetherium," Brenn said, lifting his head, "you put it back where you found it. That you return what you stole."

Reny's brows lifted, alarm flaring as her eyes snapped to Rook. He kept his face carefully blank, though she caught the flicker of surprise he thought he'd kept hidden.

"Fine." He exhaled, the motion reluctant beneath his practiced indifference.

Brenn's huff carried the faint satisfaction of victory. He turned toward the door, Aric already moving with him.

"Get some rest," Brenn said over his shoulder. "We leave at first light."

With Brenn and Aric gone, Maela stayed only long enough to fold the spare leathers and smooth what had been left in disarray before slipping out and closing the door behind her.

Night pressed against the windows, the sea a distant roar beyond the glass.

Rook turned, attention sweeping over Reny with a painful, costly kind of restraint. Every line of him was control, but the effort behind it showed.

"Drop the wall," he commanded. "From the bond. Now."

"No." Reny tipped her chin up, defiant despite the quickening of her pulse.

He moved toward her until the space between them ceased to exist, his shadow falling over her. In the same breath, he struck down the bond, all his power colliding headlong with the iron wall she'd built to keep him out.

The impact reverberated through them both, an echoed pulse that left their bones trembling. She winced, trying to ignore the splitting pain in her chest.

His jaw tightened as he leaned into her, pressing his forehead to hers. "Why are you doing this?"

"I need time," she whispered, eyes squeezing shut. "To understand what it means. What you—"

"What I am?" His voice was raw. "You *know* what I am. Who I am."

"Knowing and accepting aren't the same."

He struck again. Harder. The iron shuddered beneath the weight of him, groaning like a gate battered by a storm.

Reny. Please.

Her name echoed through the bond, desperate and demanding. He struck again, throwing every ounce of himself into tearing it all down.

A force inside her rose to meet him. Not anger. Not defiance. Something far older and fiercer, flooding her veins like molten light. It filled every seam of iron with flame until the wall became unbreakable.

And then she pushed back.

Absolute stillness poured through the bond and seized him where he stood. Rook's breath caught, muscles locked, every limb frozen mid-motion as if he'd been turned to stone. His eyes went wide, storm-gray drowning in the gold reflection of her stare.

The first time she ever saw him look afraid. It nearly dropped her to her knees.

"Reny—" Her name escaped him in a ragged whisper, half plea, half reverence.

She held it, trembling from the effort to subdue him, tears burning at the edges of her vision, though she refused to let them fall. Her chest ached with everything she refused to say. Everything she was choosing to bury behind iron and fire.

"I need time," she managed, straining. "Before these walls come down."

When she released him, he staggered forward, catching himself on the bedpost with a sharp exhale. His chest heaved as his face found hers again, eyes searching for what she would not give him.

"Wrong kind of walls, Reny," he warned. "I can't protect you this way."

The words struck deep inside her. An old ache, familiar and unwelcome.

"I'm doing what I need to do," she whispered fiercely. "And I don't need you to protect me anymore."

The silence between them stretched, awful and heavy, until Reny turned away and reached for the door. Beyond it, the wind howled through the cliffs, and the sea thundered its endless vow against the sandstone.

She didn't look back.

Rook watched her go, pain knotted tight in his chest.

She had locked him out. Refused his entry, wielding a power against him and the bond he hadn't known was possible.

And still, he followed her out the door as the blade at her back.

The corridor stretched before them, torchlight catching the sea-stone accents of her armor, the dark fall of her hair. She moved like someone who had finally remembered what she was. What she had always been.

A goddess reborn. Flame given form.

And he was the fool who had lied to her, manipulated her, dragged her across a continent under false pretenses. Only to fall so completely that the truth of her had undone every lie he'd ever told himself. He had chosen his own undoing the moment he chose her. The bond hummed between them, muted and aching, her iron wall a constant pressure against the place in his mind, in his soul, where she should have been.

But he knew she was still there. Distant, burning. But untouchable.

Sunlight he could see. Warmth he couldn't feel.

Perhaps that was fitting. *What he deserved.*

But he would stay, and he would follow. Vowed silently, as they moved through the corridor, to stand between her and every evil that dared to reach for her.

Even if she never let him close again.

He didn't just find the flame. He'd found his salvation wrapped in fire and fury. Found a tragic, beautiful becoming he hadn't known he was searching for until she burned through every defense he had. Burned through everything he ever was before.

Even if it only ever left him in darkness, he'd found the new dawn. And he'd chase it for eternity, no matter the cost.

Epilogue

The Endarian legion had marched for days through winds that stripped flesh from bone, stopping only when exhaustion claimed them. The generals gave no quarter, driving the lines north.

Toward the North Gate, where they would strike the Aetherian bastards while they were weakest.

By dawn, the storm broke as it passed over the valleys. Pale sunlight bled across the frostbitten fields, the air crisp and biting. After so many brutal days, it felt like a rare kindness.

For an hour, maybe two, the men felt warmth again.

Flinn tightened the straps of his ill-fitting armor, the metal still slick with rain. The plates hung too large, the helmet loose enough to rattle when he moved.

It was all they had. All they'd given him.

He fell into step beside hunters, smiths, and fishermen. Ordinary men pulled from quiet lives to fight along a border most had never seen. Men who would put their lives on the line for reasons they barely understood but would die for anyway, because the land they loved demanded it.

The recruiters had promised an easy battle.

When Reny left, Flinn felt it. The pull in the center of his chest.

A call to arms. A summoning to stand for something that mattered more than fear, more than himself.

Garron had told him it was a bullshit feeling to have, then ordered him to stay far from the recruiters. The lecture started at sunup and went through lunch.

"War is not an honorable adventure, boy. It will take far more from you than it will ever give."

But Flinn had already made up his mind.

If Reny could head off into a great unknown for the sake of protecting them, well... so could he.

He'd waited until Garron was head down in the chicken coop that afternoon before slipping away to meet with the recruiters. After he signed the ledger, he packed a bag in secret and waited for nightfall—for Garron to be snoring in his chair by the hearth—and then left.

He'd rallied all his courage that night on the bridge, too. Kissed Maren right on the lips. The warmth of it, her startled laugh after, had carried him through every muddy march and mile since.

Flinn meant well. Always had.

But meaning well didn't prepare him for reality. For the weight of a sword that made his arm shake, the blisters that bled through his boots, or the way grown men wept in their sleep when they believed no one could hear.

When his mind wandered to dark places, he clung to memories of River's Edge. To the family who had accepted him. Bound not by blood, but by love, choice, and loyalty.

He hoped he would see them again.

See home again.

The man beside him, a grizzled fisherman from the eastern coastal plains, spat into the frozen grass. "You ever been in a real fight, boy?"

"Once or twice," Flinn lied.

The fisherman grunted. "Keep your head down. Don't try to be a hero. It's always the heroes who die first."

Flinn nodded, though he wasn't sure he believed it. Reny had been a hero. She'd left, forced to be brave for a greater good.

That had to count for something.

Ahead, the Old Wood rose. Black, ominous titans against the horizon. Somewhere beyond it, the North Gate waited. War waited.

Flinn's stomach tightened. Around him, men checked their weapons and muttered prayers to gods Flinn had never bothered learning the names of. The darkness of the foreboding tree line drew ever closer.

He thought of Reny, wherever she was, doing whatever impossible thing she had to do, and wondered if she'd made the same mistake he had.

If she'd believed, like him, that courage would be enough.

His breath misted white in the frozen air. Each step drew him closer to those deep and hungry shadows.

Farther from everything and everyone he'd ever known. Farther from River's Edge. But he marched on anyway, head held high.

He'd gladly face whatever lay ahead if that's what it meant to keep them safe.

The cliffs slept, but Reny did not.

She waited until the deepest hours of night, when even the wind and the sea held their breath and the rest of the world fell still. Agreed to share the bed with Rook on the condition that he stay on his side and keep his mouth shut.

Easier to keep watch over him that way.

Before she slipped from the warmth of the linens, she tested the wall she'd forged over the bond. Silence so absolute that Rook would feel nothing until it was too late. She pressed a mental hand to the iron, letting her warmth seep through. Into the connection.

Into him.

I do love you. Whatever happens... know that.

Her flame chased away every nightmare that plagued him, keeping him lulled in deep, peaceful sleep.

From a shadowed corner of the room, she watched him as she slid on her armor. Secured every strap and weapon she'd chosen earlier in the day. Made no sound as she slipped through the chamber door and closed it behind her. She moved through the darkened corridors like smoke, tracing the path she had memorized hours before when she'd insisted on confirming plans with Brenn.

An easy ruse.

The turns, the descents, the narrow passage that opened onto the cliffside rather than the guarded heights where the others expected to meet her at dawn. Along the path's edge, the sea roared far below. The wind clawed at her, bitter, alive. Full of salt and sorrow.

Reny closed her eyes and reached for both ember and resolve. They rose to meet her, flooding her veins with heat and steadying her pulse with a power she was only beginning to understand.

I have to go home.

She opened her eyes and raced up the stone path until it met the tree line. The silver pines welcomed her, their ancient branches forming heavy drapes that closed behind her. The thin trail wound down through root and stone, away from the cliffs, away from the sea, away from the dawn that would soon break without her there.

She didn't look back. Didn't let herself think of the shadow still sleeping in the bed she'd left behind, or the storm he would become when he woke to find her gone.

Let his thunder roll out to the sea.

As furious as Rook would be, he could protect himself. He'd be safe.

But Malorith had threatened River's Edge. If he truly knew how to find it, then the family she loved was already in danger. And no matter what man or fate or prophecy expected of her, she would put them first.

She had to warn them. Fight for them. Burn herself down to ash for them, if that's what it meant to keep them safe.

Pushing through the endless dark of the silver pines, Reny headed south. Headed home.

Before everything that she swore to protect crumbled to dust, before the man who'd claimed her discovered what she'd done.

And tore down the world to bring her back.

About the Author

L. J. Nicolson

Author Headshot: Darcey Walthes

L. J. Nicolson has been putting words on pages since she was a child, when her poetry appeared in the *Friends I've Never Met* anthology and on her mom's refrigerator. A lifelong lover of all things magic and fantasy, she eventually traded short verses for full worlds. *Of Ember and Stone* is where that obsession finally landed and came to life. It's her debut novel.

She is also a homeschooling mom, a photographer/editor, a devoted dog mom, and completely incapable of functioning without iced coffee and heavy metal—and she would not change a single thing about it. She lives in York, Pennsylvania with her husband and family.

LOVE NOTES

This book is the product of a lifetime spent half inside my own head, wandering through the real world while dreaming up grand fantasies.

When I was a little girl, I loved listening to stories. Eventually, I loved writing them. My Nana told me, constantly and without question, that one day I would be an author. She was my earliest and most devoted believer. The kind of woman whose faith in you becomes the foundation you build upon. She modeled the relentless work ethic I carry to this day, and her certainty that I could do this taught me to be certain too. Cancer stole her from us in 2009, and my heart breaks that she isn't here to hold this book. But she lives on in the magic and heart I pour into every page.

I did it, Nana. I wrote a book.

To my Mom and Dad—my most reliable and enthusiastic fans throughout my life: thank you for your love and your unfailing support no matter what life brings. You can't put this one on the fridge with a magnet like the story I wrote you on stapled index cards when I was little, but now you'll have one for the bookshelf. No one is more eager for the sequel than you, Momma, and I love you for it. Dad—every little poem you ever wrote for me is carried with me wherever I go.

To my grandfather—"Daddy", as I've always called you, because Momma did first, and that's exactly who you are. You have always been a pillar of strength and persistence, a get-it-done kind of man no matter what life throws at you. I may have never said it plainly enough: watching you shaped me more than you know. I am so grateful for you.

To my three incredible children—all of you are still too young to read this book, but you had a front-row seat to the making of it. Thank you for every hug at the computer, for asking "How's your book going, Mommy?" and for sitting beside me in the office while you wrote books of your own. Believe in your dreams and chase them with everything you have. I will always be right behind you, rooting for you—just as you have done for me. The three of you are my sunshine and always will be.

And to J—my own stone-and-storm of a husband, the love of my life. Nearly twenty years together, and what a journey it has been. You have been a constant advocate for my happiness and for going after what I want. Rooting for me, calling me out when I needed the tough love, and, as it turns out, providing excellent inspiration for my MMC. We built an incredible life together and there are so many more wonderful things yet to come.

And to everyone else who played a part along the way: Candy, my mother-in-law, who said good morning every day even when I was face-first in the computer and helped wrangle up the kids when I was "almost done with this last chapter". My editor, **Ashleigh Worley**, who took on this manuscript with devotion and care and was always a steady, supportive voice. And to the friends who were relentless in their unwavering support, who gave me a resounding *hell yeah* when I announced I'd written a book, you have no idea how much your support means to me.

Thank you all. I love you.